"SO," HE SAID SOFTLY,
"THE CHASE IS OVER."

Raw terror tingled icily up her spine. Her every muscle tensed for flight, and every instinct screamed a warning.

His mouth curved in a teasing grin. "I know you wish to do me in, and I give you fair credit for trying, but you're a hellishly poor excuse for a murderess."

Unbidden, her gaze traveled up the proud breadth of his chest and shoulders, the handsome planes of his face. "I nearly killed ye," she whispered, "yet ye won't be punishin' me f'r it?"

"Why should I?"

Again that quick smile as he wrapped her black tresses around his wrist and drew her face close to his, and she felt his fingers burn a hot trail of fire down her neck ...

Master of my Dreams

DANELLE HARMON

AVON BOOKS ◆ NEW YORK

MASTER OF MY DREAMS is an original publication of Avon Books. This work has never before appeared in book form. This work is a novel. Any similarity to actual persons or events is purely coincidental.

AVON BOOKS
A division of
The Hearst Corporation
1350 Avenue of the Americas
New York, New York 10019

Copyright © 1993 by Danelle F. Colson
Inside back cover author photograph by Thomas F. Keegan
Published by arrangement with the author
Library of Congress Catalog Card Number: 93-90230
ISBN: 0-380-77227-2

First Avon Books Printing: September 1993

AVON TRADEMARK REG. U.S. PAT. OFF. AND IN OTHER COUNTRIES, MARCA REGISTRADA, HECHO EN U.S.A.

Printed in the U.S.A.

RA   10 9 8 7 6 5 4 3 2 1

This book is lovingly dedicated to my friend and pastor,
Reverend Edwin A. Trench, Jr.

I would also like to thank Karen and Trena,
the inestimable Pesha and Marjorie,
the present-day Menotomy Minutemen,
and especially,
Robert Hamilton,
for his determination to "make me famous."
Thanks, Grampie!

Prologue

Ireland, 1762

The press gang was in.

One could tell by the way a thick pall had spread its shivery fingers over the land, cloaking it with darkness and shadow like mist snuffing out the noonday sun. One could tell by the way the little village that clung to the sea's edge grew quiet and seemed to huddle within itself, the people slamming shut the doors of their whitewashed cottages, and fearfully watching the roads from behind slitted curtains. One could tell by the way the taverns emptied and the young lads fled into the hills that climbed toward the majestic purple ridge of the twelve mountains, where they would hide until the threat was past.

And one could tell by the big, three-masted man-of-war that filled the harbor.

England was still at war with France—and not everyone wanted to fight.

It was an infrequent but not unheard-of threat, the Royal Navy seeking its unwilling recruits from this bleak, storm-tossed area of western Ireland that even God seemed to have forgotten. No able-bodied young man was safe from the press gang. And so it was that little Deirdre O'Devir, holding tightly to her mama's hand and clutching with pale white fingers the ancient crucifix that hung from around her neck, solemnly bade her older brother good-bye. Roddy had blown her a careless, laughing kiss; then the door had banged shut behind him as he ran to join the steady stream of young lads who cheerfully whistled and sang as they headed into hiding at the ruins of the old, haunted castle, far up in the hills where even the dreaded English would dare not go.

Then she and Mama had bolted the door and, huddling together beside the snapping, smoking peat fire, waited.

Roddy had said they had nothing to fear, for the press gang didn't take lassies. But as Deirdre stood at the window and looked off toward the sea, where she could see the towering masts of the man-of-war silhouetted against the misty western sky, curiosity got the best of her. She had to see for herself just what was so terrible about the English and its Navy, which everyone so feared and hated.

After all, her dear cousin Brendan, who'd been raised right here in Connemara, was a midshipman in the Royal Navy, and despite having a British admiral for a daddy, was as much an Irishman as she or Roddy. Sometimes it was hard to believe that English blood ran in his veins. But surely, if Brendan was in the Navy, it couldn't be as evil as everyone said it was . . . could it?

Raising her delicate chin, Deirdre made up her mind. Mama would never know if she sneaked out . . . for just a bit. She was a wee mite, even for a nine-year-old; it was a simple thing to crawl out her window once she had made an excuse to steal off to her room. Once outside, she vaulted over the stone fence and rode away on Thunder, her own, well-loved pony.

She waited until she was well away from the cottage before she kneed the pony into a hard gallop and raced him headlong toward the sea. The pungent scent of peat fires singed the air, mingling with the fresh, heady tang of the ocean. Clouds scurried overhead, and the drifting mist, cold and damp and penetrating, moved stealthily down from the mountains.

Night was coming on, and with it would come a storm.

Deirdre urged Thunder faster. Already the wind was picking up; now huge black clouds were filing in from the ocean, casting shifting shadows and colors over the rocky pastures, dragging patterns of light and dark over the gray sheet of the sea. Recklessly, she pressed her heels to the

pony's flanks, not pulling him up until they breathlessly
crested the last rocky hill.

There she sat, a pale little thing with thick, spiral-curling
black hair whipping around a face dominated by the innocently wide eyes of a child. Far below, where the sea
swapped kisses with the base of the hill, waves thundered
and boomed and sent up great silver mists of spray that
dewed her cheeks and tasted like salt. Here, high above the
sea, the wind was gusty, strong, and peppered with the
promise of rain.

A flock of rooks, shrieking, winged suddenly away, and
in the distance she heard the mournful bleating of sheep.
Wind sang in her ears, snatched at her damp hair. Behind
her, a stone, loosened by the pony's hooves, skittered down
the hill, the sound cleaving the tense stillness. Deirdre gave
a start and spun around, her skin crawling with the uncanny
feeling that she was being watched.

But there was no one was there.

Wind blew thick tangles of hair across her heart-shaped
face, and floated a snarl of raven curls about her frail little
shoulders. Deirdre clawed the wild tresses out of her eyes
and looked anxiously toward the darkening sea.

There, a half mile out in the bay, the British warship lay,
majestic in all its dread, frightening in all its beauty.

Deirdre's eyes grew huge. She reached up to touch the
crucifix of hammered gold and inlaid emeralds that hung
from around her neck, but the talisman was no comfort. The
man-of-war seemed to fill up the sea; the sky, ominous and
black to begin with, was even blacker behind its towering
masts.

She crossed herself. The pony tossed his shaggy head and
pricked his ears forward, while Deirdre watched something
approach out in the rising surf. A boat had been lowered
from the ship and was headed toward shore, plunging
through the rolling breakers and barely avoiding the dark
rocks that rose from the surf.

She felt the beginnings of panic prickle along her spine.
Run, Deirdre, run! But she could do nothing except stare
at the boat, forgetting the oncoming storm, forgetting the
menace of the press gang, forgetting the fact that it would

soon be dark and the banshees would come out—and forgetting the awful feeling that she was being watched.

The boat was nearing shore now, its crew having a rough
time of it in the rising seas as they steered it through the
dark, deadly rock clusters that reared out of the crashing
surf. But even the rocks, which had guarded this ancient
coast since time began, were helpless against invading Englishmen. Oars rose and fell in perfect rhythm, and every so
often the boat's bow would nose up as it plowed a wave,
drenching the men and the tall officer in the stern with
spray. Deirdre felt sorry for them. But the oarsmen's smooth
strokes never wavered, the boat wasn't dashed against the
rocks, and steadily it drew closer.

A cold drop of rain hit her cheek. Another splashed upon
her hand. Deirdre urged the pony to the edge of the hill—
and it was then that she noticed the officer in the boat had
a telescope to his eye and was training it on *her.*

With a cry of fright, she wheeled Thunder around—and
ran straight into a group of the most evil-looking men she'd
ever seen in her life.

"And wot 'ave we 'ere, Jenkins? A wee Oirish lassie wi'
purple eyes an' the fairest 'air ye ever did see!"

Deirdre's heart stopped, and bounced sickeningly down to
her toes. Wildly, she looked behind her—but there was only
the sea at her back, and nowhere to go.

She whimpered and began to cry.

" 'Ere now, wot's this, tears on ol' Taggert 'ere?" One of
them grabbed the pony's bridle, causing the animal to yank
its head back and roll its eyes in fright. "Would ye lookee
'ere, Jenkins. Ye must've spooked her with that ugly face of
yours." Taggert grinned, showing a mouthful of prominent
buckteeth that only frightened her all the more. An oily
black braid hung down his back, tied at the end with a piece
of leather, and tattoos competed for space on his thick,
strapping arms.

"Let me go," she whimpered, struggling to pull away.

But they simply laughed, fearsome and ugly men with
long, greasy pigtails brushing shoulders that were bare and
sunburned. Fumes of rum clung to their breath and some of

them carried clubs; others had cudgels and one or two held cutlasses.

"Hold on to that nag's bridle, Taggert! With yer luck ye'll not be seein' another lass for some time to come!"

"Aye, she's the best ye're gonna do!"

Bursts of hearty guffaws followed their remarks, and their harsh English voices were foreign and frightening.

"Might as well take advantage of 'er before the lieutenant gets here!"

"Let me g-o-o-oooo!" Deirdre sobbed, kicking out at Taggert's thigh with her foot.

He merely laughed, plucked her from the pony's back, and set her on the ground. His big hand clamped around her wrist, nearly breaking the fragile bones and hurting her when she tried to fight and pull away. "Now, wot're ye doin' out here by yer lonesome when it's startin' to grow dark, eh?" He poked a huge, grimy finger beneath her chin and forced her face up. Quivering, she stared into his eyes, too terrified to move. "Ain't ye got a momma to watch over ye?"

Above, the clouds massed, stalled, and began to spit more rain. One drop. Another.

"Gorblimey, Taggert, it's startin' to pour. We've work to do, and the lieutenant ain't gonna be too happy if he catches ye messing with a mere child."

Suddenly, the men behind Taggert went still and stared with something like terror toward the hill's edge. Talk stopped abruptly. Faces went pale. Eyes widened; gazes were cast down.

And far off in the distance, thunder rumbled.

"Indeed," said a cold, hard voice, "I damn well won't be."

Taggert gasped and abruptly shoved Deirdre away.

There, a British sea officer stood silhouetted against the sky, leaning on his sword and watching them with eyes as cold and gray as the storm clouds that gathered behind him. His blue coat was soaked with spray, his lips were set in a severe line, and his features were as hard as stone.

"We've come here to press seamen, Taggert, not *im*press

little girls. Unhand her this moment before you feel the bite of my anger—*and* my sword."

Recognizing him as the officer who'd watched her from the boat, Deirdre felt her knees begin to shake. Whimpering, she huddled closer to the pony's shoulder, her eyes growing huge with fright at the sight of the boat's crew gathering behind him, huffing and puffing as they came up the hill. There was amusement in their eyes as they caught sight of her, and much rib-jostling between them. But the officer did not seem amused at all. One sharp glance from him was all that was needed to instantly wipe away their smiles. They looked down at the ground, obviously respectful of his authority and unwilling to displease him.

Even Taggert, grinning foolishly, backed away from the pony, his hands raised as though in truce. "Sorry, sir."

Pointing with his sword, the lieutenant snapped, "Get your carcass down that hill, drag the boats free of the surf, and, by God, mind that they're well hidden! We've king's business to conduct and no bloody time to be dallying with diversions, damn you!"

"Aye, aye, sir," Taggert sputtered, and fled.

With a sharp and precise movement, the officer sheathed his sword, the scrape of the blade against the scabbard sending shivers up Deirdre's spine. She stared at him, taking in the smart naval uniform and thinking that if he wasn't so frightening he might actually look handsome in it, even if he *was* a Briton. Not a speck of lint flecked the dark blue coat; not a smudge of dirt marred the sharp whiteness of breeches and waistcoat—

But then he came forward, and Deirdre's eyes went wider still with fear. The fearsome, rough-looking men parted, wordlessly letting the tall and polished officer through their ranks and following him with respectful, if not worshipful, eyes. Cold sweat broke out along the length of Deirdre's spine and she trembled violently. A strange buzzing noise started in her ears, drowning out the crash of surf, the rising moan of the wind. Her fingers went numb and the feeling began to fade from her toes, her feet, her legs. . . .

The lieutenant caught her when she would've fallen, his

touch jerking her back to reality and stark, choking terror. She screamed in fright and struggled madly.

"Let me go!" she shrieked, kicking out at him. "Let me go-o-ooo!"

Holding her easily, he let her struggle, her childish strength no match for his. Finally, she wore herself out and stood before him, frozen with fear and sobbing pathetically.

"Poor little wren," he said, his voice deep and rich and soothing. He knelt down to her level, his thumbs coming up to brush away the tears that streaked her damp cheeks. She flinched, squeezing her eyes shut and trembling violently. "I daresay we've frightened you."

Trembling, Deirdre opened her eyes. She stared at him, taking his measure from close range. His brows were blond and haughty, his cocked hat covering bright, gilded hair that was caught at the nape with a black ribbon. He had long golden eyelashes, eyes the color of fog, and a profile that reminded her of a hawk.

Smiling, he took off his hat and tucked it beneath his elbow. His fair hair, contrasting sharply with the deep tan of his handsome face, was bleached and silvery at the curling ends, as though he spent a lot of time in the sun. His body was lean, his posture straighter than any she'd ever seen, and his lips were decidedly English, thin and haughty and tightly set. Her gaze flickered back to his and she swallowed the choking knot of terror that had lodged in her throat. But then he smiled at her once more, and little crinkles appeared at the corners of his eyes, the sides of his mouth.

She smiled back, hesitantly, childishly.

"Is this your pony?" he asked, still holding her and inclining his fair head toward Thunder.

Her gaze still locked with his, she nodded, too afraid to speak.

"And what is his name?" He smiled again, heedless of the way his men were once more elbowing each other and grinning as he smoothed away the last of her tears.

"Th-Thunder," she whimpered, her voice high with fright.

The blond brows drew together in a puzzled frown as he caught sight of the crucifix hanging from around her neck.

He reached out and hefted it in his hand, studying it keenly while she went rigid with terror. "Thunder . . ." he murmured absently, rubbing his finger over the ornate Celtic cross. "A jolly good name, what?" Then, letting the crucifix fall back to the end of its chain, he sat back on his heels and gently cleared the snarls of damp hair from her face. "D'you know, I used to have a pony once, just like yours, except I called him Booley. He was a devilish fellow, though, full of naughty mischief and pranks. Why, once he even broke my arm when he refused to take a fence and tossed me right off his back and onto a pile of wood! Hurt like the devil, it did!" He smiled again, shot a glance toward the gathering storm clouds, and let his thumb rove over her cheek. Then his gaze grew serious once more. "So we have Thunder, here. And might I ask *your* name, little girl?"

Her gaze darted to the grinning seamen, then back at the handsome lieutenant, who didn't seem to care that the skies were about to open up. "Deirdre," she whispered.

"Deirdre," he repeated, the name sounding strange on his foreign tongue. "A pretty name for a right pretty lass, what?"

"If ye say so," she mumbled, swallowing hard and staring down at his dark, sun-bronzed hand, still clamped firmly around her wrist. But his grip was gentle, not harsh like Taggert's had been. Little golden hairs sprang from his fingers, the back of his hand, and his palm was as hard and callused as Roddy's palms. But it was a warm hand, a strong hand, and under his gentle touch, Deirdre's heart steadied and its pounding echo began to fade from her ears. She could hear the wind again now, feel the wet mists against her skin, the random drops of rain upon her cheeks.

"Oh, but I *do* say so." The Englishman smiled at her, and for a moment she could almost imagine him as a knight from a fairy tale, so handsome was his face, so reassuring and kind were his gray eyes. Childishly wiping the back of her hand across her running nose, Deirdre gathered her courage and took a deep breath.

"Be ye in th' Royal Navy?" she blurted innocently.

He laughed, and a twinkle appeared in his gray eyes. "Aye, that I am, little wren."

She lifted her chin. "Me mama says only pirates, thieves, and tyrants be in th' Royal Navy." Her black brows drew together in a frown and she peered closely at him, searching the depths of his face for some proof of her mama's words. "But I think me mama be wrong."

"Do you, now?" He loosened his grip on her wrist and gently straightened her cloak, fussing over her as Daddy used to do when he was alive. The corners of his mouth were twitching, as though he was trying awfully hard not to laugh. "And why d'you say that, foundling?"

Deirdre caught her lower lip between her teeth, her eyes shining with a childish secret. Then she dimpled, tucked her chin, and giggled shyly. "Because me cousin Brendan be in th' Royal Navy, and he's th' kindest, handsomest man in th' whole wide world." His sudden laughter bolstered her courage, and she puffed out her chest importantly. "And he's not a thief, an' not a pirate! His daddy was an admiral, and Mama says that someday Brendan will be, too."

"An admiral, you say?"

Beyond the lieutenant's broad shoulder, Deirdre could see Rico Hendricks leaning against his club and grinning crookedly. Without even turning around, the lieutenant snapped, "For God's sake, Hendricks, don't just stand there! Go find O'Callahan and let us be about this devilish business!"

"No need to, sir. I think I hear him coming now."

"Cor blimey, Hendricks," joked one of the seamen, "the whole blighty village must hear him!"

Rising abruptly, the lieutenant clapped his hat on his head and turned toward the road. Deirdre stared at him, her eyes reverent. He was so tall that the storm clouds seemed poised on his hat, the darkening sky balanced atop his shoulders. He cast a wistful glance toward the distant ship, as though he regretted being here and wanted more than anything to be back aboard the man-of-war. Then he looked once more toward the road. His jaw bunched, his lips tightened, and when he looked down at her again, his gray eyes were filled with determination and resolve.

"Time for you to run along, little wren."

She stared up at him, puzzled, her brows puckering in

confusion. "But don't ye want t' hear about me cousin Brendan?"

Smiling ruefully, he reached down, put his hands around her waist, and lifted her up to the pony's back. The motion was quick and sure; the manner in which it was done brusque and businesslike. Numbly, she allowed him to stuff the wet reins into her hands, noticing that he was no longer smiling, and that his mouth was tight and strained.

"Next time, foundling." He gave her hair, damp now with mist and rain, one last tousle before turning away. "Now, off with you, before it gets any darker."

"Jesus, Christian, she'll spread the alarm!"

"A pox on you, Hendricks!" he barked with sudden, unexpected anger. " 'Tis far too late for any alarm. Hail O'Callahan's party and let's be done with this. By God, 'tis miserable enough business as it is, without having to spend the entire bloody night in this godforsaken hellhole, damn you!"

Deirdre shrank back, the lieutenant's swift change of mood confusing and frightening here. The rain was falling steadily now, gathering momentum, growing colder by the minute and pulling little curls of steam from the pony's neck. She looked at the lieutenant, standing there in the rain, and waited for him to come back and talk to her again—but he did not. Hurt and the pain of rejection filled her and she bit her lip to keep from crying. Her nose burned with suppressed tears. Her eyes wounded, she hesitantly urged the pony forward, thinking to ask him why he was so angry. But if he was sharp with her again, she might cry, and she didn't want to cry in front of someone she barely knew.

Tears filling her eyes, Deirdre was just about to turn Thunder away when she heard the sounds of men coming up the road. The blood went cold in her veins. She couldn't see much through the rainy gloom, but the sounds that came to her were frighteningly sharp and clear: the stamp of boots and rattle of muskets; dragging feet and angry shouts; the click of a flintlock, the whack of a club against flesh, and a man's howl of rage and pain. English laughter . . . an Irishman's swift curses.

Another blue-and-white-clad officer was in the lead.

"Lieutenant!" he called, detaching himself from the group. "I've got some for you, prime lads who'll do the ship proud!"

The fair-haired lieutenant had drawn his sword; now he smiled tightly and sheathed it, relaxing somewhat. "By God, that was quick."

"Aye, well, being born an' raised in this part o' the world sure has its advantages." The man's voice was Irish, familiar and dear among the strange tongue of the Englishmen. As the British seamen approached, Deirdre saw they had a smaller cluster of men with them, herding them like frightened sheep and threatening them with swords and clubs to keep them in line.

She frowned and craned her neck, her hands tightening on the wet reins. The rain was coming down hard now, heightening the musky scent of earth and grass and the warm smell of the pony's hide, pitter-pattering against the rocks. Somewhere out to sea, she heard the low rumble of thunder.

"And where were they hiding, O'Callahan?" The English officer strode toward the new arrivals, his dark coattails hanging down the back of his white-clad thighs and nearly touching his knees.

"Just where I thought they'd be. Out in th' hills, and drinking themselves senseless in the ruins of an old castle."

"Splendid work, O'Callahan," the lieutenant said, yet there was an odd tonelessness in his words. "I shall make note of it to the captain."

But Deirdre's horrified gaze was not on the lieutenant, not on O'Callahan, not on the group of English seamen. She stared at the frightened, angry men whom the English tars surrounded. Their clothes were dirty and torn, their steps weary, their faces cut and bleeding. Yet there was no mistaking who they were. Seamus Kelly . . . Patrick O'Malley . . . the brothers Kevin and Kenny Meeghan. . . .

And Roddy.

It took a moment for the truth to hit. Before she knew it she was off the pony, screaming as she raced across the wet grass. She slipped on a rock and went down hard, scraping her chin and knocking the breath from her lungs. "Roddy!" she sobbed. *"Roddy!"*

Her brother's head jerked up, and she saw horror in his purple eyes at the sight of her—horror that changed quickly to rage. Without a second's hesitation, he slammed his fist into the jaw of the nearest seaman and sent another sprawling with the deadly hook that had earned him many a free ale at the village tavern.

Chaos erupted.

Deirdre scrambled to get up. In a daze, she heard the shouts of the Englishmen, the barked commands of the lieutenant, the wild yells of her neighbors. Fists slammed against flesh; guttural groans and curses broke the night. Managing to get to her feet, she ran headlong across the grass, only to be neatly snared by Hendricks. Sobbing wildly, she saw Roddy struggling between three burly seamen, spouting curses and kicking savagely out at their legs, their groins. A sharp cuff across the face stunned him; then, someone kicked him in the belly, and a cudgel's blow brought him to his knees.

With Roddy retching and coughing, the rest of the Irishmen quieted. They looked hatefully at O'Callahan, then at the fine English lieutenant. Their eyes were sullen, their backs rigid with pride and fear.

"Take them to the boats and let's be off," the lieutenant commanded in an angry, toneless voice. "The captain, damn his eyes, shall be most pleased."

Numbly, Deirdre felt Hendricks release her, and she stood frozen as the seamen hauled Roddy and his friends down the hill, slipping on wet rocks and cursing the Irish rain, the Irish cold, the Irish seas that awaited them. She stared dazedly at the proud profile of the English naval officer, suddenly realizing just what he had done.

No fair and handsome knight was he.

A tear rolled down her cheek, was washed away by the rain.

"Me brother!" she wailed, throwing herself at him and raining blows on his back. "Please, don't take me brother!"

He turned, caught her flailing fists, jerked her up, and

held her away as she tried to kick him. "By God, I said go home, foundling!"

"But ye can't take Roddy! Ye just *can't!* He's me brother and I'll never see 'im again if ye take 'im away from us!" Tears scalding her damp cheeks, she struggled madly against the grip of his iron fingers. "Roddy!" she screamed as the last seaman disappeared over the side of the hill. *"Roddy!"*

Her struggles quieted, and hanging from his grip, she collapsed in great, convulsing sobs of terror and grief. She heard the wind moaning across the dark pasture, and the voices of the seamen fading to a few barks of laughter, a curse, then nothing as they reached the beach far below. Her cheeks streaming tears and rain, her wet hair hanging in straggly spirals around her face, Deirdre raised desperate eyes to the lieutenant. He stared down at her, an anguished look on his handsome face, and for a moment she thought he was going to recall the men and release her brother. Then his jaw turned hard and unyielding, the set of his mouth determined. "We are at war with France," he said harshly. "And while I despise the methods our Navy must employ to obtain its seamen, as an officer I know that my loyalty and duty lie with my country, not with my own inclinations." His eyes softened. "I'm sorry, little wren."

Then, abruptly, he released her and turned on his heel, striding down the hill without a backward glance. She watched his white breeches melt into the darkness, heard his footsteps fade, until she was all alone with nothing but the sad patter of falling rain and the mournful crash of waves against the beach.

Moments later, she saw lights bobbing out on the sea, fuzzy and dim in the mist, as the boat headed back toward the man-of-war and carried her brother away forever.

Deirdre stood there for a long time, the wind blowing her hair in wild, wet tangles around her shoulders as she watched the lights fade to tiny pinpricks in the foggy darkness and then to nothing. At nine years of age, she had just learned there were more frightening evils in this world than the banshees whose low moans could even now be heard through the darkness of the lonely night. Choking on a last sob, she wiped her eyes, gripped in both shaking hands the ancient crucifix that had once belonged to her formidable ancestress, and raised her chin, her gaze fixed on that point beyond that had swallowed up the lights of the boat.

Someday, she'd be old enough to go to England by herself, seek her cousin Brendan, and obtain his help in getting her brother back.

Someday, she would find that English lieutenant and make him pay for what he'd done.

Someday, she vowed—she would see that English lieutenant *dead*.

Chapter 1

England, thirteen years later

The narrow, cobblestoned streets of Portsmouth were not the safest of places, but Captain Christian Lord, Royal Navy, was well able to defend himself from the pickpockets, thugs, and other rabble that haunted the waterfront area. A heavy boat cloak hid his handsome blue-and-white uniform and protected it from the sleety drizzle, but, just as his well-groomed demeanor made it obvious that he was a man of breeding and affluence—and therefore an appealing target—one would have to be stupid or blind not to recognize the military bearing that marked him as one capably employed in some service of the king. Indeed, he was well used to fighting bigger threats than those that lurked in the shadows around him, and the powerful breadth of his shoulders, the confident manner in which he carried himself, the sword that hung at his side—and the frosty anger that shone in his eyes—were enough to deter any would-be assailants.

The streets, rimmed with filth and plagued by icy puddles, were polished by a cold rain that rode a bitter southeasterly out of skies gone leaden and gray. Buildings, huddled together as though for warmth, seemed to close in on either side of him, growing darker, seedier, sadder as he neared the waterfront. He shifted the warm, whimpering bundle he carried under his arm to protect it from the stinging drizzle. Already he could smell the Solent; a moment later he could see its frothy expanse, and the anchored ships riding a chain of cruising whitecaps.

15

He paused near the shelter of the stone wall, his eyes, as cold and gray as the stormy Channel itself, sweeping the harbor. In his arms the little dog whimpered and gently he set her down, keeping a watchful eye on her before turning his attention toward the Spithead anchorage where ships tugged at their cables, their dark forms obscured by sleet. The captain yanked his hat down over his brow, and pulled up the collar of his boat cloak. His profile was hawkish, its lines unsoftened by the chilling drizzle. A carefully rolled and powdered wig, just visible beneath his hat, hid the handsome silvery-gold shade of his hair and gave him a rather stuffy look of English pomp and arrogance. But there was nothing stuffy about Captain Christian Lord. Standing just over six feet two inches, he was an impressive, powerful figure, with wintry gray eyes and a tight-lipped mouth that rarely softened in a smile. Harsh cheekbones emphasized the leanness of his tanned face, and he exuded an air of aloofness that made him a hard man to know, let alone like.

But he hadn't always been like this. Tragedy and grief had extinguished the twinkle his eyes had once held, and now, on the day before the Black Anniversary, they were more tormented than ever, the suffering of his heart as keen and wrenching as it had been on that awful night, five years ago tomorrow. . . .

He stared bleakly out to sea, his gaze traveling beyond the anchored ships, the mist-shrouded Isle of Wight, the horizonless gray gloom of the Channel . . . and into the past.

"Emily," he murmured, shutting his eyes against the sting of emotion.

Just as quickly, the image was gone, and he was left standing alone in the rain, a forlorn, wind-whipped figure with nothing but his haunted memories to accompany him.

And then his gaze fell upon the frigate he would soon command and swift, righteous anger swept in to drive the memories away.

Damn the admiral for ordering him to Boston, a bleeding sewer of malcontents and rabble-rousers if ever there was one. His hard jaw went harder yet. America, land of taxes, massacres, and tea parties! By God, England was being far too lenient with the disobedient bumpkins, and ought to enforce discipline before the situation there got out of hand. And to think that Sir Elliott was assigning him to a frigate—not just any frigate, but *Bold Marauder*—after he'd commanded mighty ships of the line, served as flag captain for two admirals, and been proclaimed a hero for his actions in the Battle of Quiberon while still a lowly lieutenant during the Seven Years War. . . .

But no, Elliott had insisted, nay, *ordered* him to take command of the thirty-eight-gun frigate, with the excuse that he was the Admiralty's last hope of bringing law and order to a ship that everyone else in the Navy had all but given up on.

The captain turned abruptly, the boat cloak billowing about him and anger seething through his blood as he resumed his quick pace. No doubt, giving him command of the Hell-Ship was Rear Admiral Sir Elliott Lord's twisted idea of taking his mind off the Black Anniversary. Christian was not at all grateful. In fact, he'd been downright furious to find, upon his arrival in Portsmouth yesterday, that his shrewd older brother had obviously had the thing planned for some time, for HMS *Bold Marauder* was already refitted and provisioned for sea.

He heard a frightened bark and paused guiltily at the sound of skittering claws on the cobblestones behind him, allowing his new acquisition time to catch up with him. He had found the little dog rifling through a pile of frozen garbage some three streets back and immediately had taken pity on her. Now she reared up on her hind legs and, whimpering, furiously licked the back of his hand, grateful that he had not abandoned her as someone else had obviously done. He bent down, picked her up, and cradled her to his chest, half wishing that those in the Service who thought him cold and emotionless could see him now. But although the spaniel brought a fleeting smile to his hard mouth, even she could not relieve the captain's vexation with his admiral for assigning him to the Hell-Ship.

He heard the crash and hiss of waves on the sand below, tasted blown spray upon his tightly compressed lips. Narrowed gray eyes sought, and found, the distinctive shape of

the frigate. She was anchored at Spithead, well out beyond
the harbor, and far away from the other vessels as though she
carried the plague. *As indeed she does,* he thought, his temper going black. A rebellious vessel with the worst reputation
in the fleet, HMS *Bold Marauder* was not his idea of a fitting reward for the twenty years of honorable service spent
in the king's Navy!

"Damn you, Elliott!" he swore from between gritted
teeth, his words torn away by the stiff wind. He set the dog
down, then dashed away the rain that dampened his cheeks,
anger heating his blood until the heavy weight of the boat
cloak became unbearable. Impatiently, he threw off the
bulky garment to reveal the proud blue-and-white uniform
of the Royal Navy—and at that very moment a last dying
shaft of sunlight broke through the thick clouds.

It glinted off the twelve meticulously polished gold buttons of his blue coat, set in threes to denote his captain's se-
niority. It shone grandly against the intricate detail of gold
lace strewn lavishly around his buttonholes, pockets, and
cuffs. It made his scrupulously clean waistcoat and breeches
seem whiter than snow, as indeed they were, and gilded the
planes of his hard face, the buckles of his shoes, the hilt of
his fine sword.

And then the captain's steely gaze again found the frigate,
and like a bad omen, the sun was snuffed out by heavy
mists.

HMS *Bold Marauder.*

Her first captain, Richards, had been a lazy, drunken lout
who'd allowed his crew the free rein to do just about anything they damn well pleased. Three men since the slovenly
Richards had tried to turn her company into a fighting pack
the king himself could be proud of. The first had come back
insane, and it had required three marines to drag him from
the cabin; the second had begged transfer to a seventy-four-
gun ship of the line; and the third had resigned from the
Navy altogether.

Of course, the fact that the frigate's officers were a tightly
knit pack of wastrels—some the sons of peers of the realm,
others the offspring of admirals ranked high on the Navy
list—guaranteed the granting of their fondest desire. And

that desire was that they were not to be separated and sent to different ships—a solution, Christian thought wryly, that would have solved the problem of HMS *Bold Marauder* immediately.

The severe line of his jaw went tight and his eyes hardened to flint. Well, the crew was in for a big surprise if they thought they could pull any nonsense on *him*. Drawing his telescope, he rapped it once against a palm, lifted it to his eye, and studied the frigate's decks with a seemingly detached stare that belied the anger in his frosty gray gaze. Sleet hit the glass lens, streaking the circular field, the frigate's dark form. He moved the glass, bringing it slowly down the length of the ship, his keen eyes seeing all and missing nothing—not even the figurehead, a brown-and-white bird dog crouched beneath the bowsprit, its foot raised to its chest as though seeking elusive game.

A hunter, Christian mused, but this particular ship had never fulfilled such promise. He trained the glass on her decks. What he saw only raised his ire all the more, for even from this distance it was frightfully obvious that HMS *Bold Marauder* fell short of the high standards of spit and polish that he, as an officer in the king's Navy, demanded of the vessels under his command.

He shut the telescope with a brisk snap.

A condition that would soon change, by God!

Scooping up the spaniel and wrapping her in his boat cloak, the captain continued on, his long mariner's stride conveying his ill temper. The streets were nearly deserted, those who were wise, or able to afford it, taking shelter in drier places and huddling next to crackling hearths. But still, he was not alone. A group of seamen caught the glint in his cold gray eyes and respectfully touched their hats as he passed; a thug with a hang-gallows look saw the sword peeping dangerously beneath his coattails and stepped aside; a pack of young boys, engaged in a fistfight, paused to gape at the brilliance of his uniform with its handsome gold trim, then fell reverently into step behind him, trailing at a respectful distance, dodging into alleyways, hiding behind trash heaps, and trying in vain to keep up with him. But the captain paid them no heed. Straight to the quay he went—and came up short, his severe features darkening with rage.

The boys fled.

Captain Lord had every right to be furious. He had sent orders out to the frigate that its gig should be here, waiting to bring him to his new command—but the boat was no-where in sight.

He was left embarrassingly stranded.

Either his orders had never been received or, more likely, they had been blatantly ignored by the crew of rebellious rascals whom it would soon be his duty to command.

"Troubles already, Captain Lord?"

A young lieutenant stood there, nervously eyeing the tall and forbidding captain and noting the reason for his anger.

"Aye, but not for long, Lieutenant—*not for bloody long!*"

His temper turning to black fury, Captain Christian Lord turned on his heel and stormed down the quay. He would find a way out to the frigate, and when he stepped aboard her for the first time, there would be all hell to pay.

Chapter 2

Captain Christian Lord wasn't the only one on his way out to the frigate *Bold Marauder.* While he was trying to procure passage to his new command, another had al-ready done so and was waiting to be rowed out to the war-ship.

Deirdre O'Devir had arrived in Portsmouth with nothing but her name, her pride, her meager life savings, and a can-vas bag containing everything in the world that was most precious to her: a miniature of her dead mother; a tiny model of a sailboat that Roddy had made when he was a lad; and an old sliver of wood, part of the wreckage of Pa-

pa's little boat, all that had washed ashore after the sea
storm in which the angels had come to bring him home so
long ago.

Had those been the only revered occupants of Deirdre's
canvas bag, it would've been sadly empty. Carefully wrapped
in linen to guard against breakage was the vial of Irish seawater she'd taken from the beach at Connemara on her last
day there; a felt pouch containing sand and shells scooped
from that same shore; a pebble from the rocky pasture outside the little cottage that had been her family's home; a tuft
of wool snipped from a neighbor's sheep; a tightly corked
glass flagon, seemingly empty, but full of Irish air; and, of
course, the loaf of bread—made of wheat flour grown on
Irish pastures and milk gleaned from Irish cows, and baked
over the heat of a good, Irish peat fire.

It didn't matter that the bread had grown stale during her
journey to England, for it was not to be eaten. Just as Deirdre O'Devir would never empty the water from the vial or
the sand and shells from the pouch, just as she would never
throw the pebble away or, God forbid, uncork the flagon of
Irish air and let it escape—she would never eat the bread.
Nor, she thought, reaching up to finger the ornate, pagan
cross that hung from the chain around her neck, would she
ever take Grace's crucifix off.

She stepped closer to the edge of the quay. Below, the old
tar she had paid to take her out to the frigate was busy
clearing space for her in his little boat. Taking advantage of
the moment, Deirdre raised a hand to shade her eyes from
the watery sun that had just broken through the clouds. She
peered across the water to the frigate. At the thought of her
impending voyage, she felt her heart jump with fear, but she
hid it well—just as she'd hidden the secret of her gender beneath a loose linen shirt, woolen jacket, and seaman's trousers. With her wildly curling tresses stuffed beneath a cap,
there was little to give away the fact that the tall, raw-boned
lad with the fair complexion and bold black brows was actually a female.

Her face, a striking contrast of beauty and strength, de-
noted the courage of Celtic blood and showed none of the
frailty that was often associated with her sex. Her nose was

straight and bold, her lips full, her cheekbones high and proud. Only her eyes, the color of the winter sky at dusk and reminiscent of that deep, mysterious purple of the heavens just before the final curtain of day is drawn, betrayed her fear and grief, for even here her mama's deathbed words, uttered not one month before, haunted her. . . .

"Deirdre. . . . Go t' England and find m' son. Go t' England . . . go wherever ye hav' t', girl. But go, find m' lad . . . an' bring him back home t' Ireland so I can rest in peace. . . ."

She had gone to London first to enlist her cousin's help, only to learn that Brendan, a captain in the Royal Navy, had been sent to the American port of Boston. He and his younger sister, Eveleen, were all the family Deirdre had left—and Brendan with his naval connections was her only hope of finding Roddy. She would follow him to America, then . . . even if the thought of crossing the stormy Atlantic terrified her.

Again she reached up to touch the heavy crucifix that hung from a chain of beaten gold around her neck. It had belonged to her ancestress, the formidable Grace O'Malley, and long, long ago, Deirdre had vowed never to take the cross off.

The crucifix had come down to Deirdre through her mother's people, and to her, it not only symbolized her beloved homeland—it *was* her homeland.

"Ye ready there, bucko?"

The old seaman was waiting for her, reaching up a gnarled hand to help her down into the boat. For a moment Deirdre hesitated, the wind bowing cold and lonely off the Solent and dragging a shiver of apprehension down her spine. But then she felt the reassuring presence of her canvas bag, the neck of which was clenched in her damp and clammy hand, and courage infused her again. As long as she had her precious bits of home with her, she would never be alone. No matter where she went, no matter what lay ahead, they would always be with her, to sustain her, to strengthen her, to remind her of who she was.

She touched the crucifix again, bitter tears of homesickness pricking her eyes. Home might be far away, but it seemed as though Grace's spirit was right here with her in this foreign, frightening place.

One month ago, Deirdre had made a vow to her dying mama to find Roddy and bring him home to Ireland. Thirteen years ago she had made a vow to *herself* to find and kill the fair-haired English lieutenant who had stolen him from them.

And now the time had come to fulfill those vows.

Sustained by her thoughts, she crouched down and allowed the old seaman to help her into the boat.

"First time goin' to sea?" he asked, amusement lighting his wizened face as he noted her frightened eyes and shaky hands.

She nodded, not trusting herself to speak, for there was a lump in the back of her throat and the harbor had blurred behind the sudden tears. Again she saw Mama, lying in bed with her eyes, once as deep a violet as her children's, faded like a piece of fabric left out in the sun for too long. She'd been dying—but then, Deirdre figured she'd been dying ever since the English lieutenant had come with the press gang and taken dear Roddy away from them. *I'll find that poxy son of a bitch, Mama,* she'd silently promised herself as she'd held her mother's small hand and felt the life fading out of her. *By all that's holy, I'll find him an' kill him, destroy him like he did you an' Roddy. . . .*

Hastily, she dashed the hot tears away so that the old tar, setting his oars, wouldn't notice. But the memories were still too fresh, still too painful, and she could still hear her mama's last, dying words. . . .

"*. . . go, find m' lad . . . an' bring him back home t' Ireland so I can rest in peace. . . .*"

Deirdre swallowed hard, her chest quivering with pent-up sobs.

Bring him home to Ireland.

Then, with an effort that would have done her ancestress proud, she fiercely brushed the tears away and jerked her chin up in defiance. She was strong. She had to be. There would be time for weeping later—*after* she had fulfilled her vows.

And fulfilling those vows would start with boarding the frigate.

Clutching the boat's damp gunwale, she stared out at the countless lighters, barges, and ships of every size and shape that clogged Portsmouth Harbor and, beyond it, the white-ruffled anchorage of Spithead.

And then her gaze found the frigate.

A seaman would've immediately noted the differences that set her apart from her neighbors. She was a warship, designed for striking fast and hard, a far cry from the bluff-bowed, tub-bodied vessels that surrounded her. A seaman's trained eye would've admired the sleek lines that marked her as a fighter, the clean rake of her masts, the efficient and businesslike design of her hull, the row of gunports that ran along her sides. But Deirdre was oblivious of such details, for to her, the ship would serve only one purpose—and that was to carry her to Boston and Brendan's help.

The mist had parted and was dispersing to the wind, leaving low-hanging clouds rolling across the leaden sky like giant white balls of dust. It would be a fine day after all, and the seaman whistled as he rowed, his wizened eyes scanning the harbor. He nodded at an acquaintance in a passing boat, then turned and caught her eye.

"Ye sure ye be wantin' to go out to *Marauder?*" he asked, flashing a toothy grin.

Deirdre shrugged. "Well, ye said she was goin' t' Amerikay . . . t' Boston, and that I could get by in her without doin' much work."

"Aye, that ye can, bucko." He stared over his shoulder, his eyes suddenly gleaming. "I reckon ye could certainly do worse fer yer first ship. Why, every jack's happy to serve on *that* frigate—most loosely run ship in the fleet!"

"But . . . isn't she a king's ship? A Royal Navy vessel?"

"Aye, that she is," the old man wheezed, leaning on his oars, "but that don't matter none. She's the *Bold Marauder.*"

The way he said the vessel's name made it sound as though *that* explained everything. Was the *Marauder*'s reputation for laxity so well known that she, Deirdre, was the only "sailor" on the wharves who was unaware of it?

Frowning, she gazed out across the rough Solent to the distant hump of the Isle of Wight—

—and nearly dropped her precious canvas bag in shock.

Not a stone's throw away, a boat was ferrying a group of grinning, gaping tars in the direction of the *Bold Marauder,* and in their midst sat a painted, yellow-haired doxy whose breasts were the size of ale jugs. Deirdre's eyes bulged. Sweet Jesus, not only were they *huge,* they were shockingly exposed, the creamy flesh swelling above the low neckline of her gown, only the nipples hidden by the fabric. As Deirdre stared, gaping and appalled, the woman threw back her head with bawdy laughter, rested her hand on the crotch of one of the sailors, and leaned into the arms of another.

"Sweet God in heaven," Deirdre whispered. Then she blushed to the roots of her hair as one of the sailors shamelessly plunged his hand beneath the woman's neckline, only causing her to laugh harder. Mortified, Deirdre yanked her cap down over her eyes.

Noting her reaction, the old tar cackled with glee. "Better get used t' such sights, bucko!" he wheezed. "This is the Navy yer goin' into!"

But there were no doxies being rowed with queenly splendor out to any of the *other* ships. . . .

Swallowing hard, Deirdre wrapped her hands around her canvas bag and tried not to think of what horrors might await her aboard the vessel that would be her home for the next month. Then she consoled herself with the reasons for choosing the frigate. After all, she *did* want a ship where she wouldn't arouse suspicion. Perhaps the *Bold Marauder,* with her obviously indifferent captain, was a good choice after all.

But still, a nagging feeling of uneasiness lodged itself beneath her breastbone, and the fear she had so bravely concealed was beginning to make itself felt in her damp palms and racing heart.

She stared at the approaching wall of the frigate's side and shakily touched the crucifix.

Just what was she getting into?

* * *

"Snivelin' blue blood, who the blighty 'ell does 'e think 'e is, any'ow? We ain't never 'ad to polish the bleedin' brasswork before!"

"You think that's bad? He had *our* watch out there swabbing the deck. Ye'd think he means for us to *eat* off it, so clean did he order it!"

"Scurvy bastard!"

"Imagine!"

"Ye didn't oblige 'im now, did ye, Skunk?"

"Christ, no! Ye'll see me rottin' in hell before I swab a bloody *deck!*"

"Well, he won't last. We've scared off three captains before him. Besides, if he's so lily-livered he won't even come aboard, but has to send his orders through his bosun, you can bet your arse he'll not last out the day."

They stood huddled near the rail of His Majesty's frigate *Bold Marauder,* the officers high-born and privileged, the crew, an evil-looking lot made up of the worst of Bristol's streets, Cornwall's pastures, and the scrapings of just about every dockyard from London to Land's End. Some wore the garb of the Royal Navy seaman: loose-fitting trousers with red-and-white stripes, short blue coats, red vests, and carefully knotted kerchiefs. Others were clad in the blue-and-white uniforms that marked them as officers, and one—the frigate's first lieutenant—was even dressed in the manner of a Scotsman, with a bonnet, black-and-red-checked hose, buckled shoes, and a brightly colored plaid. The outfit might've looked striking, had its wearer not thrown a blue-and-white lieutenant's coat over it in a halfhearted attempt to meet dress regulations.

The effect was totally ridiculous.

Above, the mist had cleared, leaving pale sunlight to poke down through the cold winter sky and shine upon the frigate's decks. The harbor was a mean, unfriendly blue, and a nippy wind snuffled about, stirring the waves to whitecaps, driving beneath heavy clothing and setting teeth to chattering. But despite the cold, tempers were so hot they could've melted the ice in the water casks below.

The gunner, a hulking, malodorous, grimy bear of a man with ribs like a ship's hull, defiantly folded his arms across his barrel-like chest. "Well, all I know is that I ain't polishin' no bloody brass, nor decks, nor the buttons on 'is Highness's fancy bleedin' coat! If our new *Lord* and *Master* wants anything done, 'e can damn well do it himself!"

"Aye, ye can tell him that when he finally comes aboard, Skunk!" cried the Scottish, red-bearded first lieutenant with a hearty guffaw. Brawny and tall, he had a jovial smile, a booming laugh, and no talent at all for playing the strange-looking instrument that was his most prized possession. Now he leaned against the bulwarks, carefully polishing it; it was called bagpipes, he'd told them, and it was supposed to make beautiful music—but so far, all that Ian MacDuff had managed to get out of the instrument was a horrible screeching noise that sounded like a cow in the throes of agony. That noise, however, had done wonders for driving the captain succeeding Richards into an insane asylum, and Ian—along with his shipmates—had high hopes of accomplishing the same with their new Lord and Master. "Better yet," he said, "won't ye be getting Elwin tae do the scrubwork? Ye ken how, as surgeon, he is about cleanliness."

"On your life, Ian!" snapped Elwin Boyd, a gawky little man who walked with his neck out like a chicken waiting for the axe. He hefted a vinegar bottle and shoved it in the big Scotsman's ruddy face. "This is for keeping germs down, not cleaning. I told you that long ago!"

"Here, now," snarled Skunk, "we're supposed to be discussin' 'is bloody Lordship and how we're gonna get rid of him, not brawlin' amongst ourselves!"

"Ah, yes, the *Ice Captain*," sneered Milton Lee, the purser, a bald, sharp-faced little man with a stooping, lanky body and a nose like a parrot's beak. His eyes watering in the sharp wind, he glanced toward shore. Their new commanding officer, whom none of them had met, would soon find that the boat he had sent for would not be waiting for him, but was instead still snugged securely in the waist of HMS *Bold Marauder.* It was the least they could do to irritate him. Already the new Lord and Master had had his fancy, claw-footed bed brought aboard *their* ship, as though he had every intention of staying; already he'd taken it upon himself to give *them* orders, as though he actually expected them to obey him! Sneering, Milton echoed the sentiments of his companions. "He's supposed to be the Navy's last hope of straightening us out. Ha! I give him one hour, Skunk, before we have him going over the side screamin' for mercy!"

"I give him ten minutes if Ian here hauls out those blasted bagpipes!"

"Ten minutes? He won't last five, I'm tellin' ye!"

"Here, now!" Ian protested, his Scots temper on the rise.

"Aw, piss off, Ian, we're just teasin' ye," Skunk said, waving his hand. "Hey, Hibbert! Ye made sure our sweet Delight was well hidden, didn't ye? We wouldn't want 'is bloody Lordship to find 'er and keep 'er all to 'imself, eh, bucko?"

"Aye, I hid her in the brig," the midshipman said conspiratorially. His fourteen-year-old face was feral and sharp, his eyes beady and cunning, and despite the fact that his father was a highly placed Lord of the Admiralty, there wasn't a clean spot on the uniform that he wore with such disdain. "The captain'll never look there!"

"Good job, m'boy!" Skunk hooted, clapping the youngster on the back. "And you, Russ! Ye're bein' awful quiet over there! Wot d'ye make of our new Royal Highness, eh?"

"What do *I* think?" Russell Rhodes said, taking off his hat to rake his hand through oily black hair gone silver at the temples. "Why, given his past record, I think our new Lord and Master's going to do his damnedest to succeed where his predecessors have failed."

"Won't never happen," growled Arthur Teach, just coming up from the brig, where he'd gone to check on the "welfare" of their lady passenger. At a height of six and a half feet, Teach towered over even the burly Skunk and Ian MacDuff. Rumor had it that he was a grandson—illegitimate, of course—of the infamous Ned Teach, alias Blackbeard, a fact that Arthur was overwhelmingly proud of, and one that he went out of his way to mention to anyone in the unenviable position of having to hear the story of how his illustrious pedigree had come about. With his bristly black hair and beard that tickled the belt of his trousers, he was hideous enough of both temperament and appearance that his presence alone had been enough to drive Captain Number Three from *Bold Marauder* with his tail between his legs.

Getting rid of Captain Number Four had been a collaborative effort on all of their parts—but this fifth one just might be a problem. . . .

"Well, all's I know is that we ain't even *met* him yet and the bloody bugger's already overstepping his bounds," growled Skunk.

"Imagine what he'll be like once he gets aboard the ship!"

"Imagine what he'll be like once we put to *sea!*"

"Aw, 'tis cowing he'll be, just like the rest of them," Ian scoffed, tucking his bagpipes under his arm and ignoring the suddenly wary looks from his shipmates. "Anyone wantae hear the new tune I learned?"

"Spare us, *please.*"

But Ian made a rude gesture, flipped his bagpipes over his shoulder, and put the blowpipe in his mouth.

Everyone backed up.

Ian grinned. "Ye sure, now?"

"Yeah, save it for his bloody Lordship!"

"Give 'im a concert he'll not likely forget!"

They howled with laughter until Ian, crestfallen, slammed his fist into Teach's jaw and Teach reacted with an equally hard punch to Ian's mouth that bloodied his lip. Fists flew, curses resounded, and in the ensuing chaos Elwin, fearful of germs, tossed the entire contents of his vinegar bottle at the big Scotsman.

"My pipes, damn ye!" Ian cried, going for Elwin's scrawny neck. Teach drew his knife and charged gleefully forward. Skunk began to bellow, Milton to howl, Hibbert to cheer—and at that moment, a frightened shriek split the air.

"What the hell was that?"

"Don't know. Shut up and maybe we'll hear it again!"

"Christ, Arthur, get that bloody knife out of my *face!*" bellowed Skunk.

The cry came again.

As one, they looked up and toward the entry port. There,

pale and shaken and skinnier than a sea worm, stood a young lad. An oversize cap covered his head, his cheeks were white as fresh sailcloth, and he had that innocent, lost look that just *invited* abuse.

The lad's terrified gaze was fastened on Arthur Teach. "What're ye gawkin' at, ye snivelin' whelp?" Teach roared in his best pirate's voice. "Go on, hie yerself out of here before I carve out yer liver and toss it to the gulls!"

The youngster went whiter still, and glanced anxiously back toward the entry port. But his chin came up, and timorously, he came forward.

"I said, off with ye!"

The lad kept walking. He looked terrified, but he came, and even the cool Russell Rhodes lifted a sardonic brow.

"Jesus," grumbled Skunk, "that one don't scare easy."

"He will. Let me have at him for a bit!" Teach stalked forward, hunching his shoulders and thrusting his great, hairy head down into the lad's face. He raised his cutlass and, in the best imitation of his grandfather, roared, "I said, get yer scrawny carcass off my ship, ye miserable pack of fish bones, before I—"

"Excuse me. I'm lookin' for the captain o' this boat?"

They stared. They gawked. It grew so quiet one could hear the waves lapping gently at the hull so far below.

"Boat?" roared Skunk, his eyes bugging from his grimy face. "Ye bloody boglander, ye callin' this here fighting ship a *boat?"*

"Aye, that he did," said Ian, quirking a red brow and nodding sagely.

"I'm sorry." The lad gave a quick, fleeting grin and ruffled nervously through a canvas bag he carried under his arm. Teach's bristly brows snapped together. Ian's mouth formed a perfect O within the red mat of his beard. Elwin picked up his vinegar bottle, dropped it, and picked it up again. Even Skunk went silent as the boy, muttering to himself, fished through his bag. Finally he produced a scrap of paper filled with notes, glanced at it, and tucked it sheepishly into his pocket. "Aye, I be terribly sorry," he repeated. "Ye're absolutely right, sir. 'Tis not a boat, but a frigate o' th' sixth rate."

"Fifth!" roared Teach, with as much fury as he could muster.

Rhodes, who'd been watching the drama, finally shoved off from the railing and came forward. "What do you want?"

"T' see th' captain. Is he . . . here?"

"Nay, he ain't come aboard yet, thank Christ. But I'm sure the Lord and Master'll be here shortly, just in time to weigh."

"Weigh what?" Deirdre began, and caught herself—too late.

The piratical one reached out, grabbed her by her collar, and yanked her forward until his beard stabbed her tender cheek. Fumes of rum hit her in the face, and it was only by sheer will alone that Deirdre kept herself from fainting with fright. "Ye ain't no seaman, so ye got no business bein' on a king's ship! Now get your puny carcass off this here vessel before we toss ye to the sharks!"

"Aye! Toss him to the sharks!"

Deirdre's knees went weak. She shut her eyes, suddenly wishing she'd ignored the advice of the old sailor and found a different ship that was going to Boston, even if it took months. Sweet Jesus, if the crew was such a pack of bloodthirsty brutes, what would their *captain* be like?

Then she felt the weight of Grace's crucifix, hidden beneath her shirt and lying against her rapidly beating heart, and her courage returned. Her chin came up with stubborn purpose, and maintaining her brave front, she said, "Well, if th' captain is no' 't'aboard, could I speak wi' his assistant?"

"Assistant?" the pirate roared.

"He means first lieutenant," said the other bearded one, who was almost as big and had a Scottish brogue that was oddly comforting amidst this collection of West Country and London dialects. He was carrying a set of bagpipes, of all things, and Deirdre frowned as she noted his outrageous manner of dress. But the Scotsman merely cuffed the pirate away, grabbed her wrist, and said, "I'm Lieutenant Ian MacDuff, the man ye'll be wantin' tae see. Now, what is it I can be doin' for ye, laddie?"

She swallowed, carefully set her canvas bag down beside

her foot, and tried very hard to look important. "I want t' sign aboard."

"Sign aboard what?"

"Why, this boa—I mean, ship, o' course."

He stared at her as if she'd gone mad. "Ye mean, ye actually want to *volunteer?*"

"Isn't tha' th' way it's done?"

The Scotsman glanced at his companions, took off his cap, and scratched his head. No one spoke, until at last, the handsome man in a lieutenant's uniform cleared his throat. He moved with the silken grace of a snake and had cold, sullen eyes containing about as much warmth as the bitter wind that cuffed the Solent into a mass of frothy white horses. "I'm Lieutenant Russell Rhodes. You want to sign aboard, eh?" He seized her canvas bag and, heedless of her frightened gasp, tossed it to the Scotsman before Deirdre had time to protest. "Well, then, let's see if you qualify. Climb that mast and don't stop till you reach the maintop—using the futtocks, of course."

Futtocks? It was all she could do not to reach for her notes to see what a "futtocks" was. "But ... but don't I have t' sign somethin'?"

"Just get your ass up that pole!" roared the pirate, stepping forward and brandishing his cutlass.

"Aye, that's all the signing we'll ask of ye!" snarled a big, dirty hulk of a man covered with a mat of brown hair. His odor alone was bad enough to send Deirdre scurrying to the mast.

"Jesus," said the Scotsman, slapping his broad forehead. "The tyke don't even know how to climb it!"

"Go to the gangway and use the shrouds, ye idiot!"

The pirate waved his cutlass in her face. Digging her nails into her palms to keep from crying, Deirdre looked up at the tall mast and choked back her fear, for it seemed to hold up the clouds themselves. Then the Scotsman shoved her toward the network of black, tarry ropes that ran skyward like narrow, tapering pyramids from the side of the ship.

"*Those* are the shrouds," he said gently. "Use them like a ladder. Ye ken, laddie?"

Deirdre pressed her hand to her shirt, seeking the comfort of the crucifix. Then, biting her quivering lip, she nodded, grasped the tarry, ice-coated shrouds, and began to ascend. She climbed one step. Two. Three steps up, she looked down and, shivering, found the tip of the pirate's cutlass two inches from her nose. He was grinning evilly.

There was no going back. Not now.

Whimpering and nearing hysteria, Deirdre took a fourth step, clinging to the harsh ropes like a treed cat afraid to move. The deck was only a few feet beneath her, but she was off its solidness now, and she could feel the sway and movement of the big ship right through her hands and up through the soles of her feet.

"I can just see him in a storm," muttered the Scotsman, shaking his head.

"Hell, I can see him when our bloody Lord and Master makes us do sail drills."

"Sail drills? He wouldn't!"

"You doubt him?"

"No captain's *ever* made us do sail drills!"

"Well, from what *I've* heard, doona put it past this one." The Scotsman sneezed, pulled out an enormous handkerchief, and waved it at Deirdre. Raising his voice, he yelled, " 'Tis climbin' higher than that ye'll have tae be, laddie, if ye want tae reach the maintop!"

"I'm ... catchin' me breath."

The foul-smelling one stepped forward. "You ain't gonna have *time* to catch yer breath when you 'ave a storm howling up your ass and the bosun's mates laying the rattans across yer back! Now, *climb!"*

Deirdre pressed her face against the ice-encrusted ropes, smelling the pungent aroma of tar and sea salt. She was terrified and fighting tears. One slip, and she would fall into the water so far below. One slip, and she would be dead. Already the chill wind was singing in her ears, and she had a long way to go before she reached what had to be the maintop. *Oh, God,* she sobbed, digging her frozen fingers into the shrouds and fighting dizziness. *Oh, God, please help me. . . .* She took a deep breath and pulled herself up a little farther.

But as she took another step, then another, she realized that the crew's attention was no longer on her. A boat was coming from shore, a feather of white at its bow, a militaristic figure dressed in blue and white in its stern.

Every man on the deck below had turned to stare at it.

"Christ, here comes the bloody captain now!"

"Quick, look busy!"

Deirdre flattened herself against the shrouds, shut her eyes, and swallowed the thick lump of dread. Oh, God. Oh, dear God. Now what? Stay here and be seen? Go back down and face the captain?

Or—her fingers bit into the shrouds as the ship swayed slightly, sickeningly, beneath her—go up?

She made up her mind, for there was no time to do otherwise. Desperate with terror, Deirdre tilted back her head, scurried skyward, and didn't stop until she reached the hole that led into the maintop. She hauled herself through it and lay there on the platform for a moment, breathing hard and not daring to look down. Then she mustered her courage and, trembling, made the mistake of peering over the edge.

It was a good thing she was on that platform when she looked down, for at that moment she fainted, and therefore missed Captain Christian Lord's arrival.

"Blind me, what the deuced hell is *wrong* with these people, Hendricks?!" Christian snapped, his gray eyes hard with fury as he stared up at the gently curved tumble home of *Bold Marauder's* black-and-gold hull. "This is a king's ship, damn them, and as such they should bloody well know the meaning of *respect!"*

"Aye, sir," the dark-skinned Jamaican bosun said, a bit ashamed that he'd been away from the frigate when his friend and captain had sent the request for a gig. Had he been aboard, he would never have allowed such a thing to happen. Rico Hendricks, a former slave, had been with Christian since the captain's days as a midshipman, when the young boy-officer had rescued him from the gallows after Rico's involvement in a scheme to overthrow his cruel master in Jamaica. Christian had changed little over the years in *that* respect, Rico thought as he took the squirming,

wet bundle from his captain's arms. He might be harder, he
might be harsher, but he still had a soft spot for the unfortunate and the abused.

And swift and fitting justice for the kind of pranks the
new crew was up to.

Rico had been ashore, procuring some spare cordage,
when he'd found Christian stalking the quay in a towering
rage. From the interactions *he'd* had with the officers and
crew of HMS *Bold Marauder,* Rico knew his captain was
going to have his hands full with this bunch. Not only had
his request for a gig been blatantly ignored, there was no
one at the entry port to welcome him aboard his new command. And for a man who detested *any* slur on the king's
Navy—be it a sloppy uniform, ungentlemanly behavior on
the part of an officer, or any breach in discipline that would
weaken the chain that was the Service—the simple denial of
a welcoming party was a declaration of war on the part of
a crew who had yet to learn just *whom* they were dealing
with.

It was not a good beginning.

The boat's crew, a sloppy, sorry bunch of malcontents
who looked like dregs out of Newgate, made several halfhearted attempts to hook onto *Bold Marauder*'s main chains
before finally succeeding. Furious, Christian looked up, still
expecting the customary shrill of pipes, the smart rectangle
of marines presenting arms, the roll of a drum, and the organized fanfare a ship was supposed to give its captain.

But there was nothing. Not even a soul at the entry port.

Fuming, he scaled the ship's side, vowing that such nonsense would not be tolerated under *his* command. Behind
him came Rico, cradling the captain's new pet in the crook
of his arm, grinning to himself, and anticipating spectacular
fireworks. At last, Christian reached the entry port and
stepped smartly onto the frigate's deck.

There was no one there to receive him, just a seaman
lounging insolently against the bulwarks and watching him,
picking his teeth with the blade of his knife.

Christian saluted the quarterdeck with tight efficiency, respectfully doffing his hat. Then he slammed it back atop his
bewigged head and marched past a row of mutinous-looking

men who sneered at him and spat on the deck in disdain after his passing. Straight up the ladder to the great, double-spoked wheel he went, his sword slapping against his well-muscled thigh, his eyes blazing. A seaman stood at the rail nearby, with a licey-looking mat of black hair and a beard that reached to his waist. He gave Christian an insolent glance. Then he went right on with what he was doing—nonchantantly carving his initials into the gunwale with a knife that could've skewered a cow from one end to another—with total unconcern. Without breaking stride, Christian reached out, spun him around, and, grabbing the man by the unsightly black growth that sprouted from his jaw, yanked him forward.

"Your name, sailor!"

"Arthur Teach," the seaman sneered. ". . . *sir.*"

"Well, Mr. Teach, fetch your first lieutenant and bring him to me," Christian snapped.

"Don't know where he is."

"Don't get uppish with me, you devilish bit of rabble! My patience has already been sorely tested and I warn you, the consequences of its being lost will not be pleasant for you or anyone else!" He yanked Teach forward by the beard until their eyes were inches apart, and snatched the knife from his hand. "Furthermore, I shall abide no defacing of property that doesn't belong to you, and no facial hair adorning the faces of my crew. Do I make myself clear?"

Teach made a rude gesture, tried to turn away—and had his neck nearly broken as the captain, still holding him by the beard, jerked his head around and hacked the evil growth off with one swoop of his own knife. Then he flung both the weapon and the beard to the deck, his eyes hard as he stared up into those of the stunned Teach.

"*Now* do I make myself clear?"

Teach stood gaping, his mouth opening and closing, his hands slowly coming up to feel his jaw. His face went white with shock, then red with fury, and Christian heard the hushed whispers from the group that was now gathering near the mainmast.

"Jee-zus, he just hacked off Teach's beard!"

"*Holy Moses,*" another breathed.

Christian seized the seaman's sleeve and roughly shoved him forward. "I gave you an order to bring me your first lieutenant," he barked. "Now, *move!*"

Teach staggered away, dazed, his hands cupping his shorn jaw. Out of the corner of his eye Christian saw Hendricks, still holding the little spaniel and watching him in gleeful approval, ready as always to step in and assist him should the need arise. But Christian was well able to take care of himself. He watched the men rushing up from below, gathering by the boats in the ship's waist, talking excitedly and staring at him in shock, disbelief, and open rebellion.

But he was in no mood to put up with further nonsense.

"Now that I have your undivided attention," he began, raking them with his gray stare, "allow me to clarify something for you. This is a king's ship and, as such, is part of the most powerful Navy in the world. She was designed by a colleague of mine, a naval architect who is a master at his trade, and therefore should wear her name with *pride,* not disgrace. I intend to give her back that pride, and I intend to start here and now. Henceforth, you shall behave as seamen in the service of your king, honoring both this ship and her officers by showing them *respect!*"

The crew eyed him balefully. Someone spat. Someone else belched.

Christian ignored them.

"The next time I enter this ship, I shall expect a proper and ceremonious welcome. You will pipe me aboard and you will stand at attention when I come through the entry port. As it will be a good month before I have to do so again, you should have plenty of time in which to practice this simple ritual." Drawing his sword, he clasped his hands over the hilt and rested the point against the deck, his smile cold and forbidding. "Is that understood?"

Silence.

The wind played with the powdered white locks of his periwig, ruffled the lace at his wrist. "After I read myself in, we shall weigh anchor and begin our journey to the American colonies, where *Bold Marauder* is under orders to hunt down and capture the Irish Pirate who's become such a damnable nuisance off the New England coast. We are also

expected to lend our assistance to Vice Admiral Sir
Geoffrey Lloyd in easing the mounting tension in Boston."
He paused, feeling their hatred crackling through the air like
lightning in an electrical storm. "Do I make myself clear?"

No one moved.

"Splendid!" He threw back his shoulders, his bright tone
belying his cold, hard eyes. "I see that we have already arrived at an understanding. And I expect that we will *understand* each other even better by the end of this voyage.
Should you demonstrate obedience and loyalty, you will
find me a most agreeable commander. In the meantime, do
not test my patience, for I warn you, you'll find it devilishly
short."

The crew, all one hundred and fifty of them, stared at
him, their eyes filled with loathing.

"Any questions?"

No one moved. The seaman who'd spat did so again.

Without pause, Christian ordered, "You may get the
bucket and clean that up."

The seaman stared at him.

Christian locked gazes with him. "I'll not repeat myself."

The offender looked to Teach as though for
permission—or, more likely, permission for refusal—and,
finding no response from that quarter, walked slowly to one
of the buckets lying near the bulwarks.

"Lively, now!" Christian prompted.

Every eye was on the seaman as, scowling, he picked up
the bucket and swaggered back to his former spot. With a
curse, he let it drop to the deck. Dirty water splashed out
and made a pool at his feet.

"You may clean that up, too, sailor. And when you have
finished you may give the mop and bucket to Mr. Teach so
he can remove that devilish mess of black hair that is even
now fouling my decks. This is a fighting ship, not a barbershop!"

With that he turned smartly on his heel, marched past
them, and, ducking his head beneath the deck beams, went
below. There should've been a marine stationed outside his
cabin door, and it didn't surprise him to find that there was
not.

Another thing that would have to change, of course.

Entering the cabin, he slammed the door shut, but not before allowing the little spaniel, who had followed him belowdecks, to slip into his quarters. Christian released his pent-up breath, his fists opening and closing as he allowed his anger to abate. It would not do to be in such a black rage when the first lieutenant arrived. He picked up the little dog, who trembled and turned her face against his chest. Gently stroking her fur, he went to the stern windows and looked out over the harbor, knowing he was going to have his hands full with *this* crew. Already they had challenged his authority—but, by God, when HMS *Bold Marauder* dropped anchor in Boston, Sir Geoffrey Lloyd would see a ship that the Navy could be proud of!

But as he stared out over the anchorage, the memories crept under his guard and drove away the troubles of his new command, for the rebellious crew was of little consequence when compared with the real devils that haunted him.

Tomorrow was the Black Anniversary, five years to the night since *she* had died.

He took a deep, shaky breath, his mind drifting back in time as he hugged the little dog closer to his chest. He tried to block the memories, but they came flooding back—just as they sometimes did during his waking hours, just as they always did during his sleeping ones. But such hours weren't filled with dreams. They were filled with nightmares, nightmares that would haunt Captain Christian Lord for the rest of his life.

He swallowed, helpless against the silent tears of agony coursing down his cheeks. *Emily.* If only he'd stayed at home and been there for her, instead of off commanding ships of war, maybe things would've been different. If only he hadn't made a career out of the Navy, maybe she wouldn't have sought the arms of another. *If only he didn't still love her. . . .*

"Dear God," he moaned, burying his cheek against the spaniel's soft ears, then raising his head to drag his arm over his eyes. The proud captain's insignia on his sleeve blotted the tears, but not the memories. "Dear God, Emmy, forgive me my failures. As a friend. As a lover. As—" He swallowed the thick, burning lump that caught suddenly in his throat. "As a husband."

Chapter 3

Deirdre opened her eyes and saw a sky smeared with clouds behind a web of spars and lines. She sat up with a gasp, looked down, and pressed herself back against the mast, her vision reeling and her hand clutching her stomach as she willed herself not to be sick.

She'd taken only one quick glance, but it had been enough. Far, far below, men scurried like ants on a deck that looked hideously narrow from this far up. Birds flew *beneath* her, not above. The waves on either side of the ship were tiny with distance, and she was so high up that she could look across, and down at, the rooftops of the buildings that framed the waterfront.

Shaking convulsively with both cold and fear, Deirdre shut her eyes in raw terror. *Oh, God,* she thought, swallowing against the rise of bile in her throat and barely able to move her paralyzed throat muscles. *Oh, Jesus, Joseph, an' Mary.* Trying not to cry, she reached up and wrapped shaking hands around Grace's crucifix. *How was she going to get down?*

But the shrouds were quivering as someone climbed skyward. Her heart racing in mounting terror, Deirdre plastered her spine against the mast. A head appeared, capped by a great, oily mop of brown curls that looked as though it had never seen soap. The body that followed it looked—and smelled—no cleaner.

It was the man she'd heard the others refer to as Skunk. Grunting, he hoisted himself up beside her and frowned as he studied her bloodless face. "Best get yer arse down there before the bloody Lord 'n' Master finds ye slouchin' off."

"Th' Lord an' Master?" she squeaked. "D'ye mean our captain's a titled gentleman?"

"Titled, my ass. Damned if I know or care. Hell, I forgot, ye're a bloody landlubber, aren't ye?" He shook his head. "Lord 'n' Master's a name we tars give to the captain of a ship," he explained. "But we also use it as our own *fond* nickname for that bastard below, after 'is own surname. Fittin', though. Ye'd think 'e's a bloody nobleman, the way 'e struts around here givin' orders an' expectin' 'em to be obeyed!"

Deirdre was trembling violently. "But isn't tha' 'twhat a captain's supposed t' do? Give orders?"

"This here's *Bold Marauder*," Skunk pointed out, his chin jutting stubbornly. "We don't take orders from *nobody*."

"Oh," Deirdre said in a small voice.

"Anyhow, I came up here to drag ye down. I knows yer scared, and 'is bloody Lordship'll be topside any moment. Pompous ass—we're all in for a hard pull with the likes o' that one in command. Why, I'll be bettin' my eyeteeth 'e don't know a damned thing about sailin' a ship; prob'ly got where 'e is by *who* 'e knows, not *wot* 'e knows, God rot his bloody, pampered hide!"

Not knowing the captain, Deirdre could not offer comment.

"Cruel bastard. Ye know what 'e did? Hacked off Teach's beard, right in front of the whole bloody crew. Hacked it right off! I'm tellin' ye, 'e'd better watch 'is back now, 'cause Teach'll be out for him. 'Course, we already got 'im good—ever hear of sabotage?—but he won't know 'bout that for a bit; besides, it ain't nothin' compared to what ol' Arthur's planning. Some night the captain'll wake up with 'is throat slit, and *that's* if 'e's lucky!" Skunk moved easily to the shrouds. "Here, gimme yer hand, bucko. That's it, slide on up behind me, put yer hands around my neck and hold on tight. Not that tight; yer chokin' me. Watch yer head there. That's it."

Holding her breath, Deirdre shut her eyes and put her face against Skunk's broad back, wondering how long she could hold out before fainting—either from lack of air or from the strong odors coming from her savior's unscrubbed body. But they were going down, and that was all that mattered.

"He think's he's gonna impress his admiral by straightenin' us out, but he's got a thing or two to learn about us, and *we've* got a thing or two of our own to show the admiral! You just wait till we set sail, hee-hee-hee!" Skunk descended as easily as if he were going down a flight of stairs and Deirdre breathed a prayer of relief as the faces of those below grew larger and larger. "Aye, you wait. We don't take no rubbish from no one, mark me well." He swung himself onto the deck and, kneeling, put her down. "Now, run along, boy, and don't let the Lord an' Master see ye, else he'll flay the skin off yer back and smile while doing it."

Deirdre needed no urging. Humiliated, and keenly aware of the smirks, sneers, and taunts of Skunk's shipmates, she snatched up her canvas bag and fled forward, where she melted safely into the group of seamen gathered in the forecastle. They stared at her as though she had grown a horn in the middle of her forehead. Finally she found a hatch and ducked below. Dear God, the ship wasn't even out of port yet and she was already in trouble. How on earth would she last the passage to America?

She reached up and touched the crucifix through the layers of her clothing. She had to.

Brendan was in America, and he was her only hope of finding her brother—and the hated British lieutenant who'd pressed him.

"Get the ship under way, please, Mr. MacDuff."

Captain Christian Lord stood near *Bold Marauder*'s great, double-spoked wheel, his hands gripping the hilt of his sword and his eyes in shadow beneath the brim of his hat. His militaristic figure emanated authority and discipline, and the Royal Navy couldn't have boasted a more capable commander.

The men hated him.

His hat, turned up in the back, sporting a black cockade, and nearly spanning the width of his shoulders, was edged with gold lace and set smartly atop his periwig. His blue coat, its buttons winking in the sun, was open to show his scrupulously clean white waistcoat and breeches. His neck-cloth was smartly tied beneath his haughty chin, his sleeves were frothed with lace, and not a speck of dust marred the shiny blackness of his buckled shoes.

He looked every inch the naval captain that he was. But only he knew of his trepidation at the thought of his admiral, and his peers, watching from the shore, the signal tower, and the decks of other vessels. Some of them, he knew, had delayed their own departures, obviously unwilling to miss what promised to be quite the spectacle.

He tightened his jaw, vowing there would *be* no spectacle.

Beside him, his first lieutenant stood, anxiously watching the anchor party. Christian glanced up at the snapping mast-head pennant and tried to ease the tension between himself and his first officer. "A fine day to put to sea, eh, Mr. MacDuff?"

Ian looked very nervous. "Aye, *sir,*" he muttered, slinging something over his shoulder and catching his captain's eye with the movement.

Christian turned, a dark frown spreading across his tanned brow. "Pray tell, what *is* that hellish contraption, Mr. MacDuff?"

"Bagpipes . . . sir."

"And what is their purpose, Lieutenant?"

"Er, tae make music, sir."

"Have they any place in a battle?"

"No, sir. Not in a sea battle, that is. . . ."

"Very well, then. I'd prefer that you leave them in your cabin when you are in the capacity of your command."

"But—"

Christian grinned to cover the steel in his voice. "Mr. MacDuff, that is an order."

Christian tightened his lips. *Bagpipes?* By God, what the *devil* was the Navy coming to! Still shaking his head, he glanced at the sailing master. A heavyset man, Tom

Wenham had great, jutting ears that seemed to hold up his hat. Several fingers were missing from his left hand, and the tip of his bulbous nose was raw and sunburned. Beside him stood a feral-looking lad dressed in the dirty and stained uniform of a midshipman, a slate in one hand, a pencil in the other.

Christian put his hands behind his back and rocked on his heels. Ian MacDuff was eyeing him nervously and stroking his bristling red beard, as though fearful that it would meet the same fate as Teach's. MacDuff had damned good reason to be nervous. As the frigate's second-in-command, he should be setting an example, not provoking more rebelliousness. Facial hair would *not* be tolerated—and neither would that outlandish Scottish garb.

Sudden anger inflamed Christian. By God, this was the *Navy,* not a damned circus show!

But he would wait until they were at sea before addressing the matter of Ian's beard—as well as Hibbert's filthy uniform and a score of other embarrassments he'd already noted in his log. Weighing anchor and getting the ship under way was a delicate enough operation without further complicating matters by alienating his first officer. And as for the crew itself . . . they hated him now, yes, but they'd hate him even more once they got away from England and the ocean rolled beneath their keel. . . .

He smiled to himself. Not that it bothered him, for he was not a man who courted friendship or popularity. For now, all that mattered was getting *Bold Marauder* safely away from Portsmouth without mishap in sight of his acquaintances, his peers, or—God forbid—his admiral.

His apprehension built. The wind was blowing fresh, and it wouldn't take much to land *Bold Marauder* in trouble—literally. But the tide was going out, and he could delay no longer. Mentally pulling himself up, he laced his fingers together behind his back and took a deep breath. Forward, the anchor was nearly hove short, the men swearing and straining at the capstan, the great cable thundering and clanking through the hawseholes. A bosun's mate stood astride the bowsprit, his greasy pigtail whipping in the cold wind, one hand wrapped around a stay, the other circling in indication of how much cable was left to bring in.

Suddenly the man raised his hand, and Rhodes, who'd been supervising the capstan party, yelled, "Anchor's hove short, sir!"

Christian gave the barest perceptible nod. He glanced quickly at the signal tower on the shore, where flags fluttered in the wind, giving him permission to proceed.

Yes, they are all watching. The whole bloody harbor. . . .

"Bring it in," he commanded.

But something was wrong. He knew it even as the men at the capstan heaved, swore, and glanced in mock confusion at each other. He knew it even as he heard several amused guffaws. And he knew it even as he saw several men exchange glances and turn away to hide their sudden grins.

Above, the wind blew impatiently, and out of the corner of his eye Christian saw the glint of sunlight against a telescope from shore.

"Is there a problem, Mr. Rhodes?"

Rhodes turned, a helpless look on his face that was directly at odds with the glint in his eye. "Uh, the anchor seems to be fouled, sir."

Bloody hell. Christian closed his eyes and mentally went through a vocabulary of much bluer naval language. "Are you sure, Mr. Rhodes?"

The lieutenant was peering over the bulwarks, his blue coattails waving in the breeze. Christian heard the crew snickering, and his apprehension turned to raw fury.

Sabotage.

Rhodes straighted up, feigning innocence. "Aye, sir," he called. "Seems to be caught on something."

Silence, with only the wind and the lap of the waves. Christian thought of those who were watching: Sir Elliott . . . the men in the signal tower . . . the hundreds of spectators, as well as other captains, officers, and seamen in and around Portsmouth Harbor and Spithead—

"Your orders, sir?" Rhodes called, smiling benignly.

The embarrassment of losing an anchor couldn't have come at a worse time, and there were only two things he could do: either delay his departure and try to retrieve it, or cut the cable and get the bloody hell out of there.

He thought of all the eyes watching from shore, from the other ships, and wasted no time on a decision.

"Hands aloft to loose tops'ls."

From below the quarterdeck rail, he heard fierce whispers that he did his best to ignore and vowed not to forget.

"This'll *really* make him look bad!"

"Aye, 'twill bring his bloody Lordship down a tuppence or two!"

His order was repeated through speaking trumpets. Men ran to the braces while others scrambled up the ratlines and out along the yards. Sail spilled down, rolling in the wind with a noise like thunder. The wind was blowing strong, and he knew he would have only a few short moments to get the sails properly set before the frigate was swept dangerously close to shore and the other anchored vessels. He would have to move fast, for once the cable was cut—

His heart began to hammer in his throat. From shore, another telescope glinted in the sunlight. Another, from an admiral's flagship. . . .

He saw Rico, watching for his next order; he felt the frigate trembling deep in her bones. He took a deep, steadying breath, stared nervously at the land, and snapped, "Prepare to lose the anchor."

The cable was cut. Like a bird trying out its wings for the first time, the frigate reeled drunkenly, her canvas flapping her yards jumping, the men aloft yelling with alarm, and some with fear, as their precarious footholds jerked and bucked beneath them.

"Look alive on those braces!"

On deck, swearing, shouting men were laid nearly on their backs as they heaved and hauled at the braces. From above came a yell of alarm as a topman slipped on a foot-rope and nearly feel. Christian stared at the land drawing closer and closer. *"Get those bloody tops'ls set!"* he roared.

The shore was now so close that he could see the people lining the docks and watching the magnificent sight of a king's ship getting under way; it was so close that he could hear the jeering hoots of ridicule from a moored sloop of war whose crew knew that the sight wasn't the least bit magnificent; it was so close that he could see the windows of an inn, and the glint of sun off another telescope. Another . . .

"Loose fore and main courses!"

Ian had been picking at a callus on his knuckle. "Huh?"

"Loose fore and main courses!"

"Oh. Aye. Uh, aye, *sir.*"

But just then the men, leaning on their heels and nearly horizontal to the deck as they hauled on the braces, sent up a great cry of distress and tumbled onto their backs.

A line had parted.

Another.

And then more cries of dismay as a brace gave way with a sound like a pistol shot.

Great God above!

Above, acres of canvas flapped in out-of-control fury. Lines snapped to and fro like the tails of a whip, yards jerked and quivered—and HMS *Bold Marauder,* out of control, headed directly for shore.

"Assume the deck, Mr. MacDuff!" Christian yelled, already running down the quarterdeck stairs and racing forward to take control of the confusion.

But it was too late. Ian, standing dumbly beside the wheel, suddenly realized the magnitude of responsibility his commanding officer had just shoved on him. "Christ, laddies, *do something!* Where's Skunk? *Skunk!* Jesus, don't just stand there—"

Skunk stood just below the quarterdeck railing, grinning and idly picking at a tooth. "Piss off, Ian. Just because ye've been given a bit o' power, ye don't have to take it out on the rest of us!"

"Yeah, leave us out of it!" Teach yelled.

"Move!" Ian roared, seeing the shoreline coming closer and closer. "Saints alive—*Christ,* Wenham, there's a moored boat coming up on the larboard bows—"

"What boat?"

Ian grabbed the wheel and spun it hard, but with the sails flapping helplessly, it was no use. And the wheel—

"The steering's gone!" he cried, curling his hands into claws and raking at his hair. *"The bluidy steering's gone!"*

The little boat cringed beneath the shadow of the oncoming frigate, and Ian clapped his hands to his ears as it was helplessly smashed beneath the great bows.

"You tampered with the rudder!" Ian yelled, going for Wenham's throat, and the sailing master ducked as the Scot's huge fist swung in a flying arc. Ian didn't see his captain desperately shoving men aside as he fought his way back to the quarterdeck. He didn't see the crew tossing down what lines *hadn't* been tampered with and surging aft to view the fight.

And he didn't see the imposing wall of old Admiral Burns's proud flagship looming up off the leeward bows, the admiral himself standing on the quarterdeck in appalled shock—

Sighing, the frigate sank her bowsprit into the man-of-war's rigging, plunged through spars and masts, and then slammed hard against the massive hull with a stunning, grinding crash. The impact knocked everyone off his feet and sent the seamen flying against pinrails, railings, and the deck itself.

Lieutenant Ian MacDuff's hot Scottish temper exploded. Ducking, he squeezed his eyes shut and came up swinging.

Skunk caught the first blow, dealt the second. Teach, seeing a good fight and furious at being left out, dove into the melee. Fists flew. Grunts and groans and curses split the air. And the new, rawboned little recruit raced up from below, saw her chance of escape from what she'd long since decided was the *wrong* ship to take to the colonies, and made a wild dive toward the rail.

"Get back here, ye miserable little worm! 'Tis all your fault we're gonna get in trouble!"

"His bloody Lordship's gonna have poor Ian's hide!"

Ian smashed a fist into Teach's jaw, raised his head, and bawled, "Damn right he is, and I'll nae suffer his temper alone, ye miserable pack of lazy, good-fer-nothing bastards!"

"Hell, don't take it out on us—it's that little pisser's

fault!" howled the rat-faced midshipman, pointing at Deirdre.

"*My* fault?"

They came at her in a pack.

"No!"

Screaming, Deirdre bolted for the railing, tripped over a coiled pile of rope, and went down hard, scraping her palms and smashing her chin against the deck. Her precious bag of Irish mementos skidded away. Stars exploded across her eyes. Her tooth cut into her lip. The coppery taste of blood filled her mouth and desperately she scrambled to regain her feet, only to fall once more as a booted foot caught her behind the knees. A hand yanked her to her feet; another shoved her violently toward the shrouds. "Get yourself up that mast and start cutting us loose—*now!*" shouted Hibbert, the rat-faced little midshipman.

There was no way in Satan's hell she was going up that mast again—nor, since she was leaving, any reason to. "Get up it y'rself, ye poxy, bleedin' bully!"

His fist crashed into her cheek. Dizzily, she swung back, lashing blindly out and managing to catch him in the mouth. Pain shot up her hand and mixed with blood—her blood, Hibbert's blood—and he came at her again, a stream of crimson pouring from his lip. Grabbing her wrist, he twisted it savagely behind her back. "He hit an officer!" the boy raged, his eyes wild. "He *hit me!*"

"Can't let such a crime go unpunished!"

"Aye, punish him! Last him to the mast and give him Moses' Law!"

"Lash him good, I say!" Someone threw the middie a whip. "Strip the skin from 'is bleedin' back!"

"Give 'im two dozen!"

"Give him three!"

Deirdre kicked and fought and screamed as they seized her wrists and tied them to the mast. Her teeth sank into someone's arm and she tasted grime and sweat. A hand cuffed her sharply across the jaw. Behind her, the men were in a frenzy, desperate for a scapegoat so they wouldn't get the punishment their captain and his big Jamaican henchman would surely have in store for them.

"Four-dozen lashes, Hibbert!"

"Make it five!"

It became a chant. "Five! Five! Five!"

"No!" Her desperate cries rang in her ears as someone tore the jacket from her back and Hibbert grabbed up the cat-o'-nine-tails.

"No-o-o-ooo!" She writhed in terror, the rope biting into her wrists as she waited for the horrible, agonizing fire to slam between her shoulders and drive the breath from her lungs. Hibbert, his eyes maniacal, drew back his arm, and she screamed as someone tore her shirt away and cold, bitter wind swept in to lash against her bare and tender back—

Hibbert's arm froze above his head.

"Holy God in heaven," someone breathed. "It's a *woman.*"

Hibbert dropped the whip. A hush fell over the ship. The tears racing down her dirty cheeks, Deirdre collapsed and hung by her wrists, her wretched sobs the only sound. Then, through the haze of fear she saw the captain striding toward her, his jaw tight and angry, his face obscured by the shadow of his hat. This was the man they hated and feared. This was the man whose word was God's aboard the vessel. This was the man who controlled their lives, their actions, their destiny.

This was the Lord and Master.

The crew, silent and still and rigid with fear, wordlessly parted, letting him pass. Straight up to her he came. She felt a knife sawing at her bound wrists. . . . Strong hands lifting her up . . . A solid, hard, comforting chest . . . Movement beneath her and faces passing, gaping, staring. She reached up, clutched the stainless white lapels, and huddled protectively against him, sobbing piteously and smearing that fine white shirt and waistcoat with blood and tears. His hand stroked her hair, held her protectively close. Then the sunlight was cut off as she was carried below. . . .

"Easy, foundling." His voice was deep and rich and soothing, rumbling up out of his chest just beneath her cheek. " 'Twill be all right. Easy, now."

She dug her fingers into his lapels and cried harder.

They passed bulkheads, alive with checkerboards of dark

and light, and then the great, imposing door, where a grim-faced marine with a musket stood guard outside. Horrible, choking terror rose up in her as they approached that sacred domain.

Then they were through the door and into the cabin. He set her down upon the deck flooring and she stood there in a daze, shivering, her arms coming up to shield her bare breasts, tears of fear and shame coursing down her face.

The Lord and Master's back was to her. He had broad and capable shoulders. Gold insignias on his sleeves, gold lace on his cocked hat, and gold trim decorating his coat.

Then he turned, and the blood drained from Deirdre's face. She staggered backward, hit a table, and sank to the floor.

It was the young lieutenant she'd vowed to find and kill. Except he wasn't a lieutenant anymore.

He was the captain.

Chapter 4

"No...."

She stared at him, denying the truth, yet feeling a hot, dizzy rush of sensation sweep through her blood as recognition set in.

He was broad through the shoulders, lean through the waist, and solid muscle in between. Smart white breeches emphasized long, powerful thighs, and hard eyes the color of fog perused the world from a sun-seared face with the proud, harsh features of an aristocrat.

He wore a carefully powdered and rolled white periwig, but there was no mistaking the haughty brows, arrogant nose, thin, English lips, and hawkish profile that could've been carved in stone. She felt that if this man smiled, that rigid, disdainful face might crack.

He smiled and it did not.

"The devil take me," he murmured, raking her with chilly gray eyes. Their color was that of the ocean beneath stormy skies, but as he moved, sunlight slanted across the irises and brought out the barest hint of green. "A woman. Life is full of bloody surprises, is it not!"

"You. . . ." she breathed, pulling herself to her feet. Her mouth gaped open, and unconsciously, she dropped her arms from her breasts—giving Captain Christian Lord an unobstructed view of the first female charms he'd seen in five years.

Hot, lancing desire left him momentarily helpless, for he hadn't felt anything for a woman, *any* woman, since Emily had died, and now was not the bloody time—

Raw fury swept through him and he tore off his coat.

"Pray, madam, cover yourself!" he barked, shoving it angrily at her harlot's body and moving toward the door.

She flung it back at him, her eyes glassy with unshed tears. "I'll rot in hell before I wear th' king's coat, ye bleedin' English *dog!"*

"By God, I haven't the time to play nursemaid with a bloody doxy!" he snarled, flinging the coat back at her and tearing open the door. "You'll wear this deuced garment, by God, or I'll put it on you myself!"

"Ye so much as touch me wi' yer filthy English hands and I'll make ye regret th' day you were *whelped,* ye poxy, bleedin' bastard!"

He whirled on his heel, his brow dark with fury, but just then the current swung the two ships together with a crash. The girl lost her balance, struck her soft thigh against his table, and with a cry tumbled to the floor.

She burst into tears.

"Bloody *hell,"* he swore, her pitiful, wretched sobs driving straight into his heart. For a brief moment he stared at her, a muscle in his harsh jaw jumping with anger; then, damning the frigate to hell, the tall and forbidding captain—hero of Quiberon, hope of *Bold Marauder,* and savior of the helpless and abandoned—went to her, dragged her to her feet, and gathered her roughly up against his broad and mighty chest.

Outside the door came voices and the warning thump of Evans's musket against the deck.

"Let me go, ye slimy, scum-suckin' *dog!*" the girl raged, sobbing and struggling in his arms. "Let m' *go-o-o-o!*"

"Evans!" he yelled, fighting to keep her still, and painfully aware of the press of her bare breasts against his waistcoat. "Keep your station at that bloody door, mind you, and allow no one to enter, is that understood?"

"Uh—aye, sir." The marine hesitated. "But—"

"No 'buts,' Evans. That is an order!"

"But, sir—"

The girl was shrieking at the top of her lungs. "I'll see ye in hell, ye rotten blackguard, ye worthless whelp of a stinkin' cur, ye—"

"Captain, *sir!*" Evans cried urgently.

"Bugger off, Evans!"

"But, *Captain—*"

With a savage curse, Christian shoved the girl away from him. "Damn you, Evans, *wait a moment!*" he roared, but he no sooner turned his back on her when she grabbed his water pitcher, hurled it at him, and dove beneath his desk. Behind him, glass crashed against the bulkhead.

"Captain, sir!" Evans shouted from behind the door. "This is *most* urgent!"

"I said *in a moment!*" Christian shouted, reaching blindly beneath the desk and trying to grab the girl. He caught her hand and felt her nails scratch his skin. Teeth sank into his wrist and, cursing, he reached in with the other hand, managing to snare a coarse and curling tress of her hair.

He held on tight, her screams of rage piercing his head as he dragged her out from beneath the desk. It was like taking a tigress by the tail. She went wild, fighting him with all of her strength and soul, shrieking, kicking, and cursing him in a scalding torrent of both Irish Gaelic and English. Her foot lashed out, hit a chair, and sent it skidding across the deck to crash into the bulkhead. She twisted around, sank her teeth into his wrist, managed to free her hand, and, slamming it into his jaw, dove for the door.

He caught her before she could reach it and jerked her around, her bare breasts slamming up against his chest.

"I hate ye, ye miserable son of a bitch! I'll see ye die, ye bleedin', poxy bastard!"

Twisting against his grip, she lunged once more. His wig went askew, tumbling to the floor even as she brought her knee up and drove it savagely into his groin. Christian doubled over in agony, white-hot pain exploding behind his eyes, only to feel her fist smash against his jaw. He staggered backward, slipped in the shards of glass and water, and went down heavily on the deck.

"Sir, is everything all right in there?" Evans yelled.

"All is—ugh! *ouch!*—quite well, thank you, Evans!" Christian grunted as the girl kicked him solidly in the shoulder; then, fighting his own haze of pain, he lunged forward as she went for his pistol, catching her arm just in time and shoving it upward. The gun exploded, the ball taking a hefty chunk out of the deckhead above—

and the door crashed open and exploded against the bulkhead.

Christian froze and the girl went stiff beneath him. Evans stood there, sheepish, anxious, scarlet-faced, and more than a little terrified. And just in front of him, resplendent in a blue-and-white uniform bedecked with a dazzling array of glittering medals, badges, and gold lace, was an officer.

Not just any officer.

"Well, well. If it's beyond me to distinguish this touching scene between tranquil serenity or soon-to-be-slaked lust, then damn me for a bleeding idiot." The admiral clapped a hand to his ornamented chest in an exaggerated gesture of affront. "Really, Christian, I'd expected more from *you,* of all people!"

Elliott.

The blood drained in a sickening rush from Christian's face.

"What the devil sort of laxity *is* this, Captain Lord?!"

The admiral stood with his weight slung on one hip, his graceful hand resting against the doorframe, and his lids hooding lazy eyes that were either amused or enraged. With Elliott, it was impossible to tell.

But then, with Elliott, it had always been impossible to tell.

Now his gaze, as gray as Christian's own, roved nonchantantly over the cabin, taking in the damning scene: the black-and-white canvas smeared with what could only be virginal blood; the girl lying helpless beneath the captain, her lip bleeding and her cheek bruised—injuries no doubt sustained when she'd tried to fend off Captain Christian Lord's lust—and Captain Christian Lord himself, spread-eagled over her nearly naked body in a *most* compromising position.

Too late, Christian recovered himself. Burning with humiliation, he leapt to his feet, grabbed his hat, and bounced it off the top of his head in a hasty salute to his admiral. The girl, sobbing, shot back beneath the desk and huddled there, her arms clasped over her breasts and her eyes glittering with hatred and tears.

Elliott put two and two together, and came up with five.

Behind him, several captains had gathered, craning their necks over their admiral's shoulder as they tried to peer into the cabin. Their brows shot clear to their hat lines, and glancing amongst themselves, they began to snicker in amusement.

Christian, his ears burning with embarrassment, pulled himself up to stand rigidly at attention.

Elliott, as usual, was at his best—and enjoying himself immensely. "I say, Captain Lord, this is most humiliating—to the Royal Navy, to this ship, and, of course, to your name," he drawled. "Heathmore, would you please go topside and assist the first lieutenant in freeing this poor vessel from her helpless berth? God strike me, what is this world coming to!"

"Dammit, Elliott—" Christian said tersely, trying to explain.

"Really, Captain Lord, that is no way to address your admiral."

The corners of Elliott's mouth were twitching, and sheer will and years of discipline were all that kept Christian from leaping forward and strangling him. He clenched his fists at his sides and through clenched teeth gritted, "Forgive me, *sir,* but what you saw was not what it appeared—"

"What I see, Captain Lord, is a young woman whose virtue has been sorely compromised, and a ship that has been helplessly abandoned by her commanding officer! I say, Admiral Burns is *most* upset! The impact knocked the old dog to his knees and I fear might have even fractured one of them. Really, Christian, I had expected more from you! Neglecting your vessel so that you can molest a young girl . . . *you,* a much-decorated sea officer! Tsk, tsk. Now, please collect your coat, Captain, and come with me. I'm sure your poor victim will be quite safe until someone can tend to her injuries." He strode into the cabin, tall and elegant and handsome, and bent down before her hiding-hole beneath the desk. "Won't you, my dear?"

She stared up at him, her purple eyes glassy with tears, her lips trembling, and her arms locked protectively around her bare breasts.

The admiral removed his hat, revealing rich, sandy-gold hair that curled boyishly around his ears. "Too frightened to speak, are you? Poor little dear. Please, don't think that *all* of our naval officers behave thus. We do have our share of *gentlemen* as well."

He got to his feet and fixed Christian with a sharp look of reprimand. "Really, Christian, seducing innocent virgins—"

"I didn't seduce her. I rescued her from a fate worse—"

"Yes, yes, I'm sure you did," Elliott said, waving his hand in a lofty, amused gesture of dismissal. "Come along, please, Captain Lord. You've much to answer to!"

Christian felt white-hot anger rip through his veins; then he seized his coat and strode toward the door, limping badly. From beneath the desk, the girl smiled a triumphant grin. It faded abruptly as the handsome admiral, turning for a last look at her, bowed elegantly from the waist, gave her a heart-melting smile, and closed the door behind the captain.

For a moment, Deirdre didn't move. She listened to the footsteps fading away, the angry protests of *Bold Marauder*'s captain. Reaching up, she dashed away hot tears and stared hard at the closed door. She hoped the *Lord and Master* would face a court-martial. She hoped he'd face demotion of his rank. She hoped he'd face the rest of his days beached, where his slimy, scum-sucking ways wouldn't put anyone else at his mercy!

"Bastard," she whispered fiercely, her hands wrapping around Grace's crucifix as the tears poured down her bare arms.

Above her head, she heard the shrill of pipes and the smart thump of muskets upon the deck as the officers left the ship. She waited another moment, then crawled nervously from beneath the desk, surveying her surroundings and glancing about for a weapon with which to defend herself.

Sunlight, reflecting from the water beyond the panoramic stern windows, shimmered peacefully against the white-painted beams and deckhead. Deirdre opened the captain's armoire and slipped into one of his shirts, her eyes moving around the cabin, but there was nothing there with which to fend off the Lord and Master when—and if—he returned. Rich green leather-backed chairs, grouped around a fine table; a wine cabinet set into one corner, an armoire in another, a desk of dark mahogany against a bulkhead; and in a smaller, partitioned area off to the side, a large, claw-footed bed that reigned supreme—and contained a small, shivering, obviously pregnant dog who stared up at her with frightened eyes.

Deirdre stared back at it, wondering if she was seeing things. A *dog*?

Then she turned away—and her gaze fell upon the far bulkhead.

Her eyes widened, and adrenaline slammed through her blood.

The captain's dress sword.

It rested there on two pegs. Heedful of the marine stationed just outside the door, she crept across the room and pulled it down. Pushing the dog aside, she slid the weapon beneath the sheets, turned the sharp edge away from her body, and crawled carefully in beside it. Then she closed her eyes and, smiling, reached up to touch the crucifix that rested comfortingly against her heart.

Grace, she thought triumphantly as she stared up at the deckhead, *you'd be proud of me.*

And she'd be even more proud if Deirdre could slay her English enemy.

Still smiling, she lay back against the pillows, wrapped her hand around the hilt of the sword, and waited.

Chapter 5

"Jeez, Christian, the wench nearly killed you, let alone your career! And now you want to go back there and *help* her? What are you, daft in the head?"

"Bugger off, Rico. She was merely frightened, 'tis all."

"Frightened, my arse! She was out for blood, and by the looks of you, she got it!"

Christian didn't bother to respond. It had been several hours since *Bold Marauder*'s disastrous attempt to get under way. Now the frigate lay out in Portsmouth Harbor, her taff-rail lantern glowing softly upon the water and making a beacon in the night. Heathmore, apparently, had been successful in freeing her from the old admiral's flagship, but the damage done to her—and to the crew's respect for their new commanding officer—remained to be seen.

The crew he would deal with, in his own time and way. It was the girl who had Christian most distressed; the girl, and his own passionate reaction to her.

At the edge of the wharf he slipped, bone-weary and exhausted, onto a bench to await the gig. Dropping his chin into his neckcloth, he wrapped his arms around himself against the cold wind, and thought back over the afternoon.

It had been a nightmare. Long hours spent undergoing

rigorous questioning by a panel of five captains presided over by Sir Elliott himself; endless waiting, pacing the floor, while in the adjoining room his past was dissected and his future decided; anger with himself for trusting in a crew who didn't deserve it, and fury with his own personal weakness regarding poor, wretched souls who ranged from the likes of starving spaniels to Irish urchins.

That weakness had nearly cost him his career—not to mention his ship.

The girl. His chin sank lower into his neckcloth and he closed his eyes to shut out the dark stain on his lapel, left by her bleeding lip. By God, she was one deuced hell of a spitfire, that one. His leg hurt, twisted when he'd fallen on it. His coat was wrinkled, his breeches smudged with dirt. He felt out of sorts without his wig, his pride groveled beneath his feet, and his groin . . . he winced in remembrance of her well-placed knee.

For a man who was known to be a strict and polished disciplinarian, both with himself and his command, he looked anything but.

"Here comes the gig now, sir," Hendricks said offhandedly as the boat cut through the darkness toward them.

"Thank God." Christian opened his eyes and, not lifting his head, stared down at his white breeches, his mind many leagues away.

"I know you're thinking about *her,* sir," the bosun said, in reference to Christian's dead wife, "but maybe you ought to go out and get yourself soused tonight, if you don't mind me saying so."

"I *do* mind you saying so," Christian retorted, angry with himself that it had been the girl he'd been thinking about, not his wife, and mentally steeling himself for the torturous nightmares he knew lay ahead. "And getting myself soused will not relieve the pain, or bring her back."

"Sorry, sir. It's just that—well, I hate to see you suffer—"

"Hendricks—"

"And there *are* other women in this world."

"Hendricks!"

The bosun smiled a teasing smile, his teeth flashing white

in the darkness. "Of course, if you *were* to interest yourself in that Irishwoman, no one has to know—"

Christian's sharp glance silenced him. "You have a devilishly impertinent tongue, Rico!"

The bosun bowed mockingly. "Thank you, sir."

"And one of these days I'm going to ship you out on another vessel and let someone else deal with it."

"After you've cut it out, sir?" Hendrick's eyes twinkled at the old joke.

"Aye, Rico." Christian smiled. "*After* I've cut it out."

Together, they watched the gig, the striped shirts of its crew now melting out of the darkness. Its presence boded no happiness for Christian. Soon it would carry him back to *Bold Marauder,* and he dreaded all that awaited him there— the girl, the crew, the humiliation, and always, the nightmares that would engulf him once he succumbed to the sleep his weary body so craved.

But tonight, he knew, those nightmares would be worse than they'd ever been—for tonight was the eve of the Black Anniversary.

The gig bumped against the wharf. Christian stared down at his buckled shoes and murmured, "Damn, what I wouldn't give for a tall glass of brandy and a warm bed."

"Don't know about the brandy, sir, but I'm sure the warm bed, at least, will be awaiting you. . . ."

"Rico?"

"Aye, sir?"

"Shut up."

The bosun grinned. "So," he ventured, casually, "who do you think she is, anyhow? The Irish girl, that is?"

Why do I even bloody bother? Christian thought, tipping his head back over the bench and staring up at the stars with increasing annoyance. "Damned if I know. Her identity is beyond me."

"I'll bet she's a seaman's trollop, a doxy, come aboard for the mutual amusement of herself and the crew."

"Balderdash, Rico. I thought so, too, at first, but not now. She was anything but amused when I found her. Besides, she seems too. . . ." He paused, frowning as he tried to find the right word.

"Innocent?" Hendricks offered, one mocking brow raised.

"Aye, innocent."

"Well, next time you're tempted to believe that heap of rot, remember what she did to you. Then think of what her *innocence* nearly cost you, as far as your career goes. Why, if it weren't for your flawless record—"

"Hendricks—"

"And the fact that Sir Elliott is your own—"

"Hendricks! By God, man, do you *ever* give up?"

Grinning, the bosun jumped down into the boat as it bumped against the wharf. As usual, not much perturbed the fellow, and for that, Christian was grateful. Brushing the wrinkles out of his coat, he strode to the edge of the pier, carefully keeping any trace of emotion from his stony features. Again, the image of frightened purple eyes and a snarl of raven curls rose in his mind. Bugger the girl, why did he have to keep thinking about her, and remembering the lovely charms of her young body? He'd nearly lost his career today—he ought to be planning the best way to handle that wretched lot of malcontents who awaited him, not thinking about a woman!

His behavior today had been deplorable, and he couldn't blame Elliott for his anger. As a king's captain, he was expected to conduct himself accordingly; to behave as an officer and a gentleman; to exercise sound judgment, leadership, and diplomacy in his every action; to put his country before himself; and, when and if he married, to take someone of his own station or better to wife.

Lady Emily had been that. And now she was dead. . . .

"Hendricks, are you bloody ready yet?" he snapped.

"Aye, sir," the bosun called up from below, his face lit by a lantern held by one of the gig's crew members.

Thank God. Christian climbed down into the gig and settled in the stern. Aware of the speculative glances of the crew, he sat rigidly as the oarsmen shoved off, shivering with cold, wishing he had his boat cloak, and being careful to keep his gaze nailed to the moored frigate. They would get no hint of the day's rulings from him, by God.

But as the gig slipped through the black waters of the harbor, Christian's mind drifted back over the day's events,

and again settled upon his memory of the girl's proud
Gaelic face. Something like hysteria, crazy and unexpected,
swept through him, and it was all he could do not to bend
his head to his hands and sob out his anguish.

"Emily, love," he whispered, staring fixedly out into the
darkness, "pray, forgive me for even *thinking* of another. . . ."

His dead wife's face, still sharp despite the passage of
time, rose in his memory, driving a raw knife of guilt into
his heart. He squeezed his eyes shut, his laced fingers tightening desperately over themselves. *She doesn't compare to
you, Emily,* he thought vehemently. *No one does.* He stared
bleakly at the approaching shape of the frigate. *No one ever
will.*

Yet as the gig cut through the dark water, he couldn't help
but wonder why the Irish girl had even been *aboard* the
frigate. Unlike Hendricks, he didn't believe her to be a paid
doxy; besides, no doxy would've shielded her breasts with
her arms, as the Irish girl had. No, she was probably some
orphaned waif who'd accepted a coin or two from his crew
in return for making his life hell.

No doubt, he thought on a sudden intuition, the "whipping" had been carefully staged, too!

His jaw tightened with sudden anger. God rot him for a
blind idiot! Why hadn't he seen it before? He shook his
head, his eyes going cold and flinty. She probably *was*
working for the crew, a party to their malicious attempts to
rid their happy ship of her newest commander! No doubt
they'd all spent the bloody day laughing their arses off over
his complete and total humiliation!

Christian squared his shoulders and took a deep, steadying breath to control his mounting fury. His fingers began
an agitated tattoo against the gunwales of the gig. Laugh,
would they? Bugger the lot of them! There'd be hell to pay
after this, by God!

He had worked himself into a fine, fuming rage by the
time the gig nudged against *Bold Marauder*'s hull, a dark
wall that loomed above them like a small fortress. As the
coxswain hailed the frigate, Christian looked up, saw the

ship's yards and rigging silhouetted against the starlit sky, and—wonder of wonders!—movement near the entry port.

"The devil take me," he breathed and, despite all, was unable to prevent a smile from spreading over his grimly set lips. Well, then, this was a start, wasn't it? A devilishly *good* start after a ghastly day. Finally, a proper ceremony for the captain as he boarded his command!

His spirits lifted, ever so slightly, and despite his aching leg, his sore groin, and his wounded pride, the weary, grateful smile remained on his lips.

Until he hauled himself through the entry port and saw what awaited him.

No.

It couldn't be.

But it was. Lieutenant Ian MacDuff, decked out in that ridiculous Scottish cap and plaid, standing at attention with a single, foolishly grinning marine—Evans—smartly presenting arms.

"Welcome aboard, *sir!*" Ian beamed, and before Christian, flabbergasted and shocked, could call a halt to this lunacy, the Scotsman tucked his bagpipes under his arm, slammed his elbow into the bag, and, grinning at the loud, droning hum that blasted forth, shoved the mouthpiece between his lips.

"Sweet God in bloody heaven," Christian murmured. And then he forgot the events of the day, his dread of the inevitable nightmare, and even the girl who awaited him in his cabin as the first ear-shattering notes came bawling out of the bagpipes at a volume loud enough to drown out everything but his own agony.

"Enough, Mr. MacDuff!" he yelled, over the noise.

His face puffed up and red with effort, Ian, launching into a tune that might—with a little imagination and a lot of brandy—have been "Rule Britannia," never heard him.

"By the grace of Almighty God, *stop!*"

Christian waved his arms in a final attempt to get his lieutenant's attention—then swiftly turned and beat a hasty retreat aft.

Ian raced after him, crestfallen. Leaping over a coiled line, his eyes filled with hopeless despair, he cried, "Sir, wait! 'Tis trying I be, honestly!" He shoved the mouthpiece back between his lips and, catching the last sigh of raucous air as it exited the bag, took up where he had left off.

"Hendricks!" Christian yelled over his shoulder. "I cannot for the life of me imagine a more ghastly sound!"

"What?"

"I said—oh, go on with you. I'm going below!"

"What? I can't *hear* you!"

There was no point in trying to be heard. His ears ringing, his head pounding, Captain Christian Lord dove to the hatch, ducked beneath the low deckhead beams, flung open his door—

—and was nearly decapitated by the sword that came singing out of the darkness to chop viciously into the bulkhead just beside his ear.

Chapter 6

Oh, dear, I've done it now, Deirdre thought wildly. She'd missed.

In the faint dust of moonlight, she saw the English captain stumble back against the bulkhead, momentarily dazed by the viciousness of her unexpected attack.

Then he came for her.

With a shrill scream, Deirdre dropped the sword and lunged behind the table, her eyes terrified. "Get away from me!"

His gaze dipped, blazing right through her stolen shirt and finding her nipples. They tensed in response, and then his eyes flashed back up to her face. "Come here, foundling."

Deirdre swallowed hard, her panicky eyes darting from side to side. "I said, *get away from me!*"

He stood unmoving, every muscle tensed to spring. Raw, primal terror rose in her throat, choking her, and she bit back a terrified sob, for even in the darkness she could see the cold glitter of this flinty eyes, the harsh set of his unforgiving mouth, and the savage anger in his stance—anger he held barely in check.

Deirdre burst into tears.

"Really, my dear, you are putting both of us through exertions that are quite unnecessary, I'm afraid." His hands reached for her, stretching closer. And closer.

"L-leave me alone!" she cried, her voice rising on a scream as she stared into his cold eyes, saw his fixed smile.

"In good time, love." He feinted to one side, Deirdre dove to her right—and smashed directly into his chest.

It was like hitting a wall of brick.

"No! Let m' go!"

The desperation that had brought her to England, the courage that had come down to her through her formidable ancestress—both rushed in to save her, and before his arms, strong, steely bands of icy heat, could close around her, she reacted. With all her strength, she raised her foot and drove it down atop his toe. Then she lunged for the door, knowing she'd never make it in time.

He caught her as her hand hit the latch and she fell hard, rolling painfully.

"Filthy English *dog!*" she raged. "I'll see ye *dead!*"

"And I'll have some answers from *you* if it damn well kills me, by God!"

"Good, I hope it does!" She freed a foot, kicked at him, and smashed her toe painfully against the side of his desk. "Ow!" she yowled, jerking her leg back and shrieking in pain.

Taking advantage of the moment, he hauled her, kicking and screaming, across the cabin by the ankles. His face was a mask of fury and cold determination, and he didn't stop until he'd dragged her into the separate sleeping compartment. There, with a lack of dignity that stung her already wounded pride, he picked her up and tossed her across the great, claw-footed bed, his eyes blazing as he saw the gap in her shirt where, during their struggle, the buttons had loosened and spilled her breasts to his gaze.

With savage anger, he grabbed the blankets and flung them angrily over her.

"Cover yourself, damn you!"

She flung the covers back, determined to defy him to the end. "I'll not wear yer bleedin' coat, and I won't take yer bleedin' orders!"

"But you *will* cover yourself, by God, before you pay the bloody consequences of flaunting your charms!" he raged, hurling the covers back over her.

She angrily flung them away. "Go t' *hell,* ye filthy English *dog!*"

Before he could help himself, Christian, cursing, was on the bed with her, his hands snaring her flailing wrists and jerking them high above her head. His powerful body crushed her ribs, pinning her helplessly to the sheets. He felt the wild pounding of her heart through his clothes, the sharp stab of her talisman driving against his chest, the silken press of her breasts against his heart. Desire stirred in his loins, shocking him, appalling him.

And Deirdre, pinned helplessly beneath him, saw the heat beginning to lick at the icy depths of his gray eyes, saw something change in his face; but she was too innocent to recognize desire, and too infuriated to do more than glare up at him in a battle of wills she had no intention of losing.

"Do you know how devilishly long it has been since I've had a woman?" he ground out.

His body was crushing hers, but she refused to quail beneath his hard stare. "I'll see ye in hell."

He laughed, his breath warming her skin, his hair tickling the cup of her shoulder until she trembled uncontrollably. His hand, rough and hard and callused, dragged down her arm, her ribs, her flesh. His palm was hot, his fingers masterful and gentle. Her skin prickled in response, and in horror, she felt her heart beginning to race. *No!* she cried to herself, desperately. It was nervousness, anger, nothing more!

"See me in hell?" he murmured, his breath hot and warm against the sensitive shivery skin at the base of her shoulder.

"I think not . . . for you see, my Irish tigress, I've *been* in hell these past five years . . . and now I would like a taste of heaven."

He saw her eyes fly open. Then he lifted one spiral-curling tress, his smoky gaze drifting over the glorious black curls that fanned out over the white pillow and framed her pale face. Never, he told himself, had he seen such magnificent hair, such fiery, purple eyes, such fair and flawless skin—

But then Emily's face appeared in his mind's eye, her eyes accusing, and he felt the fire begin to cool in his blood as quickly as it had flared to life.

"Damn it all!" Anger, swift and savage, washed over him, and, desperate to hold on to something he hadn't felt in over five years, he plunged his fingers into the girl's snarled hair and jerked her head toward him. She tried to twist away, but he held her ruthlessly, claiming her soft lips in a hard, savage kiss. She whimpered deep in her throat, her struggles only fanning his determination to drive away the devils that had tormented him for so long—and to prove to himself that he could still, by God, function as a man.

"No!" she screamed against his mouth, her struggles leaping to life.

His tongue stabbed out, driving her lips and teeth apart to plunge into the sugary sweetness of her mouth. Her head twisted wildly on the pillow; her wrists strained against his hand. He drove his mouth against hers, hating himself for what he was doing, hating her for the desire she'd awakened in him—a desire that Emily had robbed from him and taken with her into the grave.

Beneath him, the girl struggled, fighting him madly, until he finally swung one well-muscled thigh over her legs to pin them to the twisted sheets. But it was no use. The quick, fleeting fire was already cooling. What had been hard and rigid and swollen was now shriveling away in retreat.

Cursing, he tore himself from her and leapt from the bed, furious, appalled, and now, ashamed by what he had just done. He turned away and grabbed a lantern, his hands shaking.

Slowly, deliberately, he saw her reach down and pull the

sheet up over her bare breasts, her lips red and swollen, her face a study in hatred. "Slimy English *dog*," she whispered, her voice trembling with rage. Then she rose up on her elbows and, reaching up, cracked her palm across his cheek.

"Your behavior, *m'Lord and Master,* is most disgustin' f'r one who is supposed t' be a *gentleman,* an upstandin' and *honorable* representative o' England's bleedin' *king!*"

Stormy purple eyes clashed with angry gray ones. "My behavior is devilishly *appropriate* as befitting a man who finds a bare-breasted *whore,* ready and waiting, in his cabin!"

Deirdre drew herself up, trembling with rage. "I am Irish," she said proudly, her eyes glittering and defiant, *"but I am no doxy!"*

He stared at her, his nostrils flaring with wrath.

She swung her arm, catching him off guard and managing to drive her fist into his temple. Pain shot through his head at the impact. His grip on her hair loosened, but didn't let go, and he reeled, falling to the floor and taking her with him.

"Bastard!" she cried as his back slammed against the deck. Dazed, Christian felt the girl land atop him, her knee driving painfully into his belly. The breath burst from his lungs, and before he could recover, she'd snatched up his pistol and pointed it directly into his face.

His blood turned to ice.

He heard the click of the pistol as she slowly brought it to half cock. He felt a bead of sweat gather at his brow and slide into the hair at his throbbing temple. He saw a smile curve her lovely mouth as he stared fixedly at the measured, deliberate movements of her thumb.

Slowly, she cocked the pistol.

"For thirteen long years," she whispered, shakily pushing her hair off her forehead, "I've waited f'r this moment. Twelve long years, I've waited t' kill ye."

The sweat pouring from his brow in rivulets, Christian stared into the ominous dark mouth of the pistol, two inches from his face and coming closer. *Don't move,* he thought dazedly. *She's a bloody madwoman.*

"Thirteen long years, me fair *lieutenant,* t' avenge th'

wrong ye did me family . . . and now 'tis time f'r *you* t' pay th' consequences!"

Cold metal touched his brow—and then he heard the mad skitter of nails as the spaniel shot from the bed and across the cabin. In a single, swift movement, the girl jerked the pistol around—

"Don't!" Christian cried, and she swung back to face him, her eyes panicky.

He swallowed hard, and shut his eyes. ". . . Hurt my dog."

Her mouth fell open and she stared down into his face, confusion, astonishment—and something else—marring her smooth brow. He saw her throat working, her eyes going glassy with moisture. Slowly, shakily, she lowered her arm, her eyes huge and dark, a single tear slipping down her pale cheek to drop upon his chest. Bright moonlight streaked through the windows, caressing shiny black curls that cascaded past her face and tumbled down her shoulders, fanning his chest and seeming to merge with the darkness.

With a cry, Deirdre flung the pistol across the room and burst into tears.

"Damn ye," she murmured, staring down at her hands as the dog fell upon the captain, licking his face in frenzied love and devotion. He wrapped his powerful arms around the little body, hugging it close. Scalding, salty tears of frustration and anguish ran down Deirdre's cheeks, spattering the white lapels of the Lord and Master's coat and dropping upon the dog's back.

Finally the spaniel quieted, cast a last, apprehensive glance at Deirdre, and padded off across the cabin.

Deirdre swallowed with difficulty, her throat choked with emotion, her heart pushing painfully against her ribs. The English captain lay unmoving beneath her, his body hard against the inside of her thighs. The feel of him brought a strange heat to her blood, but before she had time to ponder it, he reached up and hesitantly touched a long black curl that hung over her shoulder and dangled near his nose.

"Thank you," he said softly.

Her throat was working, and it was all she could do to speak. "For *what?*" she spat scathingly. "Not killin' ye?"

"No . . . for not hurting my dog."

Hysteria rose up in her and she threw back her head in wild laughter.

"Is that so devilishly funny?" he asked, his voice harsh with anger and hurt.

His words jolted her back to reality. Her laughter stopped abruptly, and as she stared down into his confused eyes, his handsome face, the tears burst forth again. "I'm . . . a failure," she wailed, her hands coming up to clutch the crucifix. "I can't sneak aboard a ship without gettin' caught, I can't try t' kill ye without makin' a total fool o' meself, and . . . and *I wish t' God I'd never left Ireland!*"

Hot, crystalline tears splashed down on Christian's cheeks, his brow, and he felt something huge and tender welling up in his chest. He reached up and put his hands on her sides, just above her hips. Her head fell back, and the tears, running in torrents down the sides of her face and throat, dropped quietly upon the crests of her breasts. He swallowed tightly, feeling her pain as his own, and slid his arms up her body until they were locked around the back of her neck.

Then he slowly drew her down and gently, thoroughly, kissed her.

She was sweet and salty, soft and compliant. She made an attempt to pull back—first a forceful attempt, then a feeble one—but he held her head close, his fingers buried in her hair. With a last whimper, she sank down atop his broad chest, helpless beneath this sweet torment, and unable to fight it. Tenderly now, his tongue traced the outline of her swollen lips, softly coaxing, gently demanding, until finally, with a little sob, she opened to him and gave herself up to the kiss.

Deirdre felt delicious warmth flooding her veins, emanating out from the sizzling spot where lips met lips, and flowing in a river of heat downward . . . into her tingling breasts . . . into the chambers of her suddenly pounding heart . . . and down, down, into the dark, awakening regions of her womanhood. Dazedly, she felt his hands, hard and strong and masterful, warmly caressing her back, skimming the sensitive groove of her spine, the narrow span of her shoulders.

The kiss deepened, growing hotter, wetter, more demanding. Of their own accord, her hands came up to cup the sides of his face, feeling the warm roughness of his cheeks, the strength of his jaw, the pulse beating beneath her fingertips. Surprise darted through her, for she had not expected to find such familiarity in an Englishman, someone who was supposed to be her enemy, and therefore quite inhuman.

But no, he was warm and alive, not a monster or an icy demon at all—but human. Male. Full of raw power and masculine fire.

His tongue filled her mouth, tracing the ridge of her teeth, mating and melding with her tongue. His arms wrapped fiercely around her shoulders, pressing her body against his and crushing her breasts against his chest. Something hot and wet flowed from her soul, filling the tight, throbbing space between her thighs, and a detached voice, buried somewhere deep in a part of her mind that still functioned, fought for her attention.

This is madness . . . he is your enemy!

Weakly, she tried to pull away, her hands pressing against a chest that was hard as oak beneath the soft linen of his snowy waistcoat. But there was no force to her efforts, and she felt her will melting, her heart hoping shamelessly that he would not stop. His hands were hot, the night air cold, against her damp skin, and she shivered in delicious response. Then, lost in the kiss, she felt him touching her breasts, cupping them, balancing them in the palms of his callused hands. Fire raged through her blood and she tore free of his kiss, gasping as his rough thumbs skimmed the dusky nipples and coaxed them into taut buds of desire.

"Stop," she gasped, suddenly terrified. She grabbed his wrists, feeling the tight play of muscles and tendons in the backs of his hands. "Stop . . . I—I hate ye."

He grinned, his mouth roving over her lips. "I daresay."

"I said *stop!*"

This time, Deirdre's mind—and will—won out over the puddle of syrup her body had become. With a desperate sob, she leapt to her feet and bolted across the cabin, only to be brought down by the corner of the desk as her hip caught it in passing.

"Oooow!"

She sank to her knees, her sobs piercing the sudden stillness. Behind her, she heard the English captain rise to his feet, and the soft squeak of the flooring as he crossed the deck to her.

She cringed, terrified that he would touch her again, terrified because her body had so wantonly responded to him, and terrified that if he so much as laid a finger on her, she would give in to those strange feelings once more. She tightened herself into a ball, huddling pitifully in the corner, her hair falling over her trembling shoulders and her arms locked around her knees. She felt the heat of his powerful body as he moved closer, standing beside her now, and she heard the rustle of fabric as he bent down, trailed a hand through her hair, and gently touched her shoulder.

"Come to me, dear girl. Pray, you may trust me. I shall not avail myself of your charms, delightful and dangerous though they may be. . . ."

Sobbing, she turned her face from the hot and moist curtain of her hair and looked up at him. There was no anger in those gray eyes, no lust, nothing but compassion, concern, and what looked to be regret.

"Ye won't . . . be kissin' me again? Ye won't"—she swallowed, fighting the hot sting of tears—"*touch* me?"

"No."

"Ye sure?"

He smiled, sadly, and placed a hand against his heart. "My word, dear girl, as a gentleman."

She stared at him, helpless. He gazed down at her, rubbing one thick and spiraling curl between his thumb and forefinger. "Don't get me wrong," he added, still holding her gaze. "I would *like* to, foundling, if only to prove to myself that I can still enjoy a kiss, a touch, a tryst, as much as the next fellow . . . but nay, I shall not." His voice was sad, and his hand dropped defeatedly away from her hair. He gave a great sigh, and as he turned away, blinking, she saw the raw emotion in his gray eyes. "You see, I loved a woman once . . . but she was taken from me, and I shall never feel such things again. Love has no place in my dead heart, and lust, no place in the disciplined order of my life." He looked at her, his eyes dark, haunted, and vulnerable. "Therefore, my girl, you are quite safe with me."

Gently, he slid his arm down behind her legs and, easily lifting her up into his arms, cradled her against his chest as he carried her across the little room. She curled her lips between her teeth, desperately containing fresh sobs, as his heart thumped steadily beneath her cheek.

At the bed, he paused, cradling her in the curve of his arm as he bent and straightened the covers. Then he lowered her to the sheets, his arms lingering beneath her legs for a long moment, his eyes still averted from her breasts, her face. Stunned, Deirdre could only stare up at him as he made a great deal of fussing over her—pulling the blankets up over her thin shoulders, smoothing her hair, and then reluctantly turning away to light the lantern that swung gently above his head.

A soft glow filled the room. "You will be safe here," he said, "and to prove to you that my character is a noble one, I will sleep on the bench seat in my main cabin. Do not hesitate to summon me, dear girl, if you need me for any reason."

She stared, watching as he adjusted the lantern and hung it near the canvas screen that separated the two areas of the little room. "Tomorrow," he continued, "I shall have my first lieutenant escort you from this ship and back to the pier. I would do so tonight, but there are riffraff fellows about on the waterfront, and I would not subject you to their whims."

He straightened up, gazed at her for a long, searching moment, and turned to walk away.

"Th' lantern," she said, staying him with her hand and feeling his arm tense beneath her fingers. She stared from his face to the glowing flame. "Are ye goin' t' leave it burnin'?"

"Aye."

"Then . . . thank ye," she said, closing her eyes against fresh tears and silently thanking him for trying to dispel any nightmares she might have.

He nodded and, picking up the little dog, moved behind the canvas screen.

It never occurred to her that he was trying to dispel his own.

Chapter 7

It was nearly midnight, several hours later.

While their captain had faced his admiral's wrath, the crew had worked all day to replace the damaged spars and rigging suffered by the collision with Admiral Burns's flagship and now, exhausted but triumphant, sat around a table in the wardroom, laughing over the embarrassment they had caused their new Lord and Master.

The door opened.

"Mr. MacDuff, sir?" The youngest of the frigate's three midshipmen poked his tousled head into the crowded wardroom and then darted inside, shoving through seaman and officers until he came to Ian. The big Scotsman sat on a sea chest, polishing his bagpipes with a square of linen and half watching a card game that took up the entire table.

Ian glanced up, scowling. "Hugh, laddie! 'Tis past your bedtime, and there be things in here ye shouldnae be seein'!"

But little Hugh's eyes had already found the thing they shouldn't be seeing, and gaping at the scantily clad woman who sat atop Milton Lee's knee, he managed to blurt, "Captain's compliments, and he requests your presence in his day cabin!"

"Uh-oh, you're in for it now," Milton Lee predicted darkly, sliding a hand up the doxy's thigh. "The admiral's probably taken the Lord and Master down a peg or two and now he's looking for someone to put the blame on!"

Skunk roared with laughter and dealt a new hand of cards, the movements of his arm sending a cloud of stench across the table and making those nearest to him gag. "An' looks like yer it, Ian!"

"Aye, fine job you did, getting us under way this afternoon," said Russell Rhodes with a silky smile of admiration. He leaned against one of the twelve-pounders that competed for space in the wardroom, his eyes as black as the cold, heavy iron.

"And a fine job *you* did, my handsome lieutenant," the woman purred, sliding from Lee's lap and sauntering across the cabin to Rhodes. She touched his arm, letting her long nails drag up his sleeve while she tilted her head flirtatiously and stared into his eyes. "Hiding me down there in your brig. . . . such a perfect place for a friendly liaison, no? Why, I can't wait"—her husky voice dropped to a rich, throaty whisper—"to have you *all* to myself!"

"Delight, please, have me first!" cried Midshipman Hibbert, grinning foolishly and sweeping off his stained and dirty hat.

As the room erupted into laughter, the woman turned her bold gaze on the fourteen-year-old, letting it drift slowly down his filthy, wrinkled uniform and pointedly toward his groin, until young Hibbert's pink cheeks began to turn red. "Why, Hibbert, *chéri,* I just love young boys . . . their energy is so tireless, their enthusiasm so refreshing, no? But I think I shall wait till tomorrow . . . and then eat you for breakfast!"

Hibbert went scarlet. Raucous guffaws split the small room and Skunk clapped the midshipman across the back. Only the beardless Arthur Teach, who'd spent the better part of the evening sulking in the corner, did not join in their laughter. Now he sat sullenly polishing a tomahawk, taken in trade from an Indian chief he'd once met in the American colonies. The blade glittered dangerously in the lantern light.

"What, have ye no comment tae make, Arthur?" Ian prodded, getting to his feet and twirling his bonnet on his thumb. "Nothing tae say about our new Lord and Master?"

The seaman looked up, his black eyes gleaming with

menace. Slowly, he ran his finger down the flat of the tomahawk's blade.

"I'll kill him," he vowed softly.

Stunned silence reigned. No one moved. Skunk exchanged nervous glances with Ian. Hibbert paled and looked at his feet. Even the yellow-haired woman paused, her hand freezing on Rhodes's arm.

Outside, the winter wind blew, cold and dark and whispery.

The young midshipman finally broke the heavy silence. "Er, Mr. MacDuff, sir?" he squeaked, moving fearfully away from Teach. "The captain's waiting. And, begging your pardon, sir, he's not in a good mood, I don't think."

"I shouldnae think he would be," Ian murmured, frowning. He raked a hand through his thick red hair, donned his cap, and prepared to face the music.

Unable—and unwilling—to sleep, Captain Christian Lord sat in his day cabin, thinking about the girl in his bed such a short distance away. He was trying, unsuccessfully, to take his mind off her by reading *Bold Marauder*'s log under her previous captain when the thump of Evans's musket on the deck outside announced the arrival of Ian MacDuff.

He shut the leather-bound book with a snap and looked up. The Scotsman, framed by the swinging deckhead lantern behind him, stood at the door, nervously twisting his bonnet in his hands.

"Do come in, Mr. MacDuff. I dislike having conversations that involve only myself and an empty table."

Bobbing his head, Ian entered the room, aware of the raw disapproval on the Lord and Master's face as the chilly gray eyes moved over his plaid. Ian had worn it both in strict defiance against Navy regulations and in proud display of his heritage, but now, under the scrutiny of that cold gray gaze, he felt rather ridiculous. Especially with his blue coat thrown haphazardly over the whole thing and his knees, sprouting red hair, peeping out from beneath.

"I do trust you will discard that *ridiculous* attire and dress yourself accordingly," Christian remarked dryly. "I daresay you test the limits of my patience with the beard, but I cannot abide both. Choose one or the other, Mr. MacDuff, and we will get along famously."

Taken aback, Ian stared at him, for he'd expected a sharp reprimand for both the beard and the plaid. Eyeing the captain warily, he pulled out a chair, his gaze falling upon the screen that divided the day cabin from the captain's sleeping area. Was the Lord and Master keeping the young Irishwoman in there? He grinned slyly; if so, the knowledge would be wonderful fodder for the lads back in the wardroom. . . .

Armed with the thought, Ian glanced at his new commanding officer, only to find the gray eyes quietly assessing him, taking his measure. Ian's grin promptly faded. He returned the stare with innocent defiance, trying in vain to discern the strengths and weaknesses behind the captain's cold eyes. The Lord and Master was a handsome man, but Ian was not jaded into thinking that was all he was. *Bold Marauder*'s notorious exploits were well known, the captain's uniform well decorated; there had to be a reason that the Admiralty had assigned *him* to their ship.

The big Scot chewed the inside of his lip. He was no fool; he recognized, and respected, the power in the Englishman's militaristic shoulders, the intelligence behind those frosty eyes, the determination in the severity of his mouth, the discipline reflected in the scrupulously neat and clean state of his uniform.

As for weaknesses, Ian MacDuff could discern none.

He felt the first twinges of alarm. He and the crew might not have an easy time of it, winning their ship back from such a man as this.

"Concerning this afternoon, Mr. MacDuff, there is no need for you to be on guard with me," the Lord and Master said abruptly. He smiled, but a note of steel laced his tone. The cold gray eyes settled unnervingly on Ian. "Mistakes do happen, do they not?"

"Aye, sir," Ian said.

"Of course, they only happen once. Twice, and they are put down to incompetence—and incompetence, we all know, has no place on a fighting ship."

"Aye, sir." Ian said again.

The captain eyed him. "You have my forgiveness for what happened this afternoon. The mistake, of course, was mine, for trusting my command to a crew whose strengths and weaknesses I've yet to discern—and whose loyalty I've yet to secure. But it shall not happen again. Tomorrow I shall carry out a complete inspection of this vessel before weighing. We will leave Portsmouth under *my* hand"—he eyed Ian coldly—"and I expect your cooperation in seeing that our people behave in an organized, well-disciplined fashion."

"Aye, sir," Ian repeated.

Christian leaned across the table, poured brandy into two glasses, and pushed one toward Ian. "As I said, I did not summon you here to chide you for your earlier behavior, so please, rest easy."

Ian bolted the brandy, growing more and more nervous under the captain's flinty stare.

"I summoned you, by God, because I would like an explanation as to who is responsible for bringing that trollop aboard this vessel!"

Ian nearly choked on the liquor. "T-trollop, sir?"

"That deuced Irishwoman, damn you!"

Anger glittered in the Lord and Master's frosty eyes, and his mouth was a severe slash across his well-tanned, harsh visage. *Thank the gods he hadn't been referring to Delight,* Ian thought, sweating with relief. Surely he would've confiscated her and put her aboard a proper merchantman for the passage back to America!

"I, uh . . . doona ken, sir."

The captain glared at him, a muscle ticking in his jaw. "I daresay you don't, Mr. MacDuff!"

"Honestly, sir, 'tis tellin' ye the truth I be! I doona ken who the lassie is! Ye see, sir, we was havin' an argument when all of a sudden there she was, all dressed as a laddie and begging for us tae let her sign aboard!" Quailing beneath the captain's icy stare, Ian grabbed the brandy bottle and dosed himself with more of the fiery liquor. "I didnae ken she was a 'she,' sir!"

The gray eyes narrowed.

Ian gulped his brandy. "Next thing I know, ye was

wantin' tae get the ship under way, and, well, with all the, um, accidents, sir, things got a wee bit tense. The steerin' went, a fight broke out, and *Bold Marauder* hit the admiral's flagship—" He grabbed the brandy bottle. "The lad—I mean, the lassie—well, they just needed a scapegoat tae blame for it, so they turned on her—"

"And I suppose you don't know her identity, either, eh, Mr. MacDuff?"

"No, sir, never saw her before in my life!"

"And, to your knowledge, has anyone else aboard this vessel?"

"I doona think so, sir. She's as much a mystery to us, sir, as she is tae you."

The Lord and Master stared at him for a long time. Finally he sighed, poured two more glasses of brandy, and leaned back in his chair. "Blind me, but I find it devilishly easy to believe you," he said quietly.

"I wouldnae lie tae ye, sir."

"No, Mr. MacDuff . . . I believe you wouldn't." Absently he took a sip of his own brandy, then continued. "Tomorrow, we weigh. But first, I personally entrust *you* to remove that girl from this ship and see that she is safely put into the care of the fellow who owns the Spindrift Tavern." He shoved a pile of silver across the table, his eyes as aloof and unreadable as his very bearing. "This should see her on her way handsomely, I should think."

Ian was stunned by the Lord and Master's generosity. "Ye be wantin' me tae do that tonight, sir?"

"Tomorrow morning, Mr. MacDuff."

"But I doona have the watch then—"

"Then see that Mr. Rhodes escorts her ashore. I trust that he, as an officer, will behave himself accordingly." He rose to his feet, his back rigidly straight, his wig perfectly combed and white in the glow from the lantern. "That is all, Mr. MacDuff."

Gratefully, Ian got to his feet. He was halfway to the door when the Lord and Master's cold voice stopped him.

"And, Mr. MacDuff? We shall weigh the moment Mr. Rhodes returns, so relate my wishes to him accordingly. As for getting under way, it will be done without mishap. I shall expect"—he picked up a pair of navigational dividers and rapped them against the table for emphasis—"this company to be in top form."

"Sir?"

He tossed the dividers onto the desk. "Remember, Mr. MacDuff. I allow no mistakes to happen twice. Now, be off with you."

Behind the canvas partition that divided the sleeping area from the main cabin, a very homesick Deirdre O'Devir lay unmoving in the big bed, one hand wrapped around the crucifix at her neck, the other clutching her canvas bag of Irish mementos that Skunk had returned to her. Tears ran slowly down her cheeks, and trickled into the mass of raven curls that framed her white face on the pillow.

He had kissed her. He, her enemy, had put his filthy English lips against hers and *kissed* her.

And she had enjoyed it.

Silent sobs racked her breasts and she put her palm over her mouth so that the Lord and Master, speaking quietly to his nervous lieutenant in the adjoining room, wouldn't hear. Damn him! Damn his bleedin' hide to hell and back!

Viciously, she wiped her hand across her lips, but it could not erase the warm feel of him, the answering fire in her blood that even the memory evoked.

"I hate ye," she murmured scathingly, defying the sudden, mad thump of her heart, the rush of sensation in her blood. She stared up at the dark and shadowy bulkhead. "I should've killed ye when I had me chance!"

But she could not have. Even as she remembered his face, rigid but calm beneath the wavering mouth of the pistol, she knew she could not have pulled the trigger and put a ball between those steady gray eyes.

Coward!

Steady and calm, those eyes . . . until she'd swung the weapon on his little dog. Not that she could've harmed the spaniel, either. But the fact that the Lord and Master seemed to care more for his pet's life than for his own brought fresh, confusing sobs bubbling up in the back of her throat, for what kind of man put an animal's life before his own?

She turned her face into the pillow to muffle her soft, wretched cries.

If only she had never left Ireland. If only she were back home right now, safe in the little cottage she'd known since birth. She hated England, she hated the English, and she hated the English captain who had dared to kiss her, to defile her with his lips—

She flung herself onto her stomach, nearly suffocating in hot tears, thick pillow, and coarse, dampened hair. *Do not think o' him,* she told herself. *Think o' home instead. . . .*

Home.

"Oh, Ireland," she whispered to the pillow. "If only that bastard wasn't out there, I could get up an' go t' the windows and find th' North Star. If only I could know which direction ye lay in so that I could go t' sleep wi' me head facin' home. . . ."

Beyond the screen, she heard the slam of the door as the Scottish lieutenant took his leave . . . the sounds of the Lord and Master extinguishing the lantern . . . the soft murmur of his deep voice as he spoke to the little spaniel . . . the creak of the deck as he moved across the cabin . . . the whisper of his clothing as he stepped into the small sleeping area . . .

He was standing directly over her, his soft breathing the only sound.

Deirdre froze, feigning sleep and hoping he couldn't hear the sudden, wild thump of her heart. She tensed inside as his hand lifted a thick tress of her hair, then gently let it fall back across her shoulder. He stood there for a long time; then he gave a deep, ragged sigh and she heard him moving back through the darkness toward his day cabin.

Trembling, she rolled onto her back and pressed her fingers against her swollen lips. Again the tears began to flow, scalding her cheeks and dropping softly onto the already moist pillow. She gripped the coverlet and pressed the crucifix down hard against her breastbone, wishing it could quiet the too-loud thumping of her heart.

Ye have t' kill him, ye know. He'll go back on his word an' touch ye wi' his dirty English hands . . . again an' again an' again.

Her hand crept out, seeking the canvas bag. Her fingers

found the bulge that was her flagon of Irish air, and with it, comfort.

He'll touch ye . . . and ye won't deny him.

She swallowed tightly, suddenly cold and afraid. *Kill him?* She had already bungled the first two attempts. But the pistol would've been too merciful, the sword too bloody. There were other, less gruesome methods of disposing of an enemy. . . .

From the darkness, she heard the rustle of clothing as he shed his clothes and readied himself for bed. Wicked, forbidden images sprang to life in Deirdre's mind and she was powerless against the direction of her thoughts, the hot response such images evoked. Her skin dampened with perspiration and she pressed the coverlet against her mouth to still her wild breathing. From the next room came the squeak of leather as he settled his tall body down on the bench seat at the window, the soft words of a quick prayer, and the snap of his fingers.

She frowned. Snap of his fingers?

Then she heard the drum of claws upon the floor, a happy bark—and the captain's soft crooning as he comforted the little animal and settled down for the night.

He sleeps with the bleedin' dog?

She lay back against the pillows, listening to him toss and turn until his breathing grew heavy and rhythmic in the darkness. What sort of man could steal good Irish lads from their native home, and in doing so, shatter the trust of a little girl, chastise his first lieutenant in a way that provoked respect and obedience—and then take a frightened and abused animal to bed with him?

Her eyes flew open.

Just how many hours would elapse before that same man took a frightened and abused *Irishwoman* to bed with him?

Chapter 8

L ieutenant Ian MacDuff returned to the wardroom, feeling flattered, confused, guilty—and torn.

They pounced on him like a school of piranhas.

"So wot did 'is bloidy Lordship say, eh?"

"Did ye get yer comeuppance, Ian?"

"C'mon, man, out with it! What'd the bastard say?"

Ian waved them off. His eyes troubled, he turned and picked up his bagpipes. Oh, how he wanted to tell them all about his meeting with the Lord and Master! How he wanted to bask in all the attention it would get him! But a sobering thought kept him from doing so.

Lieutenant Ian MacDuff did not want to betray his new captain.

Christian Lord had given him what no other commanding officer aboard HMS *Bold Marauder* ever had—the chance to redeem himself after making a serious mistake.

Ian's chin went up a notch higher. He, Ian, was the frigate's first lieutenant, and his captain *needed* him.

The others pressed close, their faces eager, their eyes bright with excitement.

"C'mon, Ian, what did the bastard say to ye, eh?"

"Did the admiral knock him down a peg or two?"

Even Delight raised a perfect golden brow, her silky gaze sliding down the length of his torso, pausing at his groin, and making him feel as though she could see right through his plaid. "Yes, Ian, sweet," she purred seductively, *"do* tell us. . . ."

But Ian turned away. "Aw, shear off, laddies!" he mut-

83

tered, the good-natured tone of his voice belying his troubled eyes. "He just wanted tae find out who the boglander lassie was, 'tis all!"

"C'mon, Ian, there must be more to it than that! What did 'e *say?*" Skunk persisted, giving a great, toothy grin.

But the big lieutenant was already on his way out the door, taking his bagpipes with him.

"Well, now, what d'ye make of that, eh?" Skunk said, frowning and shaking his head.

But the others just shrugged.

"Emily. . . . Dear God, Emmie, no. . . . *No!*"

The sharp, tortured cry penetrated Deirdre's sleep, bringing her quickly awake. For a moment she lay staring into the darkness, confused and disoriented, the sheets fisted in her hands, her bag of Irish keepsakes pressing comfortingly against her thigh. Then she remembered. She was on the king's frigate *Bold Marauder,* and lying in its captain's bed. *The Lord and Master.*

He didn't sound so high-and-mighty now. In the darkness she could hear his harsh and erratic breathing, the sound of his tossing and turning, and the little dog's soft whimpers—whimpers that the captain never heard, whimpers that he never heeded.

"Emily? Dear Lord, Emily, where are you? For God's sake, don't do this to me. . . . Emmie. . . . Emmie!"

The terror in his voice frightened her; the agony in it tugged dangerously at her heart.

"Poxy, bleedin' bastard," she muttered, flinging herself onto her side and clapping her hands over her ears. But it was no use. And now even the little dog was growing distraught, her soft whimpers progressing into nervous whines.

Deirdre couldn't take it anymore.

She pushed aside her canvas bag, swung her legs out of the bed, and, grabbing a blanket to wrap around her shivering body, marched through the darkness and into the day cabin. The agony in the captain's voice frightened her, but she crept forward, her bare feet moving soundlessly over the black-and-white-checked canvas that covered the deck. Moonlight made a lantern unnecessary. Shapes materialized out of the dusky gloom: a tall wine cabinet . . . a bowl and pitcher set on a little stand . . . the captain's cocked hat, resting beside it—

And the captain himself.

She gasped and stood staring down at his restless form, feeling as though she was trespassing on something deep and private and personal. He lay on the bench seat, one arm flung over his eyes, his powerful chest bathed in moonlight and looking as formidable and strong as she'd imagined it would be. It glistened with sweat, heaving with his tortured breaths as he fought to draw air into his lungs. *"Emily. . . . Emmie, dear God, please, Emmie, come out. . . . You can't die. . . By God, Emmie, I won't let you!"*

Deirdre cringed at the raw agony in that voice, the desperate racking sobs that convulsed that mighty chest. His head thrashed on the pillow, and his fair hair was pale in the moonlight. His lips moved soundlessly, mouthing words that only he understood.

Then, in the gloom, Deirdre saw a silver, glistening track of moisture leading down his cheek from beneath his broad wrist.

Deirdre pushed her fist against her mouth, feeling his despair, his terror, as though it were her own. She had never heard a man cry before. She had never heard such a depth of agony and suffering in a person's sobs.

And she hoped to never hear it again.

His sobs were growing weaker now, fading into exhaustion. His fist clenched once, twice, the knuckles showing white in the darkness. Then his hand opened, the fingers growing loose, and something dropped upon the floor with a dull thud.

Frowning, Deirdre fastened her eyes on that powerful chest, on the harsh and tortured features, while she reached for the object that had fallen from his hand. She picked it up, and saw that it was a miniature, a portrait of a woman.

This Emily person?

Then he kicked his feet, and the sheets dragged down his torso and slid to the deck flooring.

Jesus, Joseph, and Mary—

He was stark naked.

Her eyes widened, filling her face, and she abruptly dropped the miniature. Gaping, she stared at the hair between his long, powerful thighs—and at the pale bulge of male flesh that lay nestled in its midst. She gulped, feeling something hot and rushing slam through her blood. Her vision dimmed, her skin broke out in sweat, and she realized she'd forgotten to breathe.

Get away from him, she thought desperately.

She tore her gaze from that alien part of his anatomy, and felt the sweat begin to race down her spine. But try as she might, Deirdre could not look away from the captain's chest, crossed with a T of golden hair that stood out in the darkness—a T of golden hair that trailed down his flat belly and pooled between his strong thighs, where his manhood lay nestled in those soft and golden curls.

She gulped and took an involuntary step backward, her face flaming. She felt as if someone had her in a throat-hold and was squeezing tightly, robbing her of breath. Her heart was racing in her chest, her feet poised for flight.

But she was unable to move.

"Emmie...." he moaned thickly. Then he gave a great, defeated sigh, and his whole body relaxed as he slipped back into the peace of oblivion.

Deirdre fled back to her bed and lay staring up in the darkness, her chest heaving, her mind stamped with the image of what she had seen. She heard his breathing grow deep and rhythmic once again; she heard the little dog whimper, then sigh with relief; and she had a sudden, wicked picture of that strong and handsome body, lying helplessly caught in the throes of a nightmare that only he could see.

That strong, handsome, and still-*naked* body.

Deirdre heard her heart thundering like a herd of runaway ponies.

Moisture collected on her brow, dampened the curls there. She swallowed tightly, once, twice, again. She flipped onto her stomach, dragged the pillow over her head, and tried in vain to block out the sound of his breathing ... and the thought of that powerful body, sprawled in the darkness such a short distance away.

Naked.

Deirdre punched the pillow, hoping the noise would rouse him enough that he might cover himself. He didn't stir. She punched it again, muttered an oath into the warm stuffing, and bit back a scream of frustration.

Nothing.

Finally she flung back her coverlet and stormed across the cabin. Reaching down, she picked up the sheets he'd kicked off and flung them angrily over his naked body.

He bolted upright, blinking.

Oh, Almighty God.

Deirdre stood frozen, her jaw agape. "Urchin?" he murmured thickly, throwing back the sheets.

Horrified, Deirdre backed up. "G-get away from me."

Heedless of his nakedness, he staggered to his feet—over six feet of solid male muscle, power, and beauty.

"I said, *get away from me!*"

He smiled in the darkness, raking a hand through his rumpled hair. "Dear girl, do you always make it a habit to watch a gentleman while he sleeps?"

"And d-do *you* always m-m-make it a habit to sleep in the nude?"

"Most certainly." He straightened to his full height, completely awake now, tall, forbidding, and most definitely dangerous. Deirdre saw the anger burning in his eyes and stamped on his severe features—and knew that if he caught her, it would be all over. Her gaze darted down, her eyes widening at the sight of his maleness. She gasped. Was it possible that that alarming part of him was growing larger, taller, straighter, thicker? And ... and *it was standing up!* She crept backward, toward the door. Her hand groped behind her—and came up against a pitcher of water, lying on his desk.

Her fingers closed around it. With all her strength, Deirdre hurled it at his head.

Too late, his arms came up to fend it off. Deirdre didn't stay to see the results of her actions. With a shrill cry, she dove through the door, hearing behind her his groan of pain, and the sound of his heavy body hitting the desk, then the deck flooring.

She was past the drunken marine, up the companionway stairs, and halfway across the moonlit deck when unseen hands caught her roughly by the shoulders and yanked her brutally around. Instinctively, her hand came up to deliver a vicious blow, and was caught in a meaty fist.

Skunk.

"Hush, girlie, before ye wake up the whole ship! Christ, I ain't never heard such a bloody racket in my life! Wot the hell is goin' on down there, eh?"

"Get yer filthy hands off o' me!" Deirdre spat, wrenching free and glaring defiantly up at him. Already, others were melting out of the darkness: Teach, not quite so fearsome without his beard; Elwin, the surgeon, stretching his chicken-neck as he tried to see around him; Hibbert, the midshipman she'd scrapped with earlier; Russell Rhodes, dark and sinister in the moonlight; and several others whose names she didn't know, and didn't care to know—including the voluptuous, lustily endowed doxy.

"Where's 'is bloody Lordship?" the big gunner demanded, his eyes narrowing. Beside him, Hibbert stood gawking at Deirdre's bare legs, until Skunk cuffed him sharply in reprimand.

"*Sleepin'*," Deirdre shot back, glancing apprehensively behind her. "What th' bleedin' hell else would a body be doin' in th' middle o' the night!"

"I might ask you the same question," murmured Ian MacDuff, emerging from below and holding up a large fragment of the pitcher that Deirdre had just hurled.

She paled, and would've fled if not for Skunk's restraining hand on her arm.

"What's this all about, Ian?"

"I doona ken, Skunk," Ian said, frowning. "Found our commanding officer in a rather sorry state."

"Sleepin'?"

"Aye, most definitely," Ian returned, taking off his cap and scratching his head. He pointed an accusatory finger at Deirdre. "For such a wee kitten, lassie, 'tis one hell of a wildcat ye be!"

Skunk wrapped a large, grimy arm around Deirdre's thin shoulders. "What's yer name, girlie?"

Ian stepped forward, scowling. "Skunk—"

"Aw, piss off, Ian," Skunk said, waving him away. "This is important!"

"Deirdre. Deirdre O'Devir."

"Well, Miss Deirdre, we already got us one lady stowaway, might as well 'ave two. Ye can keep each other company on the passage over. This here's Dolores Ann Foley—"

"But I go by the name of Delight," the woman purred, rubbing her hand up Ian's arm.

Deirdre stared at her. "Delight *Foley?*"

The woman—who, up close, didn't appear to be any older than Deirdre—gave a rich, husky laugh. "You got it, *chérie.* As in *delight-fully.*"

"*Skunk. . . .*" Ian tried again.

Skunk ignored him. "We knows Rhodes here has orders t' put ye ashore tomorrow, but we figure we can just hide ye down below with Delight till we're a ways out to sea, then bring ye both out when it's too late to take the frigate back to England. Oughta rile the new captain right nicely, eh? Hell, 'e's gonna make our lives hell for the next month, might as well return the favor!" The big gunner laughed, elbowed his grinning mates, and leered down at Deirdre. "By the way, we really admire yer attempts to end his Lordship's life, though ye *could* use some advice on how to kill someone." He grinned. "Teach here can help ye with that, eh, Arthur?"

A chorus of guffaws went up.

"So, girlie, what d' ye say?" Skunk prompted. "Ye wanna stay with us or go back ashore?"

Deirdre thought of her cousin Brendan, whose help she so desperately needed to find her brother. "I do have t' get t' Amerikay," she said slowly. Then her eyes narrowed. "But I'll be warnin' ye. If ye be thinkin' t' see me at the same trade as Delight *Foley,* ye'll find out I don't need lessons from Teach or anyone else about how t' kill someone!"

"Nah, nah, ye're quite safe. We won't be touching ye," Skunk said, boxing Hibbert's ears as the boy tried to see down Deirdre's shirt. "Now, if we can only get Ian here to quit being such an old fart, we'd be all set."

"I willnae be a part of this conspiracy!" Ian raged, clenching his fists at his sides. "Ye hear me? Ye keep yer bluidy schemes tae yerselves!"

With that he stormed angrily away, leaving a confused silence behind him.

Skunk stared after him. Then he shrugged and shook his grimy head. "So what do ye say, girlie? Ye got anythin' better to be doin' for the next month? We told ye *our* purposes. Now why don't ye come down to the wardroom and tell us *yours*, eh? You help us"—he grinned—"and we'll help you."

Deirdre stood unmoving. They were offering protection, friendship, and safe passage. Her hand came up to touch the crucifix. Even the yellow-haired girl, sliding her hands up young Hibbert's arm until the boy began to gulp, was offering a conspiring, challenging smile.

"Well?" Skunk said.

Far beyond the harbor, the first streaks of dawn pinkened the cold eastern sky. Deirdre thought of her cousin Brendan, a shining vision of hope, somewhere across the sea in a distant land called America. She thought of her promise to her dying mother, and of her long-lost brother.

Then she thought of the English captain, strong, handsome, and virile.

She swallowed hard. Next time, he would not go easy on her. But getting to America was worth the risk. And in the meantime, this rebellious crew would protect her.

"Can I go back t' th' cabin so I can get me belongin's?"

"Don't need to." Milton Lee stood there, holding up her bag of Irish mementos. "It's already been done."

"And you can borrow one of my gowns, *chérie,*" Delight offered.

"Well, then . . ." Deirdre returned their grins, and her eyes were suddenly proud and determined as they met Skunk's. "Just lead th' way," she said and, hugging her arms around her breasts to preserve her modesty, followed her escorts below.

Chapter 9

Given the ship's history, the brig of HMS *Bold Marauder* had never been used for its intended purposes, and indeed, if the vessel's builders could've seen what it was being used for now, they would've fainted dead away in shock.

A floor-length mirror was set up against one bulkhead, rows of fragrance bottles filling an area one foot long and two feet deep covered the top of an ornate dresser, and a beautiful Oriental screen of black lacquer portioned off a corner of the small room. The cloying scent of exotic French perfumes choked the air, and a light dusting of powder coated the coarse decking, imbuing it with lilac and rose and other flowery fragrances. And behind the screen was a soft velvet and satin-draped creation that looked as though it had come straight out of the boudoir of a French courtesan. It was Delight Foley's pride and joy.

She stood eyeing Deirdre up and down, her hands on her voluptuously curving hips, her shockingly large breasts straining against her daring décolletage, and one long, elegantly painted nail tapping thoughtfully at the corner of her red mouth as Deirdre held up a stunning velvet gown of a beauty and elegance the likes of which the Irish girl had never before seen in her life.

It was also of a color that Deirdre had never before *worn* in her life—deep, shocking, blood-red scarlet.

The shade alone was enough to make her blush hotly.

"You like, *chérie?*" Delight asked, tilting her head to one side and smiling.

"I—I can't be wearin' *this!*"

"Lo, you have the most *delightful* brogue! You'll just *have* to teach it to me, no? Ah, yes, the gown. Let's see what else I have." Delight tossed the rich garment over the bed, pawed through her trunk once more, and with an exclamation of triumph, lifted another, her eyes dancing.

"Aha!"

The blood drained from Deirdre's face, abruptly flooding back into her flaming cheeks. "I can't be wearin' *that,* either," she cried, shocked. "There's ... there's no *bodice* on it!"

"Oh, there's a bodice. See? It's just—transparent."

Deirdre hugged her arms to herself. In comparison, the red gown didn't look so bad after all. Echoing her thoughts, Delight tossed the second dress back into the trunk and grinned. "These two are my most ... modest, honey. Personally, with that black hair and white skin of yours, I think you'd look quite devastating in the scarlet."

The scarlet it was. Moments later, Deirdre found herself wrapped in the sinful, wickedly seductive gown as Delight, with a needle and thread, took in the bodice to accommodate Deirdre's significantly smaller bosom. At last she stood back, and clapped her hands in glee. "Aah, you look *magnifique*—here, have a look!" she cried, and laughing in triumph, she hauled Deirdre to the mirror.

Deirdre's mouth gaped open. Never had she worn, or expected to wear, such a beautiful gown in her life. Its blood-red color was a striking complement to her black, wildly curling hair, setting off the fine translucency of her skin just as Delight had predicted it would. The neckline was cut shockingly low, lifting and flaunting her breasts; the waist was tightly nipped, flattering her already tiny waist. In style, design, and color, it was not a dress that any respectable woman would wear, and thoughts of being seen in it brought a hot suffusion of color to Deirdre's already pink cheeks.

Thoughts of the Lord and Master seeing her in it deepened that blush to a scalding crimson.

"Aah, you will melt our handsome Ice Captain for sure with this, *chérie!* Perhaps your hair should be up ... no, no,

let's leave it *down*. Oh, this is great fun. I never dreamed
such a dreary passage might have such wonderful possibil-
ities! And look at you." She lifted one of Deirdre's spiraling
curls. "Aah, to have hair like that! And that crucifix you
wear is the *perfect* complement to your loveliness, rather
pagan, just like you, no? Wher*ever* did you get it?"

"It belonged to me grandmother," Deirdre said, "who
lived some two hundred years ago. She was a pirate queen."

Delight's hand clapped dramatically to her generous
bosom. "A pirate queen!"

"Aye. Grace O'Malley," Deirdre said proudly.

"Do forgive me, sweetie, but I've never heard of her. The
only pirate queen *we've* ever had is Anne Bonney."

"Where in France was she from?"

"France?" The vivacious Delight threw back her head and
laughed, her voice full-throated and gleeful. "Sweetie, I'm
American. I merely went to France to get an . . . education!"

Deirdre stared at her, confused.

"But I take it as the highest compliment that you thought
I was *French!* Lo, I must be doing something right! Do you
know, I've been practicing my accent for a month. Had everyone in England fooled!"

"Ye're not French?"

"Nay, and I'm no courtesan, either, though I *am* trying to
hone my skills as one. Lo, I'm glad to see I had you fooled
there, too! Don't look so shocked, *chérie!* The French are the
world's greatest lovers—where else would I go to learn the
best ways to pleasure a man? It's all in the technique, sweetie,
getting a man's body to harden with passion and respond to
you with all the lust of an untamed stallion."

Deirdre was shocked. "Ye mean ye crossed th' sea just t'
learn how t' . . ." She couldn't even say it.

"I had to, you see." Delight touched her generous bosom
and affected a stern look that was totally out of character
with her vivacious behavior. "Such scandalous ambitions
would never be tolerated back home, and certainly not by
my papa! In fact, if he had known the *real* reason I wanted
to go to France—I told him and Mama it was to hone my
social skills, you see?—he would've moved heaven and
earth to drag me back! Of course, had he sent the Irish Pi-

rate, I would've willingly come—but *not* back to Papa's. You've heard of the Irish Pirate, no?"

"The ... Irish Pirate?" Deirdre shook her head, still in shock over Delight's admission.

Delight cast her eyes heavenward and touched her breast. "Aah, *there* is a *man!* Hair as black as yours and a face to *die* for ... like our Lord and Master's, no? But the Irish Pirate—he is a hero back home, you know, and the sooner I can get him into my bed so I can practice on him all that I've learned, the better! But as for my *education,* I went to Paris to learn my skills as a *woman,* to London to learn my skills as a *lady,* and to Portsmouth to practice everything I'd learned on some of the most notoriously wicked and *wonderfully* lusty seamen on the planet! And we all *know* that there is no more notoriously wicked, wonderfully lusty lover than a sailor, no? Aah, it sets my hot blood on fire just to think about it!"

Deirdre's head was reeling.

"Lo, I simply can't *wait* for this voyage to begin! Just think, Deirdre, I've a whole ship of sailors to practice my new skills on before I get home. And by the time I get my *claws* into the Irish Pirate, I'll know more than any of my *teachers* back in Paris, no? But seriously, you like my new accent? I've worked so hard at perfecting it. Men just *love* this throaty, nasal sound, and if you lower your voice to a whisper—like *this*—and touch your man a lot, while talking to him and stripping him with your eyes, why, it'll just set him on fire! The combination is lethal!"

Unbidden, Captain Christian Lord's handsome face flashed before Deirdre's eyes and she found herself blushing once more. Then she thought of Delight, practicing her *skills* on him, and she felt a stab of something that was dark, ugly, and not at all pleasant.

That *something* dismayed her greatly, for she instantly recognized it for what it was.

Jealousy.

She turned away to hide it. "What are ye goin' t' do when th' captain ... finds out ye're aboard?"

Delight laughed, her voice rich and throaty. "Oh, I have a few things in mind, *chérie!* But till then, I doubt I'll have a problem hiding myself away from him. . . . Ah, too involved in his own affairs is our handsome captain, no?" She snapped the lid of her trunk shut. "And in the meantime, I can work on my *education*. Let's see . . . one hundred and fifty men in the crew—that's five per day, if you figure it should take about a month to make the crossing. Why, by the time I see the Irish Pirate, my education shall be quite thorough, though I dare not let that foul-smelling one *near* me! Lo, what a stench! In any case, when I've exhausted each man of the crew, *then* I shall turn my charms on our handsome commanding officer. I think the Ice Captain will be the ultimate test of my skills . . . why, if I can get *him* to melt to butter in my hot little hands, I should think I'll have no problem snaring my Pirate back home."

Laughing gaily, she flung the lid of the trunk back open and lifted out the gown with the transparent bodice. Then, with a wicked grin, she held up a pair of elegant silk stockings.

"Now if you'll excuse me, *chérie,* I've work to do!"

Topside, Captain Christian Lord was just coming on deck to take command of His Majesty's frigate *Bold Marauder.*

Dawn was a new visitor to the day, shining over the harbor with a pale salmon light. It reflected itself in a million little diamonds over the water's surface as the frigid wind arrived with it. But the frigate's crew was heedless of the dawn. The seamen were too busy staring at the Lord and Master.

With no outward sign of the injury that had felled him earlier, he looked terribly proper, scrupulously well groomed, and the epitome of what a naval officer should be. His uniform was meticulously clean, the gold buttons and gilded lace sparkling in the early sunlight. His periwig was carefully rolled and tied beneath his cocked hat, and his face was freshly shaved. His coat was as blue as the ocean, and his waistcoat, breeches, and stockings were whiter than sea foam.

"*Holy Moses,*" Skunk muttered, exchanging puzzled glances with Rhodes.

No emotion touched the hard set of the captain's mouth,

nor softened the harsh lines of his face, and the expression in his gray eyes was guardedly aloof. He made a quick tour of the decks, his keen gaze checking the rigging, the furled sails, the guns lashed in double rows along the frigate's sides. Mounting the stairs to the quarterdeck, he solemnly doffed his hat, then strode abruptly to the helm, where Wenham stood beside the wheel, the tips of his jutting ears already red with cold.

Wenham's shocked gaze roved his captain's face. "Er, how ye feeling this morning, sir?"

"Fine and proper, thank you, Mr. Wenham. We shall be getting under way shortly, so please see to it that *Bold Marauder* does us proud this day."

On the gun deck below, Skunk and Rhodes swapped puzzled glances. Aside from a tiredness around his eyes and a slight swelling on his cheek, their commanding officer looked right as rain.

"Now what?" Elwin hissed from the rail.

"Shut up and look busy, else ye arouse his suspicions. He'll be lookin' for the girl soon enough."

But the Lord and Master seemed more concerned about his frigate than he did about the hellion who'd laid him out cold on the deck of his own cabin. He glanced up at the wind-whipped pennant, then at the feral-faced midshipman, Hibbert, standing faithfully beside Wenham.

The middie's uniform was stained and filthy, as if it had never been washed. Christian eyed it flatly, then pulled out a chart tucked near the binnacle.

"I trust you have another uniform, Mr. Hibbert?"

"Several." The youth's tone was impertinent, his eyes challenging, for he hadn't recognized the dangerous, silky tone of his captain's words. "Down in my sea chest . . . *sir.*" The last word was as insulting as if he hadn't used the respectful form of address at all, and the boy, snickering, glanced slyly at Skunk for approval.

Christian was still unrolling the chart, his eyes moving over it. "Then pray, go change out of those rags and into something clean, and report back to me no later than ten minutes hence." He looked up, his eyes now cold and angry.

"By God, this is a king's ship, damn you. Take some pride in that fact—and in yourself, for that matter!"

He looked back down at the chart. "Mr. Rhodes? A moment, please."

The second lieutenant, very aware of the suddenly anxious looks of his shipmates, strode to the helm. He respectfully touched his hat. "Sir?"

"That—*Irishwoman.*" The Lord and Master did not look up. "I trust you saw her safely ashore this morning?"

"Aye, sir," Rhodes lied, without the slightest twitch of an eyelid.

"Very well, then." The captain ran his finger over the chart, his hat casting the paper in shadow. "You may go forward to take charge of the capstan, please. And, Mr. MacDuff? Please man the mizzenmast with those who are the least nimble—the older fellows, the new recruits, and, of course"—he grinned fleetingly—"the terrified. There is also a sloppily coiled line on the gun deck that is sure to foul itself. See to it, please."

Ian bobbed his head and rushed away, but his companions were not so genial. Out of the corner of his eye Christian could see them gathering in groups, muttering amongst themselves and casting hateful, rebellious glances his way. Towering over the lot of the buggers was Arthur Teach.

Christian marked his place on the chart and glanced up, his gaze steady and unwavering as he met the hostile eyes of the big seaman. "Mr. Teach? We are not in engagement with an enemy. Therefore, I see no need for three pistols, five knives, a cutlass, and"—his eyes narrowed and he lost his place on the chart—"pray, what *is* that ghastly thing you are carrying? An axe of some sort?"

Without warning, that "ghastly thing" came hurtling through the air with vicious intent. The Lord and Master ducked a moment before it would've taken off his head.

The ship went dangerously, ominously, still. Even the gulls overhead fell silent.

"Jesus," someone whispered.

The captain straightened up. For a long, terrifying moment he said nothing, though he went white around the mouth and his eyes began to blaze. With shaking hands, he slowly, carefully, set a pair of navigational dividers atop the chart.

Then the hard gray eyes of the Lord and Master deliberately settled on Teach.

Teach looked away.

The big Jamaican bosun melted from the shadows, and went faithfully to his captain's side. Christian lowered his gaze to the chart, his expression carefully veiled. "Hendricks," he said tightly, without looking up, "please have one of your mates escort Mr. Teach to the brig, and station a marine at the door." Cool and detached, he took a pencil from Wenham and made a notation on the chart. "As soon as we are well under way, I shall require all hands to lay aft to witness punishment."

"The *brig?*" someone yelled.

"Hell, that ain't *fair!*"

"How come he gets to go and not me?"

Christian lifted his head, wondering if the girl had knocked something awry inside it with the force of the blow. They *wanted* to go to the brig?

What the devil was *wrong* with these people?

Christian shook his head, trying to appear unfazed. The movement only reminded him of the raging headache that pounded behind his eyes and the jagged cut high on his temple, hidden now beneath the periwig but throbbing most devilishly.

He felt the sailing master staring at him. "Is there a problem, Mr. Wenham?"

"Er . . . no, sir."

"Then please prepare to loose heads'ls," he snapped.

Rico Hendricks, wearing a silver whistle around his thick neck, had returned from forward and now stood several feet away. "I checked everything, sir," he said respectfully. "No signs of foul play this time."

"Very well, then, Hendricks."

The bosun's dark gaze raked over his friend's taut, composed features. Christian had not only survived the Black Anniversary, he'd also survived his first night aboard HMS *Bold Marauder,* and had come through both with what looked to be flying colors.

As for the incident with the Irish girl in the predawn hours (which Rico had slept through, but heard all about), he could only grin to himself. He almost wished the girl *hadn't* been put off the ship. She was just what Christian needed. . . .

"Get the ship under way, Mr. Wenham."

Moments later, HMS *Bold Marauder* came alive as pipes shrilled, orders were passed, and the seamen, goaded by Hendricks's threats and the reminders of the rattan, scurried to carry out their captain's order. And if they hustled so, it was not in deference to their captain's authority, but in hopes of being the first from their watch to escape below— where Delight waited in the "brig" to receive them with open arms—

And, it was hoped, with open legs.

"Heave short."

Forward, men gathered around the capstan, throwing their weight against it to the song of a chanteyman. Slowly the cable leashing *Bold Marauder* to the land began to chink and clank as it came up through the hawseholes, dripping mud, water, and weeds.

Christian's eyes narrowed.

"Anchor's hove short, sir."

He tensed, remembering yesterday's fiasco. "Loose tops'ls, Mr. Wenham. Smartly, please."

The orders were repeated. Again came the shrill of pipes, the drum of pounding feet, and then the flapping thunder of canvas dropping from aloft.

So far, so good.

"Man the braces, please."

Christian set his jaw, his keen eyes assessing the crew's efforts. *Frightfully incompetent,* he thought grimly. But men were scurrying aloft, sails were flapping with wind, and the frigate was beginning to fidget. He nodded smartly to the sailing master.

"Up and down, sir!" came the cry from forward.

"Break her out," Christian snapped.

The anchor came wearily free of the water, dripping mud and water, and glistening in the sun. *Bold Marauder,* impatient, heeled over on her side and began to thread her way carefully between the other vessels, her shadow sliding over them with stately grace. In the near distance, buildings shone in the morning sun, their windows glowing with pale, lemony light.

Christian gripped his sword hilt, waiting for something to break, something to go awry. But the frigate continued slowly forward, finding speed, finding confidence, and slowly, he began to relax. Elliott would find no fault with him this day.

He glanced up at the masthead pennant, wincing as pain stabbed through his aching head. The urge to slide his fingers up and touch the painful gash at his temple was hard to resist, but he was determined not to show even that bit of weakness in front of the crew. The blow had been a hellishly nasty one, but soap and water, his periwig, and the shadow of his hat hid such things from inquiring eyes.

They were almost out of the harbor now.

"Hold her steady, Mr. Wenham."

High above, the canvas made great, billowing curves that stole wind and sunlight both as *Bold Marauder* pushed toward the narrow mouth of the harbor, where Christian could see several spectators standing on the headland.

Beside him, Wenham was also staring ashore, grinning and waving his hand in farewell to a group of doxies.

Christian swung abruptly away.

"See to your ship, Mr. Wenham!"

The sailing master looked at him, his eyes blank.

Firmly, Christian said, "In future, I would prefer to see more speed and skill in setting the sails. Starting tomorrow, I intend to make it a vigilant practice until such maneuvers are performed to, and beyond, my satisfaction."

He thought he heard the master groan.

"Excuse me, Mr. Wenham?"

"Er, nothing, sir. Just a frog in my throat. . . ."

Many men began filing below. Those who remained were going about their tasks with a vengeance, scurrying out along the yards, coiling lines, yelling encouragement to each other. His eyes critical, Christian watched them, finding their performance sloppy but acceptable. Perhaps they could do better; in all likelihood, they could not. But at least the bloody buggers hadn't dared to sabotage the ship today. His jaw tightened, but a smile touched his mouth. Perhaps there was hope for them after all. And when they returned to England, the crew of HMS *Bold Marauder* would be something the king himself would be proud of.

That, Captain Christian Lord vowed on his very life.

Forward, the anchor was catted amidst a chorus of curses and blasphemous oaths, and Christian sighed in relief as *Bold Marauder* showed her heels to Portsmouth.

They were free.

His smile broke into a downright grin.

Then he saw the tomahawk, savagely impaled in the wood of the mast, and the smile faded abruptly from his lips.

At the appearance of the first tar—a blushing boatswain's mate holding his hat in his hands while Arthur Teach towered impatiently behind him—Deirdre decided that Delight's *classroom* was the last place she wanted to be.

Keenly aware of the hot stares that she herself, wrapped in the scarlet gown of crushed velvet, was receiving, Deirdre hastily made her excuses and fled into the bowels of the ship. She stumbled through gloomy darkness that stank of mildew and bilge, and finally ducked into a small chamber that could only be the surgeon's domain, where she huddled against the damp timbers and clutched the crucifix in her trembling hands.

Beneath her, she felt the ship moving, and fear gripped her heart. They were leaving, about to cross an ocean under nothing but Captain Christian Lord's command, and she would probably never see Ireland again. Homesickness swept her heart. Tears stung her eyes, and swallowing a bitter lump of grief, she hugged her arms around her legs and bent her brow to her knees.

Ireland.

The sharp edges of the crucifix pressed into her breast, reminding her that she was not alone. She had her bag of Irish mementos beside her. She had her crucifix, a powerful reminder of the courage that had been *Granuaile*'s. And, she thought, running her fingers over the sensual red velvet of the gown, she had her pride.

Just touching the gown reminded her of how shockingly wicked it made her look, and caused her to think, unbidden, of the English captain. Heat drove through her at the memory of his kiss, his hands, the strength of his arms, the power of his mighty chest.

What would he think if he saw her in it?

Would a fire kindle those cold gray eyes, soften the lines of that harsh face?

Appalled, she began to sob in anger and confusion, vehemently wishing she'd killed him while she had the chance—as she had vowed, for thirteen long years, to do. Maybe she didn't have her ancestress's warrior blood in her veins after all. But surely, it wasn't her fault that she'd failed! So her aim hadn't been true when she'd flung the pitcher at him. So she'd misjudged it when she'd tried to take his head off with his own sword. After all, it *had* been dark in the cabin.

But then that other thought came to her, cold, unwelcome, and rebellious.

Maybe she hadn't really *wanted* to kill him.

Her fingers tightened around the crucifix in denial, the points of the metal pressing into her palm and bringing fresh tears to her eyes. For thirteen long years she'd kept his face alive in her memory, only so that she could destroy him. Of course she wanted to kill him! She just hadn't had the chance.

But she *had* had the chance. While she'd stood over him, watching him toss in the fitful throes of a nightmare, he'd never been so vulnerable. She could've plunged his sword into his black heart and ended it right then and there. She could've gone back after knocking him senseless with the pitcher and shot him with his own pistol.

But she had not.

And in her heart, she knew that she didn't have it in her to be a murderess.

Maybe she just didn't have Grace O'Malley's strength after all.

She tightened cold fingers around the crucifix and pressed

it to her breast. "Oh, Mama," she sobbed, the tears stream-ing down her face and making her hair cling to her cheeks. "Oh, Roddy . . . I'm a *failure*. I'm not strong enough, not *brave* enough!" Her fingers slipped into her canvas bag and withdrew the little bottle of seawater, taken from the beach at Connemara, from Ireland—

From home.

Her face crumbling, she pressed the cold bottle to her damp cheek and succumbed to long, keening wails of ag-ony. "Oh, Mama, I just want t' come home. . . . I don't want t' be on this cursed boat. I don't want t' go t' Amerikay, useless land o' savages an' rebels. I just want . . . just want . . . just want . . ."

She raised her screaming face to the darkness.

". . . t' go *ho-o-o-o-o-me*. . . ."

Beneath and around her, the ship's movements were no longer gentle and rocking, but a harsher, deeper surge as she nosed into the open sea.

The little bottle of water went rolling across the deck into the darkness. Deirdre scrambled to find it, her wet hair tan-gling in her face. Then the ship righted herself, slowly, sick-eningly. Reaching her knees, Deirdre fell back against the timbers, desperately clutching the crucifix and wailing at the top of her lungs.

"I want to go ho-o-o-o-me! Sweet Jesus, I just want t' go h-o-o-o-oooome. . . ."

From somewhere came a noise. Not the squeak of a rat. Not the steady creak and groan of timbers.

But footsteps.

Her head jerked up, her cries ceasing abruptly. In sudden terror, she clutched the crucifix. "Skunk?" she whispered, her chest convulsing on a pent-up sob.

Footsteps. Coming closer.

She whimpered, deep in her throat. They were not heavy enough to be Skunk's footsteps. Not heavy enough to be Ian's, even.

These were different. Precise, measured, and purposeful.

A door opened somewhere, and lantern light glowed softly upon the dank timbers around her. She pressed back against them, suddenly wary, her eyes huge and fearful.

The footsteps never wavered.

Steadily, the light grew stronger, until the lantern itself appeared, blinding her with its brightness and making the tears on her lashes sparkle like crystal.

Shaking violently, Deirdre flattened herself against the damp wood. She couldn't see a face. She couldn't see a form. She couldn't see anything—just that raised lantern and, below it, a dark coat and long, hard-muscled thighs wrapped in white breeches.

The lantern lowered, and a man's face shone cold and triumphant above it.

Captain Christian Lord's.

Chapter 10

"So," he said softly, his voice deep and dark and dangerous, "the chase is over."

Raw terror rose in her throat, tingled icily up her spine. Her every muscle tensed for flight, and every instinct screamed a warning. But she was frozen, unable to move.

She saw his eyes moving coldly over her, taking in the wild black curls that lay in disarray over her thin shoulders, the upthrust roundness of milky-white young breasts, the long, shapely thighs shockingly revealed beneath the scarlet gown's hem—and the gown itself.

He stared at it, his eyes narrowing, as though the sight of her in it displeased him, and displeased him greatly. She didn't like the look in those eyes. There was no heat there. No warmth. And certainly no admiration. Nothing but coldness, and a total lack of emotion that frightened her.

Somewhere in the darkness, a rat scurried.

"I am trying devilishly hard to control my temper," he said, his voice rimmed in steel.

She shrank back against the damp timbers, her frightened gaze fastened to his.

"And I am trying devilishly hard not to thrash you to within an inch of your life. You are fortunate, dear girl, that my conduct is dictated by the high esteem I have for the phrase 'officer and a gentleman.' Were it not, I can assure you that you would be a very sorry creature indeed."

His gaze raked the vibrant scarlet gown with mounting fury, making Deirdre wish she could shrink herself up in a little ball and roll into a crack.

"I am also trying devilishly hard to discern the reasons for your hatred of me. My crew's, I understand—they're merely a bit riled because they've no wish to abide by my strict codes of discipline and authority. Because I know the cause of their hatred, I can address it. Yours"—he impaled her with his hard and icy gaze—"I don't understand. That's exceedingly unfair, don't you think?"

He saw her throat working, her hand coming up to clutch the strange, pagan crucifix that hung from around her neck—but she remained silent, her face very white, her eyes very wide, and her breasts very bare above the vulgar, indecently low neckline of the flaming-red gown.

He'd just come to believe her young and innocent; seeing her wrapped in the garb of a whore made him feel strangely betrayed, and stoked the flames of his anger to life. "When I address you, I expect an answer!" he snapped.

"Ye can take yer poxy English hide and go t' hell!"

He set his jaw, fighting to keep his temper. "Blind me, but I suppose I should've known better than to trust my crew to carry out the simple order of removing you from this vessel! And I suppose I should've known better than to allow you to spend the bloody night aboard my ship!" he snarled, reaching down to haul her to her feet.

Deirdre whimpered in terror.

Something changed in his face. For a long moment he merely stared at her, his eyes unreadable; then he slowly set the lantern on the deck, his movements precise and controlled, his gaze holding hers. Her eyes, huge and purple, filled her face and went glassy with moisture, and as she stared fearfully up at him, the lantern light caught a single tear rolling down her white and bloodless cheek.

Slowly, Christian lowered his tall body down to the deck across from her, wincing a bit as he stretched his legs before him and leaned his back against the stout leg of the surgeon's operating table.

"Forgive me," he said quietly.

He saw her chest convulsing with pent-up sobs, her soft breasts pushing against the devilishly shocking gown.

"You think I've come here to punish you, don't you?" he murmured. Slowly, carefully, so as not to frighten her by quick movements, he reached up and removed his hat. Lantern light caught the purple swelling at his temple, the cruel gash, and the dark area of newly dried blood, a stark contrast to the whiteness of his wig.

The look in her eyes went from terrified to stricken.

"Yes, my dear girl, I know you wish to do me in, and I give you fair credit for trying. You're frightfully determined, aren't you?"

Deirdre couldn't answer, for she wasn't sure anymore just how determined she was. The sight of the wound filled her with guilt and self-loathing. She swallowed a few times, looked away, and whispered, *"Did* ye come down here. . . . t' punish me?"

"Heavens, no. I came down here because your bloody bawling made even Mr. MacDuff's *bagpipes* sound quiet!" A smile touched his lips, one with a trace of warmth, perhaps even humor, and in that fleeting instant, Deirdre saw again the man who had bent down and soothed the frightened little girl she'd been thirteen years ago; she saw a man who, without that stuffy English periwig and harsh demeanor, might actually be quite handsome.

Quite handsome indeed.

His mouth still curved in that teasing grin. "You're a hellishly poor excuse for a murderess, you know. Mayhap you should take lessons from Mr. Teach."

"Is that an insult?"

"Nay, merely an observation."

Unbidden, her gaze traveled up the proud breadth of his chest and shoulders, the handsome planes of his face, the purple-and-red gash at his temple. She winced, and quelled the overpowering urge to soothe that wounded area with the gentle touch of her finger. "I nearly killed ye," she whispered, "yet ye won't be punishin' me f'r it?"

"Why should I?" Again that quick smile, as though humor was something he was unaccustomed to, and perhaps even afraid of. At her confused and teary look, he said, "My dear girl, I am plagued by ghastly nightmares every night. They make it deucedly hard for me to find rest, let alone sleep. Thanks to you, early today was the first time I've slept so soundly in five years."

She gave a small, terrified grin. "Do ye want me t' be hittin' ye again, then?"

He actually laughed. "The rest is not worth the headache, thank you. And the next attempt on my life will have to merit a punishment, I'm afraid. Poor Mr. Teach is already in the brig, awaiting his."

She choked and grabbed for her throat.

"I daresay, my girl, did I say something wrong?"

"He's in th' *brig?*"

Christian frowned. "Pray, what is it about this brig—"

"Nothin'!" she cried too hastily. "Nothin' a'tall!"

The gray eyes narrowed.

"'Tis where th' crew hid all o' me—me personal belongin's," she sputtered. "Ye don't want t' be goin' in there. Ye see, I—I—" She cast about quickly for the first thing to come to mind and colored furiously. "I have me . . . me menses."

His face went as crimson as her gown. "And Mr. Teach has been brought there?" he thundered.

He slammed to his feet, his long stride already carrying him across the room. Too late, Deirdre saw the bottle of precious Irish seawater, still on the floor. Too late, she saw his path taking him toward it. Too late, she knew that he would never see it—

She screamed just as his foot crunched down on the glass.

"I say, what the bloody hell was that?"

Deirdre burst into choking, full-blown sobs and scurried across the little room on her hands and knees, her black hair spilling over her white shoulders. "Me *water!*" she wailed, desperately smearing her hands into the sad, spreading pool as though she could scoop it back up. But it was too late. She raised her face, her eyes streaming hot, scalding tears, her palms wet with the contents of the bottle. "Ye stupid, heartless son of a snail, tha' 'twas me *water!*"

Then she fell down over the little pool of moisture, laying her face to it, embracing it with her arms, and sobbing wretchedly.

Christian's jaw fell open and he stared at her, thinking she was quite mad. He stared at her crumpled, pitiful form, at the pool of spreading water, and clenched his hands at his sides in confusion.

"Don't cry," he demanded harshly.

"Ye broke me water bottle!" she cried, her voice muffled through the black curtain of her hair.

Yes, he thought, *definitely mad.*

"If you do *not* stop crying, foundling, I shall be forced to come over there and comfort you. Don't make me do something you may not enjoy."

Still hunkered down on her elbows with her little red-clad rump pointed in the air, she raised her head, her features contorted in anguish. Her face was puckered, wet, and as red as her gown. "Tha' 'twas seawater . . . from . . . from—" She fell back on her haunches, her hands gripping the crucifix so hard the knuckles turned bloodless. *"I-I-I-I-I-reland. . . ."*

So *that* was the reason for the awful, keening wails that had seemed to permeate every corner of the frigate. The reason for the awful, keening wails that were now permeating every corner of his throbbing skull.

She was *homesick.* And as he stared at the white, offered arch of her throat, the perfection of her lovely bosom, his gaze fell upon the crucifix—a heathenish ornament etched with a Celtic design and studded with emeralds. His frown deepened, became a scowl. Something rubbed at his memory, something distant, yet close, something he was very close to understanding but couldn't quite grasp, something he was very close to remembering. . . .

That crucifix. That hair. Those eyes—
Ireland.

Dear God above.

The Lord and Master reeled backward, his mouth dropping open in horror as the realization of just who this lovely, sobbing young woman was—

Thirteen long years, she had said yesterday, and he hadn't picked up on it.

"Dear God, forgive me," he whispered, his voice lost beneath the ragged sounds of her sobbing. Swallowing with difficulty, he rushed toward her, his arms outstretched, his heart full of pity for her and anger at himself for not having recognized her earlier.

"Get away from me, ye filthy English *dog!*" she screamed, raising her head. "Just *get away from me!*"

Savagely, she kicked out at his leg, wincing as her bare toe struck hard, male muscle.

"Ouch!"

In a flash, his hand snaked out and caught a thick handful of her hair, anchoring her head so that she couldn't move. Wrapping the coarse black tresses around his wrist, he drew her face close to his, his mouth taut and hard, his eyes frosty with anger.

"That," he said softly, dangerously, "was not wise, my girl."

"Go t' hell, ye poxy, bleedin' blackguard!"

"Don't fight me, foundling." His voice was low, cold, controlled. His fingers tightened on her hair, close to the scalp, and she felt his thumb grazing the soft underside of her nape, the sensitive area behind her ear. She shut her eyes, trembling with fury as his hand came up, and his knuckles grazed her wet cheek.

She winced and, with a vicious lunge, tried to tear herself away. The force nearly ripped the hair from her head and she cried out in pain.

"I said, do not fight me." Slowly, he dragged his knuckles down her cheek, tracing the strong bones beneath, the shape of her face, as he studied her with keen gray eyes. *Yes,* he thought, sickeningly, *it's she. That same little Irish girl whose brother I'd press-ganged.* But she could not know the direction of his thoughts, the enormity of his discovery, though it was obvious now to him that she'd known who *he* was for some time.

She glared at him, her cheeks stained with anger as he stroked a black curl, the wrath in her amethyst eyes raising an answering heat in his blood. She was a beauty, he thought. Wild as the wind, this one. Proud, courageous, and fiercely determined.

Irish. With a spirit to match the land that had spawned her.

She struggled against him, twisting in his grip, trying to bring her hand up to strike him. But he had grown wise to her ways, and easily caught her arm.

He had treated her dreadfully in the past; he would treat her gallantly in the future. But for now, he would treat her like the wild creature she was, until he won her trust. With kindness, but also a firm hand. With gentleness and patience, discipline and strength.

She glared defiantly at him, her eyes stormy and purple, sparkling with tears.

"The chase is over," he said softly, repeating his earlier words. "For you as well as for me."

"What?"

"I know who you are, foundling. I daresay it took me a spell, but I know who you are."

Her eyes went wide, her cheeks white.

"You're the little Irish girl from Connemara . . . the one with the pony . . . Thunder, I believe his name was? The same little girl whose brother we took with the press gang, the same little girl who—I see—has not forgiven me these many years, but has returned to avenge the wrong."

He saw her lovely face crumple. Thirteen long years dropped away, and he was again the anguished lieutenant, doing a deed he had no stomach for, following an order he had no choice but to obey. Thirteen long years dropped away, and she was again the frightened, grief-stricken little girl. Thirteen years dropped away—and came full circle.

Overwhelmed with emotion, he pulled her up against him, crushing her to his chest as though he could also crush that awful, guilt-ridden memory, drive away that tragic little face that had haunted him for so many years. "For thirteen long years," he said harshly, "I remembered your face. For thirteen long years I lived with the guilt of that memory, wishing it could've been otherwise. My dear girl, I would give anything to right the wrong, do anything to be able to go back in time and change my actions of that day. My God, if you could only know how much it has tortured me. . . ."

Deirdre tore herself out of his arms, furious. How did he dare think to apologize? How did he dare think to relieve his own *imagined* guilt over that day by declaring such lies? She had heard his nightmares, had heard him call out in his sleep, and it damn well wasn't the memory of that day in Connemara that tortured him!

Viciously, she spat, "Liar! Filthy, black-hearted *liar!*"

He stared at her, taken aback.

"I beg your pardon?"

"How dare ye stand here an' say that yer crimes against me family are what torture ye? I've heard yer nightmares! I've seen the miniature o' some red-haired hussy that ye keep like a shrine on yer desk! 'Tis not yer despicable deeds toward an innocent Irish family that torture ye, but yer dear, darlin' *Emily!*"

He stared at her, shocked, the color draining from his face and leaving it pale and shaken. Then his lips went white with anger, his voice shaky with rage. "Do not speak her name in my presence, damn you!"

"Emily, Emily, *Emily!*" she spat hatefully, taking twisted pleasure in hurting him and cruelly mimicking the tortured words of his nightmare. " 'I didn't mean it, Emmie. Dear God, please don't take her—' "

His fingers biting into her hair, he jerked her savagely against his chest, the heat of his body scalding her skin, burning her breasts. He drew her toward him, closer and closer, until she could see shards of ice glittering in the depths of his cold, frosty eyes.

She did not back down. Slowly, deliberately, she taunted, "Emily . . . oh, God, Emmie, *please* don't die—' "

His mouth slammed down atop hers, crushing her lips against her teeth and wringing a sob of pain from her throat. She struggled, fighting for breath, her fists beating uselessly against his chest. She was no match for his strength, his fury. His hand in her hair held her head to his; his hard thighs pinned her straining legs. Her vision began to dim, to reel, to burst in brilliant shards of color.

He ground his mouth against hers, his tongue stabbing into the tender recesses of her mouth, until her screams became whimpers; her whimpers, moans.

Grace . . . help me.

But there was no one to help her now. No one to protect her against his savage strength and fire. No one to save her but herself.

I will not yield t' ye, she vowed, even as his fingers burned a hot trail of fire down the side of her neck, and answering heat sang wildly through her veins. *Ye can abuse me, hurt me, rape me, kill me, even, but I'll never yield! Never!*

But her body was already responding to his savage kiss, his primal, male hardness and heat. Her bones were already going to water, her heart to erratic flutters of sensation.

Then, against her chest, she felt the force of his body pressing Grace's crucifix into her tender skin. With a desperate, valiant thrust, she placed her hands on his lapels and shoved up and outward, managing to tear her mouth free of his lips.

"Bastard!" she yelled, and with all her might, slapped him harshly across the face.

Instantly, the fire went out of his eyes, leaving them cold, angry, and hazed with echoing ripples of pain. Then even that faded as he stared at her, until nothing remained but frosty aloofness.

"It would seem," he ground out, his voice harsh and emotionless, "that I am hellishly unable to conduct myself as a gentleman when I am around you. Take your bloody charms and be damned!"

He spun away, grabbed the lantern, and strode angrily toward the door.

"Then don't come near me again, or I *will* kill ye!"

He paused, turned, and gave a cold, mocking smile.

"As you wish, my dear." His eyes were carefully veiled, the long, pale lashes masking any emotion he might have felt. "I will gladly stay away from you. In fact, the next time I think I'm doing you a favor, I'll reconsider. The next time I'm tempted to do you a kindness, I'll resist!"

She stared up at him, angry, confused, and upset. "A . . . favor?" Her eyes narrowed into hard slivers of amethyst. "What possible *kindness* could ye possibly think t' bestow upon me?"

The English captain picked up his hat and slammed it down atop his periwig, covering the bruise at his temple once more. "The coast of Ireland soon passes far off our starboard beam," he said softly. Then his voice turned hard. "Forgive me, but I merely thought you'd like to see it a final time!"

Then he turned smartly on his heel, tromped through the sad puddle on the floor, and was gone.

Chapter 11

Topside, every mouth slammed shut as the Lord and Master came on deck. Every eye followed him as he mounted the quarterdeck ladder, crossed the deck, and strode to the frigate's big, double-spoked wheel.

And every man knew just what had him so riled.

He had found the Irish girl.

The sailing master, standing beside him, took one look at the raw fury in those cold gray eyes and said carefully, "Course west by southwest, sir. Full and by."

"Very well, Mr. Wenham. We will remain on this tack until the end of the watch."

"So, er, we're not going to . . . uh, head back to England?"

Christian raised a pale brow and regarded him with a flat stare. "Pray, Mr. Wenham, what for? Does your little Irish stowaway rate so highly that she would interfere with the business of a *king's* ship? I think not!" He pulled out a chart of Boston Harbor, laid it on the binnacle, spread the damp paper flat with his palms, and stared down at it, his eyes roving over the carefully drawn figures. "Since you are all so eager to keep her here, you can begin making accommodations for her *tonight.* Mr. Rhodes may move himself out of his cabin so the girl may move herself in."

"H-his cabin, sir?"

Christian glanced up. "Yes, Mr. Wenham, his cabin—the one next to mine, in case you don't remember!" He let the chart snap shut. "Now, where the devil is the bosun's mate?"

Ian was just coming aft, his red beard blowing in the wind. "I believe he went down to get Mr. Teach, sir—like ye asked."

"That was twenty damned minutes ago! Where the bloody hell did he *go?*"

Ian flushed and looked away. "Uh . . . the brig, sir."

"Send Midshipman Hibbert to fetch the both of them, this bloody instant. In the meantime, please have all hands lay aft to witness punishment."

Like shot from an enemy's guns, his words stunned the deck into silence.

"P-punishment, sir?"

"Pray, does everyone on this ship have a bloody speech problem today? Yes, *punishment!"*

Ian's ruddy face went white. "But, sir, we've never had a whipping aboard *Bold Marauder* before—'tis not well the men will take tae it, sir!"

Christian gave a hard smile. "I do believe, Mr. MacDuff, that is *my* problem, not yours."

"But, *sir,* 'tis startin' a mutiny ye'll be! I beg of ye tae reconsider!"

"Do not challenge my orders, Mr. MacDuff."

Christian swung away and went to the weather side of the quarterdeck, his head pounding, his mouth tight. He had no right to take out his anger on the crew, especially not on Ian. It was the girl who deserved it, that bedeviled, *Irish* girl. It was bad enough she'd had the frightful audacity to stow herself aboard a king's ship, *his* ship; it was bad enough that she'd tried twice to kill him. But she had insulted the memory of his dead wife—and worse, had awakened feelings he'd thought he no longer had. Even now his loins throbbed as he thought of her in that obscenely low-cut, vulgarly form-fitting scarlet gown. Damn her, she had no business making him feel such things. *No one* did.

It was Emily he'd loved, Emily he would *always* love!

Behind him, he heard the shrill of pipes and the sudden roar of angry protest as the crew, herded by Evans's nervous marines, began to head aft. Even from here, with the wind in his face and half a deck to separate them, he heard their words.

"Bloody son of a bitch, just who the blighty hell does he think he is?"

"We ain't never had no one whipped before!"

"So much for yer damned hero worship of the bloke, Ian!" he heard Skunk yell. "And so much for yer damned praise for Admiralty for sending us Captain Christian Bleedin' Lord! He's a bloody *fool!*"

"Cruel, high-bred, spawn of a whore! How dare he think to whip one of ours, lads! 'Tis cause for mutiny, I say! *Mutiny!*"

The word caught like flame set to black powder.

"Mutiny!"

"Mutiny!"

Christian remained unmoving, even as the cold finger of dread tickled his heart. Their resentment was a live thing, a rippling undercurrent of loathing that intensified with each sweep through the men now gathering aft.

Calmly, Christian took one last look out to sea and, turning abruptly, went back to the helm. "How fares the weather, Mr. Wenham?"

The wind had risen, teasing the waves and coaxing them high; now, white foam was breaking at their crests, the spray flinging itself high over the frigate's decks with every dip and plunge of her bows. But the sailing master, his nervous gaze darting to the angry, shouting mob, appeared not to have heard the captain.

"Mr. Wenham, the weather, please!"

The big man was still staring at the massing crew. "We'll be in for a blow before nightfall, sir."

Where the devil was Hendricks? His hand sliding beneath his coat to touch his pistol, Christian looked up at the mast-head pennant streaming so far above, then down at the binnacle where the needle held steady on the compass card. He nodded curtly, his eyes as gray and forbidding as the sky above. "Thank you, Mr. Wenham. I shall keep that in mind."

The bellowing of the seamen had reached a deafening roar.

"Mutiny, lads, mutiny!"

"We'll not let no captain get away with this, Hero of bloody Quiberon or not!"

"String 'im up to the yardarm and let 'im swing!"

"Off with his bleedin' head!"

"Mutiny! Mutiny! *MUTINY!*"

Ian took off his cap and held it nervously in his hands, his eyes desperate, tiny beads of sweat rolling down his face. "Sir, 'tis a-beggin' ye I be tae reconsider the wisdom of having Arthur whipped! We've nae had a murder aboard this ship, but if you insist on going through with this"—he gulped and swallowed—"this—"

"*Folly*, Mr. MacDuff?" Christian smiled, seeing the big Scot go pale beneath his ruddy skin. "Pray, do not think to deny me the one bright spot in what has turned out to be a hellish nightmare of a day."

Ian shot a desperate glance at Wenham. In Christian Lord, Ian thought he'd finally found a commanding officer he could look up to, a captain he could *respect*—but he'd been wrong.

As one, the two officers glanced at the aloof face of the man who was about to sign his own death warrant, both knowing that the moment the dreaded cat-'o-nine-tails slashed down across Teach's back, it would be all over.

Not for Teach—but for the Lord and Master.

Hearing the uproar on the deck somewhere above her head, Deirdre, frightened, grabbed an amputation knife from Elwin Boyd's box of instruments, picked up her skirts, and fled topside, following the light trickling down through the hatches until at last she emerged, breathless, onto the frigid, wind-whipped deck.

Fighting the pitching deck, she made her way to Midshipman Hibbert's side and grabbed at his dirty sleeve.

"Hibbert! Tell me what's happening!"

The youth swung around, gaping and flushing at the sight of her in the blood-red dress. He saw the gooseflesh on her arms and gallantly handed her his coat. Then, regaining his composure, he said, "Our Lord and Master is about to prove his stupidity, that's what!" He watched as two frightened bosun's mates rigged a grating, their eyes darting between the captain and the swelling masses assembled aft. "You wait, he'll have a mutiny on his hands before the hour's up!"

Rhodes, passing, snapped, "He won't last the hour, mark my words! Soon's that whip comes down on Arthur's back, it's all over for him!"

Gasping, Deirdre gripped the crucifix. *Bold Marauder*'s captain stood at the rail, detached, aloof, and alone. Sudden, unwanted fear for him drove through her heart, but she willed it away. Bleedin' wretched bastard, he deserved whatever he got!

He turned his head and saw her. Their eyes met and held. She saw pain and anger in those cold depths, detachment, torment, and a total lack of warmth. There was no forgiveness in those eyes. None at all.

Then he turned away, leaving something awful and empty coiling in the deepest chambers of her heart.

A midshipman, white-faced with fear, came running up from the hatch, fiercely gripping a leather book. He pounded up the ladder to the quarterdeck, remembered to salute it at the last minute, and reverently handed the book to his captain.

"The Articles of War," Hibbert murmured reverently as the Lord and Master's deep, clipped voice began reciting the unfamiliar words.

Aft, a man lunged forward, shouting, to be quickly subdued by a marine.

The captain, unfazed, never looked up. At last he closed

the book, with a sound like a coffin being shut for the last time, and handed it back to the quivering boy. Above, dark clouds began to gather above the spires of the masts, but the Lord and Master seemed oblivious to the threatening storm. His gaze met Hendricks's. "Bind the prisoner, please," he ordered.

A horrible, terrifying roar arose from the crew. Teach went wild as he was dragged, kicking and screaming, to the grating. He twisted, his black eyes boring into the cool gray ones of the captain. "You're the scum of the earth, you vicious, bleedin' pig! So help me God, I'll have your black heart on a platter to feed to the sharks! I'll have your head on a pole to parade through the—"

Christian nodded to Hendricks. "You may commence punishment."

Teach was lashed to the grating—not by the wrists, as was customary, but by the ankles, in what looked to be a new method of torture.

Hendricks loosened the red baize bag and gave it to his mate.

Teach went ashen, the sweat rolling in rivulets down his brow.

And the captain, leaning on his sword with his hands crossed loosely over the hilt, smiled as the bosun's mate reached into the bag, shook it upside down, and stared at that which came slithering out to fall upon the deck.

"What the hell . . ." the man said, looking up as though he'd been the butt of a cruel joke.

For it was not the dreaded cat-o'-nine-tails that lay there, but an oily pile of rags.

There was no sound but the hiss of spray at the bows, the whine of rising wind through the shrouds. In the shocked, ensuing silence, Rico Hendricks threw back his head in laughter, bent, and casually tossed one of the rags to a stunned Arthur Teach. Then he turned as two bosun's mates, sweating and swearing, dragged a huge chest across the deck and up to Teach's bound feet. With his foot, Hendricks broke the latch and kicked the lid wide.

The crew stood frozen, motionless, silent.

"God strike me," someone murmured.

In the chest was a gruesome collection of axes, pistols, knives, and boarding pikes. As the crew stared, gaping with shock, the big Jamaican reached inside and handed the first weapon he came to—a boarding axe—to a bug-eyed and gaping Teach.

Several feet away, the Lord and Master leaned casually on his sword and watched with victorious eyes.

And then the crew of HMS *Bold Marauder* witnessed the most unorthodox—and effective—punishment the Royal Navy had ever doled out, as, with each roll of the drum, an oiled rag and a weapon from the chest were given to Blackbeard's hapless grandson, and he was forced to clean every axe, knife, tomahawk, and pike it contained.

Two hours later, Teach was finished. Wearily, he oiled the last pistol, tossed it back into the chest, and, wiping his brow, glared up at the Lord and Master. But in his black eyes was something that hadn't been there before—a wary gratitude, a grudging respect.

The Lord and Master had not whipped him.

The captain met his gaze. Then he picked up his little dog, who had come waddling up on deck to join him, and, cradling her to his chest, swept the crew with his hard gray eyes.

They stood huddled against the cold, exchanging confused glances and staring at him with amazement and shock.

"I cannot abide abuse," he snapped, his voice rising over the wind. "But I *will,* by God, have obedience and respect from the lot of you! Test my patience, and I promise you that punishment will be swift—*and* fitting to the crime."

Overhead, black storm clouds came together and the first raindrops began to fall, as if they, too, had obeyed the will of the Lord and Master.

His flinty gaze swept over Deirdre, passed on.

"You are all dismissed," he said coldly and, touching his hat to them, went below to his cabin.

Chapter 12

❦

"**T**wenty-two years at sea and I ain't never seen anything like it!"

"Bloody bastard the captain is," Skunk exclaimed, slamming his mug down atop the wardroom's scrubbed mess table, "Arthur'd've been better off with a whippin'! At least there's *dignity* in that!"

"Aye, dignity," Russell Rhodes muttered as he dealt a fresh hand of cards to his shipmates. He slapped his palm down atop them, holding them as the ship tilted in a steep swell and then crashed down into the trough. " 'Twas a humiliation, making Arthur clean all those weapons. . . . Wasn't it, Arthur?"

Teach, sitting moodily in the corner with his back propped against a bulkhead, looked away, unwilling to take a stand for or against what the Lord and Master had done to him.

Or, more correctly, what he had *not* done to him.

Rhodes glanced sideways at Teach. "Well, don't forget what he did to your beard, Arthur."

The big seaman looked down, his thumbs grazing the blade of his knife. But the fury had gone out of his eyes, and that had Rhodes, Skunk, and the rest of the die-hard intractables more than a little worried, for Teach, normally full of fire, was behaving like a tame bear in a traveling fair.

And he wasn't the only one. Ian MacDuff, still topside with the watch, had shed his Scots garb and donned a proper lieutenant's coat for the first time in anyone's memory, and the Irish girl, who'd come aboard vowing to kill

120

their new captain, was strangely quiet, her lovely eyes troubled.

No, things were not going well at all. The Lord and Master was a cunning strategist, ruling with a hand whose iron was veiled by kid gloves—and no one knew quite what to do about it.

Skunk, who'd been leering at—and down—the diaphanous bodice of Delight's gown, leaned over and leered down Deirdre's instead. She flushed, yanked the shawl that Delight had given her around her shoulders, and leaned away, to escape both his eyes and his scent. But Skunk only laughed and laid a grimy paw over her hand. "Yer lookin' a bit pale around the gills, girlie. Scared? Sick? Now, don't ye worry none 'bout this little storm. 'Tis just a mere blow and it's gonna get worse before it gets better. The ship'll be all right. After all, the Lord and Master *commands* it, eh, lads?"

Laughter met his remark, but it was guarded, and despite her rising fear, Deirdre sensed that something had changed about the crew's feelings regarding the captain.

Something she couldn't quite put her finger on.

Something that was changing within herself as well.

The thunder rolled again and she laced her fingers together as the ship began to climb the next towering swell, there to hang suspended before thundering down into a trough.

The Lord and Master. She closed her eyes. Sweet Jesus, if only she could be safe in his warm and comforting arms right now, feeling his assurance that *Bold Marauder* would not go down—

Her head snapped up, what color she had left draining abruptly from her face. Dear God, what was she *thinking* of?

"Th' Lord an' Master," she spat, in defiance of her thoughts. "I hate that poxy bastard!"

"Well, I'm glad to see that not *all* of us've taken leave of our senses!" Rhodes said, with a sidelong glance at Teach. "By the way, Deirdre"—his silky gaze dropped to her bodice, then back up again—"Elwin tells me you helped yourself to one of his amputation knives. You wouldn't be thinking of involving it in your next murder attempt, now, would you?"

"Murder attempt?" Skunk cried gleefully. "On his bloody Lordship? Why, show us the knife, girlie!"

"Aye, show us the knife!"

Slowly, she picked up her canvas bag, which she'd put protectively beside her leg. One by one, the objects came out and were carefully, reverently, placed upon the table. The loaf of Irish bread. The flagon of Irish air. The pouch of Irish sand and shells. The wool of an Irish sheep. The pebble from Irish land. Blinking back tears as she thought of the jar of Irish water—which *he* had so heartlessly broken—Deirdre at last found the knife. "Here," she said, shoving it across the table toward Skunk and hastily gathering the objects together.

"Murder weapons?" Delight asked, staring at the odd collection and grinning as her hand roved down Teach's side and over his thighs.

"No. Keepsakes from home." Deirdre said tightly, her tone of voice forbidding further discussion about the curious items she was quickly stuffing back in the bag.

Skunk grabbed the knife and held it up for all to see. "Now, have ye ever seen a finer weapon, buckos?" He swung around, his raised arm overpowering them with fresh stench. Then he shoved the blade's hilt into Deirdre's cold and clammy hand. "Now, when his bloody Lordship comes down from the deck, ye'll be waitin' fer him in the cabin, just like ye did before. But this time ye won't fail, girlie. When he opens that door, bring yer arm back, like this." He gripped her wrist and pulled her hand up and back. "A real vicious chop to the throat oughtta do it."

"Go for his jugular," Elwin hissed, his eyes maniacal.

"Aye, don't stop till he's dead and twitchin' at yer feet!" Hibbert added, hiding a grin as he elbowed Edgar Hartness, a freckle-faced midshipman who was making his first cruise on *Bold Marauder.*

Teach came alive, pounding a fist against his massive chest. "Then plunge it into his heart for good measure!"

"But first, *do* avail yourself of his handsome body," Delight said, her voice thick and husky as she rubbed herself against Teach like a cat wanting to be petted. " 'Twould be a dreadful shame to let such a fine specimen of a man go to waste, no?"

Deirdre stared at her, temporarily forgetting her fear.

"Of course, if *you* don't want to, I'd be happy to oblige," Delight added with a wink. "I'd find great *delight* in melting our Ice Captain!"

Again thunder boomed outside, echoing up through the timbers of the ship and drowning out the sounds of their laughter. Deirdre swallowed hard, picturing hundreds, maybe thousands, of feet of cold, merciless ocean beneath them. If *Bold Marauder* went down, the sea would swallow them up like the whale with Jonah. *Dear God,* she thought, shivering. Her very life depended on the sturdiness of a scant bit of wood and canvas, the seamanship of a crew whose abilities she was already beginning to doubt, and the leadership, intelligence, and ability of a man they did not trust, did not respect, and certainly did not like.

The Lord and Master.

It was his will alone that kept *Bold Marauder* from going down. His—and God's.

The ship rolled atop a particularly long swell, and Deirdre's fingers fiercely gripped the crucifix.

"Ye forget one tiny detail o' importance," she said, trying to keep the terror out of her voice. "Th' Lord an' Master has banned me from his cabin an' put me in th' one next t' him. There be no way I can ... ambush him."

Skunk braced himself against a steep, rolling plunge and gave a dismissive wave of his broad hand. "That's all taken care of, girlie. Our carpenter here—where are ye, Bernie?— chopped a secret hole in the bulkhead screen between your cabin and the Lord 'n' Master's, just this afternoon. It's deck-level and just big enough for ye to crawl through, not that our fearless leader's gonna ever notice it anyhow— right, Bernie?" He clapped the beaming carpenter on the back. "Bernie here fixed it so the door opens behind his bloody Lordship's table! You ought to be able to crawl in and out between the two cabins with him bein' none the wiser!"

Deirdre's mouth went slack.

"Why, that sounds like something *I'd* enjoy doing," Delight mused. "Imagine, if our bold captain happened to be sitting at his table at the time . . . I suppose, that being deck-level, that would make me come out at just about the level of his love-organ. Lo, I can just *imagine* his surprise to feel slow fingers stroking his more *sensitive* parts as he was trying to work. . . ."

Every man in the room flushed. Young Hibbert clawed at his throat, his eyes bulging as he put his hands over his groin to hide his sudden arousal.

"Here, now, Delight, ye're disturbin' the children!" Skunk cried, hooting with laughter and eyeing Delight's hand as it roved toward Teach's *sensitive* parts.

"Perhaps, then, some children ought to be in *bed,* no?" Delight returned with a wicked smile and a pointed glance at young Hibbert's groin.

Her face flaming, Deirdre got up to leave.

"Here, now, girlie, get back here," Skunk said, grabbing her arm. "Poor Bernie didn't go through all that trouble fer nothin'."

"Fine, then, *let* Delight do 't. I hate th' man, but I can't kill him. I've already tried twice!"

"Ain't nothing to it," Skunk said, still gripping her arm. His eyes gleamed with mischief. "All ye gotta do is crawl through the hole, wait for yer victim, and then stick yer knife squarely in the middle of his bloody Lordship's gut—"

"Aye, carve his liver out and bring it up on a platter!" Elwin spat, brandishing a scalpel.

"And his heart, too! Don't forget his blackened heart!"

Sudden, awful images crowded Deirdre's mind . . . of the captain lying in a pool of blood, dying. Of his cold eyes staring up at her in death, accusing, unforgiving.

Is that what ye really *want, Deirdre?*

She stared at the glittering blade with something like horror.

"The next time I'm tempted to do you a kindness, I'll resist. . . . Ireland soon passes far off our starboard beam. Forgive me, but I merely thought you'd like to see it a final time. . . ."

"Aw, don't look so scared, Deirdre. He won't feel a thing," Skunk said, picking up the knife and forcing it between her stiff fingers. She stared at it, bracing herself against the roll of the ship and therefore missing the mischievous glance he gave his shipmates. "Now, c'mon. Let's get you up there and into his cabin before he retires fer the night. Hibbert, take her up, would ye?"

The middie, still staring at Delight's hand—which was now dipping closer and closer to Teach's groin—scrambled to take Deirdre's hand.

"I told ye, I don't think I have it in me t' commit *murder*—"

The door crashed open and Ian MacDuff poked his head inside. Water streamed from his ruddy face, his beard, his hat. "I couldnae help hearing your conversation," he said desperately. "Listen, laddies, perhaps we can reach a peace with his Lordship. . . ."

"Aw, Ian, don't go gettin' all soft on us," Skunk complained, disgustedly waving his hand and releasing a fresh cloud of stench from beneath his armpit. "Hibbert, get the girlie up there, would ye?"

Hibbert, still staring at Delight and about to disgrace himself in front of his shipmates, grabbed Deirdre's arm, shot a last bug-eyed look at Delight's hand, and bolted from the room.

Ian turned angrily from Delight's silky, inviting smile. "Skunk, you go too far. I cannae permit this, ye ken?"

"Piss off, Ian. Ye know as well as the rest of us that the girlie hasn't the will or the guts to kill his bloody Lordship. We're just havin' a bit of sport and ye know it. Hell, if'n I was serious about wanting 'im dead, I'd do away with 'im myself." He clapped a big, meaty hand across Ian's back. "Besides, ye know none of us really want to *kill* the bastard . . . we just wanna shake him up a bit. Ye know, make him a little aggravated."

"Oh, ye'll aggravate him, tae be sure. At the wee lassie's expense!"

Ignoring Delight, he stormed from the wardroom, slamming the door behind him.

At the wee lassie's expense.
Ian couldn't have issued a more prophetic statement.

Leaving a master's mate and four experienced hands at the helm, Christian exhaustedly made his way through the stormy darkness toward the hatch.

He was freezing, uncomfortable, and soaked to the skin. His hat dripped a steady stream of water that trickled icily down his face and neck. His neckcloth was tight and itchy against his throat, his white breeches clung uncomfortably to his thighs, and his boat cloak hung heavily from his body.

His thoughts were as dark as the night.

Damn her, he thought angrily, ducking beneath the hatch. Clawing off his wet and strangling neckcloth, he flung it to the deck. How did she dare taunt him with that vulgar display of creamy white flesh revealed by a gown that only a prostitute would wear? She was no better than a whore, and he rued the years that had turned the innocent Irish girl with the huge purple eyes into the soiled creature she'd become.

Emily's face appeared in his memory, shaming him for the lust he had no business feeling. His eyes hard, he pounded through the darkness, hating himself for feeling such carnal desires, hating the girl for causing them. She had no right. She *had no right!*

The storm increased in fury, the sound of rain thrumming against the quarterdeck nearly deafening him. The frigate rolled beneath his feet, lurched upright. But his steps were sure, his balance secure—until he reached the door of his cabin and nearly tripped over Evans.

He stared down at the marine's white crossbelt, a dim white X in the darkness. Obviously, the thundering rain did nothing to disturb Evans's sleep. Or his sweet dreams.

"Ah, Delight . . ." the man murmured on a sigh.

Christian frowned, rolled his eyes, and resisted the urge to rouse the marine with a sharp word in his ear. "Bugger the lot of you," he muttered, dashing the water from his brow. Then he stepped over the marine's body and stood staring at his cabin door.

It loomed ominously in front of him.

He rubbed his chin, his lips cracking in a slow grin.

Then, taking a deep breath, he drove his foot savagely against the wood and instinctively jumped back.

Thwaaack!

The knife slammed harmlessly into the wood of the door-frame.

Evans shot to his feet, blinking in confusion. Ignoring him, Christian entered his dimly lit cabin. Nonchalantly, he removed his wet hat, tossed it aside, and pried the knife—a wicked, curving blade of death—from the doorframe.

"Really, love. This is beginning to get *quite* boring."

The girl stood in the middle of the cabin, gaping at him. Her hair hung in a wildly curling black mass about her pale shoulders, and her eyes were huge pools of violet in her chalk-white face. Predictably, she reached up with shaking hands and touched the crucifix.

"I . . . I missed."

Christian brushed past her, went to his table, and poured a hefty measure of brandy into a glass. He raised it to his lips, his gaze roving over her body and dragging heat in its wake. Then his eyes flashed up to impale hers. "I daresay."

Deirdre saw no anger in those frosty depths. Nothing but a strange, dark heat, and a flicker of something that might've been amusement.

She went scarlet with sudden rage. How did he dare mock her so! Did he think this all some grand joke? That she was nothing but an incompetent ninny? The blackguard! "Next time I won't miss!" she cried, clenching her fists while tears of frustration and confusion sprang to her eyes.

"Oh?" The Lord and Master took a casual sip from his glass and leaned against the bulkhead, his weight resting on one hip as his gaze roved appreciatively over her.

"Next time I'll . . . I'll . . ."

"Save it," he said with cold indifference. He stripped off his dripping boat cloak and flung it over a chair. "Pray, I do so enjoy a good surprise—though your incompetence is begging to tire me." He hefted his glass to her and again she flushed beneath the intensity in the hard gray eyes as his gaze slid down her creamy throat, her swelling bosom, her gently flaring hips. "It saddens me to see that in the thirteen years since I saw you last, you seem to have turned into a devilishly fetching little piece who sees no better outlet for her charms than a ship full of men who know not the meaning of the term *gentleman*. I have tried to conduct my actions, and my thoughts, in a gallant and honorable way, but it appears that you are frightfully determined to break me. You think it all a game, wearing that shockingly obscene gown and making these paltry attempts on my life?" He put down the glass, his smile chilling and cold. "Well, then, perhaps 'tis time we play it by *my* rules, dear girl."

She touched her throat, alarmed by the continued indifference in his voice. "What are ye talkin' about?"

He arched a golden brow. "Oh, I was just thinking. For every devilishly inept attempt you make on my life, I will make a devilishly *adroit* attempt on your virtue."

"What?"

"I mean, since you are obviously so determined to flaunt yourself in front of me, no doubt with the intention of bringing me down to the level of an animal, perhaps I shall give you opportunity to do so." He gave her a chilling smile. "On *your* terms, of course. . . ."

"What d'ye mean, makin' an attempt on me virtue?"

He gave her a faintly disdainful, mocking look, and continued as if he hadn't heard. "You *did* enjoy the punishment I had in store for Mr. Teach, did you not? I'm told the crew feels my methods for addressing a grievance are rather . . . *unorthodox*. So, too, are my methods for preventing one."

She stared at him, sudden apprehension icing her blood.

He smiled, a cold, triumphant smile that brought her no comfort. "From now on, my dangerous little doxy, for every attempt you make on my life, I will remove one article of your clothing."

Deirdre paled to the roots of her black hair, gaping at him.

"That's devilishly fair, is it not?" the Lord and Master asked, casually swirling his brandy and gazing at the outline of her breasts as though he'd already removed the gown.

"Fair? Ye're askin' me t' become a . . . a *prostitute!"*

He merely smiled. "Dressed as you are, my dear, how could I think you are not one already?"

"I won't be barin' me body t' ye, ye black-hearted animal!"

"But, Mistress O'Devir"—he grinned and toasted her with his glass—"or, shall, I say, Mistress *O'Never?*—you do not have to. In fact, I would rather you didn't, given that my tastes do not include would-be murderesses, dockside whores, and the like. The choice is yours, don't you see? After all, I'm not asking you to persevere in these most comic attempts on my life."

Her nostrils flared with rage. "I told ye before, I be no doxy!"

"Well, I daresay you certainly *dress* like one," he said pointedly, his gaze sliding to her upthrust breasts. His voice went harsh with anger. "Such vulgarity is far more befitting a French whore than an Irish tart. Perhaps you should choose your clothing more wisely, dear girl, if you dislike the attention it may bring you!"

Her temper breaking, she snatched up and flung the nearest object—a pair of brass dividers—at him with all the force in her lithe young body. They missed his head by a mere inch, slamming into the bulkhead and quivering with the force of the impact.

Christian raised a cool brow and set down his goblet. "That, my dear girl, most definitely counts as an attempt on my life."

He smiled, his eyes as gray as storm clouds, cold, ruthless, and yet—

Promising.

Deirdre backed up, looking for another weapon.

"I do think that you now owe me that gown, my girl." His gaze flickered over her, pausing heatedly at her breasts. Fire flamed in her cheeks and she gasped in dismay. "By the way, you do recall my address to this group of rabble that considers itself a crew, do you not?"

She crossed her arms over her chest and glanced desperately at the door, fearful because he was so cold, so controlled. "About . . . ?"

"About crimes and punishment, of course. In particular, about the punishment fitting the crime."

She stared at him, uncomprehending.

The Lord and Master's hard eyes roved down her neck and over her crossed arms. Deirdre stepped backward, her face paling.

"And so, Deirdre O'Devir—since you have tried to impale me with *your* blade, perhaps it is only fitting that I impale you with *mine.*"

He put his glass down and straightened up slowly. He was more than six feet of raw power, muscle, and tightly leashed anger.

And he was coming for her.

She bolted, too late. Her throat closed up and her mouth went dry, and she screamed as his hand snaked out and snared a thick, inky curl. Wrapping it around his wrist, he drew her close, his body pressing against hers and searing her with its hard heat. She smelled damp wool and linen, saw a trickle of rain streaming down his harsh cheek. From experience, she knew it was no use struggling. Instead, she glared up at him, her eyes hot with purple fire and her words coming through tightly clenched teeth.

"G-get away from me. . . ."

"I would dearly *love* to get away from you, love, if only I could. But, alas, you make me feel things you have no business making me feel."

She squeezed her eyes shut and turned her face away, terrified of his hot touch, of his looming presence—and of her body's response to him.

"Leave me alone!"

"Pray, I wish I *could,* but you arouse me when no one has been able to do so in over five years. Naturally, I am a bit curious to learn why this is so."

She struggled, fighting his steely grip to no avail.

"You cause me to harden with the pain of wanting you," he ground out, his voice dark with an anger she didn't understand. "You cause me to want to strip that god-awful gown from your back and shower your lovely breasts with kisses. Even now they tempt me with their softness, their nearness. Even now I see your nipples in sharp, hard outline beneath the bodice of that . . . *garment.* Even now my blood is pounding through my veins, for I should like nothing more than to touch those sweet and sugary tips, to kiss them into budding peaks, to see if this heat that rages through my blood will sustain itself long enough to engage in an act I've thought myself no longer capable of. Alas, dear girl, I think it will. I may be an officer, I may be a gentleman, but I am first a *man!*"

Heat burned her cheeks, fired her blood, swirled and tingled between her thighs. Desperately, she drove her palms against his damp waistcoat, trying to shove him away, but the futile action only seemed to spur him on. Pushing her up against the bulkhead, he pinned her with his body, flattening her tingling breasts, soaking her gown, and driving the sharp edges of the crucifix into her skin.

"Let me go, ye black-hearted *bastard!*"

His warm breath fluttered the curls at her temple, making her shiver with terror and unbidden longing. His hands caught her wrists and yanked them above her head.

"I said, let me *go!*"

She tried to bring her knee up, but he was solid, unmoving, overwhelming. The deck climbed, rolled, and fell, the lantern that hung from the deck beams swinging like a thing possessed. She shut her eyes, too angry to feel sick. Trembling, she felt his lips rove down her throat, nipping the skin, setting it afire, nuzzling the warm cleft between her collarbones as they moved toward her breasts.

"Stop," she sobbed, trying to twist away and fighting the raw heat that began to surge through her blood.

"Deirdre O'Never," he murmured sarcastically, his voice silky with menace, his callused hand moving up the soft, sensitive flesh of her shivering thigh and pushing her skirts with it. "I rather like that, I think. 'Tis *devilishly* appropriate, what?"

His hand drove upward, skimming her velvet-clad belly and cupping one breast. She gasped, feeling him gently thumbing its pouting bud.

I am not here, Deirdre thought, trying to distance herself from this torment. *I am home, in Connemara. . . . This is not happening t' me. . . .*

"Ah, you like that, don't you, love?" His breath was hot against her neck, his hard fingers rasping over her pebbly nipples and teasing them higher and higher. "I've coaxed an answer from your lovely young body already ... just as you've coaxed one from mine."

His palm caressed the silken swell of her breast; his thumb swirled over the tight, darkening bud until her breathing was no longer controlled, her heartbeat no longer her own. Deirdre whimpered, clamping her legs together and biting down hard on her lip. She felt his warm mouth brushing her throat, the underside of her jaw, the point of her chin, the corner of her mouth. His tongue, wet and sensuous, traced the outline of her lips, and she tried in vain to twist away.

"Kiss me, love. I shall not hurt you," he murmured against her mouth.

She sobbed in defeat, tasting the sweetness of brandy on his lips, feeling the gentleness of his hand as he cupped her jaw and turned her face toward him. Fire burned through her breasts, between her thighs, and instinctively, she moved her hips against his, hating herself for her uncontrollable, wanton response.

"That's my girl," he breathed, claiming her mouth and gently nipping her lips with his teeth. His fierce grip around her wrists loosened, and she shivered as he gently pulled her arms down, locking his hand around her wrist as he guided it down, down, toward the hard bulge that curved the front of his white breeches.

"No ..." she sobbed, trying to escape as she realized just where he was guiding her hand. "Please, stop. ..."

His big body pushed against her, crushing her against the bulkhead, driving her shoulders into the wood, her crucifix into her breasts, his manhood into her trembling hand. Heat radiated through his damp clothes, burning her skin. His breath rasped harshly against her damp temple.

"Touch me, love," he murmured hoarsely, desperately, against her hair. "Oh, God, touch me, show me that I *can* still feel. ..."

Beneath the wet, coarse breeches his manhood stirred against her palm. She whimpered and tried to pull away, but he pushed her hand against him, harder, the rigid blade of thick male flesh swelling mightily against her hand.

The hammer of rain on the deck above was suddenly

deafening, his nearness stifling. Gasping, Deirdre tried to break free.

He caught her hand and placed it against him once more, grinding himself against her palm. His tongue plunged into her mouth, filling her senses with the sweetness of brandy, the heat of desire.

Against her fingers she felt the thick sickle of flesh straining against his breeches. The kiss deepened, growing wetter, hotter; his breathing came harsher, the movements of his hands against her breasts feverish and rapid. Deirdre squirmed, helpless beneath his power, hating him for doing this to her, hating her body for responding to him.

But she could not pull away. Of their own accord, her fingers roved over him, tracing the alien bulge of hard flesh beneath the wet breeches, and becoming bolder as his breathing grew erratic, hot, desperate, his heartbeat as loud and rapid as her own. Her arm came up to cup the back of his neck, and she felt the dampness of his hair against her wrist, the stiff and scratchy edge of his upturned collar against the softness of her inner arm, the wide breadth of his proud shoulders against her shivery skin. She let her arm fall, down the back of his coat to his buttocks. He groaned deep in his throat, his fingers against her nipples growing harsh with desire.

"Harder, my girl," he murmured against her lips. "Please, press harder. . . . Oh, my God. . . ."

But she needed no coaxing. What had been frightening and distasteful was now forbidden and enticing. Her own heart pounding in her ears, she drove her hand against his manhood, her lips against his mouth, her aching breasts against his hand. She met his thrusting tongue with her own, clung to him with the fierceness of passion.

He dragged his mouth from hers, raining hot kisses over her cheeks, her fluttering lids, her damp brow. "By God, Deirdre, you have proved to me that I am whole, that I am healthy . . . oh, it's been so *devilishly* long. . . . No, don't stop now . . . touch me. Ah, love, there. . . ."

Caught up in the thick, wet swirls of heat that radiated from her thighs, she murmured unthinkingly, "Do I, then, cause ye t' feel like *she* did . . . yer Emily?"

It was an innocent enough question on her part; a devastating one on his. He went suddenly stiff and pulled back, his face going ashen, his eyes widening, his mouth falling open in shock.

Christian stared at her, utterly appalled at what he'd just done. *Emily.* Like a jealous ghost, her face had risen up to haunt him, taunt him, at the very moment when he'd thought he'd banished it forever. In its wake, he felt his desire shrinking pitifully beneath his breeches, the fire that had coursed through his blood chilling to ice, the warmth that had so briefly stirred his cold heart fading to bitter ashes.

Cold heart?

He *had* no heart.

He couldn't even function as a *man,* and had been so determined to prove to himself otherwise that he'd abused a young girl who deserved more from a king's officer than the behavior of an animal. *A king's officer.* He had shamed the very coat he wore with such pride.

His mouth tightened and, furious with himself, he turned away to the panoramic darkness of the stern windows. Shakily, he placed his palms on the cold sill and hung his head, as though the effort of lifting it was too much for him. "As you know, Miss O'Devir, it is not at all customary to have a civilian female aboard a king's ship." His fingers tightened on the sill, his shoulders slumped with defeat. "And I have tried to address the problem in the only way I saw fit, by assigning you the cabin of my second lieutenant. I don't know how you got in here, but, by God, I only know that you cannot stay. While I had sought to protect you from the lusts of my crew, it is apparent that I am no better than they. Try as I might, I am unable to keep myself at arm's length from you."

"But—"

"Have no fear, you shall be quite safe in Mr. Rhodes's cabin. In fact, I shall post a marine outside the door with orders to shoot and kill anyone attempting to enter." He straightened up, and turned abruptly to face her. His gray eyes were cold and hard. "Myself included."

He gave a great, ragged sigh that swelled the breadth of

his already mighty chest. Then he came forward, taking her icy hands in his own and imploring her with desperate eyes. "I beg your forgiveness, Miss O'Devir. I was wrong to force myself upon you, and I shall not do so again." He tightened his jaw, and looked up at the deckhead, as though willing himself to believe his own words, words that were filled with raw anguish. "The hell of the matter is that you are really quite safe from me. I know that my . . . attraction . . . for you is nothing more than that—for, you see, I am an empty man. The attraction is there indeed, even the lust but the ability to follow it through is sadly lacking. Have no fear that I will . . . compromise you. Tonight was a mistake. It shall not happen again."

His words, his rejection, brought an anger she didn't understand. Her eyes glittering, she tore her hands free of his. "And *you,* Captain, don't have t' worry that I'll succumb t' yer *empty* desires. Ye see, I don't find *ye* th' least bit attractive. In fact, I think ye're uglier than a dead carp. I hate Englishmen, I hate fair hair, and yer touch makes me sick. So go take yer bleedin' lusts an' practice 'em on someone who welcomes 'em!"

Then, ignoring his stricken face, she turned abruptly on her heel and slammed out of his cabin.

It was only when she reached the lonely privacy of her own that she burst into tears.

Chapter 13

~~~

She awoke in Rhodes's cabin, in Rhodes's bunk, and in total darkness.

Alone.

Outside, the storm rumbled in fury, the deep, reverberating tremors of thunder shaking the very timbers of the ship.

Deirdre couldn't see the lightning, and somehow, that was worse. Against her shoulder the bulkhead pressed, cold and damp, and she realized, in the disorienting darkness, that the frigate was heeled hard over on her side.

Fresh torrents of rain whipped across the deck above. Beneath her the ship rolled heavily, creaking, groaning, and straining in the pounding seas. Shivering with cold and fighting panic, Deirdre reached out, groped for her canvas bag and, pulling it close, wrapped her arms around it and pressed it to her madly pounding heart.

Thunder crashed again and the bunk vibrated eerily against the bulkhead.

In pitch blackness, she swung her bare feet out of bed, placed them gingerly on the cold flooring, and, gripping the bunk, pulled herself up.

The frigate rose, seeming to hang suspended before crashing down over the next heavy comber with a force that nearly yanked Deirdre's feet out from under her.

Wind screamed, and the ocean roared just outside. She took one last, desperate look at the space where the little passage lay; then, sobbing with fear, she stumbled through the darkness toward the door, desperate for the comfort of someone, *anyone*.

It opened just before her hand hit the latch.

He stood there, holding a lantern, his eyes panicky, his face pale.

"Thank God you're awake. . . ."

For one brief, crazy moment, she almost flung herself into his arms with relief, before pride swept in to save her. Instead, she clutched the doorframe as the frigate plunged into a trough, and holding on tightly, to save both her balance and her pride, she faced him defiantly. "What d'ye want, Englishman? I thought yer marine had orders t' shoot anyone who tries t' enter me cabin!"

She saw his throat working. "It's Tildy," he said, his fingers biting into the soft skin of her wrist. "Oh, Deirdre, blind me for being such a bastard earlier, but you must come—"

She forget her fear. She forgot her pride. *He* was here— and he needed her.

"Tildy?"

"My dog." He glanced anxiously over his shoulder, toward his cabin. "There's something wrong with her. She's hiding in the corner, panting ... her eyes are glazed, and she's crying—" He wiped his brow and raked a shaky hand through his hair. "Forgive me, but I did not know who else to summon."

"Let me get me coat."

She tossed the heavy garment over her scanty gown and allowed him to guide her back to his cabin. Above, the wind shrieked in demonic fury, and if not for the firm support of his arm, she would've stumbled and fallen. He pushed open the door to his cabin and held the lantern aloft as she staggered across the deck to where the little dog lay wedged into a corner and whining pitifully.

The instant Deirdre saw her, she knew what was wrong.

"She's dying, isn't she?" the Lord and Master said, his voice hoarse with emotion. "My God, I knew I should never have subjected her to the rigors of a ship—"

"She be whelpin'," Deirdre said flatly.

"What?"

"Havin' puppies."

His eyes bulged. *"Puppies?"*

"Aye, puppies." Despite herself, she couldn't help but grin at his stricken, helpless look. "Animals always pick storms t' be birthin' their wee ones," she said, kneeling down to stroke the spaniel's heaving sides. "Why don't ye be gettin' me some blankets so I can make her comfortable?"

"Puppies. . . ."

"Th' blankets, Captain?"

He stumbled as the ship pitched beneath him. "Blind me, but we can't have puppies here! *This is a king's ship!*"

"I don't think ye have a choice, an' neither does yer bleedin' king. Now get me th' blankets and get out o' me hair," she commanded, sliding her arms beneath the dog and lifting her gently. Her steps were surprisingly steady as she carried the little dog to the bench seat, where the captain hastily spread the blankets before Deirdre lay the spaniel carefully down.

She was aware of his eyes on her back, caressing her, judging her, admiring her—adoring her. He, the proud ruler of HMS *Bold Marauder*, had turned to her in his hour of need, humbling himself and placing his trust in her abilities. Trust. Confidence. Need. It was a good feeling, and her heart soared inexplainably in her breast. And as he came up to stand behind her, leaning over her like a protective father, she felt the searing heat of his body and flushed hotly.

The feeling left her strangely defenseless—and scared. Turning, she snapped, "Really, Captain ... this won't be a pretty sight. Go have yerself a tot o' rum or somethin'."

He pressed closer, his eyes fastened on the laboring dog. "Bugger it, I've seen plenty of blood in my life!"

But he had never seen a birthing. And when Tildy's whimpers progressed to sharp cries of pain and the first tiny puppy emerged some twenty minutes later, the mighty Lord and Master went as white as his shirt. He looked at the bloody sac and afterbirth, and clawed at his throat.

Deirdre glanced behind her to see him leaning heavily against the bulkhead.

"If yer goin' t' be faintin', I'd appreciate it if ye'd do it elsewhere," she said, cleaning the pup with a soft cloth and placing it against the warmth of Tildy's belly. But then she looked up at him, and met his eyes. They were warm, caressing, brimming with ... admiration? Hope? *Affection?*

Something moved heavily in her chest and she looked down at the pup, blinking the moisture back and recognizing the feeling for what it was. A warming. A thawing. A sudden rush of feeling for this man who was her enemy, this man she professed to hate, this man whose touch could turn her blood to butter.

"Aye," he murmured shakily. "Perhaps I shall go relieve the officer of the watch."

She shut her eyes, feeling her hatred crumpling beneath his defenseless manner, and wishing with all her heart that she could hold on to it. But it was no use. She opened her eyes and saw the little dog's white body going fuzzy behind a blur of tears. Softly, she murmured, "Yes, do. And perhaps when ye come back ye'll have a whole new family t' welcome."

He grabbed his coat and boat cloak and fled the cabin, his footsteps fading into the howl of rain and wind and storm. Deirdre took a deep, shaky breath and shut her eyes, listening to the soft, kittenlike mews of the tiny puppy as they permeated the roar of the storm. She had witnessed the miracle of birth before—many times, in fact—but never had it seemed so precious, so holy, so achingly beautiful.

A sudden warmth flooded her and she hugged her arms to her breasts, her eyes traveling over the Lord and Master's cabin with sudden wonder and awe. But just then, Tildy stiffened in pain and, howling, began to push out another tiny bundle, leaving Deirdre no time to ponder the new and confusing feelings of her heart.

And so it went, on and on and on, until at last the little spaniel, exhausted, staggered to her feet and licked her three little newborns.

For a long time, Deirdre watched them greedily sucking at their mother's swollen teats. She reached out and gently touched each tiny, squirming body, smiling and feeling her eyes grow misty with emotion. For a brief moment Tildy lifted her head and seemed to smile in gratitude; then the little dog's head fell back to the blankets, and with a heavy, satisfied sigh, she closed her eyes.

Deirdre rose to her feet. She tucked the blankets around the new family and stumbled to the door against the violent tilt of the deck. As she opened it, a blast of raw, wet wind hit her in the face.

In the gloom, permeated only by a crazily swinging lantern, she saw Evans blinking sleepily.

"Summon yer captain and tell him he be th' proud da o' three wee babes," Deirdre said. Then, with a last glance over her shoulder at Tildy, she turned and stumbled back to her cabin, where she fell, exhausted, into her bunk.

The storm continued for a week, chasing them across the Atlantic, abating during the day, worsening at night, pounding the frigate and battering her relentlessly beneath mountains of angry water and sheets of rain, snow, and sleet. The pumps labored day and night to rid the bilge of water that streamed down through the hatches; some of the men got seasick, and the crew, still wrapped in their drenched clothes, tumbled into their damp hammocks after their watches, cold, wet, and too exhausted to do more than close their eyes and succumb to drugging slumber.

As for the captain himself, he was glad of the storm. It kept his tormented mind occupied, for with the ship demanding every bit of his attention, he had little time to think of the girl he no longer trusted himself around, the girl whose eyes followed him wherever he went, the girl who was managing, somehow, to vie with his beloved Emily for the affections of his tightly guarded heart. Such feelings terrified him and he began to go out of his way to avoid her, until the dark purple eyes grew confused, and then angry with hurt.

But he had no choice. She was too young for him. She was too innocent for him. He had done her a grievous wrong thirteen years ago, and it was far safer for both of them if she hated him. He *preferred* that she hate him. But as the second week dragged by, he found himself pausing for long moments outside her cabin in the dead of night, laying his palm against the wood as though he could reach inside and touch her warm skin, her hair, her softly beating heart.

Then he would turn away and stumble wearily to the loneliness of his own cabin—and the nightmares that haunted his troubled sleep—never knowing that, only several feet away, the Irish girl pined for him as much as he did for her.

The storm did nothing, however, to put a damper on Delight Foley's *business;* indeed, she found such twisted and convoluted motions on the frigate's part a boon to her inventiveness when it came to sexual pleasure—and positions. A true connoisseur of carnal ecstasy, Delight loved her adoring flock of lusty seamen, though she vehemently proclaimed that she would only allow Skunk near her if he dragged a bar of soap on deck with him during a particularly violent bout of rain.

Two and a half weeks after they'd left Portsmouth, Deirdre came to Delight, hesitantly knocking on the brig's door before the other girl opened it.

"Deirdre, *chérie!*" The girl's wide, pouting mouth softened in an unpretentious grin as she saw that it was her friend, not a consort, and hastily, she flung the door open wide. A pungent blast of French perfume hit Deirdre in the face, nearly choking her. "Do come in! I was just reading about a new position in my manual—here, have a look!"

Flushing hotly, Deirdre pushed the book away, for lately her own thoughts had been filled too much with the Lord and Master—and with strange, wicked notions that brought odd tinglings to her more womanly parts.

"Delight . . . I have t' talk t' ye."

"Lo, Deirdre, I just *knew* something was troubling you. You've been so quiet lately. Sit down right here," she said, patting her bed, "and tell Delight what the problem is!"

Deirdre eyed the scented sheets, the spread of red satin—and took the chair instead. She hung her head and twisted her hands together, suddenly uncomfortable and shy.

The other girl came to her, put her hands on her wickedly curving hips, and tilted her head to one side. "Let me guess," she said brightly, tapping a red fingernail against a pearly tooth. "It's our handsome Lord and Master, no?"

Deirdre's cheeks flamed and she looked away. "Is it tha' 't' obvious?" she asked, wretchedly.

"Lo, Deirdre, when you're older you will learn how to hide the lust in your eyes. It's plain as day when you talk about him, that you feel for the man."

Deirdre stared down at the floor. There was a frothy piece of lace and leather near her shoe, and it crossed her mind to ask Delight what its purpose was. Wisely, she decided she didn't want to know.

She murmured, "Ye know, I've been seein' him more an' more withou' that wig o' his. We got in a fight, and I told 'im I hate fair hair, but ye know somethin,' Delight?" She looked up at the other girl's amused face, her sparkling, vivacious eyes. "I'm beginning' t' think his hair's kind o' pretty." She thought of how it had looked last night, when he had come into his cabin as she'd been feeding Tildy. The lantern light had shone down on each glimmering strand, making the damp, slightly wavy hair so pure and pale a gold it was almost silver. It was the color of beach sand on a hot day, curling boyishly behind his ears and at his nape, and she had almost forgotten herself and reached out to touch it.

Delight came over to her and laid her manicured hand on her thin shoulder. Softly, she said, "You're in love with him, aren't you?"

Deirdre's head jerked up. "L-love—"

"There's no use denying it, sweetie. He's a fine man, strong and gallant and chivalrous, though a bit too righteous and noble for his own good. But mark me, there are none finer on this vessel, perhaps none finer, even, in England. You want *my* advice?" She laughed. "Set your sights on him, *chérie*. He is a good catch, your man."

Deirdre dragged her head up. "But, Delight . . . he's no' 't'interested in me. I be Irish. A commoner. He be an English gentleman, master o' a king's ship, well learned an' educated."

"So?"

"He avoids me."

"So?"

"He . . . he's got rules he lives by, Delight. He's . . . he's an officer an' a gentleman. I'm just—"

"The woman he could fall in love with."

Miserably, Deirdre shook her head. "Nay. He be in love wi' someone called Emily."

"Aaah," Delight said knowingly. "His dead wife." She laughed at Deirdre's surprised look. "Lo, don't look so shocked! Rico told Ian, who told me. Happened five years ago, it did. The poor dear died in a fire. But really, Deirdre, do not let *that* stop you. You can't compete with a *ghost*, no?"

"There *is* no competition. Every time he . . . he shows me some, uh, affection, he remembers *her* an' gets all mad at me, an' starts sayin' things I don't understand. . . ."

"Such as?"

Deirdre bit her lip. Such as being less than a man. Such as being unable to function as one. But, inexplicably, she did not want to repeat the Lord and Master's strange words to Delight. Although she did not understand them, there was something private about his disclosures, something, she felt, that had been meant for her ears, and her ears alone.

"Oh, nothin'," she murmured, and rose shakily to her feet. "I thank ye, Delight. Ye . . . ye made some things clear in me mind, ye did."

The other girl shrugged and smiled brightly. "Well, anytime you want advice, you come here to Delight. And when the time comes for you to lure the Lord and Master into your bed, you just let me know. I have all kinds of *devices* to make the task go easy for you, no?"

On that note, Deirdre went scarlet and fled the brig, Delight's amused laughter ringing in her ears.

Emily.

His wife came to him, as she had every night for the past five years, waiting until he was deeply asleep before exploding into his slumber.

Christian's blood went cold, and he trembled, curling himself beneath the blankets and whimpering deep in his throat. But there was no hiding. No escaping.

"Emily?" He was dreaming, he *knew* he was dreaming, but nevertheless it was all happening again, just as it had that long-ago night in the English countryside, and there was nothing, absolutely nothing, he could do to change it.

He opened his eyes, hearing the soft chirp of crickets outside. Something had woken him. He reached out for her in the darkness, again finding their bed empty.

He sat up, his hand still resting on the cool spot on the sheet where his wife should've been.

"Emmie?"

Worried, he swung himself out of bed, stumbling as his feet touched the icy tiles. After so many months at sea, he was well used to a rolling deck, not cold marble, plush Persian rugs, and a solid floor that didn't move. But no, he was not aboard his ship, *Titan,* but at home at the fine country estate in Hampshire that had been in the Lord family for centuries.

He stood for a moment, swaying in the darkness and getting his bearings. Beneath his feet, the floor felt cold and alien—not unlike the way *she* had behaved toward him since *Titan* had dropped anchor in Portsmouth a week before.

"Emily?"

He stumbled along, slightly disoriented, the rich, ornate furniture with which she had filled their bedroom looming up as huge, dark shapes in the gloom. The furniture was ugly and far too grand for his tastes, but she had wanted it, and it wasn't in his heart to deny her.

"Emmie?" he said again, the haunting emptiness of the house chilling his spine. With her legs crippled from a childhood illness, she couldn't have gone far. He paused, listening. From downstairs came the sound of a clock; from beyond the window, the shriek of a night bird. Land sounds, unfamiliar to his mariner's ears. Outside, an owl hooted, once, twice.

A frown marred his brow. Where the devil *was* she?

It was as his hand groped for a flint that he heard it: from downstairs, the tinkle of her laughter.

He froze, the blood chilling in his veins.

His hands were shaking, his heart pounding as he tried once, twice, to light a candle. Shielding the wavering flame with his hand and gripping the candle's base so hard that his knuckles turned white, he crept out of the room and down the steep and twisting marble staircase.

Voices came drifting through the hall. "Really, James, I prefer it when you touch me there . . . oh, yes, *there*. Oh . . . oh, *God*. . . ."

Raw devastation swept through him. . . And then—blind anger. He rushed forward. His foot slammed into the parlor door and sent it crashing back against the wall.

And by the dim glow of a candle, he saw it all. Emily, her hair spread beneath her on the sofa, her long, frail legs opened wide, her thighs wrapped around her lover's back as he pumped and strained madly above her.

With a hoarse cry, Christian charged forward.

Deirdre O'Devir awoke with a start.

Something had roused her. She sat up in bed, her eyes wild and probing the choking darkness.

The Lord and Master.

Through the canvas screen, she heard him thrashing in his bed, his harsh breathing ripping through the stillness, blotting out even the ceaseless moans of the wind and sea outside.

Deirdre flung the covers aside, ducked through the little hinged door, and padded on silent feet across the checked canvas that covered the deck flooring.

The storm clouds were parting, and by the light of a full moon, she saw the English captain, sprawled in a tortuous position on his bed. The sheets were twined around his legs, sweat sheened his heaving chest and glistened between the darker mat of hair that covered it, and his mouth was open in a silent scream.

She gripped the crucifix, the barely remembered face of her brother rising up before her eyes to remind her of her forgotten vow.

Kill him, Deirdre. . . . Kill him . . . remember what he did to us. To you and mama. . . . Remember your vow, Deirdre!

"No!"

She clapped her hands to her ears, squeezing her eyes shut and choking on a sob as she tried futilely to push the images away, to block them out.

Kill him.

Never would she find the Lord and Master more vulnerable.

"I *can't!*" she cried, clawing at her cheeks.

"Emmie . . ." he moaned brokenly, his voice no longer a plea, but awful, choking sobs that tore at her heart. "Dear God, Emmie . . ."

Her hands shaking madly, Deirdre took a deep breath.

Then she reached behind her, her fingers closing over the letter opener that rested atop his desk and glinted coldly in the moonlight.

"I'll see you in hell, by God!"

Christian dove forward, hearing his wife's scream as her lover lunged to his feet and fled from the room. Blinded by rage, Christian pounded after him, her desperate voice echoing behind him.

"If you weren't at sea all the time, you wouldn't have forced me to take a lover! If you were half the husband you ought to be, I would never have strayed! Dammit, Christian, *don't do it!*"

Red, blinding rage. . . . His breath roaring through his lungs. . . . The man's pale, naked form rounding the corner into the hall, racing through the elegant drawing room, stopping only long enough to snatch a lamp from the wall and hurl it backward with all his strength—

The room exploded into flames. Fire whooshed up the curtains in a deafening roar, sending Christian reeling back, away from the vicious wall of searing heat. The rugs went up in a bright inferno, and savage, hungry flames leapt up the fine paper that covered the walls.

In minutes, the house was ablaze.

Servants pounded past, screaming. The angry roar grew deeper, stronger, louder, deafening as he pounded back down the hall. *"Emily!"* he screamed hoarsely. "Emmie, dear God, where *are* you!"

The parlor was empty.

Thick, black, choking whorls of smoke smothered him, blinding him, drove the breath from his aching lungs. Heat blasted against his skin, his eyes, his feet. He coughed, fell, and stumbled, the flames chasing him as he tore madly through the house.

"Emil-e-e-e-e!"

Pounding up the stairs, he crashed into the bedroom and found nothing. He half ran, half fell, down the spiraling staircase, hearing her sudden screams of terror.

"Christian! *Christia-a-a-a-an!*"

Where was she? Sobbing, he kicked open doors that were already in flames. He bolted through rooms crackling with savage heat, engulfed in brilliant fire. The acrid stench of burning fabric, plaster, and wood seared his nose. Flame singed his hair, clawed madly at him as he raced past.

Her voice rose to a shrill scream. *"Christia-a-a-an!"*

There, huddled in a heap at the far end of the hall, he saw her, her frightened face glowing orange in the leaping flames, her frail body lying where her crippled legs had finally given out.

He raced headlong down the burning hall, her screams of terror guiding him blindly through flames that tore at his face, smoke that stung his eyes and exploded into his heaving lungs.

"Christian!"

He was almost there. *Almost there!* Another few feet and—

With a sudden bellowing roar, a fiery wall of timbers crashed down around him in an exploding inferno of showering sparks and leaping flame, forever separating them.

Emily! Emile-e-e-e. . . .

He heard her unholy, dying screams.

Then nothing.

Deirdre stood above him, the blade clenched tightly in her white and shaking fists, its point hovering several inches above his bruised temple.

She leaned her head back, crying with him, crying for him.

"Emily. . . ."

Harsh, racking sobs broke from his chest, so desolate, so desperate, so full of raw anguish that her own heart felt like it was being torn asunder.

Setting her jaw, Deirdre wrapped both hands around the blade and raised it high above her head, tears streaming down her cheeks as she stared at the soft swirl of fair hair at his temple.

With a cry, she brought the weapon savagely, brutally, down.

And at the last moment, her hands jerked sideways and hurled the blade to the floor, where it bounced harmlessly away.

She couldn't do it, just as she'd known all along that she couldn't, *wouldn't*, do it.

"Emmie," he sobbed, wadding the sheets up in one hand, his tears darkening the pillow. "Dear God, please, take me instead. . . ."

Harsh, agonized sobs cleaved the stillness of the cabin.

Deirdre stared at him for a long moment, seeing the Lord and Master as none of the others had seen him.

Alone, tortured—and defenseless.

Swallowing over her tears, she peeled back the covers, slid gently in beside him, and wrapped her soft arms around his heaving shoulders, holding him tightly until at last his breathing leveled, his muscles relaxed, and his anguished sobs faded to nothing but the sheen of tears upon harsh cheeks that shone silver in the moonlight.

Chapter 14

Dawn's light, pale and pink and shimmering upon the sea, shone softly through the salt-streaked stern windows and probed the bright expanse of the day cabin.

The Lord and Master awakened.

Above his head, morning painted the white deckhead and beams in its soft glow; it shone salmon against the white checks on the canvas spread over the flooring. Just overhead, he heard footsteps crossing the deck, and Ian MacDuff's gruff orders to lay the frigate over onto the other tack. Everything was well. Everything was as it should be.

Except for the woman asleep in the bed with him.

He sat up with a start and stared down at her, heat pulsing through his blood.

By God, she was beautiful. Hellishly so. Thick, coarse black curls cascaded around the pale skin of her lovely face, tangling in soft, sweeping lashes the color of charcoal. They tumbled around her neck, swirled around creamy, rawboned shoulders, fanned around her head, and sprayed across the whiteness of the pillow. They spiraled across her breasts, spilled over her back, brushed against the curve of her bottom.

His eyes following the dark tresses, he wondered if the

curls between her long, shapely thighs were just as lush and glossy.

He tried to crawl out from behind her, but, he could not do so without waking her. The narrowness of the bed did not leave much space between them, and the Irish girl seemed determined, even in slumber, to capitalize on that fact. Her arm, soft and white, lay draped over his hips. Her lips were parted, resting against his chest in an unconscious kiss.

The Lord and Master swallowed hard, as helpless as a square-rigger caught all aback.

She was wearing nothing but baggy trousers and a long, lace-wristed shirt, probably borrowed from one of the midshipmen. It had ridden up during the night; now it lay bunched and twined around her tiny waist, exposing a flat, creamy belly that was a band of temptation above the trousers, and more of her lovely young breasts than was decent. He had thought the lewd scarlet gown to be vulgar. Now he realized that with such a shape as hers, it wouldn't matter *what* she wore.

Desire. It rippled through his loins, cruel, unwanted, and unfair. It caused his manhood to grow stiff and swollen, his blood to thicken and tingle right out into the tips of his fingers. He heard his breathing coming faster, felt himself breaking out in a fine sheen of sweat that wilted the sheets where they touched his skin.

The girl sighed softly in her sleep, unconsciously driving her inner arm down over his lightly furred thighs until her fingers, resting in the thick mat of pale, golden curls between his legs, lay a mere two inches from his throbbing shaft.

God bloody rot it.

Lust. It was nothing but *lust,* he told himself. Emily might have done him wrong, but *she* was his love, his only love, and always would be. He would not betray his wife by allowing his head to be turned by this scrawny, spitting, Irish girl, who probably *wasn't* a doxy—but who could definitely mean the swift and sorry ruin of his career if he got tangled up with her.

He was English.

She was Irish.

End of discussion.

His staff pushed against the girl's hand and he clenched his teeth together, groaning deep in his throat. The sensation filled him with longing—and with despair, for he alone knew that he could not carry out the love act itself.

Not with Emily still coming to him every night. Not with Emily's face still rising up before his eyes at the first ripples of desire for another. Not with Emily's death still filling him with raw, torturous guilt that he had not been able to save her. . . .

But that long-dead face did not appear in the haunted rooms of his mind as he tentatively reached out and, trembling, touched the Irish girl's spiral-curling black hair. It was coarse, wiry, as willful as her spirit, and just as wild. His thumb began a gentle caress, crushing the lock in his fist, as something huge and painful welled up in his chest. He gently laid the long curl over her white shoulder, his gaze straying down her softly rising bosom to follow the chain that lay slackly around her neck. The crucifix, glinting in the dawn's light, rested atop one swelling breast, mocking him with its blatant reminder of their differences in religion.

He was Anglican.

She was Irish Catholic.

End of discussion.

There were those who would frown upon a highly respected naval officer taking a papist to wife. There were those who would think her coarse and unsuitable as the bride of an English nobleman. There were those who would have nothing but contempt for this *Irish* lass. Damn them, damn all of them who would put her, the only woman he'd so much as even *looked* at since Emily, out of his reach! It didn't seem fair, it *wasn't* fair.

And then he realized where his thoughts had been leading.

Wife.

"Blind me," he murmured, dragging a shaky hand through his rumpled hair.

Bride . . . .

He shut his eyes, and broke out in fresh sweat. *Behave yourself, Christian. You are an officer.*

An officer. A gentleman. As such, he was supposed to conduct himself in a stellar manner. To do otherwise would be to bring disgrace upon his king, his country, and the uniform he wore with such pride. The embarrassment of Portsmouth, and being found in such a *compromising* position, still rankled, and rankled deeply. Another such incident could bring about his ruin.

Desperately, he glanced at the little wooden box beneath the bench window that the carpenter, Bernie, had made for Tildy and her puppies. The babies were still asleep, but sensing her master's stare, Tildy raised her head and looked at him, seeming to grin.

"Ha, ha," the little spaniel seemed to say. *"Now what are you going to do?"*

The girl's hand was curled three inches from his thigh. He tensed and shut his eyes, the sweat gathering on his brow, between his shoulders. How he wished she'd move that little hand closer; how he longed to feel her soft, whispery touch moving silkily over the raw, aching length of him, stroking it, coaxing it, harder and higher, until—

Sudden, violent anger slammed through him.

What the devil was he thinking of? Twenty years of naval service lay behind him. It was bad enough that he was forsaking the memory of his dead wife by harboring lust for the girl, but if he acted upon that lust and the Admiralty got wind of it—

Cursing, he crawled out from beneath her, no longer caring whether or not he woke her. He did not. Breathing hard, he stood naked on the slightly angled deck, his powerful chest rising and falling and running with sweat as he tried to rein in his thoughts, his *desires.*

He stared out the sweeping windows of the stern gallery. The sea was deep and blue and ruffled by wind, reflecting against the deckhead in a pattern of myriad dancing stars like sunlight through a thousand diamonds. He passed the back of his wrist across his brow, then clenched his fists at his sides, unable to keep his eyes off the girl.

"Damn you!" He turned away, his hard body magnificent

in the golden light of morning and rippling with muscle. Very aware of the girl's presence, he rushed through his morning ritual, cursing when the angry, choppy motions with which he swept his razor over his face brought a trickle of blood from his chin. He grabbed his wig, arranged the rolled curls over his faintly bruised temple, and donned his uniform with a haste he hadn't shown since he'd been a fourteen-year-old midshipman who, cocky after his first night with a cheap doxy, had shown the bad sense to arrive late for his watch.

Cursing blackly, Christian stuffed his shirttails into his breeches, grabbed his coat, and slammed out of the cabin without a backward glance.

"Er, Ian? I really think you ought to have let her go for another hour or so before tacking," Wenham said, scratching one jutting ear as he peered up at the set of the sails with a critical eye. *Bold Marauder* was quite comfortable, driving along on a larboard tack under reefed topsails and courses, but he knew that the Lord and Master would have the hands piped for sail drill as soon as he came on deck.

That would mean, of course, that the men would have to go aloft to reset the sails for the second time this morning. Wenham groaned. Why work the crew any more than needed? he thought, watching the thin curl of smoke that rose tantalizingly from the galley funnel and feeling his stomach growl in anticipation of breakfast.

Ian puffed out his chest. "The captain left *me* in charge, Thomas," he said, hoisting his bagpipes and squeezing the bag beneath his brawny elbow. The big Scot missed the looks of alarm that spread amongst those standing nearby, for Ian's talents at playing his instrument had not improved in the slightest. "And *I* think it was time tae tack, so doona question my wishes!"

Rhodes, leaning against the rail, rolled his eyes as Ian stormed off. "The captain!" he sneered with a derisive glance at the hatch. "If he were any sort of commanding *officer*, he'd be up here on deck, seeing to his ship!"

"Prob'ly fussin' with that stupid wig," Skunk remarked.

"Or feeding treats to that sap-eyed dog," Elwin spat.

Hibbert, who'd spent a very educational hour in the company of Delight Foley, gave a sly grin. "Or tumbling the Irish girl."

A dark shadow fell over the deck. "That will be all, Mr. Hibbert."

Hibbert's head shot up, the blood draining from his face at the sound of that icy, dangerous voice. Abruptly, the officers snapped off guilty salutes; then all turned hastily away and pretended to be engrossed in their duties.

Christian wasted no time in pleasantries. His jaw hard, and the very wig they were ridiculing carefully combed and tied at his nape beneath the wide brim of his cocked hat, he crossed to the weather side of the ship and stared out over the brilliant azure sea. The wind was cold and biting. Spray was almost crystalline. Foam rode high on the tumbling waves and flecked the ocean for as far as the eye could see. He stared up at the masthead pennant, a dark serpent-shape against huge, fluffy white clouds bracketed by the frigate's yards.

The ship nosed into a swell, and a huge sheet of spray drove over the rail and drenched his coat. He heard someone howl with laughter before Ian's sharp reprimand abruptly silenced him.

He ignored them, though his gray eyes narrowed and a vein throbbed at his temple. Let them have their little fun. They'd learn, soon enough, that his patience for putting up with nonsense was limited. Squaring his shoulders, he strode to the wheel, keenly aware of the hostile glances the two helmsmen bestowed on him as he studied the compass.

Wenham was right. Ian *could've* left the frigate on the starboard tack for another hour.

He glanced at his first lieutenant, thinking to mention the matter to him. But there was such a hopeful look in Ian's eyes, such an anxious look about his mouth, that Christian, despite his black mood and better judgment, decided to let the matter go.

He saw Skunk, his grimy hair caught in a long pigtail at his nape and hanging between his beefy, tattooed shoulders. Several of the other troublemakers—Teach among them—stood nearby, carefully upwind of the big gunner. Skunk's gaze was on Christian. So was Teach's, Wenham's, and that of every tar from bowsprit to poop.

Watching him. Judging him. Searching for some flaw in his character, some weakness they could exploit. Christian smiled, though his jaw tightened and his sharp gaze raked over them with the keenness of a well-honed blade. They would find no flaw to attack, no weakness to exploit.

And, he thought wryly, no blemish upon his behavior. Regardless of how the Irish girl had ended up in his cabin, he had not taken advantage of her.

He began to look about him. Ian had seen fit to at least *try* to make the frigate look smart after the buffeting she'd taken during the past two and a half weeks; her sails were drawing well; the guns glistened in the morning sunlight, some of them sparkling with spray; the men were bright-eyed and ruddy-cheeked, and all turned out in proper uniform, and the decks—

Christian's jaw fell open and his gray eyes widened in shock.

"Mr. MacDuff!"

The big Scotsman's head jerked up at the sharp tone of the Lord and Master's voice and instinctively he tightened his elbow over the bagpipes. "Yes, sir?"

Christian was staring, incredulously, around him. "Who had the morning watch?"

Ian paled. "Er . . . uh, no one, sir. . . ."

"No one? And who has the watch now, Mr. MacDuff?"

"Er . . . Mr. Rhodes, sir," Ian said lamely.

The crew exchanged nervous glances, wondering what had so riled the Lord and Master.

They soon found out. "Blind me, but *look* at these decks! Torn cordage, seaweed, slime—why, this is an *embarrassment,* not only to me, but to this ship!"

He glared at his officers, the raw anger in his eyes causing them to take an involuntary step backward. "What the bloody deuce is the matter with you all? This is a *king's vessel!* Take some pride in that fact, and in yourselves!"

They stared at him, totally uncomprehending.

"This is a king's vessel!" Hibbert mimicked, smirking.

"Silence, the lot of you!" Christian snapped, his eyes

hard beneath the shadow of his cocked hat. "Mr. Rhodes, set your people to scrubbing, and when they have finished, have them wash down the deck with seawater and vinegar."

A low grumble of angry protests swept through the crew as the sharp scents of frying pork wafted up from the galley and drifted on the wind. "But, sir," Ian ventured, trying to intervene, "what about *breakfast?*"

"Breakfast will keep, Mr. MacDuff. In future, perhaps the crew will remember that if they wish to eat their breakfast on time, such *mundane* tasks as scrubbing the deck are to be performed before sunup!"

Such a threat was enough to send even Skunk running for a mop. Christian watched the crew attack the job with a vengeance. *Another small victory in this little war,* he thought smugly. And he hadn't even had to enlist the help of his bosun.

Speaking of Rico . . .

Slowly he descended the quarterdeck companionway and strode among the men, moving upwind of Skunk. The gunner was attacking the grime from beneath the hulking shadow of a cannon, his arms glistening with sweat as he swore and scrubbed and grumbled. Rhodes was watching him with a mixture of indignation and rebellion. Hibbert was supervising a group of swearing, laboring seamen, his hands on his hips, his uniform unacceptably filthy. Christian set his jaw and, coming up behind the youth, clapped a hand over his scrawny shoulder.

"Mr. Hibbert?"

The midshipman whirled, paled, and shrank back.

"Pray, have you seen my bosun?"

Hibbert's face changed, becoming smug with a private grin. "Aye."

"That's aye, *sir,* and don't you forget it lest I box your ears and send you to the bloody brig!"

"The brig? I would like that, sir—"

Too late, Hibbert realized his mistake. A grin of triumph seared the harshness of his commanding officer's face. The ship quieted, the mops stopped, and only the hiss of spray at the bows broke the sudden silence.

The Lord and Master's cold gray eyes narrowed. "The

brig. 'Twould seem that is a most *popular* area of the ship, is it not, Mr. Hibbert? Pray, am I missing something down there that I should not be?"

"N-no, sir! Not at all!"

"We shall see," Christian said coldly, and abruptly turned on his heel.

The crew froze. As one, every seaman, every warrant officer, every petty officer, every marine, watched him go, each man's eyes desperate, his heart racing with anxiety.

The Lord and Master was headed for the hatch. The Lord and Master was going to find Delight. The Lord and Master was going to put a swift and abrupt end to any chance of enjoyment this cruise might harbor.

For the crew of HMS *Bold Marauder,* it was the beginning of the end.

Down into the bowels of the frigate he went, descending hatches, walking slowly down companionways, his eyes purposeful, his stride never faltering.

The brig. It loomed up in front of him, its door shut tight. Without pausing, the Lord and Master drew his fine flint-lock pistol, lifted the latch, and, placing a palm carefully against the door, pushed it open.

He blinked once, twice.

The pistol fell from his hand and landed painfully on his foot.

On the walls—and ceiling—were enough mirrors to send his reflection back at him from every point of the compass. On the deck was a rich purple-and-red carpet strewn with pillows. In the middle of the room, draped in sheets of dark red satin, was a bed.

And reclining on the bed, her legs spread casually, was a woman.

She was reading aloud, in French, from a book she held before her nose, and did not see him. But he saw her. Wickedly long, shapely legs, bent at the knees and lazily spread to reveal enough of her to make his face flame with heat. Black garters that disappeared beneath the hem of a short shift. Daggerlike, red fingernails lazily tapping the top of the book, and a sultry, husky voice that was meant to be felt, not heard.

If Captain Christian Lord was stunned by the discovery of what the "brig" contained, he was downright shocked by the discovery of what its occupant was reading. For he understood French, and understood it well, and what the woman was reading was no dignified work of an educated scholar.

". . . 'after tying your man up, preferably to all four posts of your bed with a length of rope'—hmm, being a ship, *that* should be an easy commodity to come by!—'move your tongue over every square inch of his skin, thoroughly wetting him and then blowing coolly upon the wet areas until he is hot and hard and begging for release. Work every area of his body, moving your tongue slowly into the folds of his ears, sucking on his earlobes, and then letting your tongue drag down his neck, over his shoulders, lapping his nipples, even the inside of his navel. It is very important to pay particular attention to this area before proceeding to his—' " She stopped, lowered the book, and without faltering, purred, "Why, hello, Captain Lord. *Do* come in and join me. I've been waiting for you."

He stared, his jaw hanging, his body unable to move.

"What, is our bold and handsome commanding officer shy and inhibited?" She laughed, a rich, husky, throaty sound that sent shivers rippling through his blood. He kept staring, fascinated and appalled at the same time, as she set the book aside and came to her feet in a single fluid, feline movement.

She crossed the room in a slinky, sinuous float, her eyes never leaving his. In their blue depths was a raw, hungry invitation that had his heart pounding long before her long fingernails even touched his white waistcoat, his broad shoulders. She dragged them seductively down his chest, flicking them around each gold button and undoing them as she went. "Aah, such a handsome uniform . . . a sea warrior you are, no? Such a brave and noble man you must be . . . here, darling, let Delight show you how much she *appreciates* brave and noble men. . . ."

He recovered enough to shove her away. "How the bloody *hell* did you get aboard my ship?" he thundered.

"Lo, I just *love* a man when he's angry," she purred, sauntering around behind him and letting her hand rove down his spine. "Makes my love-juices flow, no? Here, darling, take my hand and let me lead you to my bed . . . I do need someone to practice my new techniques of bondage on."

"Get away from me!"

"Ta, Captain, you hurt poor Delight's feelings with such words! You do not have to act the part of a gentleman with me, you know? Let me touch you . . . let me taste you . . . let me do things to you with my tongue that you wouldn't dream could be done. Wouldn't you enjoy the feel of my lips around your forbidden parts, Captain? I know *just* how much pressure to exert in order to give you the most enjoyable climax. . . . Do you know, I have sent lesser men than you to the *petite morte*. Come, let me play with you . . . I'm very good, you know."

The Lord and Master was turning purple. *"Rico!"* he bellowed hoarsely as her hand slid over his breeches and flickered suggestively, boldly, across his groin.

"Dear Rico, aah, if he should come visit me, I know he would leave here quite, quite exhausted. . . . I have *just* the lady for him when we reach home."

"Home? Damn you, we're going to the colonies, not France!" He caught her hand and stared, horrified, at her probing fingers. "By God, this is *a king's ship!"*

She wrestled her hand free. "Yes, darling, I know . . . but the king's proud officers need their just rewards, too, no?" Long, skillful fingers toyed with his manhood through the breeches, and angrily he caught her wrist once more.

"Damn you, I asked you how you got aboard this ship!"

"Why, Captain, I merely asked and your men brought me aboard. They took pity on me, you see, because I needed passage home to Boston."

"Boston?" he roared, shoving her hand away from his groin.

"Yes, darling, Boston." Her husky laugh rippled over him. "Had you fooled, no? I'm not French, I'm American.

I only went to France so that I could learn, from those who know them best, the finer techniques of pleasuring a man, though if dear Papa knew, he'd surely get apoplexy, if not something far worse. *He* thinks I went to learn my social graces, so if you run into him when we get to Boston, please, do not tell him."

He gaped at her, unable to move, watching in frozen fascination as her probing fingers skimmed with shivery expertise over his slowly rising tumescence.

"You see, Captain, going to France was the only way I could think of to make myself competitive, as all the young *ladies* back home want the same man I do. I *had* to learn things they did not, so that I would have the advantage over them."

"A-advantage?"

"Yes, darling, *advantage*. . . . You see, I am in love with a dashing rogue back home, a handsome scoundrel who calls himself the Irish Pirate, and I will do anything, *anything*, to get him into my bed and firmly entrenched between my legs. . . . Captain Lord? Captain Lord, are you all right?"

His mouth had gone slack with shock.

"Come, my handsome captain, you simply must lie down, no? You have grown pale, and if you fall here, you may hurt yourself. Lo, you are so big and strong I do not think I could lift you . . . though, if you prefer, I would be most happy to practice a little something right here. Have you ever heard of *pattes d'araignée*, Captain? Most do it only with their fingers, but I have grown most skillful with my toes. . . ."

"My God," he said, coming to his senses. He grabbed her wrist as she cupped his manhood and massaged him through the fabric of his breeches. "How *old* are you?"

"Ta, Captain, don't you know you should never ask a lady her age? But if you *must* know, I am nineteen . . . a very *mature* nineteen, no?" Her wrist slithered out of his grip, her hand touching him once more, the pressure of her fingers growing stronger and sending bolts of feeling shooting up through his loins and into his blood. "Ah, you like that, no, Captain? Yes, it is pleasure spot that will bring even the most gallant of men to his knees."

He backed up, trying desperately to escape. "You cannot stay here, by God!"

"Then by all means, my sweet, let us go to your cabin instead. Surely, 'twill take the pressure off our poor little Irish girl, no? She is so innocent and naive, why, you should have seen the shock on her face when I gave her that gown to wear ... poor little thing, I thought she would faint dead away!"

By God, I have to get out of here, Christian thought, beginning to panic. Desperately, he caught her hand and yanked it up and away from him, wincing as her other hand slid out to run dangerously up the inside of his thigh. Swearing, he caught that one, too, and shoved her forcefully away. "This is a *king's* ship, madam, and I will not tolerate such lascivious behavior! I give you ten minutes to get out of that ridiculous attire and into a proper gown, and if I don't see you up on deck within the hour, so help me God, I'll make you rue the day you met me!"

She pressed her body against him, rubbed her bare foot up the back of his calf and, tilting her head back, allowed her lips to curve into a sensual, feline smile. "I should dearly *love* to come on deck, Captain ... I *do* need to find myself some rope. . . ."

"And furthermore," he thundered, reddening with rage as he tried to pry her away from him without releasing her hands, "you can collect your belongs and prepare to move them! I'll not have a floating *brothel* aboard my command, do you understand? This is a—"

"Yes, darling, I know. It is a *king's ship* and you simply *must* uphold the standards that are set for you."

"Do not try my patience, woman!" Freeing himself from her clutches, he put out his hand to keep her at arm's distance, but she merely smiled and ground her breasts suggestively against his palm. "And do not think to toy with me, do you understand? I've had a devilish bellyful of conniving women! For the rest of this hellish voyage, you will confine yourself to the cabin next to mine, and the Irish girl whose innocence you so obviously disdain!"

He snatched up his pistol, spun on his heel, and stormed off, more angry—and aroused—than he'd ever been in his life.

A crew who was determined to make his life hell, an Irish girl with a chronic case of homesickness, and now, an American brat aspiring to be a French whore.

Hell and damnation, would this bloody voyage end soon enough?

Crunch, crunch . . . sniffle, crunch, crunch. . . .
Deirdre O'Devir yawned and stretched as soft whines and strange noises slowly penetrated the blissful haze of her slumber.

She turned over and drew the warm woolen blankets up over her shoulders. Her hand slid across the sheet, where dim memories of a hard, warm body still lingered. There was no warmth there now, and slowly, lazily, her purple eyes drifted open.

Crunch, crunch . . . sniffle, crunch. . . .
The dog, she thought. No doubt Tildy was gobbling up one of the treats the Lord and Master was fond of sneaking her, a fact that would soon have her as fat as she was just before she'd whelped.

"Go away," Deirdre mumbled sleepily, her fingers tracing the wrinkled sheet where the Lord and Master's powerful shoulders had left a soft indentation. A slow, languorous smile of contentment curved her lips as she gazed drowsily at the spot. Then she jolted awake as the memory of last night drove through her.

"Dear God," she breathed, a flush of horror pinkening her cheeks.

Had she really stood above this very cot, the cruel blade braced in her shaking fists, intent on killing the Lord and Master? Had she really brought it savagely down, flinging it away at the last possible moment before she would've ended his life forever? And, sweet Mary, had she really crawled into bed with him, to comfort him and wrap her arms around his back as he lay suffering in the tormented throes of a dreadful nightmare?

Dear God, she had.

"I spent a night in th' Lord an' Master's bed," she murmured, staring bleakly at the imprint on the white pillow where his fair head had rested. *"With* him. . . ."

Her face grew feverish. Her breasts tingled unexpectedly, shocking her.

Crunch, crunch. Sniffle, sniffle. Crunch. . . .

Taking a deep, shuddering breath, Deirdre rolled onto her back, her shirt twining and bunching uncomfortably around her waist. She stared up at the deckhead, as though she could see through the white-painted timbers and to the poop deck itself.

The Lord and Master. Her fingers tightened over the sheets, dragging them to her chin. Horrible, shameful images drifted into her mind and she shut her eyes against them. She had grown up in the countryside; she knew what stallions did to mares, what roosters did to hens. What had the captain done to *her* during the night, after she'd fallen asleep? Or, worse, this morning when he woke and found her nestled in his arms?

The unspeakable, unthinkable thought slammed into her innocent head. *What if he*—she gulped and swallowed— *took* me?

Surely she would've awoken, wouldn't she?

Breathing hard and biting her trembling lip, she shut her eyes and drove her hands beneath her shirt, touching trembling fingers to her breasts and running her palms over her sharply defined ribs, the crests of her hips, down the leanness of her flanks. Everything seemed as it should be. She didn't hurt anywhere, and if he had done *that* to her, surely she'd be aching somewhere . . . wouldn't she?

Heat burned her face and caused her heart to slam a wild tattoo against her ribs.

"Oh, sweet Mary," she murmured, her hands coming up to clasp the crucifix as though in atonement for a sin she didn't even know if she'd committed.

But the dream images were there, vivid, colorful, and erotic. Dreams, or—she gulped, feeling hot blood fill her face— *memories?* A rush of moisture gathered between her legs as the wicked images burned through her mind . . . of the Lord and Master's hot hands skimming her breasts, cupping them

. . . his fingers grazing the swollen nipples, and squeezing the soft mounds of flesh as his mouth came down to engulf first one aching crest, then the other, his lips branding her pale flesh with scorching heat. . . .

She sucked in her lips and bit down hard.

. . . Of his hard hands, fanning down the curves of her waist, the tautness of her belly, the supple flesh of her inner thighs, the dark junction of moist curls between them—

She pressed her hands against her eyes, trying to block the shameful images. *Had the Lord and Master taken advantage of her while she'd slept?*

Thick, choking horror, then rage, swept through her.

Crunch, crunch, crunch. . . .

She flung herself onto her side and saw Tildy, her head and shoulders in Deirdre's canvas bag, rifling through the only things she had left of her beloved Ireland.

The bread.

Deirdre bolted upright. *"Tildy!"* she screamed, diving off the bed and lunging for the furry white rump.

With a startled yelp, the spaniel shot out of the bag and tore across the cabin, her mouth clamped around the stale, fist-sized chunk that was all that remained of Deirdre's preciously guarded bread. The bag lay on its side, a sad fan of hard crumbs on the floor around it.

"N-o-o-o-o!" Deirdre shrieked, tears clogging the back of her throat as she hurled herself across the cabin and dove beneath the desk, where Tildy had fled.

Crunch, crunch, sniffle, lap, lap—

"No!" she cried, sobbing and reaching blindly under the desk. " 'Tis mine, d'ye hear me, *mine!*" Kneeling, Deirdre got down on her elbows and crawled under the desk, the shirt still entwined around her shoulders. "Give it back, ye miserable, mangy, bleedin' maggot of a *dog!*"

But Tildy had no intention of giving up the prize and scooted farther beneath the desk, until she was up against the little, hidden door that led into Deirdre's cabin.

It was too much. Sobbing, Deirdre dropped her face to her forearms and wailed with grief. She clapped her hands to her ears, trying to shut out the sounds of crunching. "Me bread," she cried brokenly as she crushed her face into the damp hair fanning out over her arms. "Oh God, me *bre-e-e-e-a-a-a-a-d!*"

Suddenly the cabin door banged open, a hand grasped her by the hem of her shirt, and she was hauled forcibly out from beneath the desk.

It was the Lord and Master, his severe features dark with fury, his eyes frosted with anger. "What the devil is this ghastly wailing all about? You've got the whole ship in one hellish uproar!"

"Leave me alone, ye son of a bitch!" she railed, twisting around to strike him. Effortlessly, he caught her hand, jerked her to her feet, and yanked her arm around behind her back as she tried to hit him with her little fist.

"Let me *go-o-o-oooo!*"

"What the *deuce* is the matter with you?" he shouted, grabbing her shoulders so hard that his fingers bit into the soft flesh.

She lashed out at him with her foot and screamed, *"Go away!"*

Desperate, he shook her, causing her head to snap back and forth until the hysteria faded from her streaming eyes. The huge purple pools widened, the soft mouth quivered, and she collapsed against his mighty chest, sobbing bitterly.

"Me b-bread," she choked, gasping and hiccuping in anguish. "Yer b-bleedin' dog ate m-me b-*bre-e-e-e-a-a-a-d!*"

Christian stared down at the top of her black, glossy head, at the hopelessly tangled curls that fell around her quaking shoulders, at the fists clenched around his lapels. Sudden, cold terror lanced through him and coiled in his gut. Horrified, he gasped, "Pray, was there something *wrong* with it?"

She only cried harder, her tears soaking through his clothing and making his chest all warm and damp.

Terrified for his dog, he dug his fingers into her shoulders. *"Was there?"*

Deirdre raised her head, clawed the web of damp hair from her streaming cheeks, and screamed, "It was from *Ireland!*"

He stared at her, gaping—and then understanding swept in.

Ireland.

"Jesus deuced Christ," he swore, shoving her away in disgust and passing a shaking hand over his hot brow. "All that ghastly carrying-on over a piece of stale bread just because it came from *Ireland?* By God, if it makes you bloody feel better, you can have a whole confounded *bag* of ship's biscuit, and with my blessing!" His voice softened as he saw a fresh glimmer of tears spring to her eyes, and he stepped forward to take her hands. "Hang it, girl, you really know how to frighten someone, you know that? Here I thought something dreadful had happened to you—"

She tore free of his grasp, her eyes blazing with fury. "Somethin' *did!*" she cried, diving into the opening he'd so unwittingly provided. "And maybe you can tell me just what it was!"

"What?"

"Ye heard me, ye quiverin', stiff-lipped paragon o' arrogance an' conceit! Last night! Don't be actin' like ye don't know what I'm a-talkin' about! Ye did somethin' t' me, somethin' vile, unspeakable, *sinful*, and I want t' know just what it was!"

The gray eyes shone with confusion and surprise, then darkened like clouds gathering for a storm. "Pray, dear girl, why don't you tell *me?*"

"Ye insufferable English bastard!" she cried, bursting into tears. Her hand flashed out to strike him, and she shrieked with pain as it slammed up against the hardness of his wrist.

"Don't," he said dangerously, "try that again. My patience with you and your tantrums is wearing thin, Miss O'*Never.*"

"Damn ye t' hell an' beyond, English *dog!*" she spat, trying to rip free of his grip.

"I am damned, Irishwoman, and not by you!"

"How dare ye stand there an' deny ye touched me last night, when all I can remember is—is—"

Her face went crimson at the thought of putting those vivid images into words.

"Remember what, pray tell?" he drawled, a challenging look in his cold gray eyes.

"Shameful things. . . Such as yer h-hands touch—" She gulped, swallowed, and choked out, *"Touchin'* me when I was sleepin'!"

"Touching you?" He laughed, but there was no humor in the sound. "Perhaps you'd like to know where *your* hand was, dear girl, when I opened my eyes this morn! To say nothing of your body itself, which I distinctly remember having assigned to the adjacent cabin, not with me in *my* bloody cabin!"

Humiliation burned her cheeks, and she pried desperately at his fingers, still locked around her wrist. "Only an animal would take advantage o' a lass when she be asleep!"

"And only an animal would consider taking a man's life when *he* is, Miss O'Devir," he countered smoothly, one pale brow arched in challenge.

She came up short, her eyes, bright with fury and tears, narrowing. "Wha' 't'are ye talkin' about?"

His fingers bit into the soft indentation between her wristbones. He inclined his head toward the floor, where the letter opener glittered dangerously in the sunlight. "I suppose that just crawled off my desk and ended up there by itself? Or let me guess. The dog did it."

"So maybe I *did* think o' killin' ye!" she yelled, struggling against the raw power of his steely grip. "Or maybe I didn't! I don't have t' be remindin' ye tha' t'yer list o' enemies on this boat is rather long, yer *Lordship!"*

"So, by God, you admit it."

"I admit nothin', 'cept th' fact that I could've ended yer miserable life an' didn't, a fact I now regret wi' all me heart! And after th' vile things ye did t' me last night—"

"I did nothing to you!" he snarled, furious that she could stand there and accuse him of something he *knew* he hadn't done, something he knew he *couldn't* do!

"Ye *touched* me!"

"You flatter yourself to think I even *dreamed* of it!"

"Oh? And what *did* ye dream about that had ye so torn wi' grief, eh? Who is it that lays th' Lord an' Master so low every night, huh?" Sobbing, she glared up into his harsh face, now turning a slow crimson with anger, and yelled *"Emily?"*

The gray eyes darkened almost to black.

"Did ye envision yer precious *wife* beneath ye when ye touched me, kissed me—"

He jerked her savagely up against his chest, his blazing eyes just inches from hers, the intense heat of his body burning through her shirt. *"I did not touch you,"* he ground out, his voice quivering with rage, "and I will make something very clear to you, once and for all. I have no intention of doing so, not now, not *ever!"* Something like pain flashed across her face, but ruthlessly, cruelly, he lashed out, wanting to hurt her as she had him. His fingers biting into the soft flesh of her inner wrist, he drew her so close that her frightened eyes were a mere inch from his nose. "And furthermore," he gritted from between clenched teeth before shoving her violently away, "as for your precious *virtue,* you needn't worry about me compromising it, Miss O'*Never!* I have been unable to feel anything for any woman since my *wife* died, and you, an ill-bred, ill-tempered, vicious little urchin, haven't a prayer of stirring lusts I no longer *have!"*

His words stung to the bone.

"Unable t' feel anythin'? Lusts ye no longer have? What's th' matter, doesn't yer *wedding* tackle work?" she sneered, her eyes roving pointedly, disdainfully, to his groin.

He went crimson, then as white as the deckhead above, and with sudden, glorious triumph, Deirdre knew her barb had hit home.

"So that's it, isn't it?" she spat, her eyes glinting with victory, her heart inexplicably sinking even as she railed against the truth revealed so blatantly in his horrified, stricken face. "Th' haughty Lord an' Master—decorated hero of Quiberon, pride o' Britain's Navy, an' master of its swiftest warship—is *useless* as a man!"

"Silence," he whispered, his nostrils flaring with rage as he stumbled backward, away from her.

"Useless!" she repeated, her stormy eyes bright with triumph. "He cannot function! He be less than a man! He doesn't *work!"*

She threw back her head and laughed, overcome with hysteria and a strange, inexplicable grief that blinded her to the unforgivable and awful thing she had just done—stripped him of every shred of his masculine pride.

With a strangled sound he stormed from the cabin, her wild laughter following him, mocking him, and chasing him into the depths of hell itself.

Chapter 15

"I tell ye, this is turnin' out to be a voyage from *hell*," Skunk spat, his foot lashing out to kick over a neatly coiled line and send it snaking out across the deck. "First he has us cleanin' the decks, then he has us practicing sail drills, then he takes our Delight from us—Christ, I'd as soon stayed in blighty England!"

It had been more than three long, miserable weeks since HMS *Bold Marauder* had shown her heels to Spithead—and things weren't getting any better. Although the marine who guarded the cabin where the two girls now stayed was easily *coerced*—by a very manipulative Delight—into admitting "visitors" while Deirdre was absent, the rebellious spirit that the ship had left England with was sadly lacking. Sail drills had everyone's back and arms aching. Gun practice had them all exhausted and had all their ears ringing. Strict attention to quarterdeck rules and Navy protocol had everyone wishing he'd taken duty on another ship. Only Delight maintained her bright and bubbly spirit, and she alone kept the men smiling when they found nothing to smile about.

The Irish girl, however, was another matter. She spent her time standing at the rail with her canvas bag clenched in one hand, her sad face turned toward an Ireland that was now nearly three thousand miles away.

And the aloof and unapproachable Lord and Master spent *his* time watching her.

Now the men, just finishing their morning task of scrubbing the decks, watched him with mutinous eyes. As usual, they were full of complaints—but that was the extent of it, for none dared to cross him. His unorthodox punishments, beginning that awful day he had forced Teach to clean all the objects in the weapons chest, were doled out swiftly and mercilessly. Hibbert, having been caught once too often in his filthy uniform, had been forced to soap and scrub the uniform of every officer on the frigate. Skunk, caught swearing in front of the ladies, had been forced to stand before his shipmates for an hour and read from the Lord and Master's prized leather Bible. Worse, all punishments were carried out to the slow beat of the marine drummer's drum, with the entire crew and officers assembled to watch. Such humiliation was enough to make even the most recalcitrant of *Bold Marauder*'s men think twice about raising the Lord and Master's ire.

But it did nothing to make them like him.

"Aye, Skunk, it just ain't fair," Teach grumbled, scratching at the chin he kept clean and well shaven—not to please his commanding officer but Delight, who happened to prefer smooth faces. He turned toward his shipmates, his huge, burly arms outstretched in a silent plea. "Why the hell did *we* have to end up with the stuffy prig, anyhow? Ain't he a ship-o'-the-line captain? What's he doing on a mere frigate?"

"Dunno, Teach, but I don't believe all that rot about him being a decorated hero for one bloody minute," Wenham muttered, staring up at the set of the topsails and sullenly tugging at his jutting ears with the stubs of his missing fingers. He risked a glance at the bosun, for Rico Hendricks was usually within earshot. "Probably made one too many embarrassing mistakes somewhere and the Admiralty thought they could squirrel him away on *Bold Marauder*—at *our* expense!"

"Decorated hero, my arse! Besides, whoever heard of a naval captain who wears a *wig* aboard ship!"

"Maybe he's got a big bald spot he's tryin' to cover up!"

"Maybe 'e's afraid wot little brains 'e has'll leak out if 'e don't keep a top on 'em!"

"Maybe he thinks he looks right handsome in it and is trying to impress the girl!"

"Ha, he's doin' a fine job, ain't 'e!"

They howled with glee, remembering the now-fading, deep purple bruise that the wig couldn't quite conceal. Every man jack on the ship had heard about the latest falling-out between the Irish girl and the Lord and Master, but only Delight knew what it was about, and *she*, as Deirdre's cabin-mate and friend, wasn't telling.

"Hero or not, I'll bet my last shilling he ain't never seen action in his life! Prob'ly *bought* all those fancy medals!"

"Here, now, Skunk, ye be mindin' your tongue," Ian chided, frowning. "Ye canna put doon the mon when ye've never seen battle yerself!"

"None of us have, Ian, but *we* ain't the ones wearin' the rank of a posted captain or carryin' a fancy dress sword, an' we ain't the ones with medals of valor affixed to our best coat! I *still* bet he bought 'em off someone, or stole 'em off some corpse. Why, I'll bet when this here ship gets into a battle—not that *I* think she ever will—our fearless leader'll go running below with his tail between his legs!"

"Aye, and leave *us* to do the fighting!" Rhodes spat, detaching himself from his place by the pinrail. "Why, it wouldn't surprise me a bit to find his Lordship hiding down in his cabin, fussing with his wig and taking tea!"

Hibbert, who'd been watching with a gleam in his eye, swaggered out from Wenham's shadow, his lips curved with mischief. "Aye, taking *tea,*" he sniffed, striking an exaggeratedly dandified pose, flaring his nostrils, and making a big show over smoothing his rumpled uniform.

The crew roared with laughter.

"Aah, ye show 'em, laddie!"

To windward, far off over the leaping wave crests that rolled endlessly toward *Bold Marauder*'s starboard bows, tiny splotches of white hung suspended from the hazy clouds that hugged the horizon.

But no one saw them, nor heard the distant echo of gunfire—not even the lookout, who, at the moment, was lying flat on his back on the maintop, with a boyishly disguised Delight straddling his belly and putting his mind on other things.

"Keep it up, Hibbert!" Skunk roared, slapping his thigh. "Christ, we could do with some blighty amusement on these here sour decks!"

Laughing, Hibbert primped his ill-kempt queue and pranced across the deck in a caricature of his commanding officer. Pinching his nostrils shut to affect an exaggerated nasal drawl that sounded nothing like the clipped, educated tone of the Lord and Master, he sniffed, "Mr. MacDuff, I daresay we're in for a *devilish* blow . . . would you please put a reef in the forecourse?"

A burst of raucous laughter went up from his mates, and several threw wary glances toward the forecastle, where Ian had gone off to use the head. Their first lieutenant was no fun anymore, refusing to join his shipmates in making jokes about the Lord and Master.

Grinning, Hibbert pushed his hat back, primped and preened some more, and then, clasping his hands behind his back, strode slowly across the deck. He sank his chin into his neckcloth and drew his brows close in a threatening scowl. "Oh, and, Mr. Skunk, please see to it that the deck is scrubbed and clean before I come topside!"

Skunk threw back his grimy head, roaring with laughter. "Ye've got it, boy! Ye look just like the blasted blue blood!"

"Aye, just like 'im!"

"More, Hibbert, more!"

On the horizon, the triangles of white began to take on distinct shapes as they detached themselves from the cloud mass.

But no one saw them.

The midshipman grabbed a boarding pike from the rack at the mainmast, and insolently leaned his weight on it in imitation of the captain with his sword. His eyes half lidded, Hibbert stiffened his back and drawled, "Oh, and, Mr.

Teach, please remove that *growth* from your face. This is a fighting ship, not a barbershop!"

"Not *fighting* ship," Skunk cried, "*king's* ship! If yer gonna do it, do it right!"

Hibbert struck a pose. "This is a *king's* ship!"

"Ha, ha, ha!"

Someone coughed.

But Hibbert, lost in the game, never saw the object of his ridicule standing in the companionway, silently watching him and holding three tiny puppies in the broad shelter of his arm. Primping his hair, the youth swaggered to the wheel and stared haughtily down at the compass. "I *daresay*, Mr. Wenham, the forecourse is not in proper trim for this wind. Pray, do see to the matter!"

"Er, Hibbert—"

"Mr. Rhodes, please do not interrupt your commanding officer," Hibbert chided, imperiously waving his hand. He turned to face the second lieutenant. "You *know* how it grieves—"

He broke off abruptly and dropped the pike on his toe. The Lord and Master was standing a mere ten feet away, coldly watching him.

"Are you quite finished, *Mr.* Hibbert?" The frosty gray eyes, hard with anger, raked the boy's face. "Pray, remind me to purchase tickets next time you decide to stage such an amusing performance."

Hibbert paled, gulped, and stared down at his shoes, a trickle of sweat running down his temple. "Aye."

"Aye, *sir.* And get your damned hide below and change out of that miserable excuse for a uniform and into something *presentable!*"

Hibbert fled, nearly knocking the returning Ian MacDuff over in his haste to escape.

"Hey, watch it, ye imperious wee upstart!" Ian roared, raising his fist. But the midshipman was gone.

Christian strode to the rail that separated the quarterdeck from the waist of the ship. His cold eyes swept the sea of angry faces beneath him, all upturned and waiting. He let the silence build, knowing that their attention was on him and him alone. Then he cleared his throat and, cradling the three puppies against the warmth of his chest, stared out at them.

"A pity," he said, his tone emotionless and cold, "that here we are, only a few days out from Boston, and you, as a company, are no closer to doing your Navy proud than you were when we left England. I had truly hoped to make a favorable impression upon the admiral there, but I'm afraid that I shall be embarrassed, not proud, to bring this vessel into that harbor and present her to my superior."

Skunk and Rhodes exchanged nervous glances.

"You think that having me as your commanding officer is the worst curse this ship could've been bestowed with, don't you?"

Skunk opened his mouth to reply in the positive, but a quick jab in the ribs from Rhodes silenced him.

The action was not wasted on the captain. He gave a hard but patient smile. "Why must you comply to discipline and tradition? you ask. What reason is there for saluting the quarterdeck, for touching your hat to your commanding or superior officers, for manning the rail when your captain leaves?" Christian's hand tightened fiercely around the rail. "Do you think me so devilishly pompous that I ask your compliance for *my* sake? Do you think me so arrogant and conceited that I demand it for *myself?*"

They stared at him, uncomprehending. No one spoke. Above, wind sighed softly in the shrouds, the gently flapping canvas.

"Death at sea can come swiftly, in any form, at any time. A sudden squall. A sea battle. A mistake in interpreting a chart, a position, an enemy's strength. At such times, when chaos may reign, there is one thing, and one thing alone, that will keep a ship together, and that, my good fellows, is called *discipline.*"

He stared at them, hard, letting them absorb his words. "Our Navy is the most powerful sea power in the world, with possibly only the French to challenge it. That strength does not arise out of the independence of each vessel, but out of unity among them all, and the men who serve them. That strength is rooted in discipline and strict allegiance to tradition—they are the cement that holds our Navy together, not something to be sneered at, scoffed at, ridiculed. Now, if everyone decided not to respect their seniors, and they, in turn, did not respect the flag that flies above their heads, where, then, would this Navy be? Indeed, where would *England* be?"

Some of them looked at their feet, visibly ashamed.

"I do not chastise you for your impertinence and disrespect to *me;* I chastise you for your impertinence and disrespect for that flag—the flag of *Britain.* Your blatant disrespect of me is not an insult to *me*—it is an insult to your *country."*

More men stared down at their toes, their faces reddening with humiliation. Even Deirdre turned away from the rail to listen.

Christian turned to gaze at the long pendant that streamed proudly from *Bold Marauder's* jack. "When you salute me, or your flag, or the quarterdeck, you are partaking of a ceremony that is far older than you are, and one which shall persevere long after you are gone. Since you are representatives of your country and king, your conduct as seamen is representative of England. By seeking to anger *me,* you disgrace not only your country, but your ship and the men who you may someday fight beside.

"Tradition, ceremony, discipline, and obedience are the matrix of a fighting ship. A fighting ship is the essence of a fleet; a fleet, the pride of a nation. Remove one chink in the armor, one link in the chain, and it is weakened. Do *you,* my lads, want to be remembered by those you love and protect back home as being that weak link?"

No one moved.

"Do you?"

They stared at him, while high above, the pendant undulated with majestic grace in the wind.

"I have nothing more to say." Turning his back on them, the Lord and Master touched his hat to those proud colors above his head, and, passing his gaping officers, his strangely silent crew, went below.

But even he did not see the distant puffs of white far off the starboard bows—puffs that might've been clouds, but were no clouds at all.

* * *

"Lo, Deirdre, I wish you'd come to me earlier," Delight said, plopping down on her satiny bed and touching a set of red-painted nails to her temple as the Irish girl came miserably into the cabin. "I told you before, I have certain *ways* of bringing a man to his knees. Surely, whatever damage you've done is repairable, no?"

"I accused him o' havin' faulty weddin' tackle," she blurted out.

Delight's hand froze. "You *what?*"

"And then I laughed at him."

"Oh, dear."

Deirdre felt a knot of ice twisting in her spine. "But ye say tha' t'all angers can be eased, right?"

"All, I'm afraid, except *that* one. Lo, Deirdre, you've sorely wounded the man's pride! 'Twill take a lot to make him forgive you. . . ."

Deirdre put her face in her hands and sank down on her bunk. "Oh, Delight, I didn't mean it, I was just so *mad* . . . I woke up that mornin'—I mean, I got in bed wi' him that night because he was havin' that nightmare that keeps him—an' the rest o' us—awake every night, but I wanted t' comfort him, so I got in bed wi' him. Th' next mornin' I woke up and he was gone, and I had all these thoughts that maybe he touched me, that maybe he might've stolen me virginity—"

"You mean, you didn't know?"

"How *would* I? I was sleepin'!"

Delight threw back her head, sending her rich golden tresses spilling over her shoulders. "Lo, child, if he'd taken your maidenhood, I can *assure* you that you would know it!"

"*Maybe* he did," she replied stubbornly.

"As I said, you'd know it. Besides, you would've found your maiden's blood on the sheets, no?"

Deirdre shrugged, her face beginning to redden.

"Ah, you are more innocent than even I would've thought. What you must do, Deirdre, is win your man back to you. He carries more scars than a battle warrior, no? Emotional ones. Someone has hurt him deeply, probably this Emily. You have a formidable opponent in this dead wife, but *she* is dead, and you are not, and our Lord and Master cannot make love to a dead woman, no?"

Deirdre raised her head. "But, Delight, it be wrong that I have such feelin's. He took me brother from me...."

"No, Deirdre." The other girl gave her a pointed stare and placed her hands on Deirdre's shoulders. "The *Royal Navy* took your brother from you, not Captain Lord."

"Besides," Deirdre persisted stubbornly, "he's English."

"I know, a stuffy, pompous race, but we cannot dictate the direction of our hearts."

"Ye make it sound like I'm in love wi' him!"

"No, Deirdre, *you* make it sound like you're in love with him." She smiled patiently. "My advice to you is to get to work *immediately* on proving to him just how you feel."

"How? He hates me, he does!"

"No, he does not hate you. He merely thinks he loves another. And you have sorely wounded his male pride. But *you* are a woman, Deirdre. A living, breathing woman. He will not stand a chance against you once you put your mind to it to go after him, no?" She gave a wicked smile, curved an arm around Deirdre's shoulders, and, guiding her to the door, scooped a gown out of her armoire. "Now, here, put this on, and make sure you tug the bodice down so that your nipples are most blatantly displayed."

"Delight!"

"Don't give me that look. 'Tis time you started thawing our handsome Ice Captain! Lord knows *I* cannot! Now go," she said, grinning. "We'll be in Boston within a few days, and the ladies there will all be falling over each other to get their claws into your man. Make an effort to have the advantage over them!"

Deirdre clutched the gown to her chest, terrified. But she got no farther than the Lord and Master's cabin, for at that moment harsh cries drove down from above.

"Two sail closing rapidly in off the starboard bows!"

She froze.

"And another, lying off the starboard beam! Jesus, it's an English ship—and it's being *attacked!*"

Chapter 16

On deck, the frightened crew of HMS *Bold Marauder* wasted no time in summoning their commanding officer. Now they stood anxiously beside him, staring into his harsh face for comfort as he took a glass from Midshipman Hartness and trained it on the three ships.

"What do ye make of it, sir?" Ian murmured, echoing their thoughts and cringing at each deafening explosion of gunfire.

The Lord and Master studied the three vessels for a moment longer, then closed the glass with a snap. Handing it back to the midshipman, he turned and walked toward the wheel. "One is a French corvette, Ian."

The big Scotsman's eyes widened with pleasure at the captain's familiar use of his first name, but Christian continued as if it were of no consequence. "The second is a sloop, flying no colors at all. And the one under attack"—he looked at them gravely—"is an English cutter."

He paused, letting his words sink in.

"But it's *peacetime*, sir!"

"I know that, Ian."

Little Edgar Hartness was jumping up and down in excitement. "Her captain is signaling for assistance, sir!" he shouted as flags broke through the smoke that hung above the three ships.

Teach shoved to the forefront of the pack. "The one flyin' no flags—I've seen that ship before! On my last voyage to the American colonies!"

They clustered at the rail, straining their eyes for a better look.

"Look, the sloop's breakin' off the engagement!"

Christian set his jaw. Through the hazy field of the telescope he had seen the sloop's captain. The man was fox-featured and laughing; he had high cheekbones, ruddy cheeks, roguish eyes, and a mane of glossy black curls caught in a flamboyant length of purple velvet. Now Christian saw the man lift his hand in a mocking salute as the sloop fell off into the wind.

"Bloody freebooter," he snapped. "I have no stomach for pirates, and even less for one who would dare attack a lone English ship!"

"What'll we do, sir?" Ian said, glancing anxiously at his captain for guidance.

"Send the women below to the surgeon, where they will be safe." He turned and looked steadily at his second-in-command. "Then clear for action and beat to quarters."

"B-beat to quarters . . . sir?"

The men exchanged frightened glances, their jaws slack and their faces white with horror. Then they stared at their captain, and saw the cool detachment in the steady gray eyes.

"Yes, that is what I said, Mr. MacDuff. *Beat to quarters.*" He smiled, and in his eyes was the look of a warrior. "Pray, we are going to fight."

Belowdecks, the two girls heard it all: the urgent tattoo of the marine drummer boy, the shrill of bosuns' pipes; the hammer of pounding feet up the companionways, across the decks; the ominous crashes and bangs, and rumblings from above as the frigate's massive cannon were rolled into place.

Deirdre, watching Delight roll bandages, didn't need Elwin to tell her just what was happening up there. "They're clearing for action now," he said bleakly, as though taking comfort from the sound of his own voice. His bony hands shook as he laid out an array of saws, knives, tourniquets, and bandages on the midshipmen's mess table.

Deirdre's stomach writhed with apprehension, and she

stared hypnotically at the gleaming instruments, at the bottles of rum that, when the wounded were brought down, would be the only respite from the pain as Elwin dug and cut and—

Her blood chilled in her veins, and she hugged little Tildy close to her chest, trying to still the mad, frightened pounding of her heart. Then she put the dog down with her crying puppies, safely nestled in their box that one of the crewmen had brought down.

"Is it goin' t' be that bad, Elwin?" she whispered.

Even Delight paused, her eyes wide and frightened.

"Might be." His hands fluttered nervously as he tied on his surgeon's apron, then positioned a wooden bucket beneath the table. Moments before, that same table had been where the midshipmen took their meals; now it might be seeing horrors she could only guess at. Above, the swinging deckhead lanterns threw spidery shadows over the operating table, the deck flooring, the whiteness of her shirt, Elwin's waxen face.

"Wha' 'twill happen, d'ye think?" Deirdre whispered, reaching up to finger her crucifix.

"Hopefully, nothing." The surgeon's voice was too quick, too fidgety. "This here ship's never been in a fight." His lips thinned and he swung away, busying himself at tearing bandages from a fresh piece of linen. "But then, she's never had a captain like this one, either."

Thunder, muffled and foreboding, boomed somewhere outside, as *Bold Marauder* drew closer to the fight.

She's never had a captain like this one.

"Elwin . . . I be scared."

His hands fluttering, the small man glanced around to see if anyone was within earshot. "So am I, girl." He swallowed, his gaze darting about the sick bay as though seeing the darkened beams for the last time. "And so, I suspect, are the others."

More crashes boomed out from the other ships, echoing right into *Bold Marauder*'s hull. Deirdre shut her eyes and wrapped shaking, sweating hands around Granuaile's crucifix. But there was no strength to be had there, no comfort.

Think of Ireland . . . stone fences and misty skies . . .

whitewashed cottages and rocky pastures . . . sheep bleating on twilit hills. . . .

With a start of horror, she realized she'd left her precious ditty bag in the Lord and Master's cabin. Cold sweat gathered on her brow and she squeezed the crucifix desperately, bending her head to hide her frightened tears.

More cannon crashed from somewhere beyond the hull, deep and reverberating and awful. Tildy cried with fear and Deirdre swiftly picked her up, cuddling her. Beneath Deirdre's chin, the spaniel whined and whimpered, shaking so violently that the vibration made Deirdre's teeth chatter.

Please, God, be with us. Please, Mother Mary, keep us safe. Be with this ship, and . . . and be with our Lord an' Master. Please, oh heavenly Father, guide him, let th' crew follow him, help him t' get us out o' this an' keep us safe. She squeezed her eyes tightly shut, feeling the misty sting of tears behind her lids. *And please, dear Jesus, I beg o' ye, please, please,* please *keep him safe.*

Here she was, praying for the safety of a man she had once vowed to kill.

Dear God.

From above came another resounding crash, and a chorus of shouts and yells. *Bold Marauder* was getting close now. Very close.

"I hope Captain Christian Lord knows what he's doing," Delight said shakily.

"They say he's been captain of many ships," Elwin murmured, echoing her own fears. "That he saved the day at Quiberon. That his last command was a mighty first-rate man-of-war carrying one hundred guns. . . . Ever see a hundred-gunner, girls? It's so big, it'd make this here ship look like a sailboat."

They heard a low, menacing rumble as a gun was hauled across the deck, a shout, and then *Bold Marauder*'s own bellowing voice as one of the nine-pounders in her bow fired a shot. The deep reverberation sent sound waves echoing through the room. Two bottles of rum clinked together, and Elwin's sallow skin went chalky.

"No." Deirdre's voice was a bare whisper. "I've never

seen a hundred-gunner, Elwin. After this, I don't think I ever want t'."

Another gun boomed out from directly above, sounding like a thunderclap striking too close. Deirdre sobbed in fear and tightened her arms around Tildy, while Delight gathered the three puppies into her arms.

Oh, dear God, please be with our Lord and Master. . . .

What went through a man's mind at a time like this? What must he be thinking? Feeling?

She thought of the hateful words she had once thrown at him.

Uglier than a dead carp. Her lower lip began to tremble, and choking back a sob, she curled it between her teeth and bit down hard. Then she raised her face, the tears sparkling in her purple eyes and making them huge and luminous in her white face.

"He's not ugly, Elwin."

"Eh?"

"He's not ugly . . . I don't hate him . . . I said awful things t' him, and now—and now it may be too late t' take 'em back—"

Her voice caught on a sob, and hot, crystalline tears splashed down her cheeks and dropped upon the little dog's head. Hastily dashing them away with the palm of her hand, she bent her head to stanch the wet flow against Tildy's soft ear, and felt the comforting touch of Delight's hand upon her shoulder.

Elwin tightened his lips and looked away.

Another gun banged out, making the instruments shake and rattle atop the table. "Soon now," Elwin said nervously, beginning to pace and wiping his sweating palms on his apron.

More pipes shrilled, bare feet stamped madly across the deck overhead, and then the floor beneath them began to tilt upright, leveling out for a brief moment before the ship angled over onto the other tack. A pair of forceps slid down the table and clattered loudly to the floor. They heard wild shouts from above, then felt the frigate pulling herself up out of the water, the hungry, surging motion as she gathered speed. . . .

Elwin shut his eyes, his lips moving in a tremulous whisper. "The Lord and Master's sending her in now. . . ."

From above came a deep, heavy rumbling, drowning out all sound . . . then a thick, expectant silence as the entire ship tensed for that first, resounding crash from *Bold Marauder's* broadside.

Deirdre clapped her hand over her ears, hearing her heartbeat thundering against her palms. *"Elwi-i-i-n!"* she screamed.

Then the world erupted in walls of thunder as *Bold Marauder* engaged the enemy.

"Topmen aloft, and men to the braces! Stand by, Mr. Wenham, and prepare to come about!"

Pipes shrilled, and men swarmed up the shrouds and out along the frigate's yards. Moments later, *Bold Marauder* was nose-up to the wind, fighting her crew and trying desperately to fall off.

"Now, Mr. Wenham!"

The deck seemed to drop away beneath them as the man-of-war flung herself onto the other tack and charged down toward the battle.

"Steady as you go, Mr. Wenham!"

"Course south by southwest, full and by!"

The Lord and Master gripped the quarterdeck rail, watching the ships drawing closer and closer through the swirling smoke. His mouth was tense and set, his gray eyes emotionless. Yet he was very conscious of Ian standing beside him and gripping a huge Scottish claymore, his red beard blowing in the wind, his eyes fierce. He was very aware of Rhodes, in place beside Skunk and the larboard battery of guns; he was very aware of the lively response of the frigate, and he was very aware of the terrified crew, their fixated, glassy stares directed ahead toward the fight. A huge ball of thick, roiling smoke hung above the three ships, broken topmasts and streaming pendants poking through it. Christian tugged at the lace of his coat sleeve. There had been one or two snickers of disdain about his "primped" appearance, but only he knew the real reason he'd donned a fresh shirt and his finest coat, and clipped his best sword to his belt frog—he was a king's officer, and if he fell today, he would do so with honor.

If he fell.

How many times had he sent ships into battle with that same thought running through his mind? How many times had he counted on the strength and loyalty of men who would blindly follow him into hell itself?

But these men . . .

By God, he would not dip England's colors to a damned Frog no matter what happened!

Fiercely gripping the quarterdeck rail, he peered across the double batteries of guns and their anxious, crouching crews. Faces ran with nervous sweat. Eyes stared up at him, terrified. Only Rhodes seemed calm. Christian met his gaze and gave the briefest of nods, then stared over the lieutenant's head. Just beyond, *Bold Marauder*'s plunging jibboom seemed to swallow up the sea as she charged down toward the smoke-cloaked ships.

"Look!" Ian yelled, pointing into the smoke at the ship that flew no colors. She was bearing up into the wind, raising more sail and gathering the spray at her bows. "The sloop's fleeing!"

Christian raised his telescope, steadying it in the crook of his elbow. The little ship swam into view, and his eyes narrowed as he trained the glass toward its helm. He saw the captain raise his hand in mocking farewell and a memory throbbed in Christian's head, for somewhere, at some time, he knew he'd seen the man before. . . .

"Shall we chase him, sir?" Ian cried, pointing at the fleeing ship.

"No." Christian snapped the glass closed. "The cutter has requested our assistance, and, by God, I shall not desert her to a damned Frenchman!"

Gunfire echoed across the water, reverberating up through *Bold Marauder*'s hull. Christian's gaze never wavered. He saw the ornate stern of the French corvette showing dimly through the smoke, her masts poking up through the thick cloud that engulfed her. More guns boomed out in flashes of orange against black, and there was a terrible crash as the small English cutter's single mast toppled, dragging rigging and screaming men with it into the sea. A great sigh of despair went up from *Bold Marauder*'s horrified crew at the sight of seamen, Englishmen like themselves, floundering in the steep waves.

"By the saints," Ian gasped, with a desperate glance at his captain.

"Mr. Hibbert!" Christian caught the midshipman's scrawny arm, his eyes on the men floundering pitifully in the swells. "Bring up more hammocks from below, make sure they're tightly rolled, and toss them to those people out there."

The middie, terrified, just stared at him.

"Damn you, do not tarry!" Christian shouted, shoving the boy into action. "Bring her up a point, Mr. Wenham, right up around that Frog's stern! I daresay, with a bit of luck we can strip the guts from her with a broadside!"

Cold spray hissed and dashed over the frigate's plunging beakhead, soaking the decks, the men, the guns.

"Sta'b'd battery, run out!" Christian yelled.

All along the deck, men strained and heaved, coaxing the big guns into position.

Not fast enough, Christian thought desperately.

"All run out, sir!"

Christian stepped forward, his face in shadow beneath his gold-laced hat. He saw every frightened gun captain staring aft, awaiting his signal, and beyond them, *Bold Marauder*'s jibboom, just thrusting into the frayed edges of the thick cloud of smoke.

Drawing his sword, he raised his arm, the girl's face swimming into his memory once more, her words coming back to haunt him.

Uglier than a dead carp.

Savagely, he brought the sword down. *"Fire!"*

The world exploded.

It was a scene from hell itself. Midshipmen, sobbing with terror, racing through the smoke to relay orders from quarterdeck to gun deck; flashes of musket fire from the French ship's poop as her marksmen tried desperately to pick off *Bold Marauder*'s blue-and-white-clad officers; iron shrieking overhead, spars and pieces of burning rigging bouncing off the nettings spread above the deck, guns belching death and destruction, and men falling, only to be dragged, screaming, away to the surgeon's knife below.

And the Lord and Master, steady, aloof, and unruffled, veteran of countless sea fights, and the one force holding *Bold Marauder*'s frightened crew together.

"Sta'b'd broadside, *fire!*"

The big guns roared out, one by one, in a resounding crash that left his ears ringing and thunder vibrating right up through the deck and into the soles of his shoes. It wasn't a timed broadside; it wasn't even close. *By God, we have to do better, or we're all done for!*

An answering boom roared through the smoke from the French corvette, and a cannonball screamed across the deck, smashed against one of the starboard guns, and exploded. Several gunners, grimy with smoke and sweat, fell screaming, blood streaming from their broken bodies and their legs kicking in death.

Through the smoke and haze, Christian saw the French ship's yards turning as she abandoned the sinking English cutter and came about, the water glistening dully from her side, her ports open and her guns poking their black snouts toward them—

"Reload and run out!" he cried, gripping his sword. "*Give them a jolly good drubbing, lads!*"

Beside him, one of the helmsmen screamed and, clutching his side, crumpled to his knees.

"*Fire!*"

Guns belched smoke and flame, recoiling against their tackle. The raw scent of sulfur singed the air. Several feet away, Teach, cursing, stumbled backward in horror as his nine-pounder slammed inboard, nearly crushing him.

Christian shut his eyes, clenching his sword hilt.

"For God's sake, sir!" Hibbert raced back to the quarter-deck. "They're killing us!"

"We'll nae win this fight, sir; they be too strong for us!" Ian yelled desperately.

Christian turned on them, his eyes fierce. "And I'll be damned if I lower my colors to a bloody *Frenchman!* Mr.

Wenham!" Cupping his hands over his mouth, he yelled, "Hard-a-lee, and prepare to ram . . . *now!*"

"R-ram, sir?"

"Yes, Wenham, *ram!*"

A pigtailed, bare-backed seaman, slamming a fresh charge down one of the starboard guns, suddenly threw his hand over his eyes and fell twitching to the deck, a musket ball buried in his brain. Guns roared from the corvette, and a pinrail evaporated in an exploding shower of wood. Then the helm went over, and with slow, stately purpose, *Bold Marauder* drove her jibboom into the French ship's rigging. The jarring smash of hull against hull hurled men to their knees, the Lord and Master against the wheel, guns onto their sides.

"Stand fast, lads, and prepare to repel boarders!" Christian yelled, his voice raw with smoke as he fought to pull himself up from the deck.

Slowly, the two vessels pivoted, locked nose to shoulder, swinging with the wind as their guns pounded each other with vicious, unending fury. The English cutter drifted away, her battered crew trying to bring her under control. Then Ian grabbed his captain's arm and pointed at the stream of yelling, cutlass-wielding seamen leaping across the distance to *Bold Marauder*'s deck.

"They're boarding us, sir!"

Shot screamed past, and Wenham gasped and slumped over the wheel. From above came a high, terrified scream and a marine fell, spiraling and kicking, to the deck. Somewhere forward, one of *Bold Marauder*'s guns banged out, and dimly Christian heard the sharp pop of muskets as his marines fired across at the enemy.

"*They're onto us, sir!*"

Thank God, Christian thought insanely. He took one look at his men—dirty, ragged, fearsome, and defiant—and in that fleeting instant, knew that his decision to ram the other ship had been the right one, the *only* one. They were inexperienced at fighting the guns of their frigate, yes; they were quarrelsome and rebellious, yes; *but they were English sailors*, and as such, there were none on God's earth who would fight harder, nor more fiercely, when it came to defending their home.

And *Bold Marauder* was their home.

He saw the bloodlust in their eyes, the savagery on their faces, and, raising his sword, dove down the quarterdeck ladder in a single bound. "To me, lads!" he heard himself shout, his blade coming up to clash violently with the steel of the first wild-eyed intruders as they swarmed over the gangway like a horde of angry wasps.

For one awful moment, the crew did not move, stunned by the courage of the man they'd thought to be nothing but an aristocratic fop.

Then they reacted.

"Jesus," Skunk cried, his eyes bulging as the Lord and Master swung his sword against a pirate's with a ringing clash, and then, pivoting with a duelist's grace, disarmed the man and hacked him across the neck. Beside him, Ian swung his claymore with deadly force, his back to his captain's as the two of them single-handedly took on the yelling, screaming boarders.

And now more and more of the French devils were leaping over *Bold Marauder*'s rails, *their* rails, their swords slashing.

"*Jesus!*" Skunk cried again as *Bold Marauder*'s crew began grabbing pikes, pistols, and axes, and, yelling in fury, raced to join their two senior officers. Not to be left behind, Skunk seized a cutlass and raised it high. "His bloody Lordship really *ain't* no peacock, no simpering blue blood, and, by Jesus, no blithering coward!"

He was at the front of his men, leading them!

Enraged, Skunk swung his arm toward the boarders and bellowed, "At 'em, lads!"

With a wild, rushing roar, the frigate's men abandoned their guns and, yelling like madmen, dove into the fray, fighting as they fought best—hand to hand, in bloody, ruthless combat.

"Take that, ye lily-livered French bastards!"

"Sons of bitches!"

Flashes of red streaked past as the marines joined the fight, their bayonets gleaming, thrusting, stabbing. A gun, then another, banged out from forward as some levelheaded soul fired into the corvette's hull. Relief swept over Christian, but there was no time to thank God that his plan had worked, that his men were finally behind him. He knocked aside the cutlass of an attacking seaman, brought his own sword chopping into the man's ribs, and, jerking it free, stumbled over a sprawled body.

He fell, his shoulder smashing painfully against a ringbolt. Then a shadow filled his vision, and, helpless, he stared up into the maniacal eyes of a pirate leaping out of the smoke.

Christian saw his life flash before his eyes as the pirate, his face wild and triumphant as he stood over the fallen English captain, brought his sword savagely up with a wild yell—

Then Teach was there, bellowing with fury, his massive arm knocking aside the pirate's cutlass, his sword impaling the man through the heart.

Christian's eyes met his for the briefest of seconds. "Well done, Mr. Teach—"

But Teach was gone, pounding across the deck as he clashed swords with another.

Dazed, Christian felt Skunk hauling him roughly to his feet. "You all right, sir?"

Christian reeled against him. "Hibbert . . ."

Swinging around, Skunk saw the young midshipman raising his pitiful dirk against the charging might of a pirate's pike. With a howl of rage, Skunk viciously knocked the pike aside. The full weight of his big body was behind the impact, and as the Frenchman collapsed onto the deck, Skunk turned back to the Lord and Master in time to see him suddenly flinch, drag off his fancy hat, and clap it over his shoulder.

"Bloody captain," Skunk joked, knocking aside a musket barrel that came swinging toward him with the ease of a child fending off a stick, " 'e don't want anyone to mark him down by his captain's hat, so he took it off!"

"Shut up, Skunk. The *bloody captain*'s the only hope we have of surviving this"—stab, thrust, stab—*"massacre!"* Ian yelled, ripping his claymore out of a man's chest and charging after his captain.

But even Ian was too crazed with excitement and bloodlust to see the color draining from the Lord and Master's face.

All he saw was that they were beating the enemy back onto its own decks.

The tide was turning.

Slash, parry, hack, chop. Whooping in triumph and glee, *Bold Marauder*'s enraged men drove the invaders back to their corvette, the fight now an attack by seamen from both English ships that had the Frenchmen screaming in fear and racing for the decks of their own vessel. Tiring rapidly, Christian fended off the sword of a seaman and, still holding his hat to his shoulder, jumped for the gangway. Someone on the corvette had already had the forethought to chop away the spars and lines tangled in *Bold Marauder*'s bowsprit, and now the corvette was beginning to draw slowly away, her officers screaming encouragement to the retreating sailors as the gap of blue sea between them grew wider and wider. Gauging the expanding distance between the two ships, Christian leapt, hearing Skunk, Ian, and Teach yelling in triumph behind him.

Protecting my back, he thought dazedly.

His feet hit the enemy's deck and he almost went down. Shouting with excitement, their swords flashing, his men rushed past him, nearly knocking him to his knees. Then Hendricks was there, lifting him by his lapels, and he was carried forward on the tide of English seamen.

His vision swam, and desperately he clutched his hat to his shoulder, terrified that his men would see the seriousness of the wound and lose heart.

Pray God, let me hold out just a bit longer, he thought. Then he slashed and fought his way toward the corvette's quarterdeck even as its flag tumbled to the deck in surrender.

A great earsplitting cheer went up from *Bold Marauder*'s men as Skunk and Teach grabbed the corvette's commander and hauled him unceremoniously toward Christian.

"Huzzah! Huzzah! Huzzah!"

"Three cheers for our Lord and Master!"

The man was shoved roughly before him.

"Here ye go, sir, the bleedin' bastard 'imself!"

Dirty, cut, and bleeding, the Lord and Master wearily accepted the other captain's sword. Then his arm fell, and for the first time, his men saw the perfect, round hole punched neatly below his shoulder, several inches away from the glittering gold buttons, and the huge stain of blood that turned the blue coat to purple.

"Devilishly well done, my lads," he said. Then he slumped against the shrouds, and slid quietly to the deck.

Chapter 17

In the surgeon's area, Deirdre choked back nausea as the wounded were dragged below. Above, the guns boomed, making conversation nearly impossible, making her ears ring with pain, making her fear the very deck was going to come crashing down—

"The captain!" she cried, overcome by sudden terror as a seaman dragged a moaning Wenham into the little room and laid him on Elwin's table beneath the swinging lantern.

"Huh?"

"The *captain!*" she shouted, trying to be heard over the crashing roar of cannon.

"Leading a boarding party ... onto the enemy. I ain't seen nothing like it. ..."

Wenham screamed in terror as Elwin, aided by two assistants, positioned him on the bloodied table. In one fluid movement they tore off his shirt and flung it to the floor.

"Nothing but a scratch." Elwin grabbed a needle and thread and slapped them into Deirdre's hand as another seaman was dragged below, this one with a terrible cutlass gash across his arm. "If you're going to stand there, then get busy, girl!" His arms were bathed to the elbows in blood, and his face was spattered with it. "Sew up that man's arm before he bleeds to death!"

From above came more firing, then a heavy wave of exultant cheering.

"We must be beatin' 'em, lads!" yelled the injured man, sitting upright. "By God, the Lord and Master must be driving the bloody Frogs back onto their own ship!"

Christian, Deirdre thought wildly, her hands shaking as she tried desperately to thread the needle. She watched as Delight, tight-lipped, washed the man's wound with a wet rag. Then, cringing, Deirdre pinched the ragged edges of flesh together and slowly sank the needle into the man's flesh. He went white with pain, and as the moments dragged on, the only way Deirdre was able to hold her breakfast down was to imagine the scene above, her lips moving in a desperate prayer for the captain's safety.

There was no use lying to herself anymore. She not only cared about him, she *loved him,* and was terrified for his safety, his life—

Suddenly Deirdre realized that the firing had stopped. Her ears were ringing, her body still tensed for each thunderous explosion. Another ragged cheer sounded, and then Hibbert, breathless, came flying into the room, his face stained with black powder, his chest heaving. "The English cutter is safe, the sloop has fled, and we took the Frenchie!" he gasped, swiping at his brow. His eyes were wild with pride. "They surrendered to our captain! To *us!*"

Ian crowded the space behind him, his ruddy face bleak and drained. "Aye, but at what price." He met their gazes and, in the sudden, awful hush, said solemnly, "The Lord and Master's down."

Deirdre was dimly aware of Delight's hand upon her shoulder; then the blood faded from her face as she looked dazedly past the midshipman to the group of men gathering there, all looking anxiously over their shoulders.

Arthur Teach's huge body filled the doorway.

The men stepped aside to let him pass, their eyes grave. The big seaman was carrying the body of an officer in his great, thewed arms, and crying like a babe. Blood ran from the officer's shoulder, seeped through his sleeve, followed the curve of his limp fingers, and dripped silently to the floor.

Deirdre stumbled back into Elwin's chest, grabbing the edge of the table for support. She didn't have to see the man's face to know just which officer he was.

Christian clawed and groped his way up through choking darkness and opened his eyes to the sight of Elwin's strained and waxen face above him, silhouetted by the swinging deckhead lantern. The pungent scents of blood, ointment, vinegar, and death assailed him, and he realized with horror that he was laid out on the operating table, its cold and merciless surface hard beneath his spine.

With a gasp, he sat up.

"Don't move, sir," Elwin hissed, pushing against his chest and trying to force him back down.

"Get your bloody hands off me. I've a ship to see to, wounded to care for—"

"The Frog pirates've surrendered, sir, don't ye remember? And Ian and Rhodes are seeing to *Bold Marauder*'s war wounds. Now, lie back and relax. You've got a musket ball somewhere in there, and if I don't get it out, you'll be a dead man by midnight!"

Christian knocked the surgeon's bony arm away. "Damn you, let me up!"

"Sir, I *must* insist!" Roughly, the surgeon shoved him back down on the table.

A voice exploded above Christian's head with a roar like a cannon blast. "Ye be easy with him, Elwin, or I'll have yer head on a pike!"

"Look, just get the hell out of here, all of ye!" Elwin spat, waving his bloodied hands and reaching for his vinegar bottle. "How's a man supposed to do his work if ye're all—"

Roaring madly, Skunk lunged forward and grabbed the surgeon's bony wrist, nearly snapping it. "You pour that on the cap'n's wound and you'll be answering to me, ye hear me, Elwin?!"

"For Christ's sake, Skunk, I'm merely washing my instruments in it—"

"What's this?" Ian barged in, his Scottish cap askew on his red curls, his bagpipes knocking rudely into Teach's cheek. "Is Elwin mistreating the captain?" He lunged forward, his hands outstretched. "So help me God, Elwin—"

"Damn you, damn all of you, just clear out and let me do what needs to be done!" Elwin raged, angrily wiping his bloodied hands on his apron. He snatched up a long, tapered, needlelike probe and, waving it at them, snarled, "Pack of useless, good-for-nothing loafers! Now, *get out!*"

Christian saw that long, wicked piece of metal coming toward his shoulder and went stiff, bracing himself for the pain. Fierce but gentle pressure tightened around his fingers, and rolling his head, he saw that someone was standing on the other side of the operating table and holding his hand, someone he now realized had been standing there and holding his hand all along.

Deirdre.

Her face was white and strained, her lips a bloodless slash across her chin, as though every bit of his pain was being transferred right up through her fingers and into her heart. Tears sparkled on her lashes, and her eyes were huge purple pools in her pale face. She squeezed his hand, fiercely, reassuringly, and the moisture in her eyes spilled over and traced a glittering track down her soft cheek. He stared at her, confused. "Miss O'Devir?"

Her thumbs pressed against his knuckles. Her black hair shone in the soft glow of the overhead lantern, and he saw her raise her other hand to hastily wipe at her damp cheeks.

"Teach carried ye down," she whispered, her soft brogue flowing over him like honey. She bent her head, and he felt the brush of her curly black hair as it draped his cold brow, the splash of a hot, salty tear upon his cheek. She gazed down at him, her eyes brimming with pain, the heavy crucifix that hung from her neck dangling near his nose. "The whole crew's braggin' about how ye led 'em t' victory an' saved th' ship."

"Damn right he did!" Skunk snarled. "If it weren't for his bleedin' Lordship, we'd all be at the bottom of the sea!"

"Or at the mercy of those French pirates!" Teach thundered, touching his tomahawk.

"Gentlemen," Elwin warned, lowering a knife to the blood-soaked hole in the Lord and Master's coat and deftly thrusting its tip beneath the fabric, "if you don't leave and let me attend to my business, you may *lose* your Lord and Master as soon as you've found him! That ball is lodged in a very vascular area, and if I don't get it out . . ."

With a flick of his wrist, he jerked upward, slicing through the sodden, heavy cloth of the coat.

Instinctively, Christian turned his head to look, but the girl loomed above, her eyes dark with compassion . . . and something else. She laid her warm palm against the side of his jaw, forcing his face toward her so that he couldn't see Elwin's ministrations. He closed his eyes, feeling the surgeon's knife ruthlessly cutting through his coat; but with the girl's soft hand against his cheek, his apprehension dimmed, faded away. "Elwin's right," she said quietly. "Th' ball has t' come out. But I'll be here, holdin' yer hand through it . . . Christian."

Christian.

He swallowed hard, several times, against the thick, sudden sting of emotion.

She'd called him by his name.

On her tongue, with her soft Irish brogue, it was music. More lovely than sea song, more lovely than fresh wind in hungry sails, more lovely, even, than what *her* voice had been like. . . .

Her voice. Suddenly, he could not recall Emily's face, let alone her voice.

Better just to drift. . . .

He opened his eyes as Skunk and Teach came forward, sliding their hands behind his shoulders and lifting him up. His chin fell forward against his chest, and he felt the girl's hand stroking his hair. Dimly, he was aware of Elwin peeling off his coat, his waistcoat, his blood-soaked shirt.

Christian, she'd said.

As they lowered him back to the table, he turned his head so she wouldn't see the raw emotion in his eyes. Then cool air swept against the exposed wound, and he didn't have to hear Delight's soft cry, or the collective gasps of dismay, to know how serious it was.

Rolling his head, he looked up at the girl and managed a smile. "Devilishly bad, eh?"

She was pure white. He saw her throat moving, but no words came out. The fierce pressure of her fingers around his was answer enough.

Grumbling, the surgeon plunged his hands into a bowl of water. "You're lucky to still have the use of that arm," he muttered, wiping his hands on his bloodied apron and picking up the long, gleaming probe once more. "And I tell you, you'd've been far better off if ye hadn't woken up, because you're going to feel this."

Low moans of pain came from elsewhere in the room, and Christian knew there were others down here in far more desperate need of the surgeon's service than he.

"See to the others first, Elwin," he said quietly, not seeing the worried glances that Skunk and Teach exchanged. "My wound will keep."

"My mates are seeing to the others, sir, and pardon me for saying so, but yours *won't* keep. You've lost a lot of blood, and I won't answer to the consequences if you lose any more. Now, hold still and don't talk!"

"I'm warnin' ye, Elwin!" Teach snarled, raising his tomahawk. "Ye make one slip and yer going to be eating steel and shittin' bullets, you hear me?"

Cuffing Teach's arm aside and ignoring the crowd gathering in the cramped space and stuffing the doorway, Elwin offered a bottle of rum to Christian. "Here, sir, I beg you to take some of this," he urged. "This won't be easy for you!"

Christian reached up, gripped Elwin's collar, and hauled him forcefully down until the surgeon's bulging eyes were mere inches away. "And have the company see me helpless beneath a haze of alcohol? Thank you, Mr. Boyd, but I happen to value my coherence!" He released the surgeon and steeled himself for the inevitable. "Now get on with it, please."

Elwin, sulking, gave a noncommittal shrug. "As you wish, then, sir." He splashed the rum into a clean rag instead and pressed the dripping cloth to the captain's wound.

Christian arched upward, sucking in his breath on a strangled hiss of agony.

Again Elwin paused above him, frowning. "You sure about that rum, sir?"

"Just *do* it, damn you!"

He shut his eyes, and only the girl, fiercely clasping his hand in hers and pressing his fingers to the crucifix at her breast, felt the tension and pain in his desperate grip. Then she brought her other hand down to his lips, her fingers gently touching his mouth and coaxing him to take and bite down on a strip of leather. He gazed up into her eyes, knowing that he could endure anything as long as she looked at him like that. He saw apology in their purple depths; admiration, kindness, and yes, even forgiveness.

Forgiveness.

Her soft fingers lingered on the rise of his cheekbones, the hardness of his jaw, the silky arch of his fair brows, the damp curls of hair that lay plastered against his forehead. He saw the three little midshipmen standing beside the anxious crew and mustered an encouraging smile. Then Elwin moved close, and he tensed in expectation of the first cold kiss of steel against his flesh.

Catching the girl's fingers, he pressed them to his lips.

"Don't leave me," he whispered.

Her eyes were soft, luminous, and filling with tears. " 'Tis a . . . a wonderful smile ye have," she said, her voice breaking.

The knife sliced against the raw edge of the wound and he flinched, his face draining of blood.

The girl bent close, her hair hanging over one shoulder and brushing his cheek, her hot tears splashing onto his brow. Her words were for his ears alone, soft, sweet, and precious.

"And ye're *not* uglier than a dead carp," she whispered, her lips moving against his temple. "Ye're a fine-lookin' man, a golden god, and I think ye're very brave an' handsome."

He felt searing pain as Elwin began to dig.

"Did ye heat that bluidy thing?" Ian roared.

Elwin whirled around, madly waving the knife. "Look, I

know my business, so get out of here, all of you!" He
swung back to his patient, the knife clenched in one fist.
"Damned interfering, nosy busybodies. . . ."

Christian felt the cold sweat running down his sides. Nausea welled up in his stomach, and white-hot agony fanned
out of his shoulder, radiating into his neck and down his
back as the surgeon probed the wound in a desperate, un-
successful attempt to locate the musket ball. Dimly, he was
aware that he was gripping the girl's hand like a lifeline;
from far away he felt her warm breath against his face, her
soft hand stroking his cheek, his hair.

"Damn," the surgeon snapped, holding the lip of the
wound aside with a two-pronged retractor as he dug and
probed. "I can't find this godforsaken thing—"

Christian sank his teeth into the leather, hearing the girl's
voice fading in and out, coming from a great distance away.

". . . I really *don't* mind fair hair . . . and some Englishmen can actually be quite nice. . . ."

Pain exploded in his head as the probe scraped against
bone, and his testicles seemed to shrivel in agony.

". . . I'll help ye o'er yer nightmares, Christian, if ye help
me find me brother. . . . I don't hate ye, really I don't. And
I'm sorry for all those times I tried t' kill ye. I'm sorry for
making yer life hell, for all th' cruel things I said an' did—"

Through slitted eyes he saw Delight, her painted nails
caught between her teeth, the crew pushing and shoving for
space behind her—and Elwin, turning back to him and
bending close with the needlelike steel probe. The girl's
tears came faster, hot and salty against his face, and her fingers crushed his as she, too, saw what was coming. He shut
his eyes, and nearly went through the deckhead as the surgeon pushed the wicked steel into his shoulder, probing the
area and touching upon raw, white bone. His molars grinding into the leather, Christian rasped, "When . . . when we
get to Boston, dear girl, I shall do all in my power to . . .
find your brother. So help me God."

Deirdre looked down at him through her tears. "Hold
on, Christian," she murmured, rubbing his cold cheek with
her thumb. Again, the probe scraped against bone. Christian's great body shuddered in agony, his hand opening

and then closing around hers in a death grip. Sobbing, Deirdre leaned close to his ear, her tears falling against his cheek. "Let go," she murmured, burying her lips against his salty, sweat-dampened skin. "Let go, Christian. Succumb t' th' darkness ... I'll watch o'er ye...."

Elwin probed deeper.

The captain nearly broke her fingers.

"Dammit, ye're hurtin' him!" she cried, grabbing Elwin's arm.

The surgeon straightened up, wiping his bloody hands on his apron. His face was tight with strain, his eyes futile. "I can't get it out," he muttered darkly, glaring at his shipmates as though daring them to defy him. "I can't even *find* the damned thing."

The crowd, held back by Teach, surged forward, already guessing the next method of treatment. "Forget it, Elwin!" Skunk raged.

"There's nothing I can do!" Elwin shot back, snatching up a huge, gleaming amputation saw. "That arm's going to have to come off. Skunk? Teach? Ian? You want to come over here and hold him down?"

"No!" Deirdre shouted as the captain's eyes closed in acceptance of his fate. Her own eyes shot angry amethyst fire. "Sweet Jesus, ye be talkin' about his *arm!*"

Elwin spun around, his eyes hard. "Look, girl, the ball's too deep. The arm's got to come off. Ye want that thing to putrefy and develop gangrene? *Ye want him to die?"*

She reeled back, stunned.

"Do you?"

"No," she whispered brokenly. Through her tears she gazed down at the captain. He was lying very still, his mouth a tight line of pain. He looked resigned. Defenseless. "No, Elwin ... please, don't let him die."

"Then stand back," he said quietly, "and let me do what needs to be done."

The Lord and Master was still holding her hand. His eyes were closed, his respiration shallow and strained, as though every breath was an effort. She stared down at him, sobbing with helplessness and despair, while the crucifix pressed against her heart, reminding her of its presence and the strength of the woman it had once belonged to.

Granuaile . . . oh, Granuaile, help me.

Elwin, resigned to his business, passed the steel saw through the fire to warm it.

Teach, his own black eyes strangely moist, shot her an imploring glance.

Deirdre shut her eyes and sent up a silent prayer.

Please, Granuaile. . . .

Elwin measured the blade against the ragged hole. Exchanging desperate glances, Skunk and Teach took the captain's arms, and Hendricks held down his legs. The saw touched the raw flesh. The captain's throat moved and he turned his cheek against Deirdre's hand.

"Hold him," Elwin said tightly, without looking up.

The first line of blood burst from the wound. The captain went rigid and Deirdre broke down. "Jesus, Joseph, an' Marry, *ye're hurtin' him,* Elwin!" she screamed, bursting into tears.

In a fit of temper, Elwin flung the saw to the deck and raged, "What do you want? He won't take rum, I can't get the ball out, and there's nothing else to do!"

"Ye didn't try very hard t' get it out wi' th' probe or forceps!"

"I can't see or feel a damned thing in there with them!"

"What th' bleedin' hell kind o' surgeon *are* ye?"

Elwin ripped off his apron and flung it to the floor. "Fine, then—if you think you can do better, do it yourself!"

He shoved past the stunned officers and crew, pushed through the marines, and slammed out of the sick bay.

In the ensuing silence, only the deckhead lantern moved, swinging eerily in the gloom.

Deirdre's jaw dropped, and for a startled moment, she could only stare blankly at those around her. Her stricken gaze moved from Teach to Skunk to Ian to Hendricks to a pale and green-looking Hibbert, who had returned and was huddled beside Evans, then to the red-coated pack of marines and to the scores of seamen pressing against the doorway.

They were staring at her. Every last, bleedin' one of them.

"It's your decision, *chérie*," Delight said softly.

Gulping, Deirdre looked down at the Lord and Master. He was fading fast, the blood, obscene and purple in the glare of the lantern light, pulsing down his chest with every beat of his heart. His eyes were half closed, glazed with pain.

"You can do it, foundling," he murmured, his thumb weakly stroking her hand. Then he dragged his eyes open to gaze at her face. "That is ... if you want to."

The others looked at her, holding their breath. Their faces were anxious, hopeful.

You can do it.

Chills drove up her spine. Her stomach fluttered with sudden panic. Suppressing a shiver, she stared down at that raw, ominous hole just beneath the ridge of the captain's collarbone, and swallowed hard.

They were waiting. All of them.

Wildly, she glanced about, but there was no help to be found.

She felt gentle pressure against her fingers. "This ... is growing devilishly sore," he whispered with a weak smile.

"Ye'd ... ye'd trust me, after what I've *done* t' ye?"

The gray eyes drifted shut, and his fingers tightened over hers in reassurance. "I would trust no other ... my dear girl."

She felt the weight of the seamen's gazes boring into her. She glanced at Skunk, and involuntarily, her hand went to her throat to touch the crucifix. The sick bay was suddenly too hot, the air too thick to breathe, her heart pounding too loudly in her ears. "I—I don't know what t' do, but ..."

"Just dig the thing out," Skunk said. "Here, we'll all hold him down. Get over here, buckos—"

The Lord and Master opened eyes that were foggy with pain. "No," he said quietly, his breath warm against her wrist. "There ... there is no need." He turned his head, his fair hair glimmering in the lantern light and curling handsomely around his ears. "So get on with it, girl." He gave a strained smile. "I have a ship to run, you know."

Aware of every eye in the room, she nodded, bit her trembling lip, and scrubbed her hands in a clean bowl of water. They were shaking badly as she held them out, allowing Skunk to pour a liberal dose of rum over them to kill any remaining germs. Hibbert tied her hair back with a strip of leather, and taking a deep, shaky breath, her lovely black brows drawn close in fierce concentration, Deirdre bent over the wound.

Christian felt the heavy crucifix brushing, then resting upon, his bloody chest. He closed his eyes as her soft fingers touched his skin. They were gentle, caring, perhaps even loving. Slowly, he let out his breath on a long sigh, his muscles relaxing as she held his shoulder with one hand and touched the ragged lip of the wound with her fingers.

With her fingers.

It came to him that she would not use the steel probe, the knife, or any of the other wicked instruments of torture in the surgeon's collection.

Her fingers.

He studied her face as she worked, watching her lovely features tighten with concentration. Once, she glanced up at Hendricks as though for reassurance; he nodded, and Christian felt her hand in his flesh once more. Pain began to throb up his neck, down his back. He shut his eyes and bit down on the leather, the inside of his cheek, until he tasted blood.

"Easy, sir," she whispered, her face so close to his shoulder he could feel the warmth of her breath feathering against his damp skin, the wound itself. Her fingers explored deeper, and chills of nausea swept down his spine as she touched the raw edge of his collarbone.

Deirdre, however, was nearing despair. She raised her face, her features white and strained as she turned desperate eyes on the others. Tears spilled down her cheeks in salty rivers and she bit her lip to still its trembling. "I . . . I can't find it."

She looked down at her bloody hand. By sheer force of will, she kept herself from fainting with the knowledge of what she was doing, what she knew she must do.

"Go deeper," Skunk commanded harshly, leaning over her and blocking the lantern light.

Hot, scalding tears ran down her face, dropped upon the captain's chest, and diluted with his blood to race down the curve of his ribs and onto the cloth upon which he lay. Her fingers dark with blood, Deirdre reached up and touched the crucifix; then, momentarily squeezing her eyes shut, she pushed her forefinger back into the hole, feeling the warm embrace of muscle, tissue, blood, and bone.

The captain moved beneath her, the sweat rolling down his temples in rivulets. "Deeper, little wren . . ."

She choked on a sob and, crying, pushed her finger in further. Further.

"Oh, m' God, Skunk, I can't—"

A hand came up and closed with steely intensity around her other wrist. It was the Lord and Master's.

"You *can,*" he bit out.

She bent her head, dashed tears and sweat from her face with her shoulder, and pushed her finger in deeper. And deeper.

Stringy tissue, bone, muscle—and then something round and hard—

"I found it—dear Jesus, I think I have it!"

The tears flowed faster. Her fingers slipped away from the slippery ball, losing it.

"Oh, oh, dear God, sweet Mary—"

She glanced down at the captain. Mercifully, he had fainted.

"Quick, girl, get it now!" Hendricks yelled, shoving forward with the crowd.

"And mind ye doona miss any pieces of his clothing that might be in there, too!" Ian cried, glancing anxiously at the Lord and Master's still face.

Her lips tight with concentration, Deirdre pushed her thumb into the hole and spread the tissue aside. Fresh blood welled up and flooded over her fingers. Sobbing, she plunged her fingers recklessly further—and found the musket ball.

Squeezing her eyes shut, she gripped it and pulled.

"I lost it!"

Teach was there, his hands against the captain's powerful chest to hold him down. "Quick, Deirdre, he's coming to—"

Desperately, she gripped the slick ball once more and, with a wretched cry of triumph, pulled it free.

Her tears burst forth in a deluge, and Teach grabbed the bloodied ball from her hand and held it up for all to see. "She did it! The lass did it, by God!"

"Three huzzahs for our Deirdre!"

The room erupted in a wild, deafening uproar of mad cheering.

Sobbing, she bent her head to the captain's broad chest, his warm blood slippery against her cheek and mixing with her tears. But she didn't care. She felt his wet, wiry chest hair folding beneath her cheek, the weak touch of his hand upon her hair—and heard the strong beat of his heart beneath her ear.

His arm came up weakly to encircle the back of her neck.

For her, that was all that mattered.

Chapter 18

Through careful questioning, Lieutenants MacDuff and Rhodes learned that the corvette's French captain, a confessed outlaw loyal to no flag, had happened upon the long English cutter while in company with his consort . . . easy prey, until HMS *Bold Marauder* had come upon the scene. But even the combined menace of Arthur Teach, Ian MacDuff, Rico Hendricks, and Skunk could not convince the Frenchman to disclose the name of his consort in the sloop, which had promptly fled at the first sign of the powerful English frigate.

As for the corvette herself, she now lay far back over the dark horizon, her people prisoners in their own hold, her new crew made up of Britons from the cutter. They would sail her back to England, where the pirate's fate would be decided by the officials of government, but out here on the open sea, other rulings had to be made by those upon whose shoulders such power rested.

And at the time, those shoulders had been Lieutenant Ian MacDuff's.

In his first decision as second-in-command of HMS *Bold Marauder*, Ian had decided not to have Elwin punished for deserting the captain in surgery, for in doing so, Elwin had inadvertently done their commanding officer a favor. In his second decree, Ian decided against pursuing the sloop. It was a decision that the Lord and Master, emerging briefly from a laudanum-induced sleep, had hazedly agreed with, for even in his condition, he knew the frigate's unseasoned gunners had had enough for one day.

Deirdre, however, was less concerned with pirates than she was with her patient, whose side she had not left since she'd extracted the musket ball six days before. She had carefully bandaged his shoulder, walked beside him as Teach and Hendricks had carried him back to his cabin, held his hand until the laudanum had taken effect and he finally succumbed to an exhausted sleep, and maintained a faithful vigil beside his bed.

Now, nearly a week after the battle, she stood on the cold deck, gripping the salt-sticky rail and watching the stars wink on in the vast sky over her head. Blown spray made her curls tight and spiraling, coaxing them into a black cloud that floated like a shawl around her thin shoulders and merged with the night around her. Moonlight frosted the sails, the guns, the deck planking; a harsh wind gusted off the North Atlantic and drove through the layers of clothing she wore, chilling her to the bone.

She felt alive, exhilarated, and strangely ... *free.*

Beneath her feet, the frigate rose and plunged and rose again in a timeless rhythm that brought with it a sense of weightlessness and eternity. Deirdre tilted her head back, letting the night wind brush its icy kiss over her bared throat, her cheeks. Her fingers, clutching the rail, were stiff with cold, and the blood tingled vibrantly in her face. From around her came the sounds of masts creaking and groaning, the whisper of spray at the bows, the splash of waves driving against the hull. She drew the salty sea air deeply into her lungs, relishing the bracing bite of the wind through her hair and ripping at her clothes. Then she gazed out over the cold sea, where the reflection of moon and stars coasted atop the restless wave crests.

"Christian," she said softly.

Her heart felt strange and barren, as though it had been flushed clean of the bitter hatred she'd carried for so long and was now an empty vessel whose deep and cavernous chambers ached to be filled with something good, something joyous, something wonderful. She reached up and touched her chest, feeling her heart beating through the thick layers of clothing.

"Christian." She stared down at the sea, which fell away in great sheets of foam that glinted in the darkness as the frigate smashed down on each rising comber. Then she gazed up at the listening stars, pounding her fist against her heart and holding it pressed there, hard. "It don't matter anymore tha' 't'ye be an Englishman, one o' th' enemy. I'm tired o' fightin' what I feel for ye in me heart. I'm tired o' tryin' t' hate ye, when I just can't anymore. I know that what ye did to me brother all those years ago was somethin' ye didn't want t' be doin'. Ye was just followin' orders, like Hendricks keeps a-tellin' me. Ye're an officer, who knows no other way o' life but discipline an' actin' on behalf o' yer country. Yer Navy asked ye t' do it, Christian—therefore 'twas *their* fault for takin' me brother, Christian, not yers! *Yer Navy's!* And I hold *them* responsible for it!"

She felt the wind whipping through her hair, stinging her cheeks.

"It was th' *Navy's* fault, Christian! And when I get t' Boston I'm goin' t' do all I can t' make 'em find me brother, an' return him t' *Ireland!* I'm goin' t' make *them* pay for takin' him, and usin' you t' do somethin' I know ye hated doin'!" Her eyes closed over sudden, scalding tears. "And t' think o' all these years I hated *you*, me love. . . ."

She surely didn't hate him now. . . . But just when had she begun to love him?

Perhaps when the Lord and Master had discovered her aboard the frigate, intervened on her behalf, and carried her to safety in his powerful arms. Perhaps with that first, unforgettable meeting, thirteen long years ago. She did not know. She did not care. But the seeds had been sown, somewhere, sometime, and that love had grown with each act of kindness and patience he'd shown her, each time she'd caught him fawning over his little canine family, each instance he would've been justified in punishing his crew with the harsh and brutal discipline the Royal Navy was famous for—but had instead reacted with understanding, inventiveness, and yes, *humanity.*

Love.

The final, annihilating revelation had come during those terrible moments in the surgeon's bay—when Teach had carried him down and she had been paralyzed with fear in thinking him dead. When fate had laid him low and placed him in her hands. When he had gazed up at her, his calm gray eyes reflecting trust and confidence that she, Deirdre O'Devir, could succeed where the surgeon had failed.

When he had trusted her with his life.

Love.

Above, the stars grew brilliant, sparkling like chips of crystal as the night grew darker, deeper. The ocean took on a mysterious beauty, and the frigate's lights spread searching fingers of gold across the waves, as though the ship was reaching out across forever toward her own destiny.

But HMS *Bold Marauder* had no one but the lonely helmsman with whom to share the beauty of the night.

The spot at the rail where Deirdre O'Devir had stood was already empty.

He had beautiful hair.

With trembling fingers, she reached out and touched it.

The Lord and Master was asleep, deeply so, aided by a strong draught of laudanum that Hendricks had craftily slipped into his tea. But it gave Deirdre the opportunity to study this enigmatic man without those cold gray eyes taking her measure and making her feel ill at ease. In sleep, his face wasn't quite so austere and forbidding; in sleep, it was handsome and youthful, the years dropping away, until he was once again the fair-haired lieutenant who'd bent down to calm and reassure a frightened little girl.

From the corner, she was aware of the puppies crying in their box, the soft sounds of Tildy quietly licking their tiny backs. Little suckling noises, then quiet. She smiled, a warm, loving feeling suffusing her heart, and suddenly she wished that *she* had a family, too. A man to love her, care for her, cherish her . . .

Christian.

A lantern swung gently from the beams above, softly gilding the Lord and Master's face, the strong column of his neck, the bare rise of his shoulders and lightly furred chest—and yes, his hair.

His *fair* hair, which she had so vehemently proclaimed to dislike.

"Nay, 'tis *beautiful* . . . Captain Lord," she whispered, carefully sitting beside him on the bed and stroking the glistening locks. They were thick and pale and wavy, the color of sunlight at the hottest part of the day. Not quite yellow, not quite white, and soft and springy to the touch. She smoothed the hair away from his brow, gazing in wonder at it and wishing he wouldn't wear that dull and pompous wig. Didn't he know he was far more handsome without it?

Her fingers moved softly over his forehead, her eyes gazing at every detail of his face. His pale brows were fine, haughty, and aristocratic, arched and silky beneath her touch; his nose was straight and proud; his lashes, thick and golden-brown, were bleached at the tips and lying heavily against high and prominent cheekbones. She'd never realized that a man could have such long lashes, that a man could have such beautiful hair; she'd never realized how handsome and vulnerable a man could look in sleep; and never, ever, in a thousand years had she thought to apply any of those words—*handsome, beautiful, vulnerable*—to the cold and enigmatic Lord and Master of His Majesty's Ship *Bold Marauder.*

The cabin seemed suddenly stuffy, the air heavy and cloying and still. Mesmerized, Deirdre let her fingers brush the burnished locks that curled enticingly at his temple, and then the faded bruise just beneath. Her touch lingered there, feeling the fragile pulse that beat beneath her fingertips.

Her eyes filled with gentle wonder.

He was an Englishman. The enemy. Part of that hated race that had been tromping on the rights and land of her people for centuries. But enemies were supposed to be cold and alien, monstrous and inhuman—weren't they? Yet this man's skin was as warm as hers. His pulse beat just as strongly as hers, his magnificently muscled chest rose and fell with the same breath, and the blood that had flowed so freely from his bandaged shoulder was just as red as hers.

She brushed the back of her hand against his cheek. And he felt pain as acutely as any Irishman she'd ever known.

Weren't enemies supposed to be ... *different?*

But no. He was wonderfully human, warm and alive and breathing. He had hopes and fears, dreams and visions, and somewhere, people who cared about and loved him. *He was no different than she was*—except he'd been born in a different place.

Deirdre swallowed a few times, her heart swelling with something thick and powerful and huge, something that threatened to bring the tears spilling down her cheeks. Quickly, she blinked them back.

I love ye, Christian. She wiped at her eyes. "God help me, I love ye. . . ."

Her hand shaking, she traced the shape of his face and the bones beneath, noting how the texture of his skin was soft in some places, rough in others; she smoothed the sun-bleached hair from his brow, let her fingers trail in it. She touched the pulse beating in his throat, the hard plane of his cheek, the rise of his lips, the stubbled curve of his throat, then gazed down at his chest, remembering how safe she'd felt when he'd gathered her against it and let her cry.

It was a splendid view of muscle and power, sheathed by bronzed skin and a mat of golden hair. She touched his bandage, then placed her hand directly over his heart, feeling its strong beat beneath her palm. Then, unbidden, Deirdre's gaze flickered downward, to the covers that lay slackly over his hips, and heat flooded her cheeks.

She did not have to lift the blankets to know the Lord and Master was stark naked beneath.

His tortured confession—that he was unable to function as a man—suddenly came to her. *The attraction is there ...*

but the ability to follow it through is sadly lacking. . . . What was wrong with him that he lacked this . . . ability? What possible defect could he have? And who, God help her, would ever know if she lifted that blanket for a wee second, just to see for herself what this horrible defect was?

She sucked her bottom lip between her teeth and shot a nervous glance toward the door. What if Hendricks came? What if Evans looked in on them? What if—

No. It was late. No one would come, and besides, hadn't Hendricks personally entrusted her with the job of nursing the Lord and Master back to health?

Her heart hammered in her breast. Hot blood scalded her face. Her palms grew damp, her breathing shaky, and between her legs, she felt something hot and tingly and gripping.

Go ahead. Look. He'll never know. . . .

Swallowing hard, Deirdre reached down and, gingerly gripping the blanket between her thumb and forefinger, lifted it.

Emily.

He tensed and braced himself, knowing it was the nightmare; he heard the same noises downstairs, crept from the empty bed, descended the stairs, and paused behind the door. He heard her laughter and saw the two bodies entwined, glistening with sweat; he heard his own howl of rage and saw the intruder flee, terrified and cowardly.

This time, Christian vowed, he'd bloody well kill the bastard.

But this time, the nightmare was different.

Her voice rang out behind him, sharp and pleading and desperate. "Christian, no! Let it go! You know what will happen if you don't! He'll throw the lantern and there'll be a fire! I'll *die,* Christian, and you'll have this very same nightmare haunting you for the rest of your days!"

She *knew* about the nightmare? Confusion drove through him. The hall seemed unreal and fantastic, and beneath his feet, the cold marble floor surged back and forth, not unlike the deck of a ship. Yes, it was a dream. But if he kept going, it would become the nightmare.

"Don't *do* it, Christian!"

He paused, hearing her lover's pounding feet as he fled the house; then, with a fierce cry, Christian turned and ran back to that closed door, knowing this would be the only chance he would ever have to love her, forgive her, put an end to the nightmare—

He flung open the door and saw her.

"Christian," she said in a husky dream-voice.

His mouth fell open and the breath caught in his throat. He stumbled back against the doorframe, shaking badly.

She was lying on the sofa. Her legs were open, her eyes were hungry, and she was naked.

Waiting for him.

Deirdre hadn't meant to do more than just *peek* at him, and briefly at that. She hadn't meant to do more than just *look* at his maleness for a moment, to see what it was about it that made him unable to function. . . .

As for your precious virtue, you needn't worry about me compromising it! I have been unable to feel anything for any woman since my wife died. . . .

Aside from him, she had never seen a man naked, let alone aroused, but she had seen stallions, she had seen dogs, she had seen cattle and sheep—and yes, she had heard stories.

Unable to function, he'd said.

And her words: *Useless as a man.*

He'd been right.

There was no big secret beneath the covers, nothing to hold one's breath over, and with an odd, empty feeling of sadness, she stared at the limp and flaccid flesh that lay buried in the patch of golden hair between his powerful thighs.

Useless as a man.

She felt pity for Captain Christian Lord, and then anger that she felt the pity. He had told her the truth. There was no way that this sad bit of pale flesh could ever do a man's work, like the proud stallion with the feisty mare. What lay beneath her gaze was slack and small and still.

Pitiful.

Her breath came out on a sigh. Slowly, she peeled the blanket back, farther and farther, finally laying it across the Lord and Master's knees and exposing the whole of his lean and naked loins to her blushing gaze. Pity, that such a proud and handsome specimen of a man—even if he *was* English—was so . . . deformed.

But here was the proof.

It must've been a strange coincidence, those times he'd been large and hard and stiff. Looking at him now, she found it impossible to believe he had ever been otherwise. Maybe she'd been just imagining it, then. After all, he had no reason to lie to her.

She reached down, thinking to pull the covers back up over his legs, but instead, her fingers strayed to the limp curve of flesh.

It was warm; quite so, in fact. Holding her breath, she nervously glanced at the Lord and Master's handsome face. He didn't move. Bolder now, she looked back at the golden thicket of springy hair, slid her finger into it and then, carefully, beneath the male flesh. She stared at it; then she stared at his still face; then she stared back at the warm flesh in her hand, and felt it give a little quiver.

Deirdre's brows drew close in a frown. Slowly, she passed her thumb over the warm flesh, and felt it quiver once more.

She gave a little start and glanced at his face, her own cheeks flaming red. The Lord and Master was deeply asleep; no doubt the tremor she'd felt against her suddenly moist palm was nothing more than some perfectly normal body function, or, perhaps, a twitch from a dream.

Her heart pounded, loud enough to echo in her ears. She bit her lip, held her breath, and slowly dragged her thumb over the limp flesh again, wondering at its soft and velvety texture.

Again that involuntary tremor.

"Oh, my . . ." she breathed, frowning. It felt different; a bit warmer, maybe, a bit firmer. She stared hard at it; then her eyes widened.

Heat washed over her face. That alien bit of anatomy was not only warmer, not only firmer—it was *bigger.*

She didn't hear the harsh rasp of her breathing as the air dragged in and out of her lungs. A bead of sweat gathered between her breasts; another trickled down her temple and dampened her hair. The Lord and Master gave a soft gasp in his sleep, and then groaned. But Deirdre was no longer looking at his face. She cupped the growing—yes, it *was* growing—length of him in her hand and watched, mesmerized and awestruck, as it began to transform itself before her very eyes, growing stiff and hard and hot in her shaking hand.

"Oh . . . oh, sweet Jesus," Deirdre said, her face steaming.

Replace the covers. Get out o' here before he wakes up. Now, before, before—

She broke off her thought and, trembling, began to hesitantly caress that hot and hard blade of flesh.

Emily.

Her hair was dark and glorious, spread out over the arm of the sofa, trailing halfway to the floor. Her thighs were open with invitation, the dark patch of hair at their center glistening, eager, and damp; her arms were raised, her eyes hungry.

His manhood stirred against the soft fabric of his robe aching with need.

"Come to me, Christian . . . you know he never meant anything to me . . . it is *you* I love, you I *want* . . . this is your only chance, darling. Your only chance to say goodbye before I leave you forever. . . ."

"Emmie! *Emmie, don't go. . . .*"

"Christian, darling, you *know* this is a dream. . . . I'm dead, remember?"

No, not dead. No dead woman looked like she did.

"Ah, Emmie. . . ." Tears stung his eyes, that he should be given this chance to make things right after all these years, even if it was a dream, even if the woman on the sofa was not the soft and shy Emily he had married, but a sultry vixen with a courtesan's eyes. With a helpless groan, he went to her, shedding his robe and letting it slip to the floor as he fell to the sofa with her.

Wake up, Christian . . . it's a dream. . . .

No. He fought the tug, the pull, to awaken.

His body hardened in response to her. Her arms came up to touch his shoulders, rove down his back, skim over his buttocks. "There now," she breathed, her voice whispering against the curve of his shoulder. "Aren't you glad you didn't chase after him? Aren't you glad you came back to *me?*"

"You're . . . this is a dream."

Her hands were on him, sweet and gentle, yet harsh where they needed to be, *when* they needed to be. One moment feathery and grazing; the next, bold and exploring. Desire rocked through him, and he sprang to rigid, fiery life in her hands, tightening in soundless pleasure, his breathing harsh, his heartbeat filling his ears.

Such gentle hands. Such sweet hands. Such *soft* hands.

He groaned, and broke out in a sweat. He felt the fog swirling around him in a thick, hot pocket of moisture, and in that weird way of dreams, the scene shifted and she was suddenly above him, no longer Emily but someone else. . . . He couldn't see her face, but that didn't matter, for his eyes were closed. He couldn't hear her voice, but that didn't matter, either, because it was a dream. The only thing that mattered was that she was loving him, and he, tortured, hardened, and anguished, had not been loved by anyone or anything for so very, very long. . . .

"There, my bold captain. See? You're not 'useless' after all . . . perfectly able to function. . . . You were always such a magnificent lover . . . when you were home."

She was pulling at him now, stroking him, cupping him and rubbing him between her hands. His teeth gritted together, and his eyes rolled up behind tightly clenched lids.

"Dear God," he said roughly, one hand gripping the sheets, the other anchored in her hair. "Dear God, please don't stop. . . ."

"I won't," Deirdre O'Devir said.

Her face burned hotter than a summer day in Hades. Her eyes were wide and staring, her breathing thick and measured. Liquid heat swirled between her thighs, and she felt a spreading moisture there, a moisture that grew hotter and more flooding with each twisted movement the captain made on the bed beneath her, with every rasp of his tortured breath, with ever twitch of his legs, his hands, his—

No limp and flaccid piece of sorry flesh, this! Sweet Jesus, the thing filled her hand and defied the span of her encircling fingers; it was hard as marble, proud and stiff and tall, and with every flick of her thumb across the engorged and purplish head, with every squeeze of her fingertips over the rigid and hot flesh, it jumped.

A small pearl of ivory gathered on the blunted tip, sparkling in the lantern light. Deirdre stared at it for a moment, then recklessly smudged it over the velvety shaft.

"Dear God . . ." he moaned, still in the throes of sleep.

Heady excitement surged through her that she had managed to bring him to such a state, that she had him in her power, at her mercy, even while he slept—and that he was far from being *useless as a man*.

"I do believe I've proved you wrong, my Lord and Master," she said, and encircled him with thumb and forefinger near the root of that proud pillar, squeezing hard.

His breathing quickened, and sweat glistened on his sleeping brow.

"Faster. . . ." he murmured thickly.

Deirdre smiled, her gaze fastened to his face, the harsh mouth that was slack with passion, the eyes that moved rapidly beneath his lids.

"Please, don't stop. . . ."

She tightened the circle of her fingers, feeling the answering heat in her own blood, in her own rapid, jerky movements, in her own thundering of heart against ribs, blood through veins. She stared down at that massive, heaving chest, the hard-muscled thighs, the thick and pulsing flesh in her hand.

"Don't stop . . . *please* . . ."

She couldn't stop even if she wanted to. Breathing as hard as he, she stroked harder . . . faster . . . velvet sliding over hot and rigid steel; up and down, faster, faster—

He gasped and cried out in his sleep, his body convulsing in great, mighty shudders, and as she froze in terror, wondering if she'd killed him, something warm and wet spurted over her hand, her wrist, her arm, his belly.

Deirdre shrieked, jerked her hand away, and leapt to her feet in horror.

The gray eyes shot open.

"Deirdre!"

Her heart was thundering. Her blood was racing. She took an involuntary step backward, away from that confused stare . . . a stare that reflected recognition, horror—and then raw, bone-chilling fury.

Chapter 19

Between his thighs, his manhood pulsed and shuddered, the flow of fluid slowing, running down his handsome thigh, dampening the bed sheets.

"By God, woman, have you no bloody shame?" he roared, mortified, as he came suddenly, and rudely, awake. His shocked gaze went first to his loins, then to her dripping hand, his face flooding with brilliant, fiery color. Snatching the blanket, he hauled it up over his thighs and snarled, "Bloody hell, girl, leave me!"

Leave him? Her body was throbbing, tingling, burning, and she had no intention of going anywhere.

"Ye can order me t' leave, Captain Lord, but I doubt ye're as strong as ye'd like t' think ye are," she said, with a pointed glance at his bandaged shoulder. "I'll not leave until Mr. MacDuff says I may."

"You will leave now, by God, or I'll toss you out on your bloody ear!"

"Christian, I only looked because I wanted t' see what ye meant when ye said ye were *useless* as a man—"

"You said I was useless as a man—I merely said I couldn't function as one!"

"—and I touched ye because ye *asked* me t'," she said softly.

He froze. Gray eyes narrowed dangerously, to chips of flint. *"Asked* you to?"

"Aye." Slowly, she wiped her damp hand on the side of her trousers, very aware that the action only brought his color up even higher. She saw the red flush spreading down his throat, and working its way out toward his bandaged shoulder. "Ye no' t'only *asked* me t', ye asked me t' squeeze it, stroke it, rub it harder."

"Deuced hell," he murmured, turning away a face that was as harsh and cold as stone. "Get out."

"I will not." Defiantly, Deirdre sat beside him on the bed, her slight weight barely bowing it. His lips were a slash of anger, his color high with mortification. Huge shoulders were darkly handsome against the white sheets, and his chest was damp with sweat, which only emphasized the sharp definition of muscle, bone, and utter male perfection. Her fingers itched to touch him, to trail through the soft, wiry mat of golden hair that pelted that magnificent chest, and it was only by a supreme effort that she was able to force her gaze away from the area of the blanket that covered that forbidden, but tempting, part of him.

The thought brought a fresh wave of heat washing between her thighs. Alarmed, she clamped her legs together, wondering what was wrong with her; her breasts were tingling, her thighs were burning and damp. "I know ye're embarrassed, and I be sorry," she murmured. Her chin came up and bravely, she met his angry, accusing glare. "But ye're th' only naked man I've ever seen before, an' tha' 'twas mostly in th' dark, and here ye've been goin' on so about how deformed ye are—"

"Deformed?" he thundered, bolting upright in the bed. "Deprived, madam, but, I can assure you, not *deformed!"*

"Ye don't have t' be yellin' at me!" she cried, her eyes filling. She tore her hand from his, but he reached out and grabbed her wrist when she would've fled, his fingers biting into the tender skin.

Their gazes clashed. A muscle jumped in his jaw. He stared at her for a long moment, then flung her hand away.

"From now on, just stay the bloody hell *away* from me when I'm sleeping!" he ordered, pushing the damp hair off his brow. His hand was shaking. "In fact, just stay away from me, *period!*"

She burst into tears. "Oh, Christian," she wailed, clapping her hands over her face, "I just wanted t' see what was wrong with ye, so I could . . . so I c-could . . . h-help ye t' get over it. . . . And now I think there be somethin' wrong wi' *me*, b'cause my—my—oh, I ache in funny places, and—"

"Bloody hell," he murmured. Damning himself for a weak fool, he gathered her close, his fingers tangling in her coarse and curling hair. He felt her shoulders shaking, her arms going fiercely around his neck. Something thick and warm wrapped around his heart, choking him, until he had to swallow several times to be able to speak. "My dear girl, there is nothing wrong with you," he said. "What you are feeling is simply a healthy female attraction and response to the male species, a feeling no doubt exacerbated by the shocking spectacle your virgin eyes have just witnessed."

Against his neck, she sobbed, "Do you . . . do you have these feelings, too?"

"Aye, Deirdre, I have them, too . . . for all the bloody good they do me," he said bitterly.

His tone immediately quelled her tears. She pulled back, her eyes questioning.

"I do not welcome the feelings, Deirdre, because I . . . because I—" He flushed, gripped her fingers so hard she thought they would break, and looked away, too ashamed to meet her questing gaze. "Oh, the devil take it, *because I cannot function as a man!*"

She stared at him, at the proud, hawkish profile, the sharp cast of his English nose, the lips that were compressed in a tight line of pain and humiliation. Her eyes narrowed in confusion, then in sudden speculation. "Bu' 't'wasn't that a manly thing ye just did while ye was sleepin'?"

"Aye," he said tightly.

"Then ye must be able t' function quite *well* as a man."

"I was asleep!" he snapped, as though that explained everything. "Awake, I fear I cannot sustain that hard state long enough to bring either one of us pleasure." He looked away, humiliated and embarrassed. "This is most uncomfortable for me to discuss. I have my pride, and you are making a devilish shambles of it by forcing me to admit that I am impotent."

"Impotent?"

"Meaning I can't be . . . stirred. I cannot pleasure a woman. I cannot make babies. Therefore, I am less than a man."

"But what just happened—"

"I was *asleep,* damn it!"

She looked hurt at his harsh tone. "Why can't ye do such a thing *awake?"*

"Because a certain jealous specter of my past—*my dead wife*—will not allow it!" His eyes were raw with pain and anguish and shame. Then he saw the wounded look on her face, and his manner softened. Quietly, he said, "You see, Deirdre, there is nothing *anatomically* wrong with me." He sighed, and pointed to his temple. "It's all in *here,* dear girl. My . . . my jealous specter, if you will. As long as I feel guilt over the death of my wife, I am of no use to any woman."

The silence hung heavily between them. Topside, the sound of voices drifted down to them, and the deck began to slant as the frigate leaned hard over onto the opposite tack. Deirdre stared down at their interlaced fingers, then gently picked up his hand, cradling it in her own. It was broad and strong, warm and pulsing with life.

"Ye are o' use t' *me,* Captain Lord, whether or not ye can . . . *function."* She studied that strong hand, the veins standing out in relief on the back of it, the fine brush of pale hair. Her hip pressed against the hard ridge of his thigh, and through the blanket she could feel his heat, his power. "Ye see, Christian"—she paused, her throat working—"I . . . I love ye."

He didn't answer, only the sudden tightening of his fingers over her own indicating that he'd heard.

"Christian?" she said softly.

He looked up, his eyes tortured, the guarded expression coming over his face once again. "You are too young, too innocent to know what love is about," he said sharply. "Now go, leave me, while I still have my pride and you your innocence! This discussion should not be taking place; it is devilishly improper!"

"Nay, Christian, it *should* be takin' place. It should've taken place a long time ago."

"By God," he snapped, *"go,* before I lose my patience as well as my damned dignity!"

Her chin came up and she faced him defiantly. Tears sparkled on her lashes. "And yer heart, me Lord an' Master?"

He stared at her, alarmed that his thoughts were so transparent that she, a mere girl, could guess them. Was his desire so easily read? And for that matter, what *was* in his heart?

" 'Tis innocent I may be," she said softly, "but I'm not stupid. I know th' look a man gets in his eyes when he sees a woman he finds bonny. D'ye think yer fair Emily has robbed ye of even *that?"* She ignored the shocked look on his face, and splayed her fingers through the golden mat on his chest, seeking his heartbeat. "About the only thing she's robbed ye of is yer confidence. I don't believe for an instant that she's made ye as *useless* as ye've led yerself—and, for a while, me—t' believe. Oh, no, I think ye're fully capable o' functionin' as well as any man."

"This is not a subject I care to discuss!"

Her eyes glinted with a silent dare. "What, be ye afraid, then?"

"Do not challenge me, girl. You may find yourself in waters over your head."

"No, me Lord an' Master, 'tis *you,* I think, who's afraid. Afraid o' settin' yerself free t' love another. Afraid o' followin' the wants o' yer heart, yer body, for fear o' discoverin' tha' t'ye *can* love someone else—someone who's not yer dear Emily. And that scares ye, doesn't it?"

His face went white with fury, his nostrils flared, and his eyes grew hard as stone.

"Doesn't it?"

"By God—"

"I'll not go, Christian!" Undaunted, she leaned close, wagging her finger in his angry face. "I'll not go, because I have a few things t' say t' ye! I know why ye're doin' this. Ye're shuttin' me out because ye feel like ye're betrayin' yer dead wife for bein' fond of another, and that makes ye feel guilty as sin, don't it? Far easier for ye t' convince yerself tha' t'ye *have* no heart, that' t'ye're incapable o' feelin' anythin' for *anyone.*"

"You presume too much for your own bloody good!"

She pressed her hand to her chest, flattening the crucifix to her breasts. "I presume on me woman's heart." Reaching down, she took both of his hands and looked deeply into his eyes, until some of the harshness left his face and his breathing leveled out. "Christian . . . please, let it go. Let *her* go. There are those who want t' make ye feel again. Those who want t' prove t' ye tha' t'ye *are* whole; those who want t' make ye feel loved, cherished. . . ."

He shut his eyes and turned his head on the pillow, away from her. His mouth was a grim slash of pain. "Go *away,*" he said.

"Nay, Christian. I cannot, and I will not. Ye need me."

"I *don't* need you. I don't need *anyone.*"

"Well, I need *you.*" Her soft hands moved over his face, smoothing his hair, stoking a fire in his blood and an ache in his heart that was becoming increasingly painful by the moment. "I need that golden-haired lieutenant who came t' Connemara, a man who laughed an' smiled an' took th' time t' calm a wee lass! Where is that man now, Christian?"

"He died five years ago," he said harshly, not daring to open his eyes and face the grim sword of truth she carried.

"Nay, I see him still. I see him in th' captain who tries so hard t' appear cold and distant, yet who croons t' and cuddles a little dog when he thinks no one be lookin'. I see him in th' man who cannot stand t' see anythin' helpless an' hurt. I see him in th' officer who follows Royal Navy customs an' rules t' th' letter, but who hasn't th' heart t' have an offender whipped. Oh, no. That man's still in there." She laid her palm across his heart and pressed hard. "Right *here.* He just needs someone t' show him out o' th' prison he's locked himself in!"

"There is no way out of this prison, this *hell*, Deirdre! Now go, damn you! Just—bloody—*go!*"

His features were twisted with pain, fear, and anger. Deirdre reached out and touched the harsh plane of his cheek, his jaw, feeling the muscles tensing just beneath. "Ye're just afraid t' be lettin' anyone even near th' door o' yer prison t' try t' fit a key t' it, Christian," she said softly. "Please, I beg o' ye, let *me* try."

"Why should you care? After what I've bloody well done to you?"

"Christian ... ye didn't *want* t' do what ye did t' me brother those thirteen years ago. I didn't know it then, but I know it now. Ye're a product o' th' Navy. Ye live by its rules, its principles. The Navy is yer life. Maybe even more so since ye lost yer Emily. maybe it's somethin' for ye t' escape t', so ye don't have t' face the pain." She felt him wince, and knew she'd struck a nerve. Her fingers tightened around his. "Ye can't hide forever, Christian. Ye got t' come out an' face life. 'Tis the only way t' get rid o' th' pain, th' guilt. Th' demons that give ye th' nightmares."

"I still took your brother. That's a ghastly, devilish fact, no matter how I feel about it!"

"Nay, Christian, th' *Navy* took me brother. If I be blamin' anyone for takin' him, 'tis them, not you."

She laid her knuckles gently across his jaw. Her fingertips grazed his cheek, brushed the soft fan of his lower lashes, and traced the severe line of his lips. "I forgive ye, Christian. I told ye that. I also told ye I love ye. Wha' 't'else do I have t' do t' get ye t' smile? T' open yer arms, yer heart ... that door to yer prison?"

She bent down and placed her lips against his brow. He shuddered violently. The crucifix slipped free of her shirt and lay heavily against his chest, the gold glittering no more than the burnished hairs it rested against. She felt him tensing beneath her, every muscle rock-hard and tight. She felt him blink his eyes, the tips of his lashes grazing the sensitive underside of her throat. She felt the pulse beating at his temple where her lips touched the faded bruise and nuzzled the soft whorls of bright hair there. "I'll be sayin' it again,

Christian, 'cause I'm a-thinkin' we both be needin' t' hear it."

He opened his eyes, trembling as she leaned back, cupped his face in her hands, and looked deeply into his eyes.

"I love ye, Christian."

"Deirdre—"

"Did ye hear me? I said *I love ye.*"

He shut his eyes against the quick sting of tears, vowing that he would die before he'd let her see him succumb to five years of pent-up emotion.

But she was determined to force it out of him. Her voice whispered against his cheeks; her fresh, soapy scent filled his nostrils. "For an Englishman, ye be very handsome, d'ye know that, Christian? 'Specially when ye smile. Ye just need someone t' make ye do it more often."

"Stop, Deirdre. In the name of God, leave me. . . ."

"And ye need someone t' bring ye laughter an' joy, someone t' be makin' a big fuss o'er ye an' tellin' ye how special ye be."

His chest quivered with the supreme amount of will it took to control his emotion.

"And . . . and ye need someone t' . . . t' hug ye." She gathered her curly fall of hair, draped it over one narrow shoulder, slowly bent down, and touched her lips to his with agonizing innocence, gentleness, and yes, love.

Don't do this to me, he thought wildly, desperately, as her arms wrapped fiercely around him, cradling the injured shoulder with overwhelming tenderness. *Don't shatter these defenses . . . they're all I bloody well have.*

Her kiss deepened, warm and soft and sweet. He felt the tears stinging the back of his throat, filling the huge, ragged hole in his chest where his heart used to lay, swelling it until he thought his ribs would burst. His fists clenched at his side, the short nails driving into the callused palms as he fought to control himself. He did not trust himself to touch her, not even to push her away. He did not trust himself to move. He did not trust himself to—

"*I love ye,*" she said, slowly pulling away.

Where her lips had touched his, it felt cold and empty and awful.

"D'ye want me, Christian?"

"Go away . . . go away, please. . . ."

He felt her thumb stroking the corner of his cheekbone. There was no friction there, only a slipperiness, and he knew he had already lost control of his tears.

"Do ye, Christian?"

"Dear God," he whispered, "I . . . I want you more than I've wanted any woman since *her* . . . maybe more, even, than I wanted—"

Emily.

"Ye can say it, Christian. I'll not be judgin' ye."

"Em"—He gulped and swallowed. "Emily."

She laid both hands against the sides of his face, and he felt her lips against his brow, her hair draping his head like a veil.

" 'Tis all right, Christian."

He was shaking like a child, terrified of a force greater than himself, a force he could not control. *She* was that force, and the weapon she wielded was love.

It was devastating him. Blowing his defenses to hell. Ripping down these last, final barriers that, once stormed, would leave his heart open and bare and as vulnerable as a merchantman's decks beneath the guns of a warship.

Her lips moved over his brows, and he felt her soft breath fluttering warmly against his skin. "What are ye afraid of, Christian? Lettin' go o' th' guilt? The chance that ye might be feelin' somethin' for another? The fact that ye just *might* be able t' perform as a man?"

He couldn't move. The final bit of mortar that held the wall around his heart together was slowly crumbling.

Tumbling.

Crashing to the feet of this young girl.

"Is it, Christian? Is it what ye're afraid of?"

She had saved his life, when she'd had every reason to hate him enough to see him dead. She had dug a musket ball out of his shoulder—not with the steel probe, not with the harshness of a cold piece of metal, but with the loving gentleness of her fingers.

She had said she loved him.

"Aye," he whispered. "That's what I'm afraid of. All of that. Not one or the other . . . but all of it."

She put her palms against his chest, and pushed herself back so that she could gaze down at his face. "Ye be a man for admittin' that, Christian. And I'll not be abusin' yer trust, nor will I hurt ye. D'ye remember how ye refused th' surgeon's rum because ye didn't want t' let down yer guard, and let th' others see ye helpless? D'ye remember how ye let down yer guard with *me?* Ye *trusted* me then, Christian, and I didn't betray that trust. Would it be so very hard t' trust me again?"

Dear God. . . .

"If ye return me love, then show me, Christian. For th' love o' God, don't be afraid o' me."

His fists were hard knots at his sides, his muscles coiled so tightly he felt them cramping. Every nerve was strung to the breaking point, and his heartbeat pounded in his ears.

Something plopped upon his chest. Something hot and wet and tickling. His eyes dragged open, and through his own blurry vision he saw tears streaming down her pale cheeks. Wetness spiked her lashes, and her proud Gaelic face was stamped with the pain, and fear, of rejection.

She tried to grin to cover it. "I also need someone t' make *me* smile," she whispered. "For ye see, Christian . . . I . . . I need hugs, too."

"I'm not worthy, Deirdre." He balled his fists at his sides. "By God, *I am not worthy!*"

"Hug me, Christian. Everyone needs t' be hugged."

He needed no encouragement, and she felt his powerful arms come up to enfold her. At first, it was merely a cold embrace, a wary embrace, a reluctant embrace; then, as though a floodgate had been opened, she felt savage, desperate pressure as he clasped her to him with a strength that nearly broke her ribs.

"I forgive ye, Christian," she whispered, burying her wet cheek against his hair. "By all that's holy, I forgive ye. Sweet Jesus, Christian, I—I *love* ye."

He clung to her, his hand coming up to cup the back of her head.

"Did ye hear me?" Her arms tightened around his ribs. "I

love ye, Christian." Her lips moved against his neck, playing with the spun strands of pale hair. "Ye don't have t' be tellin' me ye love me back, ye just have t' be huggin' me. 'Tis all I be askin' o' ye. Hug me back, Christian. . . ."

His arms tightened, nearly cutting off her breath. His powerful body gave a huge, trembling shudder, then began to quake.

" 'Tis all right, Christian." She wrapped her arms around him, hugging him, rocking him, holding him, loving him. "No wound's ever healed till th' poison comes out. Yers has been festerin' for five long years. Ain't no shame in lettin' it go."

"I . . . I've not forgiven myself, Deirdre. She haunts my dreams every night. I see her face in the flames . . . I hear her screams as she's dying . . . *dear God, I smell her burning.*" Harsh sobs racked him, and she felt his pain as her own, felt her own tears running hotly down her cheeks and splashing upon his proud shoulders.

"She's dead, Christian," she said gently, pressing her cheek against his hair. "Nothin' ye say or do can bring her back. Ain't no reason t' sacrifice th' rest o' yer life t' her memory. Ye be healthy and whole. If the good Lord didn't want ye t' live, he'd have taken ye, too. Such decisions aren't ours t' question, merely t' accept."

Her hands, gently and soothing, roved down the hard, tight curve of his back. He clung to her as though he could never let her go, ashamed that she should see him thus: he, a proud and decorated sea warrior, veteran of countless battles, laid low and sobbing in the arms of a woman.

She's dead, Christian.

The words slammed brutally into him, hard.

Dead. Powerless. Unable to enter his nightmares unless he allowed it. Unable to torment him unless he permitted it. Unable to harm him, hurt him, haunt him, unless he wanted it. For five long years he had allowed it, yes, even *wanted* it, as punishment for his failure to get her out of the burning house, as punishment for leaving her for so long while he was away at sea. The nightmares, the guilt, the grief— Emily had not done that to him; *he* had done it to himself.

Something opened in his soul, like huge black clouds fil-

ing out after a heavy storm. Sunlight broke tremulously
through, gathering brightness, intensity, until its blinding
warmth shone down upon him and wrapped itself around
his heart. He saw Emily's face, lingering briefly; then she
was gone, clean, healthy wind swirling the leaves where her
feet had been, sunlight filling the place were she had stood,
until it became so bright he couldn't look at it.

That sunshine was wrapped around him, holding him in
her arms.

Hugging him.

Loving him.

"Deirdre," he breathed, and on a broken, victorious sob,
claimed her lips with his own.

Chapter 20

She was the one to finally break the kiss, not because she
wanted to, but because she was starting to black out for
want of air.

In her innocence, she didn't realize that she was supposed
to breathe.

"Oh, Christian," she murmured, her hand coming up to
touch her lips.

He stared at her, shocked by the crushing, overwhelming
realization of love he felt for her—and the fact that his manhood had not diminished in size in the least, but had, if anything, grown harder. Larger.

His mouth went dry and he began to shake.

In her own newfound discovery of sensation, she didn't
realize what the simple act of kissing had done to—and
for—him. She glanced up, her face flushed, the tears already drying on her face. "Christian, I'd be dearly lovin' t'
do that again with ye, as soon as I get me air back," she

gasped, placing her hand over her heart and staring at him with wide purple eyes. "Truly, I would. . . ."

Her comment caught him off guard, and the corners of his mouth began to twitch. "Dear girl, have you tried breathing?"

"While *kissin'*?"

"It would certainly help."

"But . . . but *how?*"

His mouth lowered to hers, and his arm tightened around her shoulders, his fingers twining in the spiraling curls of her hair. "Like this."

Again his lips claimed hers, infinitely tender, gentle, yet demanding. She wiggled closer to him. His tongue slipped into her mouth, hesitantly at first, then growing bolder with confidence. She leaned into him, her heart beginning to pound, the strange heat between her thighs threading its way up her belly. *Breathe.* She sucked in a great lungful of air, and drove her mouth wetly, inexpertly, against his. She had it now. She was breathing, all right, and breathing hard.

So was he.

He dragged his mouth away from hers, and when she looked up into his face, she saw that his eyes were dark and hazy, heavy-lidded and intense—and that he was smiling. In relief, in triumph . . . in wonder.

"Deirdre," he said simply, and touched her cheek.

He was gazing at her as though he had just discovered something wondrous, beautiful, revered. She saw his throat move, his eyes roving over every detail of her face, and felt the deep, inner shuddering of his big body. Against her cheek, his hand began to tremble, and she shut her eyes as his thumb dipped beneath her chin, lifting it until his lips claimed her once more. His fingers stroked the soft underside of her jaw, then dragged down her throat, the slope of her shoulders, and even the length of the gold chain that hung around her neck.

Slowly he pulled away, the crucifix resting in his broad palm, his head bent, and a fringe of pale hair falling over his brow as he gazed down at the cross and rubbed his finger over the intricate design of its surface.

"It never leaves me," she said, feeling a need to explain.

"I know."

" 'Tis part o' me ... part o' me heritage ... I'll *never* take it off!"

He looked up then, smiled, and gently let the crucifix fall back against her shirt. Then he leaned close, his nearness making her blood go to butter, her bones to water. His lips touched her brow, and his breath grew warm against her temple. "Indeed, dear girl, I should not wish you to. It is as much a part of you as ... as that bottle of Irish seawater, or the bread that Tildy ate."

"Aye, Christian," she said soberly. " 'Tis more than a part o' me. 'Tis a part o' *Ireland.*"

He gathered her close, pressing her tightly against his chest. She shut her eyes again, her chin just touching his bandaged shoulder, every nerve in her body jumping, every inch of her skin tingling. Neither spoke. The silence stretched on, until it became awkward for both of them; he, knowing what he wanted but afraid of failing himself and her; she, knowing what she wanted but afraid to push him too far, too fast. The sea washed around the rudder, and they felt the gentle sway of the ship, heard the strains of a chantey from somewhere above their heads. And they became painfully aware of each other: he, of her soft, soapy scent, a strand of hair that was tangled in his lashes, the swell of her breasts against his bare chest; she, of the hard muscles of his shoulder beneath the bandage, a little scar on the side of his neck only an inch from her nose, the salty scent of his skin and the thump of his heartbeat against her own.

"I"—he swallowed hard—"I do not know if I ... if I can do this, Deirdre."

She pulled back slightly and looked into his eyes. Fear and anguish, doubt and indecision, were etched into the severe planes of his face, the tightness of his mouth. Gently, she said, "If ye can't, Christian ... there be only the two of us t' ever know abou' t'it."

He glanced away, biting his lip and staring at the checked flooring, oblivious of the shouts that drifted down from topside, the boom of canvas, the creaking of yards. Long moments went by, and she sensed the inner war he was waging; for him, the courage he had to muster for this most manly of acts, this most supreme test of his masculinity, must be far more than that of sending a ship into battle.

And then he raised his head and looked at her, his voice commanding and direct.

"Go lock the door, Deirdre."

Her heart fluttering, she slid from the bed and did as he bade. It took her a moment to accomplish the task, so badly was her hand shaking. She laid her palm against the door to steady herself, took a deep breath, and turned slowly to face him, suddenly aware of the sensuous feel of her hair, falling in thick, riotous disarray around her shoulders and back and breasts.

He smiled, a slow, lupine smile that robbed the strength from her knees.

"Come here, Deirdre."

His eyes were dark and intense. Shivering, she wrapped her arms around herself and moved back across the cabin to where he lay, her gaze never leaving his. Every sensation was heightened, acute: the scent of tar and wood and salt spray; the taste of nervous anticipation in her mouth; the fear and eagerness of the unknown; the chill of the air, the squeak of the decking beneath her shoes, the thunderous echo of her heartbeat in her ears.

He raised his hand, stopping her several feet away from the bed.

"Deirdre, dear girl. . . ." His voice was hoarse, shaky, a direct contrast to the boldness of his eye. "I think this is the last chance I shall have to tell you to leave."

She shivered and hugged herself tighter, knowing that despite his injured shoulder, his fears, and his tenuous, slipping grasp on his standards of behavior as an officer and a gentleman, he would never let her leave the cabin.

Not now.

She walked straight up to him and into his arms. "I don't *want* t' leave, Christian. Not now . . . not ever."

"Ah, Deirdre," he murmured thickly, pulling her down with him. "Against every principle I hold dear, against every rule I enforce, against every shred of my conscience, my morals, my better judgment . . . you have broken me."

She cradled his head in her hands, shamelessly kissing his cheek, his jaw, the corners of his mouth.

"By God, never did I think it would happen, but you, dear girl, have done me in."

She slid her arms beneath his neck and kissed him, her mouth moving fervently against his. Beneath her shirt, his hands—shaking with anticipation, trembling with need—cradled her breasts, teased the nipples, burned a path over her skin. She kicked off her shoes, heard them thump on the deck flooring, and broke the kiss long enough for him to coax her shirt over her head, the trousers following it on its way to the floor. Cold air swept against her skin; his palm roved over her bottom, down her thighs, and then he pulled her protectively close and under the covers with him.

The heat of his powerful body was like a furnace. She molded herself to it, his chest rough beneath her naked breasts, the rocky muscles of his arm pulling her even closer. Her toes curled with pleasure, and she quivered in eagerness as he drew the blanket up to their chins, encasing them in warmth and making her feel delightfully wicked and wanton in the knowledge that they were both shamelessly naked beneath.

She felt his breath, warm against her nose and cheeks and brow. Fire blazed between her thighs and her breasts tingled with a gnawing ache. Anticipation rocked her body, and suddenly she realized that now it was she who was shaking, he whose hands were confident and masterful.

"Yer shoulder," she said weakly.

"Bugger my shoulder." Beneath the blanket she felt his palm trailing down her arm and over the concave dip of her hip. "I know what it is capable of."

Face-to-face on the pillow, they gazed into each other's eyes, touching each other beneath the covers and feeling dampness break out on their skin. Hard male muscle burned against soft female flesh. Breaths intermingled, became one. Never had Deirdre experienced the sensation of a male body against hers, and the feeling left her deliciously weak. She was aware of the mat of his chest hair against her breasts; the heaviness of one hard, muscled leg thrown possessively over her thigh; the scrape of his foot as it moved up and down her calf, dragging star bursts of pleasure with it. . . .

And the feel of his manhood—strong, rigid, powerful, and pulsing with life—against her soft belly.

She reached down beneath the covers and touched it, feeling it throb with response; but he gently drew her hand away, guiding it upward and murmuring that she must not rush things. Her fingers splayed against the massive block of his chest, tangling in the mat of crisp hair as his hand moved over her tingling skin. Her breathing grew harsh, raspy, erratic with each new spot he touched, each previously unexplored inch of flesh.

"Oh, Christian—" She choked on a sob of pleasure. "If only ye knew how much I love ye. . . ."

Gently he pushed her onto her back and gazed lovingly into her face before bending to kiss her tears away. "And I love you, too, dear girl. I have for a long time."

Supporting his weight on his good side, he leaned over her, his hand pushing the blanket down her belly and leaving it bunched above her knees. She shut her eyes, trembling as he rained gentle kisses over her face, her lips, her fluttering eyelids.

She shivered violently, and not from the chill of the cabin.

"Relax, dear girl," he murmured, remembering that she was an innocent virgin. "Just relax. You have taught me how to hug, how to smile, how to trust. Now let me show you what it feels like to be cherished, adored, worshipped . . . loved."

Deirdre melted inside.

Unsure what to do, she settled back, quaking at the vibrant bursts of sensation each touch of his hand, each press of his lips, brought her. She felt the hard calluses of his palms rasping over her collarbone, her breasts, the rise of her ribs, and the sweet curve of her hips. His mouth grazed her cheek, leaving hot, tingly kisses in its wake; then he kissed her, gently at first, then fiercely, drawing the very breath and soul from her with the searing intensity of his desire. Fear filled her, fear that she was not behaving the way she was supposed to, that she might do something wrong, that in doing so she might upset the delicate balance that he was so afraid he would lose.

But the Lord and Master seemed to have no such concern.

He lifted his head again, his harsh breathing making the wide breadth of his powerful chest rise and fall. "I am going to kiss you now, Deirdre."

"But . . . wasn't that what ye were just doin'?"

"I have only just *begun* kissing you, love."

She shut her eyes tightly, quivering and hot inside, as his mouth roved deliciously over hers once more. And kiss her he did—her forehead, her brows, the base of her nose, her earlobes, her cheeks, her fluttering lashes, the coarse spirals of her hair. He lifted each of her hands and kissed the cups of her palms; he kissed the inside of her wrists, the inside of her elbows, the inside of her arms, until gooseflesh puckered her skin and little feathery sensations darted through her belly and twined between her thighs. Slowly, he lowered her arm, and bent to take her mouth once more. She felt his thumb rasping over her jaw, cupping her chin; she felt it grazing the wildly beating pulse at her throat as his lips left hers and began to move slowly over her chin, down the inside of her throat, nibbling here, kissing there, burning everywhere.

His breath was hot against her skin, and she felt moisture gathering in her palms, atop her brow, over every inch of her burning flesh. He nuzzled the crucifix aside and dropped kisses between her breasts, then grazed one aching nipple with his lips, his tongue slipping out to lap at the erect bud.

She bolted upright, gasping.

"Lie back, foundling."

"Are ye *supposed* t' kiss me there?"

"Yes, love. I'm supposed to kiss you *everywhere.*"

"But, Christian, I don't know if ye should. I mean it's been five years, an' ye might be forgettin' just where ye're supposed t' be kissin'—"

He bent his head once more, his laughter bubbling against one swelling mound and teasing her nipple into throbbing, aching hardness. "I've not forgotten a single blessed thing, dear girl." He looked up, touched her cheek to reassure her, and pressed firmly against her shoulder to coax her back down to the bed. "Now, relax . . . or do you not enjoy this?"

"I . . . I'm scared, Christian."

One brow arched, and his eyes were gently mocking and glinting with amusement. "Shall I stop?"

"N-nay!"

He smiled then, and never had she thought a man could be more handsome than her Lord and Master. And then she forgot all else as his head lowered once more, his lips playing with her tightened nipple until the fire between her thighs became unbearable. She sucked her lips between her teeth and touched tremulous fingers to his hair, crushing the pale locks in her fist as the pressure of his lips became a little less gentle, a little less hesitant, a little less restrained. . . .

His mouth moved to the other breast, and she gasped as she felt the hot-cool wetness of his tongue tease the pink nipple into tight, hard perkiness.

"Christian, Christian, I'm *scared!*"

"You're doing devilishly fine . . . relax."

She stiffened as his tongue traced circles over the pouting crest, his hand pushing the swelling mound up to his mouth so that he could better taste it. Her senses reeled, and with something like terror she felt his hard palm skimming down the inside curves of her waist, nearing that aching, throbbing, burning part of her that was now pulsing with every beat of her heart.

His mouth left her breast, and cool air rushed in to take its place. His hand traced gentle circles over her belly as he eased himself onto his side, resting his weight on his good shoulder while his admiring eyes swept over her.

"Do not be shy, love," he murmured. "Your beauty is unsurpassed."

"But—but, Christian, I don't know wha' 't'I'm supposed t' *do,*" she said, her voice desperate with fear.

He smiled, a soft, patient, lazy smile that warmed her heart. His hand slid over her belly, fanned her breasts, came up to knuckle her cheek. "Deirdre, you needn't *do* anything . . . yet. Next time, maybe, but for now . . . for now, just let the captain be in command . . . eh?"

She took a deep, shaky breath, feeling that male part of him pressing against her thigh like a hard board. "Aye, Christian. Ye teach, and I'll do me best t' learn." She shut her eyes, stiffened her arms at her sides, and waited.

She heard him chuckling above her, felt his hand playing with a long, spiraling curl that trailed over her shoulder as he allowed her time to get used to the feel of a man's hand and mouth against her virgin flesh.

"Shall we proceed, m' lady?"

She shivered as his thumb circled her nipple. "Aye, Christian—after one last, wee request."

He rose onto his elbow, the wide, powerful breadth of his chest and shoulders blotting out the deckhead above. "Yes?"

She gazed up at him, pressing her arms to her sides. "Which way . . . is Ireland?"

His hand stopped abruptly. *"Ireland?"*

"Aye." Sheepishly, she added, "I need t' know which direction it be in so that when this monumental thing ye're goin' t' do t' me happens, me face can be turned toward it."

He stared at her. A corner of his mouth twitched with delighted amusement. Then his handsome face crumpled and rich, heady laughter tumbled out of his chest. "Bless me, Deirdre, nowhere on this earth is there anyone like you. Ireland lies far beneath the horizon, and at your feet. Precisely where it should be." His laughter faded away, and he stared down at her, his gray eyes becoming soft with love once more. "Now, pray, is there anything else you demand of me?"

"Aye, Christian."

Her hand came up to tremulously touch his rough cheek.

"And that is, my dear, homesick little boglander?"

"I want ye t' keep kissin' me."

Laughing, he claimed her lips, drinking of the honeyed sweetness of her young and innocent mouth. Her arms wound around his neck, and he knew that his time was limited. The sweet anguish was growing harder and harder to bear, and it was all he could do to restrain himself as he moved his hands over her trembling body, soothing her, calming her, teasing her . . . arousing her.

Five long years since he'd had a woman. Five long years

since Emily had been taken from him. He cringed, waiting for his dead wife's face to appear before him and smash his desire to helpless pulp. But there was only the loveliness of the young Irish girl beneath him, only the pale and untried sweetness of her body, only the reverent adoration in her wide purple eyes that drove through his heart and wrapped itself around his hungry soul.

He pressed his face into the curve of her shoulder, burying his nose in her fragrant curls as his hand caressed her belly and his fingers twined in the soft, silky curls at the junction of her thighs. She clamped her legs together, instinctively, her whole body going tense.

"Open, love," he murmured against her neck. "Open, and let me touch you."

"It . . . it tickles, Christian!"

He drew back, forcing himself to go slow and easy with her. But his staff was hot and throbbing, driving itself against the outside of her thigh and begging for release.

Control, Christian, he told himself. *Just go slow.*

"Oh, Christian, are ye *sure* ye're doin' this right? Are ye sure ye haven't forgotten anythin'?"

Once more his fingers explored the silky triangle between her thighs, threading through the soft curls, seeking her opening. She tightened, shivering with fear and longing, the lips of her womanhood clamping around his gently questing fingers.

"I'm sure, Deirdre. It won't hurt . . . I promise you."

She relaxed enough that he could drag his fingers down, down, down . . . then she tensed and gasped as he slid a finger between the soft folds of her womanhood and stroked her gently. A groan tore from his own throat at the wonderful, heady feel of her, for she was soft and warm and wet and ready. Heat rocked his throbbing groin, and he drove his mouth against the curve of her neck, his breath hot against her hair, his fingers smearing her dampness through the silky curls of her womanhood.

She pushed herself upward against his hand. From somewhere, he heard her soft voice: "Aye, Christian . . . aye, it feels good, real good, just like ye said i' 'twould. . . ."

"It will feel better, dear girl, in a moment."

"Oh, Christian, I don't think it *can* feel better. It—it feels too good now—"

His thumb found the hard, swollen bud of her womanhood, gently kneaded it—and proved her wrong. Something like a sob burst from her and her slight body twisted, writhed, heaved upon the bed. He pressed his lips against her neck, kissing her feverishly.

Breathing hard, he raised himself and gazed at this precious, lovely creature beneath him. Her hair swirled around her face, her eyes were tightly closed, her lip was caught between her teeth. Shakily, he leaned down, kissed her mouth, and stroked her damp femininity until tears of joy streamed down her cheeks.

"I love ye, Christian . . . I love ye, Christian . . . oh, God, I love ye. . . ."

He was losing control of himself. He knew it as surely as he knew the sun would rise on the morrow, and it felt blessedly, wonderfully, beautiful—

"Oh, Christian, love me harder. Show me tha' 't'ye love me as much as I love you. . . . I *need* ye, Christian, dear God in heaven, I need ye. . . ."

May God help me, he thought, and then, on shaky limbs, the Lord and Master raised his powerful, bronzed body above her and closed his eyes, the sight of the crucifix the last thing he saw before he abandoned all hesitations, all good sense, and all gentlemanly intentions he'd sought to employ.

With a harsh groan, he leaned back and slowly drove his knee between her clamped thighs. She turned her head, her breath feathering against his wrist; he felt her lips move fervently over his skin, kissing him, loving him, tasting him, as her gentle tears ran down her cheek and wet the back of his hand.

He gazed at her perfectly formed breasts, her taut, creamy belly, the soft indentation of her navel, the silky black triangle between her thighs. Then he stared down at his manhood.

He was ready. By God, he had never been *more* ready.

"Open for me, love," he commanded.

His knee pressed harder, and she gasped as he slowly,

carefully, lowered himself. Dragging her eyes open, she saw such a tortured look upon his rigid features that swift, unexpected terror surged through her. "Oh, Christian, will it be hurtin' ye?"

The gray eyes shot open, heavy-lidded and drugged with passion. "Nay, dear girl . . . but it may hurt you."

"Do it, Christian. Do whatever ye have t', t' make me yers."

" 'Twill hurt, Deirdre . . . but I shall try my best to be gentle."

"Don't try anythin', Christian, just *do* it!"

His fair head bowed, the handsome, sun-bleached locks tumbling down over his brow as he grasped his manhood in one unsteady hand and slowly guided it to the entrance of her womanhood. She tensed, waiting for pain, feeling only gentle pressure and exquisite sensation as the velvety head slipped gently between her hot and moist folds. He released himself and leaned forward, favoring his shoulder as he slowly, carefully, slid himself into her. She felt him give a mighty shudder, as though the effort was too much for him, and saw his features go rigid with concentration.

And then he stopped, his great body quivering as if on the verge of something tremendous.

"Christian?"

She felt his hot breath against the curve of her neck and shoulder, heard it rasping in her ear. "I can go no further, Deirdre . . . without taking your maidenhead."

Sweet, delicious sensations rippled through her. "I don't *want* me maidenhead anymore, Christian. 'Tis yers. *I'm* yers. *Make* me yers, Christian. . . ."

He needed no further invitation nor encouragement. His hand tangled in her hair, anchoring her head as his mouth claimed hers and his tongue plunged between her lips. She moaned, arching upward to meet his kiss. Then he tensed, drew back, and drove himself into her.

The pain was searing, a lance of white fire. She drove herself upward, meeting it bravely, boldly, and gratefully. Slowly, the pain died away, faded away, trickled away on waves of dampness that ran hotly between her thighs, and as it left her, she realized that in its place was a depth of feeling so intense, so agonizingly wonderful, that she thought she would die from it.

And now he was thrusting himself into her, pulling out, thrusting in, and building a rhythm that made her writhe with sweet agony. His tongue melded with hers, his mouth ground against her lips, his hand gathered her hair and crushed it in his fist. Faster and faster he moved, no longer gentle and slow, no longer able to take his time. His breathing came faster. Harsher. Hotter. Moisture broke out between straining bodies. Breath mingled and mixed, became one—

"Don't *stop*, Christian!" she cried, her head whipping on the pillow. "Dear God, don't stop!"

It started. She felt it in the deepest, darkest, most hidden recesses of her body, her soul, building, pulsing, welling up and up—

"Christian!"

—peaking, climbing, bursting—

"Christia-a-a-n!"

She arched up to meet him, her senses exploding and sucking her body upward, outward, and violently into his. Her hands clawed at his back, her nails sank into his skin, and she clung to him, sobbing, as her thighs spasmed uncontrollably and her legs clamped fiercely around him. His body went rigid, his head falling back, and with a mighty, savage lunge, he drew back and slammed himself fully into her, impaling her to the root of his manhood. She felt his seed, pulsing and throbbing and ebbing inside her, and it brought another glorious release, another cresting wave of sweet agony that left her sobbing into the pillow.

Exhausted, triumphant, he sank down beside her, breathing hard. She thought she felt him sobbing, or perhaps he was laughing; she could not be sure.

Slowly, the burning sensation faded away, and something huge and wonderful filled her heart and radiated out through her blood, her fingertips, her toes, the nerve endings of her skin. He threw his arm possessively over her waist and drew her close, until she was pressed against his chest, his still-pounding heart.

"Deirdre?"

"Aye, Christian?"

A long moment went by in which the only sound was their intermingled breathing, the fading sounds of their heartbeats.

He raised his head and looked at her, and his eyes were moist.

"Thank you."

Chapter 21

"**D**on't know wot the two of 'em are doin' down there, but I think ye might wanna go get the cap'n and tell 'im we've just sighted land off the starboard bows."

"*I* ken what they be doing, Skunk," Ian said importantly. "The same thing they've been doing for the past five days. Let 'em be. A wee bit of female companionship is just what our cold and aloof Lord and Master needs to warm up a bit."

Ian turned away, shading his eyes as he stared out over the thousands of diamondlike waves, all dancing and jumping in the cold sunlight. The frigate dipped into a trough, heaved herself up again, and impatiently tossed spray over her bows. But there, it was unmistakable. A thin purplish line penciled atop the horizon of blue, blue sea.

Land.

As the two littlest midshipmen waved at a sea gull that winged overhead and then fell to giggling, the men crowded the gangway and gathered at the rail, staring out at it. The officers took out their spyglasses, bracing their elbows against the shrouds as they eagerly sought their first glance of the American colonies.

For a crew who had left England hating their new commanding officer, their change in attitude toward him and their vessel was nothing short of astounding. Ever since the heated engagement in which they'd taken the corvette, pride in themselves and their ship had run rampant. Men at their watches sang "Hearts of Oak." Hibbert was as likely to be found in a clean uniform as a rumpled one, Skunk no longer grumbled while scrubbing the decks each morning, Teach had taken it upon himself to care for Tildy and her puppies, and Ian diligently oversaw daily gun practice.

But as for their strict disciplinarian of a captain, the idea of him being in love was an endearing and vastly amusing one, and there was not a soul aboard the frigate who didn't watch the blossoming romance with a keen mental telescope—and comment upon it daily. Oddly, this rough group of seasoned tars felt strangely protective of the growing feelings between their commanding offfcer and his Irish girl, and though most of them were a good deal younger than he, they saw themselves as protectors of those fragile seeds of newfound love.

Of course, such feelings of mutual protectiveness—the Lord and Master watching over them in battle, and the seamen watching over his romance with the girl—went far to foster the sort of respect, liking, and loyalty that every captain strives for between himself and his men—and which no captain of HMS *Bold Marauder* had ever enjoyed.

Until now.

"Yeah, 'bout time someone thawed the Ice Captain," Teach remarked, crossing his arms and leaning his bulk against one of the boats snugged securely in the frigate's waist. He gave a sly grin. "God knows even our skillful Delight couldn't do it!"

"Heard she tried, though," Milton Lee put in.

"And failed."

Skunk waved his hand and scoffed, "Delight ain't his type."

"The captain and Deirdre belong together," Elwin snapped. "Any fool can see that!"

"Still, isn't it something, the two of 'em being in love." Ian rubbed his beard, and his eyes grew reflective. "And tae think how much our bonnie Irish lassie hated our very British captain when she first came aboard."

"To think how much we *all* hated him," Teach added,

with an expression of mixed shame and puzzlement that was echoed by his companions.

They stared down at their shoes, and even Skunk distractedly kicked at the deck seams. Finally he said, "Ah, but the girl's good for him. She makes him smile. She makes him mad. She makes him anythin' but emotionless."

"Aye, I've actually heard him *laughing*," Rhodes said, craning his neck as he gazed out over the whitecaps toward the distant land. "Can you imagine?"

Ian laughed. " 'Bout bluidy time!"

"Hey, Ian," Wenham said, "in all seriousness, if you want to make our commanding officer happy, *do* send someone to tell him we just sighted land. By my reckoning," he added, looking down at his chart and tracing the coastline with his finger, "it's Cape Cod. The captain'll want to make the ship presentable for his admiral."

"Presentable?" Ian drew himself up, peeved about being reminded of his duty. "What's wrong with her? I doona see anything amiss!"

Rhodes coughed and raised a mocking brow. "Salutes, and the like, Ian?"

Skunk nodded. *"Ceremony* stuff. Things *we* don't know nothin' about."

"Of course," Ian said, flushing and puffing out his chest. "Hibbert!"

Like some of the others, the youth had a spyglass to his eye. However, his was not trained toward the distant land, but up at the maintop, where Delight had gone to share a "picnic lunch" with one of the marines.

"Hibbert!" Ian roared, purpling with rage. " 'Tis angry ye be making me! Get yer wee tail over here before I thrash ye to within an inch of yer life!"

Flushing hotly, Hibbert snapped the glass closed and came to stand next to his lieutenant.

"Aye?"

"That's 'Aye, *sir*,' and doona be forgetting it!" He glared fiercely down at the boy, his hands fisted against his hips, his red beard blowing in the wind. "Now, go rouse the captain. Give him my respects, and tell him we be nearing Cape Cod."

Hibbert frowned, snapped off a sloppy salute, and with a last, wistful glance up toward the maintop, went below.

"Wot was 'e looking at, anyhow?" Skunk murmured, scowling as he tipped his oily head back and stared aloft. But there was nothing to be seen up there but acres of proudly set, pale yellow sails, bloated with wind and pushing HMS *Bold Marauder* on a steady course toward Boston.

"Christian."

He lay beside her, one well-muscled arm thrown possessively over her ribs and anchoring her slight body to his hard one, his face turned into the mass of curling black ringlets that toppled over her shoulder and spilled onto the pillow.

She hated to wake him. But the timid knocking on the door was not going away.

"Christian!" she hissed.

Sweet Mary, the man slept like the dead! She wriggled out from beneath the heavy weight of his arm, let him settle into the space where her body had been, and dipped her head to press gentle kisses atop the hard rise of his handsome shoulder, where a fresh bandage stood clean and white against his golden skin. Her fingers twined in the fringe of fair, curling hair that curled boyishly against the back of his neck; her palm smoothed it away from his temple. He was warm and heavy and heartbreakingly handsome. Just looking at him made the burning sensations start up between her thighs again.

The knocking came louder.

"Christian!" She put a hand against his arm and shook him. His heavy, regulated breathing didn't change. She stared down at him, realizing that, for the first time since she'd known him, he had not had the nightmares.

No wonder he slept so peacefully.

The knocking on the door became quiet. "Captain?"

Hibbert. Desperately, Deirdre leaned down, nuzzled aside the golden waves of hair, and put her lips against his ear. "Christian, me love. Wake up! Yer men be wantin' ye!"

He made an unintelligible noise, reached out, and hauled her close to his body. "Don't leave me, Dee. . . ."

"Wake *up!*" she hissed, wishing she could strangle Hibbert for disturbing their newfound happiness.

He groaned and turned over, his gray eyes opening to regard her with lazy adoration. "What is it, dear girl, that you invade my dreams and rouse me from sleep?"

"Yer dreams?" She laughed. "I hope I'm in them!"

He reached up, captured a thick, spiraling curl, and pressed it to his lips, smiling, his gaze warmly holding hers. "Yes, love, you are in them. I daresay you are the mistress of my dreams. . . ."

"And y' be th' master o' mine. Stop, Christian!" she gasped as he gently pulled her head down to his via his grip on her curl. "Hibbert is outside th' door."

The knocking became a downright pounding. "Captain? Are you in there?"

"Damn your bloody eyes, Hibbert, what the devil do you want!"

"Mr. MacDuff's respects, sir, and he's just sighted land off the starboard bows. Mr. Wenham says we're off Massachusetts Bay, sir, and that we'll be entering Boston Harbor soon."

Christian sighed and gave an inward groan, suddenly wishing this voyage could go on forever. "My compliments to the first lieutenant, and tell him to prepare the ship as though the king himself is awaiting us. We'll make a fine show for those rebellious colonials, eh, Mr. Hibbert?"

"Aye, sir. We'll show those colonial upstarts we're not a navy to trifle with! We'll show 'em we're a *king's* ship!"

Christian threw back his head and laughed the sleep out of his sluggish body. "Aye, we'll do that, young fellow. Now go, do not tarry. I shall be on deck shortly."

"Boston!" Deirdre cried excitedly. Impulsively, she threw her arms around the Lord and Master's hard body. "Oh, Christian. How can I thank ye enough? Just think, me cousin is there. I haven't seen him in years! He'll help me t' find me brother, Christian, ye wait an' see!"

He looked at her soberly. "And so, as God is my witness, shall I, Deirdre."

* * *

The people of Boston saw her first as another one of the king's ships, sent to quell resistance and restore order, and wasted no time in sending messengers to the rebel leaders to announce her coming. The nervous governor might rejoice over the arrival of a smart and powerful frigate, but otherwise, her appearance was unwelcome by all except the Tory population, the British troops camped out in Boston Common eager for news of home, and, of course, the crusty old admiral whose small squadron lay at anchor in the harbor.

Boston Harbor, which had been closed to colonial trade since the establishment of the hated Port Act, was a serrated expanse of gentle water dotted with numerous islands and the ominous shapes of several of His Majesty's ships. Originally deployed to the rebellious colony to enforce the unpopular Port Act, support Governor Thomas Gage, and act as a show of force to the rebels, who already had control of the Massachusetts north shore, the ships—all part of a small squadron under the command of Vice Admiral Sir Geoffrey Lloyd—were a fine and impressive sight.

Upon the flagship, a huge, double-decked leviathan boasting a murderous array of seventy-four guns, the admiral's flag snapped in the wind. The admiral himself, a stiff-lipped, crusty old salt whose long years of sea service had left him tired, achy, irritable, and dreaming about his upcoming retirement years, sat at a fine table in his day cabin, squinting his eyes and frowning as he read the latest broadside, initiated and distributed by that hotheaded rabble-rouser Sam Adams.

Lately, though, the alarming activities of the rebels were not all that occupied Sir Geoffrey's weary mind. Yesterday, he had received the distressing news that the king's frigate *Bold Marauder*—which he'd been expecting for several days now—had encountered the Irish Pirate while the smuggler, in company with the French freebooter he traded with, had been attacking a lone English ship. Although *Bold Marauder* had supposedly taken the French vessel, the Irish Pirate had managed to make his escape and bring the embarrassing news back to Boston, where it had been enthusiastically received—and spread—by the upstarts.

Outside the door, the marine thumped his musket smartly

on the deck, interrupting the admiral's musings. *"Halcyon*'s captain to see you, sir!"

Sir Geoffrey's own flag captain was ashore, and he had invited young Brendan aboard to share the mid-day meal with him.

"Send him in," Sir Geoffrey muttered, shoving the broadside away from him with a tired motion.

The door opened and Captain Merrick entered, his cocked hat held respectfully in his hands, his chestnut hair shining in the sunlight that wafted down through the hatch behind him.

"Ah, Brendan. Come in and join me for a bite to eat."

The young man was tall and handsome, an intelligent, promising young rake with a mirthful grin. Quick-witted, clever, and compassionate, the captain of the frigate *Halcyon,* anchored in the lee of Castle Island a shadow's length from the big flagship, had climbed far and fast through the naval ranks. And now, as usual, the young half-Irishman was in high spirits.

"You'll be pleased to know, sir, that His Britannic Majesty's frigate *Bold Marauder* has just been sighted, standing for the harbor."

"Bold Marauder!" the admiral exclaimed, the tiredness instantly fading from his sloped shoulders, his aching limbs. He promptly forgot about the mid-day meal. "Damme, Merrick, it's about time! Now we shall learn *just* what happened between him and the Irish Pirate, eh? But I am sure her captain has a worthy explanation as to why he failed to capture the rogue. And as for the ship herself, why, one can never have enough frigates, eh? *Bold Marauder* will be a welcome addition to our little collection of warships!"

"Faith, sir, that she will," Brendan said hesitantly.

Their gazes met. Both were well aware of the frigate's bad reputation, but a missive written by Rear Admiral Sir Elliott Lord and delivered unto Sir Geoffrey's care by a fast-sailing packet had already advised the admiral of the identity of *Bold Marauder*'s commanding officer. The frigate might be the most rebellious ship in the king's fleet—but her new captain was the most principled, disciplined, and upstanding officer the Navy had.

Something, certainly, to take heart over after the worsening situation here in Boston!

Sir Geoffrey rose to his feet with rare agility and clapped his young officer on the back, the matter of the rebel broadside already forgotten. "Ah, 'tis good that she is here, eh? And Captain Lord is a fine officer with a long and distinguished record. A capable, competent, and thoroughly dislikable chap, but one who can be trusted to bring his ship in with a fine show!"

The young frigate captain frowned. "Pardon me, sir, but I served with Captain Lord aboard the old *Londoner* and I did not find him dislikable."

"Forgive me, Brendan. I had forgotten his, er, troubles concerning his dead wife. Such things can turn the most jovial of men into dragons, can they not?" The admiral finished the last of his tea, and called impatiently for his steward.

Brendan, watching with amusement in his russet eyes, had never seen his superior happier. A normally dour old man, Sir Geoffrey was beaming with boyish excitement.

"Ah, Brendan, *Bold Marauder* is just what these Bostonians need. Captain Lord can be counted upon to put on a fine display of competence, seamanship, and discipline! He will set an example, not only for our people, but also for these colonial upstarts who think His Majesty's forces nothing but a bumbling display of misplaced pomp and arrogance." He impatiently beckoned for his steward to enter. "And these bumpkins here have grown troublesome enough, have they not? They ridicule our troops, they ridicule our seamen, they ridicule the governor, they ridicule our attempts to maintain order!" He raised his arms, allowing his steward to help him into his coat. "No, not that one, Perry, the other one. Yes, the dress coat. And my finest sword, if you please! I will not honor Captain Lord with anything less than perfection!"

From above came the excited chorus of calls and shouts as the flagship's crew welcomed the arrival of the new ship.

Silently cursing the absence of his flag captain, the admiral turned instead to the young half-Irishman. "Brendan, please see to it that *Bold Marauder* is received with highest ceremony! I want every officer in his best uniform, every tar at strict and rigid attention, and a thunderous, proper salute from the guns of every ship in the squadron. And make sure that as *Bold Marauder* comes within pistol range, our people send up a loud and rousing cheer, to validate Captain Lord's faith in us and our trust in him. I want *no effort spared*, do you understand?"

"Uh, quite well, sir."

"Fine, then! Be on your way, then, and do not tarry!"

Shaking his handsome head, the dashing young frigate captain touched his hat and strode swiftly from the bright, sunlit cabin. Three years shy of his thirtieth year, he was as much a part of his crew as he was captain of it, well loved and much respected by his subordinates. As his long strides carried him topside, the flagship's men joked and traded barbs with him, and called him by his first name, privileges that few seamen in His Majesty's Navy would've dared and few commanders would have allowed.

But then, Captain Brendan Jay Merrick was quite unlike most commanders in His Majesty's Navy.

His coxswain, a big, strapping Irishman who'd been his best friend since the days when he'd grown up in Connemara, grabbed his elbow and pointed out over the sparkling harbor toward the majestic sight of the incoming frigate. "God Almighty, Brendan, she's a sight t' make a lad's heart weep, ain't she? Don't ye just swell with pride, knowin' ye designed 'er?"

The young captain, a modest and humble sort, flushed and shrugged. "If she's lovely, Liam, it is because of the hand of her captain, not mine. He deserves the credit for making her look so smart."

The frigate was taking on shape and detail as she drew close, the tall shadows of her masts falling across the bare trees that capped a small island she passed. Her topmasts boasted proud squares of pale, gold-tinted sail, and her yards were smartly angled to make best use of the unsteady breeze. She was a glorious sight, the water curling back from her rakish bow, sparkling in the sun and gleaming upon her stem, and despite himself, her young designer experienced a quick surge of pride.

He felt a presence at his elbow and, turning, found the

crusty old admiral beside him, his face as bright as any schoolboy's, his keen and piercing eyes crinkling with humor as he gazed out at the incoming frigate. "I see, sir, that you could not resist," Brendan said, grinning.

Impatiently beckoning to a terrified midshipman, Sir Geoffrey snatched a telescope from the boy and raised it to his eye. On the deck behind them, the first lieutenant was snapping orders, and the bosun and his mates were driving the men into a state of orderly, disciplined splendor. "I may be an old man, Brendan, but not so old that the sight of a well-run, smartly disciplined fighting ship doesn't bring a tear to my eye. Damme, she's lovely." He handed the telescope to the young captain. "Leave it to Captain Lord to put on a display of seamanship our Navy can be damned proud of!"

Brendan raised his glass to his eye, barely flinching as the deck beneath his feet quaked to the might of the big guns in a welcome salute to the proud new arrival. Answering puffs blurted from *Bold Marauder*'s gunports as she returned it, the salute smartly done, and as precisely calibrated as a ball to a musket's barrel. Brendan moved the glass, saw the proud officer who stood rigidly on the quarterdeck, and smiled as he recognized the man who had taught him much about seamanship, leadership, and naval tradition.

Captain Christian Lord. Brendan grinned, keenly aware of the huge crowds gathering to watch the new arrival.

"This is *just* what we need to show these rabble-rousers what is meant by a *king's* ship!" The admiral's voice quivered with pride as he stared out over the water at the glorious, majestic frigate. "And, by God, there's Lord himself, the absolute epitome of what a king's *officer* should be! Damme, Brendan, don't keep the glass all to yourself, man! Have some pity on an old tar who's half blind as it is!"

But the young officer had stiffened, the color draining from his face.

Impatiently, Sir Geoffrey snapped, "Damme, Brendan, the glass *please!*"

Slowly, the captain brought the telescope down, blinking in shock and then horror. His face was very white. He looked at Sir Geoffrey, glaring at him. He looked back at the frigate, and had a sudden, desperate urge to hurl the telescope overboard before his admiral could discover for himself what he had seen through that circular field.

Something that, judging by the thunderous commotion from shore, the jeering crowds had already discovered.

Something that the flagship's crew was rushing to the rails to see, pushing and shoving in their haste to be nearest it.

Something that the admiral, smiling triumphantly as he raised the glass to his keen and bleary old eye, would be seeing just . . . about . . .

Brendan shut his eyes, wincing.

"Great *GOD* above!" Sir Geoffrey thundered, and the glass dropped from his fingers to smash upon the flagship's deck.

Now.

The old man clutched at his heart. "He has a . . . a *woman* in the maintop!" he croaked, his face as pale as the furled sail above. "And she's stark, raving *naked!*"

Chapter 22

"I have never been more *humiliated,* ashamed, and *embarrassed* in my life!" Sir Geoffrey raged, storming up through HMS *Bold Marauder*'s entry port with Captain Brendan Jay Merrick close behind him. He cringed as the ceremonies trill of pipes, meant to be a salute to him, rang mockingly around him.

Captain Christian Lord, splendidly turned out in his finest uniform and wearing a gold-tasseled dress sword at his hip, stepped forward to receive them. He was smiling, obviously proud of himself, and his shoulders were squared and straight. Solemnly, he doffed his hat. "Welcome, sir, to His

Majesty's frigate *Bold Marauder.* We are deeply honored to—"

"Spare me your damned pleasantries, *Captain Lord!* God rot it, you have made me the laughingstock of Boston, and I'll see you in your cabin *now!*"

"Sir?" the captain said, confusion darkening his gray eyes. At his side and slightly behind him, his first lieutenant, a broad, ruddy-faced Scot with a shock of red hair, exchanged puzzled glances with the second lieutenant. And coming up from the hatch was a fat white spaniel, who took one look at the enraged Sir Geoffrey—and promptly emptied her bladder in terror.

"I said now!" the admiral thundered.

"Yes, sir. By all means," Christian said tightly, grabbing up Tildy and wondering what the devil had riled the admiral so. *Bold Marauder* had put on a fine show, one the king himself would've been proud of. She was clean and smart and beyond reproach. Keenly aware of his men's equally confused stares, he turned abruptly and led the way to his cabin, holding himself upright and feeling his shoulder beginning to throb. The quarterdeck loomed ominously over their heads, and from long habit, he ducked. "Pray, sir, please watch your head—"

"Hold your bloody tongue, Lord, I've been on warships a damn sight longer than you! God rot it, I have *never* been so damned embarrassed in my life—"

They were now beyond earshot of *Bold Marauder*'s crew. Angrily, Christian swung around, his eyes blazing. "Pray, sir, I don't know what grieves you so! My ship is *faultless!*"

The admiral was a head shorter than Christian, but with his fine rage, his stature was considerably increased. Glaring up into the captain's gray eyes, he roared, "There is a *woman* in your maintop, Captain Lord, and *she is not wearing a damned stitch of clothing!*"

Christian stared at him. Sick, sudden horror drained the color from his face and left it white, then gray. *Dear God,* he thought. *Delight.*

Cold sweat broke out of every pore, and he turned just outside his cabin door, trying to maintain the last shreds of his dignity. The admiral's rage was a tangible thing, and

Christian was keenly aware of not only Sir Geoffrey, but also the young Captain Merrick—who looked quite sympathetic, if not a little amused.

Ian MacDuff, his own Scots temper ready to blow, came charging down the short corridor. "Here, now, Captain, 'tis looking right bonnie we be! What the saints has the old fart all riled—"

Sir Geoffrey went purple.

Quietly, Christian said, "Mr. MacDuff, please send someone up to the maintop *immediately* to fetch Delight down."

"Del—" Ian's jaw came unhinged.

"Yes, Ian, *Delight.*" He fisted his hands at his sides, feeling his career sliding into ruin around his feet. "Pray, do so now . . . before the damage becomes irreparable."

Ian left at a dead run.

"I am most grievously sorry, sir," Christian managed, lifting his head and meeting the admiral's furious glare. "I had—"

He couldn't say he had no idea. It would only pound another nail into his coffin. Besides, there was no use in trying to make excuses. He was already incriminated. Finished. Doomed to court-martial, disgrace, and the rest of his life spent on the beach. With a defeated sigh, he shoved open his cabin door, forgetting, too late, about—

"Great *God* above, Lord, do you run a goddamned brothel or a fighting ship?" the admiral cried as the lovely raven-haired girl on the bed, clad in nothing but the captain's shirt, flung aside the covers and flew across the cabin.

Christian shut his eyes.

"Brendan!" she cried. And with a happy shriek, the girl threw herself into the startled arms of Sir Geoffrey Lloyd's next consideration for flag captain.

Christian was too devastated to feel surprise that the two knew each other. He was too devastated to feel jealousy at the way Deirdre was openly sobbing with glee as she clung to the dashingly handsome Captain Merrick. He was too devastated to feel the sudden, throbbing agony in his shoulder, the hollow nausea in the pit of his stomach.

His career was finished.

"Deirdre, please address the captain with the respect he

deserves," he said quietly, lowering Tildy to her puppies and already hearing the death knell of a court-martial.

But Captain Merrick had swept Deirdre up in his arms, swung her around and around, and was now hugging her fiercely. "Nonsense, Captain Lord! Faith, the lass is my *cousin!* How very *good* of you to bring her all the way across the Atlantic just to deliver her into my care!"

"What?" Sir Geoffrey snapped, whirling.

Merrick's pointed gaze met Christian's from above Deirdre's shoulder, and Christian was quick to grasp what the shrewd younger captain had so quickly offered. Escape.

"Yes, yes, of course," he said lamely, feeling the piercing gaze of the old admiral driving between his shoulders. "She had a most trying time of it, but I daresay she made a good sailor."

"She always did, even when I took her up to Mayo in my little sailboat so she could see the castle where her ancestress lived. Never once got seasick, did you, Deirdre?"

"Oh, never, Brendan! And remember climbin' Crough Patrick, an' the awful storm that hit us on th' way home? Why, if it wasn't for yer skill as a sailor, th' angels would've collected us that day for sure—"

Sir Geoffrey glared at the two cousins, glared down at the puppies, and glared up at Captain Christian Lord. "You mean to tell me you were merely transporting this—this *girl* to Boston, Captain Lord?"

Christian met the sharp stare unflinchingly. "Yes, sir."

Hastily, Deirdre offered, "Me mama died, ye see, an' Brendan's the only family I got left."

Ignoring her, the admiral stormed, "I saw no mention of a female passenger in the dispatches from your admiral back in Portsmouth, Captain Lord!"

"Uh, Sir Elliott has had a lot on his mind lately, sir. Perhaps he . . . forgot."

"Your brother is not the type to *forget!* And this *still* doesn't explain that *female* on your maintop, blatantly waving a kerchief in greeting to the people of Boston upon your *glorious* entry!"

A commotion sounded just outside the door as the "female" in question was escorted aft.

"Oh, dear God," Christian began, graying with horror as he realized that Ian was bringing Delight in.

Just then, the door swung open and Delight, swathed in nothing but a wool blanket, sauntered in, much to the pop-eyed consternation of Sir Geoffrey.

"Why, Captain Lord, you did so spoil my fun by bringing me down from the maintop! Lo, I got the most awful burn on my *derriere* on the way down," she purred, suggestively rubbing her bottom through the blanket. "Why, hello, kind sir. . . ." Her eyes gleaming, she sauntered over to the shocked Sir Geoffrey, whose complexion had gone apoplectic. "You must be the admiral. I just *love* a man with *power,*" she crooned, sidling close to him and dragging a long red fingernail down his seamed, suddenly white cheek. "You'd just love a little romp with Delight here, no? I have the most wickedly wonderful methods of—"

"Ian, *get her out of here!*" Christian roared.

Even Brendan looked shocked, though his russet eyes were glinting with mirth.

"*IAN!*"

"Uh, aye, sir, 'tis trying I am—"

Delight rubbed herself against Sir Geoffrey's chest, her hand roving down his waistcoat toward his breeches. The admiral's face was going a bright, alarming red, a shockingly bright contrast to the whiteness of his hair.

And then Delight allowed the blanket to slip to the floor.

Christian shut his eyes and clapped his hand over his brow. Brendan Merrick gulped and nearly dropped his cousin. Delight Foley touched a hand to the admiral's groin—

And Sir Geoffrey slid to the floor in a dead faint.

" 'Twas too much for his heart, sir," Elwin Boyd said matter-of-factly, leaning over the admiral, and fanning him with a piece of paper. "But I think he's coming round now."

Sir Geoffrey, lying in the bed that Christian had shared with Deirdre not two hours past, blinked and tried to sit up, his hand going unconsciously to his heart. "Let me up, you bunch of bumbling fools!" he snarled, pushing aside their hands. The blond doxy was nowhere in sight. Young

Merrick stood nearby, his lips twitching with suppressed laughter. His Irish cousin—a comely young thing with striking purple eyes and an out-of-control mane of wild black hair—sat beside the bed, her worshipful gaze passing between Brendan and the tight-lipped Christian Lord. A loose pair of seaman's trousers now covered her bare legs, and she held a glass of water in her hand, trying to press it to Sir Geoffrey's lips.

"Here, sir. Drink, an' 'twill make ye feel better."

Angrily, Sir Geoffrey knocked it away, spilling water to the deck flooring. "God rot it, there's nothing wrong with me! Bunch of fools, treating me like some blasted invalid! Damn your eyes, Captain Lord, you have much to answer to!"

"Yes, sir." The captain turned to the frowning surgeon. "Please leave us, Elwin."

The Irish girl's hand came up to touch a strange, pagan crucifix at her throat. Lifting her chin, she fastened steady eyes on the admiral. They were beautiful eyes, stormy eyes, of a brilliant purple shade that reminded him of violets in springtime. "Please, sir, don't be takin' yer anger out on Captain Lord," she said in her gentle brogue. "He's a fine an' upstandin' officer, an' wouldn't tolerate no shenanigans."

"And what do you call that—that *spectacle* in the maintop?" Sir Geoffrey raged, more to Christian Lord than to the young Irishwoman.

Again the girl answered, her soft voice unresponsive to his anger. "Oh, her name be Dolores. She has a bit o' a problem, ye see? Her papa sent her t' France t' learn her social graces, but ye know how those awful French people are, Sir Geoffrey."

The admiral's eyes narrowed, for as a true Briton, he had no love for the French. "Yes, I know *exactly* how awful they are!"

The girl gave a sad, gentle smile. "Well, sir, they corrupted her an' poisoned her mind. She left Boston as a sweet and innocent lady o' virtue, but those awful French had their way with her, ye see, an', well ... She ended up in Portsmouth an' Captain Lord, bein' the gallant naval officer he is, took it upon himself t' deliver her safely back t' her family here in Massachusetts. He put so much time and effort int' makin' somethin' o' this crew—a real hard-t'-manage one, if ye'll recall—that' 'twasn't always easy for him t' keep an eye on Deli—I mean, Dolores. But she can't help herself, sir. 'Twas the French influence."

The admiral's eyes narrowed. "French influence, you say?"

Bless you, dear girl, Christian thought, shutting his eyes.

"Oh, aye," Deirdre was saying. "French influence. They were quite brutal wi' her, sir. No wonder she came out o' it th' way she is. Why, 'tis makin' me skin crawl just thinkin' o' the horrors poor Dolores had t' endure at th' hands o' those animals. . . ."

Brendan's eyes were dancing with mirth as he shot a conspiring glance toward the speechless Christian, though he was careful to keep his tone properly sober. "Quite right, Sir Geoffrey. An immoral and lascivious people, you must agree. Faith, I shudder to think of any impressionable young female at the mercy of their carnal ways!" He cast a pointed glance around the orderly cabin and looked up at the deckhead, as though he could see through the great beams to the decks above. "That aside, Captain Lord, please accept my congratulations on what wonders you have done with this vessel! Faith, the last time I saw her I was ashamed to admit that I had designed her. . . ." He turned to the admiral and said cheerfully, "Really, sir, don't you think that Captain Lord's success at making something of *Bold Marauder*'s crew far outweighs the, uh, little incident with Miss Dolores?"

Deirdre dramatically clasped her hands before her chest, as though in prayer. "And the sad thing is, Dolores's father has lots o' money, sir. He'll be ashamed an' distressed t' see what those nasty French people've done t' his poor, innocent daughter." She sighed, her eyes filled with ruefulness. "But those French are a vulgar people, aren't they, Captain Lord?"

Brendan, caught up in the game, answered before Christian could reply. "Faith! The whole country's a den of iniquity, if I do say so myself!"

His eyes narrowing, Sir Geoffrey snatched the glass of water from the girl's hand, and stared at his young captain. Merrick's logic, as usual, was sound, and the admiral knew that the accomplishment of salvaging the finest frigate in the king's fleet ought to count for something more than a court-martial. Granted, his pride stung, and he'd have to account for the humiliating incident before Governor Gage, but Brendan was right. Captain Lord's accomplishments regarding *Bold Marauder*'s crew far outweighed the embarrassment of Dolores's *display.*

He drained what water there was in the glass and thrust it back into the Irish girl's hand. "I suppose there's nothing to be done for it, then, but to return the chit to her father and let *him* deal with her," he muttered irately. "You say her family lives here in Boston?'

"Well, almost. She tells me her home is on the west side o' Cambridge, wherever that be."

"Less than ten miles from here," Sir Geoffrey said gruffly. "I suppose it falls upon *me*, then, to escort her back."

Brendan cleared his throat and drew himself up, his eyes suddenly eager. "Faith, sir, but I'd be happy to oblige."

"Yes, I'm sure you *would*," Sir Geoffrey snapped. "But I'll not chance the possibility of my finest officer tarnishing his name and reputation by being seen in the girl's company until a cure can be found for her . . . *condition.*" He turned to Christian. "I trust that she has something to wear, besides a *blanket,* so that she can be escorted from this ship with some degree of dignity?"

Christian paled, thinking of the trunk of gowns—and other *equipment*—that Delight had had hauled up from the brig and now lay close, *too* close, in a nearby cabin. "Er, yes, sir, though I daresay they could use some . . . uh, alterations."

"Fine. See to it that your sailmaker has them done. I want that woman off this ship by sundown."

Brendan, fidgeting, persisted. "Will you, then, be escorting her back to her family, sir?"

The admiral rose to his feet. "You seem quite bloody *eager,* Captain Merrick!"

Brendan flashed a quick grin. "Aye, sir. I wouldn't want *you* to tarnish your name, either."

"Oh, go on with you!" the admiral retorted. "I don't give a king's damn who takes her, as long as she's removed from this vessel before she can cause our Navy any more humiliation. By the way . . ." He frowned and turned to Deirdre, his shrewd eyes narrowing. "Who is this *wealthy* father who is in the unenviable position of having sired her?"

Deirdre shrugged. "All I know, sir, is that his name be Foley, and that he an' his family live outside o' Boston in a place called Menotomy."

The admiral stared at her. "Foley? *Menotomy?*"

"Aye, sir." Her pale and lovely brow furrowed in a frown. "Do ye know the family, then?"

"Oh, I know them, all right. I know them damned well!" He snatched up his hat. "Captain Merrick, you may have the afternoon to catch up on old times with your cousin, but I expect that girl to be safely delivered unto her father's care by *tonight*. You will receive additional orders shortly. And you, Captain Lord"—his harsh stare settled on Christian—"I shall see you aboard the flagship at eight bells. We have *much* to discuss!"

Christian heaved a silent sigh of relief. Then he picked up his own hat and, squaring his shoulders, followed the admiral out the door to see him properly off the ship, his shoulder aching, his head throbbing with suppressed tension.

But at the door he paused to flash his beloved a look of indebtedness and admiration.

No matter what trouble she'd caused him back in Portsmouth, here in Boston she had just saved his career.

Sir Geoffrey announced an informal dinner for his officers in the vast cabin of his flagship, the massive, seventy-four-gun *Dauntless,* whose dining area alone made the entire cabin of HMS *Bold Marauder* seem small and cramped in comparison. But the flagship was the domain of the admiral, and as such, there was more than enough room in the cabin for Sir Geoffrey, his captains, and the huge array of food brought in by stewards and nervous, smartly turned-out midshipmen.

The men were a small but diverse collection: the admiral, a cranky, slope-shouldered old man with a shrewd and piercing eye; Captain Hiram Ellsworth, a high-minded prig whose snuff habit would probably melt his nasal septum by the time he was forty; Captain Stanley Cutler, the present flag captain, sulking, drinking, and sulking some more when it became obvious to him that he'd somehow earned the wrath of his admiral; Lieutenant Peter Atkins, loud, swaggering, and boastful; a varied array of young officers—and Captain Christian Lord.

Christian sat at the polished mahogany table, watching the admiral's servants clearing away the meal which his stomach, used to the horrors of naval fare, had accepted first with glee and now with hesitation and no small degree of remorse. Its queasy condition was not helped by the openly hostile attitude of the other occupants of the room.

Cutler raised his glass and downed its contents in a single gulp. "So, Captain Lord," he said with a conspiring glance at his companions, "I'm told you made something of that worthless rabble you left Portsmouth with."

Christian's lips tightened. "I could not make something of them if there was nothing there to begin with."

Ellsworth made a snorting noise. "Huh! *Bold Marauder*'s previous captain is a dear friend of mine. He told me her officers and crew are naught but a bunch of incompetent asses who don't know a stem from a stern!"

Laughter rippled around the table, but Sir Geoffrey, thanking a nervous little midshipman for bringing him his pillow to put between his brittle old back and the unforgiving chair, didn't notice the open insult to Christian's crew.

"I say, they must *still* be a bunch of incompetent asses, Ellsworth!" Cutler said recklessly, sniggering as he poured himself another glass of port. "They've already bungled the very thing they were sent here to do—apprehend that damned Irish Pirate! Can you imagine? Why, *Bold Marauder* had the rascal right under her guns, and *still* the fellow got away! Ah, Captain Lord, I pity you, having to take command of *those* dolts!"

But the slight to his crew was lost on Christian by what Cutler had just revealed.

"The Irish *Pirate?*"

"Don't tell us you didn't know. All of Boston is abuzz with it."

Christian nearly broke his goblet as he slammed it down atop the table. "Abuzz with *what?*"

"Why, the news, of course. Brought back by the smuggler himself, no doubt, that you engaged him and the French corvette he happened to be trading with some distance off the Maine coast. You mean to tell me you didn't *know* he was the Irish Pirate?"

More snickers.

No. He hadn't known.

The room grew suddenly too hot, too stuffy, and he began to sweat beneath his fine uniform.

It was the admiral who came to his rescue. "That will be enough, gentleman," Sir Geoffrey said crossly, for he had intended to speak to Christian privately about the matter after the meal, and did not want the captain to be on the defensive. "It is a known fact that the Irish Pirate flies no colors. And as for why Captain Lord failed to apprehend him, do not forget that he had a sinking English cutter to assist, a French corvette to man, and other things to occupy him."

"That's for damned sure!" Cutler cried, hooting with laughter. "Would that we *all* had such . . . *diversions!*"

"I said, that will be enough!" the admiral barked, keenly aware of the fury beginning to blaze in Christian's cold eyes, the muscle jumping in his jaw, and the effort it was costing him to retain his beyond-reproach dignity.

"But of course, sir," Cutler said with mock innocence. "There is probably a very good reason why Captain Lord's crew didn't take the Irish Pirate. We all know how *difficult* it can be to get a shabby crew to perform to even the lowest of acceptable standards."

"Especially a crew as notoriously *bad* as HMS *Bold Marauder*'s."

"Poor Merrick. How embarrassed and ashamed of her he must be!"

"Aye, to think of his fine masterpiece crewed by a bunch of bumbling asses with nothing better to do than cause trouble and make their gloriously decorated and esteemed *captain,* whose lofty heights *we* shall never aspire to, look so terribly ghastly!"

" 'Tis not just the crew who are responsible, Cutler, but the officers! I say, *they* are the root of the problem!"

"S'death, I'd be happy to lend you some of *my* officers, Captain Lord!" Atkins said jovially. *"They,* at least, would spare you the embarrassment of having to answer for *your* pack of wastrels!"

Their laughter was abruptly silenced by the thunderous crash of Christian's fist slamming down atop the table. "My officers behaved gallantly under extreme circumstances, and I found no fault with my people's behavior, none at all! I *daresay* I do not have to sit here and suffer hearing their names maligned!"

He felt Sir Geoffrey's eyes on him, scrutinizing him, his old mouth beginning to curve in an admiring, approving smile.

Ellsworth drawled, "Here, here, Lord, we're not putting your *ship* down—after all, you *did* manage—somehow—to catch that puny French corvette that was in company with the even punier sloop of the Irish Pirate. . . ."

"Puny indeed, Hiram," Lieutenant Atkins said, watching as Ellsworth reached for his snuff and put a delicate pinch in each nostril. "But I suppose, with such incompetent rabble for a crew, one must start *somewhere,* eh?"

"I say, Lord, did you have that blond-haired doxy employed at *manning* the helm?"

The table erupted in laughter. Christian leapt to his feet, an angry retort on his lips.

The admiral had had enough. "Damme, Lord, sit down. And the rest of you, hold your bloody tongues. I daresay none of you would've fared any better. Captain Lord was at a considerable handicap with a crew that had never seen battle before, and under the circumstances, I can only commend him.

"And furthermore," Sir Geoffrey said, "regardless of the reputation of *Bold Marauder*'s crew, I have nothing but respect for a captain who will defend them even when he knows that some improvement could stand to be had. You have my sympathies, Captain Lord, for all that you have endured with them during your passage, and you have my heartfelt praise for what you have made of them during such a short time. Aside from the *spectacle* in your maintop, your ship made a fine showing upon entering the harbor today."

"So did the girl in the maintop," Cutler said, sniggering.

"I said, *enough*, Cutler!" Sir Geoffrey railed. Instantly, the flag captain quieted, and looked down at his hands, his lips twitching.

"I did not call you together to practice dissent among yourselves, and I'll tolerate no more words against either Captain Lord's character or his crew," Sir Geoffrey said sharply, unwilling to see one of his officers embarrassed, no matter how displeased he was over the incident with Dolores. He rose to his feet. "I called you together merely to share an amiable meal, and to allow you the opportunity to acquaint yourselves with Captain Lord and him with you. With tension mounting daily between the rebels and His Majesty's forces, we must work together. Dissent will get us nowhere!"

Hiram took some more snuff. Cutler reached for another glass of port, ignoring his admiral's disapproving eye.

"Furthermore," Sir Geoffrey continued, "if conflict *does* break out between us and these rebels, I would have us all be familiar with each other's character, strengths, and weaknesses."

"And women," Cutler added snidely.

"What?"

"Nothing, sir."

The admiral fixed an angry eye on his flag captain. Tersely, he said, "As you all know, Lord Dartmouth has sent orders to General Gage to arrest the rebel leaders of this so-called Massachusetts Provincial Congress. Gage has not yet acted upon these orders, despite efforts on behalf of the king's loyal subjects here in Boston to press him to do so. Therefore, men like Adams, Hancock, Warren, and Revere continue to run rampant, infecting the general populace with their polluted ideas of dissent and rebellion. They fear nothing, these men. Not only do they have the audacity to set up a government that is wholly independent of their king's, they even now are selecting a speaker to commemorate the fifth anniversary of that unfortunate event they call the Boston Massacre. A bold move, if I may say so myself, what with the town filled with our troops and supported by our ships here in the harbor, but that just goes to show the desperate and hotheaded nature of these upstarts we are dealing with. General Gage, as you may imagine, is growing *most* distressed."

"Well, if the Old Woman would get the wind beneath his coattails and *do* something about the rabble—"

"Captain Cutler, your duty is not to comment or question, but to *obey!*"

"But, sir," Cutler protested, overindulgence in Sir Geoffrey's port making him reckless, "Lord Dartmouth sent very specific orders to Gage to arrest the rebel leaders. Yet he has done nothing."

"It is not our place to discuss the conduct of the military governor," the admiral snapped, his eyes blazing with anger. "Would you have our Navy become like the troops in Boston? Openly mocking General Gage, with some of them even deserting?" Cutler lowered his head and reached for more port. "No, we must band together for strength. A division between forces will only lead to defeat should the worst happen. As it stands, intelligence tells us that the rebels are gathering arms and ammunition and secreting them in the countryside." He paused. "Tell me, gentlemen, *just who do you think they're preparing to use these arms against?*"

He raked them with a hard, penetrating stare, allowing his words to sink in. Then, quietly, he said, "Rather than bicker amongst ourselves, let us instead use our energies to quell rebel activities before they lead to unnecessary bloodshed."

Christian sat rigidly, his pain forgotten beneath the shock of Sir Geoffrey's words. He had known, of course, that matters on this side of the Atlantic were bad, but he had not known that Englishmen here were actually taking up arms against fellow Englishmen back in Britain. . . .

Sir Geoffrey's tired old face showed the strain of the day. "I believe I have gone over all that needs to be discussed here tonight," he said wearily. "The lot of you may take your leave, and with my blessing." But as he noted their hostile glances toward the tight-lipped Christian Lord, some of his fire immediately returned. "One last word of warning," he snapped. "Anyone caught discussing today's incident, or maligning Captain Lord and his crew, will answer to *me.*"

Christian had risen to his feet to follow them, but the vice admiral's sharp voice rang out behind him. "A moment, please, Captain Lord."

He paused in the doorway, his hat in his hands, his shoulder throbbing dully. He waited until the others were out of earshot. "Thank you, sir, for defending my crew's honor." His voice was hard, tight, guarded. "It is most appreciated."

"Nonsense. You have performed admirably in shaping them into a fine and respectable crew. Sir Elliott has advised me in his missives about the exact nature of what you were taking on when he assigned you to *Bold Marauder.*" The admiral allowed a hint of a smile. "Not that I had not already known."

"Thank you, sir."

"But make no bones about the matter! While I defended you before your peers tonight—who, I might add, are merely envious of your noble accomplishments—I am still *most* distressed about the incident with Miss Foley and so, I'm afraid, is Governor Gage." He smiled gravely. "However, even the worst turns of event can still bear fruit. As this one did."

"Sir?"

"Please have a seat, Captain. I did not detain you to go over something you're already aware of, but to advise you of the Navy's mission for you."

"The Irish Pirate, sir?"

"That, and more."

He sat down, gripping his hat tightly in his hands. "I am sorry, sir. I had no idea that the sloop was the Irish Pirate's."

The admiral seated himself in his chair, leaned back, and kneaded his tired brow. "Of course not, Captain. How could you? But no matter. We will catch the rogue—or, shall I say, Christian, *you* will."

"Sir?"

The admiral gave a weary sigh and gazed out the great stern windows, where the lights of Boston could be seen in the darkness. "Things here in Boston have grown unbearably tense over the past several months. Last year's Port Act—which, as you know, was intended as punishment for that dastardly Tea Party incident—met with anger and rebellion, and while meant to cut Boston's trade off from other ports and therefore starve and choke the town into submission, the exact opposite happened. It has only served to unify the rebels, and give them more strength. Relief has poured into Boston from all over Massachusetts; indeed, from all over the bloody continent."

Christian nodded, wondering what the admiral was leading up to.

"Furthermore, other *punitive* actions, meant to clip the wings of Massachusetts's self-government, have merely incited fury and open defiance among the rabble. Gage, between you and me, is a complete buffoon. He draws up declarations and refuses to enforce them, pretending ignorance while the bumpkins blatantly defy them, right under his nose. *Not* a fine way to garner respect for authority, mind you!"

Christian allowed himself a wry grin. "Captain Merrick tells me the troops are referring to Gage as the Old Woman for his failure to use force where it obviously needs to be used."

"Hmmph!" Sir Geoffrey snorted, staring irritably at the table. "Do not allow me to get going about our governor, *please.* Despite the fact that we have several warships in the harbor, thousands of troops camped out in and around Boston, and London standing on her tiptoes watching the whole bloody mess, he is loath to enforce his own orders! As a result, the rebels grow bolder and bolder. They have launched their own form of government. Their Dr. Joseph Warren drew up a set of resolutions declaring that there was no need to obey the Port Act, and implored the people to prepare themselves for a war against England. Last fall, they sent representatives to Philadelphia to partake in a colony-wide assembly of rebels calling themselves the Continental Congress, and have since proceeded to downright *steal* money from the royal collections to fund their dastardly schemes. Now morale is so low that our own troops are deserting, while others are going so far as to sell their muskets to the damned rabble just for the extra money. Putting toys in the hands of children, Captain! Things are so damned tense as it is, 'twill only take a spark to blow everything to kingdom come, and God help us all when that happens!"

"I had not realized that the situation has deteriorated to such an extent, sir," Christian said quietly. He looked down at his port. Suddenly, the fine wine looked like blood to him.

"War is imminent, Captain. The rebels have established Committees of Safety to oversee a new militia, a collection of motley rabble calling themselves minutemen." The admiral made a disgusted noise. "Can you imagine? Bumpkins—farmers, ordinary citizens, merchants—taking up *arms* against the finest army in the world. It's tragic." His tone turned wretched. "They haven't a bloody chance."

"*Minute*men?" Christian raised a brow.

"Yes, Captain, *minutemen*. Forgive me, I forget that you have only just arrived in this hellhole, so of course you would have no idea what I'm talking about. Companies of men, each led by someone designated as captain, who muster, march, and are ready to move at a minute's notice against the king's forces at the first sound of alarm. Farmers and civilians, the lot of them."

Christian looked down at his port again and, suddenly unable to drink it, slid the glass away from him.

Sir Geoffrey gave a hard sigh. "In any case, Captain, as I mentioned earlier, I was most intrigued to learn the name of this woman you took aboard as a passenger. This Miss Foley. I will be direct and to the point. Dolores Ann Foley is the daughter of one Jared Foley, a printer who lives in the western part of Cambridge, in the little village of Menotomy. He proclaims to be loyal to king and Crown, but recent intelligence has reached Gage that there has been a suspicious amount of *activity* to and from the Foley home at all hours of the day and night. Activity that is highly suspect for a man purported to be a Loyalist."

"Are you saying that Foley is a rebel?"

"I'm saying we *suspect* he's a rebel. He is most assuredly a printer, Captain, and as such, is therefore in a position to print broadsides and distribute them to the populace."

Christian sat back, rubbing his jaw. "I wonder, then, sir," he said slowly, "if perhaps Dolores Ann Foley did not go to France to learn 'social graces,' but rather to feel out French thoughts regarding the, er, plight of the rebels?"

Sir Geoffrey stared at him. "By God, Lord, you are astute! A possibility, but then, I don't know. What I *do* know is that Gage's spies have seen Foley in company with the likes of Adams, Hancock, Dr. Warren, and"—he paused, looking hard at Christian—"the Irish Pirate."

"My God," Christian said, suddenly remembering how Delight, when she'd cornered him in the brig, had professed that she was going to seduce and capture the notorious smuggler for herself.

"The Irish Pirate," Sir Geoffrey snapped, giving Christian an intent look, "is a proclaimed rebel who *must be stopped.* Were he a simple smuggler, I would not be so concerned with him, but the Americans are secretly moving guns into the countryside, and they are obviously coming from somewhere."

Christian's eyes widened. "The Irish Pirate, sir?"

"Aye, Captain Lord. Had the exchange not already been made, undoubtedly you would have found your French corvette's hold packed with crates of fine French muskets. So you see now why the Irish Pirate must be stopped. If Gage will not move against the other rebel leaders, then it falls upon the king's Navy to do what it must regarding those who fall under its jurisdiction. The matter of the Irish Pirate is under *my* control, and I am not content to sit back and watch a bloody war unfold! The Irish Pirate is more than a *mere smuggler.* He is procuring arms from Philadelphia and Baltimore, bringing them into ports north of Boston, and ensuring their delivery into the hands of the rebels. These same arms and ammunition are being hidden in the countryside with the intent of being used upon fellow Englishmen should conflict break out between the king's forces and the rebels. The Irish Pirate *must be stopped!*"

Christian said nothing, wondering, as he had so often during the past month, why Elliott had sent him here all the way from England when Sir Geoffrey might've selected his frigate captain, Brendan Jay Merrick, for the task. Surely Brendan, a fine and gallant sea officer, was more than capable.

The admiral stood up and began to pace. "There is no time to waste. Your task is to bring the Irish Pirate to heel as quickly and efficiently as possible, using every resource at your command. By your having the *misfortune* of transporting Miss Foley across the ocean, fate could not have worked in a better way on our behalf. You are well acquainted with Miss Foley, and therefore have perfect reason to call upon Miss O'Devir at the Foley home in Menotomy."

"Sir?" Christian stiffened, growing uneasy.

"With the Foleys proclaiming to be Loyalists, they cannot protest a fine and much-respected officer of the king's Navy calling upon a friend of their daughter. And regarding Miss O'Devir—and by the way, that was most gallant of you to bring her here to Captain Merrick, though I am not so old or blind that your obvious *affections* for each other have escaped me—'twould be most unseemly for her to remain upon a man-of-war amidst the company of one hundred and fifty of the king's most notoriously misbehaved tars. Especially," he added, smiling and wagging a paternal finger, "in light of how you and the girl share such *affections.*" He allowed himself a small chuckle. "Because she is the cousin of one of my most respected officers, I will do all that I can to preserve her reputation, as well as yours—which I daresay your envious peers would take delight in tarnishing. To that end—and because she may be of convenient use in reporting the activities of the Irish Pirate to us—I have arranged for her to take lodging with the Foleys."

"But—"

"The matter is settled, Christian." The admiral poured himself a glass of wine, sipped it, and put the goblet down on the table with an air of dismissal. "I had Captain Merrick escort the two women to the Foley home while we met over supper tonight."

Christian stared at him in speechless dismay.

"Captain Lord," the admiral said coldly, "you were sent here to apprehend the Irish Pirate, a lone wolf who makes his den in happy company with a nest of rattlesnakes. If Gage will not step on the rattlesnakes, then you and I must shoot the wolf. The arms shipments to the colonists must be halted immediately. Do I make myself clear, Captain? *Immediately.*"

"Yes, sir."

"I know you don't wish to be separated from the girl, but it is necessary, for *all* of the reasons I have given you. The Irish Pirate is a secret friend of Jared Foley, whose own activities are highly suspect. Your courting of Miss O'Devir is the perfect foil for this assignment, and will keep anyone from suspecting your true purpose for being in the countryside. *That* is between you and me, and no one else."

Christian took a deep breath, his hand coming up to touch his throbbing shoulder. "Does Captain Merrick know of this plan? And why was *he* not selected to apprehend the Irish Pirate? Surely he is more than capable of it!"

"Merrick is half Irish himself, Captain, and as you know, the Irish are a clannish race. I would not send him against one of his own. It would not be wise, or healthy for *him*, and though I have no doubt that he would do his duty, I would not ask such a thing of him. In fact, I think it would be in *everyone's* best interest if I send him off on a cruise to join the frigate *Lively* in patrolling the coast."

With that, the crotchety old admiral got to his feet.

Christian followed suit, his head dazed, his heart heavy. Poor Deirdre. He hadn't even had the chance to say goodbye to her, or to properly thank her for coming to his rescue this afternoon. And no doubt she was homesick, lonely, frightened, and miserable. If only *he* could've brought her out to Menotomy. . . .

The admiral walked with him toward the door. "Take heart, old boy," he said, clasping his shoulder and missing his wince of pain. " 'Twill not be forever!"

"Aye, sir."

"In fact, you might even begin calling on Miss O'Devir tomorrow. Now, that's something to look forward to, eh?"

"Indeed, sir."

But at the door, the admiral gave him a level, warning look. "Just ... watch yourself, Captain, and keep your nose clean in all of this. This assignment could be very dangerous—and damaging to your career should your name in *any* way be smeared by too close association with any of the rebels whom you might befriend, Miss Foley, of course, included."

"Sir?"

"You have a brilliant and highly praised naval career behind you. And an even brighter one before you. There are those who would delight in shooting you down, and I would not have the career of England's future admiral jeopardized!" He gave a tight smile. "Do I make myself clear, Captain Lord?"

Christian met the old man's intent gaze. "Yes, sir. *Very* clear."

"Fine, then. Enough on the matter, Captain Lord. Perhaps by week's end we'll have brought the Irish Pirate to heel and put a stop to his black activities, eh?" He paused at the door. "Now please, if you'll excuse me? It has been a *most* trying day."

Chapter 23

Deirdre hated Massachusetts from the moment she stepped onto the wharf at Boston, staggered, reached the land, and nearly fell at the unfamiliarity of solid earth beneath her feet.

It didn't take her long to discover that Boston was cold and ugly and stinking, the buildings as bleak and forbidding as the faces of the people who inhabited them. Red-coated soldiers patrolled the streets. Many of the shops were closed, some showing the effects of vandalism. Hungry, mean-looking dogs ran in packs looking for a stray chicken, a heap of garbage, their ribs showing, their teeth flashing if one came too close. Drunken seamen wearing Navy-issue slops were thick along the waterfront; some, upon sighting Brendan, saluted respectfully. But there was no such respect amongst the out-of-work townspeople who lounged idly about, their eyes angry, their faces grim and set, their expressions disdainful as they watched him help the two girls into the carriage he had hired to take them to the Foley home.

The countryside beyond Boston was just as bleak as the port town, and no friendlier. Treacherous ruts carved up roads that were muddy and half frozen. The trees were bare-branched and gray with winter. The earth was spread with a sad carpet of bare, lifeless grass that was not green, as it should be, but *brown*, and flattened to the ground like a head of dirty, uncombed hair. Here and there, snow made a tired, dingy crust upon a shaded slope, and fields divided by haphazard walls of stone loomed on either side of the road.

With each mile that brought her farther and farther away from Christian, Deirdre's heart sank. Blocking out Delight's chatter, and Brendan's responsive laughter, she pressed her nose against the glass of the carriage window and blinked back tears of homesickness and despair.

"Christian," she whispered miserably, her sad eyes fixed on hills that were purple with the nakedness of the trees. "Oh, why couldn't I just have stayed with ye? Why does yer bleedin' admiral have t' be so concerned wi' me reputation when he doesn't even *know* me?"

The admiral. He had invited, nay, demanded that Christian join him aboard the flagship for dinner, and as Deirdre had solemnly watched the Lord and Master changing into his best uniform and calling for his finest sword, she'd had no idea that it would be the last time they would be together. Her anticipation of slowly stripping off that dashing uniform upon his return had been hopelessly smashed when, shortly after he'd left, Brendan had arrived to take *both* girls to the Foley home in Menotomy.

Deirdre had protested, railed, and wept, but the only thing such actions got her was apologies from her half-Irish cousin for having to follow orders that he admittedly agreed with. Brendan had patiently explained to her that Sir Geoffrey was concerned not only for *her* reputation, but also for those of his two captains. Of course, after Delight's brazen display in the maintop, Christian's would need all the help it could get. Having a woman living in his cabin would do nothing to salvage it.

Finally, stormy-eyed and sobbing, Deirdre had gathered up her few precious belongings, stolen one of Christian's shirts from his armoire so that she'd have something of his to comfort her, and, joining Delight and Brendan, departed the only home she had known for the past month.

"Tell th' captain where I be!" she had sobbed, fiercely hugging Ian just before she'd left the ship. "Tell him th' Old Fart's sendin' me away! Tell him t' come rescue me as soon as he can!"

"Aye, lassie. Now wipe away those tears, mind ye, and hold tight. The Lord and Master'll not abandon ye!"

No, surely he wouldn't! she thought, staring out at a flaw-lessly blue sky that was strangely naked of cloud. It looked nothing like the misty skies of home, reminding her again of how far away her beloved Ireland was. But Ian was right. The Lord and Master would *not* abandon her here! He loved her! As soon as he could get away, he would come for her.

But as they traveled farther inland, she couldn't prevent the sharp stabs of homesickness and mounting despair. The sky was not the only feature of this bleak and barren land that was strange. In fact, nothing was the way it *should* be. Back home, the trees would just be starting to branch and bud. Back home, yellow daffodils would be poking up through lush grass that was so brilliant and green it hurt your eyes to look at it. Back home, the weather would be raw and moist; here, it was frigid, dry—and bitterly cold.

She glanced at her cousin for assurance, but he obviously didn't notice the alarming differences between the two lands, so caught up was he at grinning over Delight's subtle remarks and not-so-subtle invitations.

Deirdre turned away to stare out the window, her eyes blurring with tears.

"Here we are!" Delight suddenly cried as the carriage

drew up beside a squarish, two-story house painted a humble shade of brown. "Now, Deirdre, you *must* remember not to call me Delight, no? Especially after all the pains I have taken to appear ... *presentable!*" Laughing, she indicated her modest blue dress, then yanked her shawl over her shoulders to conceal the tempting swell of her bodice, which had been purposely bared for the benefit of Brendan's appreciative eyes. "And you, Captain Merrick, simply *must* join us for supper! Mama will be most distressed if you do not, and"—she trailed her fingernails down his sleeve and gazed invitingly up into his eyes—"so will I!"

"Yes, Brendan, please stay," Deirdre murmured, terrified about being left with these people she didn't even know, terrified of losing contact with her cousin, terrified about being abandoned to this bleak and foreign land. She gripped his sleeve, trying in vain to blink back the tears. " 'Tis only for supper—"

The door to the house opened and a woman appeared on the threshold. Clad in brown-and-white calico, she had a white apron around her ample waist and blond hair tucked severely beneath a muslin cap.

"Dolores Ann!"

"Mama!"

Delight leapt out of the carriage, raced across the lawn, and flung herself into the woman's arms. There was much hugging and weeping and cheek-pinching before Delight, dragging her mother back across the muddy lawn, could make introductions. Brendan had already stepped down from the carriage and now stood on the lawn, holding his fancy, gold-laced hat. "Oh, Mama, I have brought guests!" Delight bubbled happily. "My friend is in the carriage— she's from Ireland—and our gallant escort here is her cousin, Captain Brendan Jay Merrick, who was kind enough to accompany us from Boston to ensure that no harm befell us. He's in the king's *Navy*, Mama!"

That last word—*Navy*—was oddly stressed, almost as if in warning. From inside the carriage, Deirdre saw a quick, fleeting look of alarm cross the woman's face as she looked at Deirdre's cousin in his handsome uniform; then she allowed him to take her hand and bow over it, a gesture that soon wiped the uneasiness from her eyes and had her cheeks flushing pink. "How do you do, madam," he said politely, with the same grin that had already won him many a female heart. And then: "My cousin, Deirdre O'Devir."

They had to pull her from the carriage. Mrs. Foley's eyes raked disapprovingly over Deirdre's ragged appearance, taking in the seaman's jacket that covered her thin shoulders, the trousers that hid her long legs. The woman's eyes widened in shock, but then she saw the frightened tears in Deirdre's purple eyes, and her smile could've melted the frost from Deirdre's cold-numbed toes. On impulse, she reached out and hugged her as fiercely as she had her own daughter. "Oh, do come in, poor thing, you must be absolutely frozen! A cup of chocolate will restore you in no time."

"Thank ye, Mrs. Foley. I . . . I'm sorry t' be intrudin' like this. I'd just as soon have stayed aboard th' ship. . . ."

"My, you have the most *delightful* brogue!" She put her hands on Deirdre's shoulders and stood back, admiring her and pretending she didn't notice the tears welling up in Deirdre's eyes. "Why, just listen to her talk, Dolores Ann! And, good heavens, don't speak such nonsense; you're not intruding at all. Any friend of Dolores's is a friend of ours. Besides, we were expecting you; the admiral in Boston sent word ahead that my daughter had arrived and was bringing a friend. Come, come, my dear, let's get you out of those atrocious clothes and into something a bit more ladylike. And you, Captain Merrick, do come in and join us for supper!"

"Faith, that's kind of you, madam, but I really couldn't—"

"I insist! Jared is at the shop right now, but he'll be home shortly. Meanwhile, you *must* come in and tell us all about what the king's noble Navy is doing to protect us from these horrible rebels."

"Yes, Captain Merrick, you simply *must!*" Delight echoed, eyeing his lean form appreciatively, suggestively, hungrily, from behind her mother's back.

No man could resist such a blatant invitation, not even a king's officer. And so it was that Brendan found himself ushered into the Foleys' house, a pale and frightened Deirdre trailing in his shadow.

It was hours later and Deirdre, seated morosely beside Brendan and listening to the effusive Delight babble on about her travels in France (omitting the more *salacious* details), was as miserable, lonely, and homesick as Christian had feared she would be.

Outside, the night pressed gloomily against the windows, and the reflection of the fire in the hearth seemed lonely and sad. Wind moaned under the eaves, made the flames waver and jump in the grating. Home had never seemed so far away. *Christian* had never seemed so far away. It was almost as if both belonged to another time, another place.

"Deirdre? Are you all right, lass?"

She glanced up at her cousin, whose mirthful eyes were dark with worry. "Aye, Brendan. Just ... just a wee bit homesick, 'tis all."

She looked down, afraid the Foleys would all start laughing at her.

"Why, I'll bet you're just missing your handsome Lord and Master," Delight chirped, shooting Brendan a bold glance from beneath her lashes. The look went unnoticed by her mother, who had gone to the hearth to ladle more stew from the pot, and her father, who had been inconspicuously studying the naval officer all during supper.

Brendan laughed, ever his cheerful self. "No, she misses Ireland," he teased, glancing at the crucifix around her neck, the canvas bag in her lap. *"Believe* me!"

"Oh, let the poor girl alone, you two!" Mrs. Foley scolded with mock sharpness. She plunked the steaming bowl of beef stew down amongst them and reclaimed her seat. "She's been across an ocean, traveled all day, and is probably tired to the bone. No wonder she's feeling poorly!"

Poorly was not the word for it, Deirdre thought, picking up her spoon and trying to pretend she had an appetite. And both of them were right—she missed Christian as much as she missed Ireland.

Her plate blurred behind her tears. She dragged the spoon up and put it in her mouth. The stew tasted as it should, but the yellow, coarse bread that accompanied it was dry and tasteless. She stared down at it, hating it as much as she did everything else here.

Brendan reached down and squeezed her hand. She saw twinkling reassurance in his russet eyes, teasing mirth around his mouth. Imitating her dejected look, he gave a black scowl, turning down the corners of his mouth and lowering his quirky eyebrows until she couldn't help but smile. But her response was short-lived, and as soon as he turned back to his meal, Deirdre was again staring down at her lap, her eyes on her bag of Irish mementos.

Oh, Christian, she thought. *If only I was with ye right now, safely wrapped in yer strong arms an' snuggled against yer big, warm chest. . . .*

Cradling the bag with her arm, she poked at her stew, making herself take a few bites just so she wouldn't appear rude. Outside, it was awfully black, the darkness thick and alien and hostile. The wind shook a loose pane against a casing, and a cold draft whispered across the wide-boarded floor and curled around her ankles.

American stew. American darkness. American wind. American cold.

Her hand came up to curl around Grace's crucifix, and it was all she could do not to burst into tears. *I want t' go home.*

But she was able to hold her tears in throughout the meal, knowing that the time would soon come when she could be alone, free to cry out the misery of her heart. Beside her, Brendan was already beginning to fidget, and she knew that soon he would have to leave, abandoning her in this foreign, unfriendly land with a family who ate strange food and talked with a strange accent. Suddenly the tears burned so painfully she could not contain them. She looked down, blinking them furiously back, but it was no use. One fell. Another. And yet a third spattered upon the simple muslin petticoat that Mrs. Foley had found for her, while a fourth fell upon the woolen skirts of her plain, plum-colored dress.

"You all right, Deirdre?" Delight asked gently.

Deirdre nodded quickly, too quickly, hastily wiping her eyes and trying to smile. Delight's father glanced at her. No doubt he was angry that he had another mouth to feed. He had barely said two words to her all night, instead watching Brendan and her with a look in his shrewd blue eyes that did nothing to make her feel welcome.

"Sure, now?" Delight persisted as Deirdre's white fingers came up to wrap around the crucifix.

"Aye . . . just a wee bit homesick, 'tis all."

Mr. Foley returned his attention to his stew. Mrs. Foley flashed her a warm smile. Brendan gave her another mocking scowl and Delight reached across the table to touch her wrist.

Talk went on, with the elder Foleys idly inquiring what the Navy was doing to quell smuggling, and Brendan giving bland answers that disclosed nothing. And all too soon, the steam stopped rising from the stew, the flames settled in the hearth, and Deirdre caught her handsome cousin glancing repeatedly at the shelf clock standing on a nearby table. Raw loneliness filled her, and it was all she could do not to start crying.

Don't go, Brendan, she thought desperately. *Oh, please, don't go and leave me here all by meself. . . .*

But in another half hour, the dreaded moment finally came. Brendan gave a great sigh, complimented Mrs. Foley on the meal, accepted a chunk of corn bread carefully wrapped in linen for the "trip back," and picked up his gold-laced hat. Deirdre followed him outside and then, sobbing, flew into his open arms.

"Oh, Brendan, I beg o' ye, *please* don't leave me here!"

His arms, not so large and muscled as Christian's, but wiry and every bit as strong, closed around her shaking shoulders. She pressed her face against his coat, his British coat, the same one that Christian wore.

"Faith, Deirdre, such carrying-on! 'Tis not the end of the world, you know!"

"Brendan, I hate it here! Everything's different, no one is friendly, and I just want t' go *ho-o-o-me. . . .*"

"Yes, Deirdre, speaking of home, I've been meaning to ask you. Why on *earth* did you leave Ireland to come here? Wasn't the money I've been sending to you and your mother enough?" He gripped her thin shoulders and, setting her away, looked down at her, his eyes concerned and very dark in the pale starlight.

"Mama's gone t' be with th' angels," she sobbed brokenly. "And I came here to find *you*. All day I've been waitin' fer the chance to be tellin' ye, but this is the first time I've had to be alone with ye. I came to find *you*, Brendan!"

"Me?"

" 'Tis a long story—I had no one left and I made a promise t' Mama, Brendan! She was dyin' and just before she took her last breath she begged me t' find Roddy an' bring him home t' Ireland so she could rest in peace. I thought ye could help me find him, since yer in the Navy! I thought ye could *help* me, Brendan!"

"Faith, is *that* why you came to America?"

"Aye, Brendan, i' 't'is, I swear it!"

"Dear God." He embraced her tightly, his arms closing around her thin shoulders. He had grown taller, stronger, even more handsome since she'd seen him last, but he was still the laughing, beloved cousin she remembered so well— and, he carried the blood of Ireland in his veins, the brogue of Connacht in his voice, the memory of Connemara in his heart.

Home.

She clung to him, unable to relinquish him to the night, her tears wetting the white lapels of his coat. "Brendan, ye can't leave me here, please, don't be leavin' me! I only came here t' find *you*, so that ye could help me find me brother!" She gazed up at him, her eyes desperate. "Please, Brendan, don't go! Take me back with ye, hide me aboard yer ship, hide me aboard Christian's ship, hide me *anywhere*, but please, I beg o' ye, don't leave me out here wi' these people I don't even know!"

"Faith, Deirdre—"

"Oh, Brendan, if anyone can find Roddy, 'tis you and Christian! Ye've got t' help me, Brendan! Ye've got t' take me back!"

"I can't take you back, Deirdre, and you know it. Faith, must you be so persuasive?" He grinned, trying to cheer her. "Besides, I'm sure that Captain Lord will be here just as soon as he can get away. If anyone can find your brother, he can."

She stared at him. "What about you, Brendan? Aren't ye goin' t' help?"

He gave a sad shake of his head. "Sir Geoffrey is sending me back to sea tomorrow, to cruise the north shore and make sure things do not get out of hand there." He saw his cousin's crumpling face and hugged her fiercely. "But I won't be gone forever, lass. When I come back, I promise to start making inquiries amongst my fellow officers and their seamen as to Roddy's whereabouts."

"D'ye think he's still alive, Brendan?" Her eyes pooled with tears. "Do ye?"

A shadow passed over his face. "Thirteen years is a long time, Deirdre."

"He's alive," she declared, raising her chin. "I feel it in me bones. We'll find him, Brendan, ye just wait an' see. Christian already promised he would do everythin' in his power t' get him back for me. He feels responsible, as i' 'twas his press gang that took Roddy in the first place, but I don't hold him accountable now for it. He was just doin' his duty." Fire flashed in her eyes. "Nay, Brendan, 'twas the Navy's fault, and it's up t' the Navy t' return me brother t' me!"

He looked down at her, his eyes affectionate, his face belovedly dear. "Ah, lass, you certainly have the determination of our Grace O'Malley in you, don't you? Now, make her even more proud and dry those tears." He reached down and thumbed away the moisture beneath the fringes of her lower lashes.

"Aye, Brendan."

"And now I must go. Sir Geoffrey will be most irate if I dally for too long."

On sudden impulse, she flung her arms around his neck, clinging tightly to him. They embraced each other for a long time, she wearing her homesickness and loneliness on her sleeve, he well used to this strange land and uncharacteristically silent as he pondered all she had told him. Finally he stood back and grinned at her in reassurance, reminded her that Christian was not so far away, and then climbed swiftly up into the carriage. Moments later, it was fading into the night.

Weeping quietly, Deirdre stayed out on the half-frozen lawn, watching until the horse's hoofbeats had dimmed and the carriage's lanterns had shrunk to mere sparks in the distance. At last they were gone altogether, and she was alone, the wind dragging through the bare branches above her head, her face turned eastward toward Boston Harbor—and, three thousand miles beyond it, Ireland.

The tears rushed down her cheeks in scalding torrents of homesickness and loneliness. Sobbing, she ran back into the house and fled up the narrow wooden staircase to the room that Mrs. Foley had prepared for her. Someone had brought her bag of Irish mementos up and placed it on the little stand just inside the door. The bed was neatly turned down, waiting. She grabbed her bag, pulled a thick, heavy quilt from the bed, wrapped it around herself, and went to the window. After much tugging, she managed to get it open. Cold night air swept in, and still weeping, she sat down on the bare floor and gazed out into the night, imagining her beloved cousin traveling somewhere out there in the darkness, away from her—and toward Christian.

"Oh, *Christian*," she sobbed, gripping her crucifix and staring up into the dark heavens. She pulled his shirt out of the bag and pressed it against her lips, inhaling his scent and crying bitterly. "Please, come an' get me. Please, oh, *please*, don't let me rot out here."

Stars twinkled brightly above the fringes of the treetops and the low-lying hills. Woodsmoke lay heavily in the air and wafted through the window on crisp, breezy puffs of cold wind. Across the road, the windows of a tavern glowed orange in the darkness. Figures in silhouette moved back and forth behind the panes.

"Christian," she whispered, spreading her palm to the darkness as though she could reach across the miles and touch him. Her voice sounded unnaturally loud and lonely in the stillness of the night. Hot tears splashed upon the back of her hand and rolled down her arm.

Deirdre pushed her fist against her mouth so no one would hear her sobs. In her lap was her precious bag of

Irish mementos, and she touched it, her fingers moving over the odd lumps and bumps and knowing each shape in the darkness.

Far, far off in the distance, a dog barked, the sound lonely and sad in the night.

How far away from her now was Brendan? A mile? Two?

Her chest convulsed on a thick sob, and she reached into the bag and touched the soft clump of wool from an Irish sheep. That tiny connection with home—so near, and yet so far—brought a fresh torrent of hot, stinging tears coursing down her cheeks, and she bent her head, burying her face in the harsh folds of the canvas bag to contain the sounds of her weeping.

Home. Oh, God, where *was* it? In which direction did it lie?

She looked up into the night sky. Alarm spread through her when she could not find the North Star. Dear Lord, were the stars that shone over this godforsaken wasteland different from those that stood over her beloved Ireland? Sniffling, and shivering with cold, Deirdre clutched the tuft of wool and leaned far out the window, craning her neck and peering up at the peaked roof of the dark house.

There. The North Star. Choking relief swept over her, and her chest constricted on another hot wave of tears. *Thank God.* That, at least, was familiar. Wiping her eyes with the back of her hand, she leaned out the window once again, contorting her body at an unnatural angle so that her face was turned homeward.

At that moment a gust of wind came up, tearing the wool from her hand. She cried out and make a mad lunge toward it, but the lonely white tuft drifted off into the darkness, dancing on the wind, fading away until it was swallowed by the night.

Far away, the dog barked again.

She pressed wet fingers to her temples, her wretched sobs echoing in the stillness of the room. "Oh ... oh, God, no. . . ."

Ireland.

Another piece of it gone.

She wrapped her arms around her knees, bent her head,

and, clutching Christian's shirt to her heart, cried until she could cry no more.

"Heavens, Deirdre, what was all that bumping and thumping going on up there last night?" Delight asked at the breakfast table the next morning. She stuffed a spoonful of strange yellow pudding into her mouth and reached for the pitcher of tree sap—which Deirdre had been told, was called maple syrup. "I thought the house was going to come down!"

Deirdre raised her head. She didn't need a mirror to know that her eyes were puffy, swollen, and red-rimmed from crying and lack of sleep. Only when she had made some adjustments to her bed, then fiercely hugged Christian's shirt in her arms and pretended she was hugging *him*, had she been able to find sleep.

But it was morning now, and her spirits—buoyed by the hope that Christian might come to see her today—were much higher than they had been when she had finally fallen into troubled slumber upon a pillow that was wet with tears.

Mr. and Mrs. Foley were regarding her curiously. Outside, sunshine was bright across the land, making the low-lying hills in the near distance look as purple as the Twelve Bens back home. Deirdre's cheeks flamed, and sheepishly, she murmured, "I'm sorry. I didn't mean t' keep anyone awake. I was . . . movin' th' bed."

"Moving the *bed?*"

She swallowed hard, and stared down at her hands, suddenly embarrassed. "I wanted it t' . . . t' face Ireland."

Even the stern and stoic Jared Foley was hard pressed to suppress an amused smirk at that.

"Well, I never!" Mrs. Foley exclaimed. "You have to be the most homesick little girl I've ever met! You'll just have to meet Dolores Ann's Irish *friend* soon, right, Dolores?"

"Irish friend?" Deirdre asked, suddenly brightening.

"A seafarer, just like *your* man," Delight said, her eyes glinting with instigation.

"What?" Mr. Foley asked, peering at Deirdre from over the top of his wire-rimmed spectacles. "You have a suitor?"

"Oh, he is *most* handsome," Delight said. "He masters a ship, right, Deirdre?"

"Aye," Deirdre said proudly.

Mr. Foley laid down his fork and stared at her. "Which one?"

"His Majesty's frigate *Bold Marauder.* Christian is a king's officer. A captain in th' Royal Navy."

A shadow passed over Mr. Foley's face. He exchanged a quick glance with his wife and, picking up his fork, cast his gaze back down toward his plate.

"Did I say somethin' wrong?"

"No, Deirdre." Mrs. Foley patted her hand. "Not at all." Again she glanced at her husband. "We should like to, er, meet him sometime. Wouldn't we, Jared?"

"Aye," he grunted, attacking his hasty pudding.

Deirdre looked at them, wondering what she had said to alarm them. She glanced at Delight, hoping to find an answer, but her friend was looking down, smiling, and removing a shell from her eggs.

The sudden silence was uncomfortable. Bending her head, Deirdre picked up her fork and, shunning the strange hasty pudding, went for the more familiar eggs instead.

They weren't from an Irish hen, but at least they didn't taste any different.

Perhaps there was hope here, after all.

Despite Sir Geoffrey's assurances, and Christian's desire to race off to Menotomy at the first chance he had, it was two days before he could get away from his duties. Meetings with his admiral and General Gage to discuss rebel movements, and the presentation of his bold plan to net the Irish Pirate, kept him near his command. But by the third morning, when he awoke bleary-eyed, lonely, and exhausted, he knew he could delay no longer.

Tildy had left her puppies in a warm, tightly knotted mass to climb into bed with him, but though her presence was a small comfort, no one could take the place of his beloved Deirdre. Every time he'd rolled over and looked at the white pillow, he imagined his Irish girl's thick, spiraling black curls spread over it, her innocent purple eyes gazing at him with love and adoration. He hadn't realized how much he missed her until he was forced to sleep alone.

How had she fared through the nights? Bugger it, the poor mite was probably homesick as hell, out there all by herself in an unfamiliar countryside with unfamiliar people. Anger swept through him at the unfortunate circumstances that had separated them. He rose from his bed. There was no sense in allowing her to suffer any longer.

Mechanically, he went through the motions of washing, shaving, dressing. He packed a bag with a few civilian clothes, then chose his finest shirt, his best dress coat, and his gold-tasseled presentation sword. He made a handsome picture as he appeared on deck, and could not have been more pleased with the smartness and ceremony with which his men saw him over the side.

They stood by the hammock nettings, watching his gig carry him across the sparkling harbor, threading its way between the other anchored warships.

"Something's troubling our Lord and Master," Hibbert said, as though no one else had noticed.

"Aye, he be in a bad way. The Old Fart must ha'e given him a good setting-down the other day," Ian said, glaring at the huge flagship that shimmered in her own reflection. "Right, Skunk?"

Skunk slammed a meaty fist into his broad palm. "It ain't *his* fault none of us knew Delight was up there!"

"Elwin says the Old Fart was so mad he was spitting nails."

"Should've let Delight work her charms upon *him*," Teach growled, joining them. He held a fine flintlock pistol in his hand, and was cocking the empty weapon, pulling the trigger, cocking the weapon, pulling the trigger, his annoyance obvious and beginning to become annoying in itself. "Might've done the Old Fart a world of good."

"She tried," Elwin said, scowling irritably at Teach, then picking at a callus on his finger. "But it was Deirdre, not Delight, who got the old crust softened up enough that he finally quit raging at our Lord and Master. Never saw nothing like it. Had him eating out of her hand, she did."

Click, snap, click, snap, went Teach's pistol.

Wenham scratched at his great, jutting ears. "Too bad that young Irish captain had to take Deirdre from us. I'll bet that's what's got our poor Lord and Master in such a sorry state, having her stolen away from him like that."

"That young captain be her cousin, y'know," Ian said.

"Her *cousin?*"

"Aye. Ye can see some resemblance around the mouth. Same smile."

"Same way of talkin', too. Boglander brogue," added Skunk.

Click. Snap. Click.

"Christ, would ye quit with that noise? It's irritatin' as all hell!" Skunk snarled.

Teach merely grinned, and kept on doing it.

Ian cleared his throat. "Well, *I* think we need tae be cheering up our captain. What do ye all think of inviting him tae the wardroom for supper with us tomorrow night? That way he won't have tae eat all by himself. Besides, 'twill show him how much *we're* behind him, no matter what the Old Fart says or does!"

"Aye, good idea, Ian!"

Rhodes melted out of the shadows and seated himself upon the gunwales of one of the ship's boats. His tone was solemn. "When I accompanied him over to the flagship yesterday, one of the lieutenants told me our captain isn't well liked. The other commanders are jealous of his record, envious of what he's accomplished." He swept them with his black eyes. "They'll not make things easy for him here."

"Huh! Piss on *them,* I say!" Skunk said, his eyes flashing. "Sufferin' bastards, I hear *any* of 'em sayin' one bad word about our captain and I'll skin the wrinkles from their hides and stuff 'em down their bloody throats!"

"Aye!" they echoed in unison, their eyes fierce, protective, and angry.

Teach raised his pistol and pointed it at the huge flagship. *Click. Snap. Click.* "And that goes for that old fart of an admiral, too!"

Chapter 24

Christian was not sorry to get away from Boston for the day. The tense and explosive atmosphere of the town made him uneasy: red-coated troops spoiling for a fight, bored sailors lounging along the wharves, angry and resentful colonists who'd been out of work since Parliament's Coercive Acts had deprived them of their jobs and left them bitter and indignant. Now the townspeople had nothing better to do than taunt the British troops, monitor their every movement, and report back to the infamous Sons of Liberty, who were behind this whole bloody mess.

Beneath him, his horse, a strapping chestnut stallion he'd purchased at a ridiculously low price from a Welsh major eager to pay off a gambling debt, sensed his anxiety and began to prance. Christian's hands tightened on the reins. If only Sir Geoffrey hadn't discovered Deirdre aboard the frigate; he'd give anything to have her safely behind the protection of *Bold Marauder*'s guns should the inevitable explosion between colonists and the king's forces occur.

And, of course, there was the undeniable fact that he loved her. . . .

Rico had barged into his cabin that morning while Christian had been eating his breakfast. "Every man jack aboard the frigate knows you're pining for the Irish girl," his friend had said as Christian morosely toyed with his boiled egg and ship's biscuit. "Why don't you just marry her and get on with life?"

"Marry her?"

Why not? It was a simple solution to the loneliness that

285

had plagued him for the past five years. He had lived in hell for all that time, but now that he'd had a taste of nirvana, thoughts of even one more day of it were suddenly unbearable.

Deirdre. He loved her, and she, by her own word, loved him. He gazed ahead, past the pricked ears of his mount, smiling as he pictured that beloved face, that glorious fall of spiraling black curls scattered across thin and creamy shoulders, those sometimes stormy, sometimes childlike, but always loving amethyst eyes that had haunted him for the past month.

Eyes that he knew now had haunted him for the past thirteen years.

He shifted in the saddle, nudging his horse into a light trot and gritting his teeth against the sudden pain in his shoulder. What would marriage to his little Irish girl be like? Would she adapt to life in England? She'd already proved she could adjust to life aboard a king's warship; would she be happy as the wife of a king's officer?

One thing he was certain of. When at sea, he would *not* leave her behind as he had Emily. No, he would take his wife with him wherever he went, tucking her safely in the deepest abyss of the ship during battle, allowing her free run of the decks in gentler times. He couldn't face another morning like this one—empty, cold, and lonely.

He couldn't face an empty bed, ever again.

But could he, a battle-scarred, sometimes cynical king's officer who'd seen far too much of the world, make *her* happy? Was he good enough for her?

He had the ring in his pocket. He'd put it there before he'd left the ship that morning. Holding the reins in one hand, he reached down and checked to be sure it was still there. Of purest gold, the ring was a lion's body, its eyes blood-red rubies, its mouth glinting with diamond chips, its tail the band that would wrap itself around Deirdre's delicate finger. The ring was exquisite, and as ancient as the title that Christian's ancestors had held for centuries. Upon the death of their father, Elliott would become the marquess, but Elliott had ardently professed that he would sooner fall victim to a cannonball than to marriage, and had given the ring to his younger brother shortly before *Bold Marauder* had left Portsmouth.

Deirdre O'Devir Lord. *His bride, his wife.* Warmth and love softened his heart as the thought took on reality and substance, vision and hope. Oh, he wanted her more than anything, anyone. He wanted her as his *wife*.

But would she have him?

His lips tightened as his horse trotted slowly on, skirting the glistening puddles that pocked the road that led out from Boston into the western countryside. He was, after all, an Englishman she'd spent the past thirteen years of her life hating. And despite having made inquiries amongst some of the other sea officers and their men, he was no closer now to fulfilling his promise to find her brother than he had been last week, no closer to righting the dreadful wrong that he— and England—had done to her and her family those thirteen years ago.

By God, he *would* right it. He *would* find her brother if it was the last thing he did, and reunite the family that he, in the king's name, had torn apart!

"As God is my witness, I will," he vowed ardently.

So caught up was he in his musings that the miles passed beneath him without his notice that they were even gone. It seemed that he had barely left Boston before he crossed a small bridge over the Mystic River Brook, and, passing beneath the bare branches of two old elm trees that guarded the little village, entered Menotomy. His gray eyes became sharp and assessing as he took in his surroundings, for this was, after all, where Deirdre would have to live until he made her his wife.

Would she be happy here in the interim? A typical New England town, it was tiny and picturesque. Stone walls and fences bordered the road. Fields strewn with a haphazard scattering of granite, sheep, and cows rolled away into the distance, melting into gentle hills of birch, pine, oak, elm, and maple. Yet despite the lulling mildness of the early spring morning, he sensed a tension in the air that was far from tranquil.

The hairs rose on the back of his neck, and he touched the inside of his elbow to the hilt of his sword. Tranquil and

serene, yes; but he could feel eyes upon him, eyes that
watched him with suspicion and no small degree of hostility.

He slowed the horse to a walk, passing the Black Horse
Tavern and Spy Pond, where geese honked loudly and
shook the water out of their broad wings. From somewhere
he heard the distant sound of fife and drum, and wondered
if even now the so-called minutemen were mustering, preparing to practice their futile maneuvers.

The thought both saddened and alarmed him.

The Menotomy minutemen were a new unit, led by a
farmer named Benjamin Locke, whose house was farther
westward along the Concord Road. Christian gazed at the
peaceful fields and the humble dwellings that spilled smoke
from their thick chimneys. Why had things come down to
this? Why couldn't Englishmen live in harmony with one
another? Why couldn't Parliament be more sympathetic to
those who lived across the sea, and all those in power back
in England be more understanding about the concerns of the
colonists? God help the poor bumpkins if and when things
came to blows between them and the king's forces.

The haunting music was disturbing and depressing. Christian nudged his mount into a trot, wincing with each jolting
jar to his shoulder, but welcoming the sound of the beast's
hooves over the lonely fife and drum. Mud splashed up and
splattered the animal's belly, its forelegs, and Christian's
gleaming boots, but the horse shook its head, wanting more
speed. He tightened his hands on the reins, keeping the stallion's pace contained. The traffic was heavier here, the other
travelers staring at him as he passed. Seeing an open carriage with a pair of country women in it, he touched his hat
in polite greeting. Their eyes raked him with disdain and
anger. A youth no older than Hibbert glared at him with
open hostility from behind a stone wall, and a group of
farmers, leading a milk cow, spat on the ground in open
contempt. Disturbed and feeling increasingly ill at ease,
Christian continued on.

He passed another tavern, where movement at the windows indicated his presence was not unobserved. By God,
was the whole bloody village watching him? It was almost

as though people had seen him coming and had spread the news of his presence long before his horse had even reached the place. No doubt they were wondering what a naval officer was doing this far from sea and were suspicious as to the reason. In that, he couldn't blame them.

Ahead was an intersection, and as he came abreast of it, he saw a store and a small, steepled church, beyond which lay a small forest of gray gravestones, bleak and forbidding even in the bright splash of sunlight. He passed several more houses, another tavern, and there, directly across the road, stood the simple brown house that, according to Sir Geoffrey's roughly drawn map, belonged to Jared Foley.

At last.

He pulled his horse to a halt, content just to sit for a minute in the sunshine and gaze upon the girl who stood at a well in the front yard, toiling with a rope and what must've been a rather heavy bucket at its end. Instantly, he forgot his throbbing shoulder. Her bent back was toward him, her little rump outlined in a plain skirt of pine-green linsey-woolsey, her muslin petticoats barely clear of the squishy mud in which she stood. Her hair, black as pitch and caught in a loose braid, followed the taut groove of her spine and brushed the gentle rise of her hips. He saw her narrow shoulder blades working as she wrestled with the heavy rope, heard her angry curses.

"Damned poxy, bleedin' thing! I *hate* this place, I want t' go home!" A quick shrug of her cheek against her shoulder betrayed the probability of accompanying tears and abruptly wiped the amused grin from Christian's lips.

Vaulting from his saddle with an ease not usually found among mariners, Christian strode across the spongy lawn, his boots squishing in damp turf. But still, she didn't hear him. He came up behind her, grasped the rope, and began to pull, his strength making quick work of the task.

"Christian!"

He pulled the dripping bucket up just as she whirled to face him. Her mouth had dropped open, her eyes bulging with shock, disbelief, and sudden, happy tears.

"Christian!"

Holding the rope in one hand, he reached up with his

other and doffed his hat. Sunlight shone blindingly atop his hair, so fair and pale that it needed no powder, and certainly not the wig he seemed to have permanently forgone. "I daresay you could've used some help, my dear girl."

She flung herself against him, bursting into sobs that shook her shoulders and dampened the front of his coat. His arms closed around her, and for a long moment he could only hold her, burying his face in her hair while a fierce sense of protectiveness and possessiveness welled up in his chest. His heart constricted almost painfully, making it hard to breathe, impossible to think. But it was a good feeling. It was an even better one to see how happy his appearance had made her. He swallowed, overcome with emotion. How different she was, in every way, from how Emily had been.

Closing his eyes, he held her close, wishing with all his heart he could take her back to *Bold Marauder* with him. Tonight. Now. Forever. She smelled like road dust and spring sunshine, clean wind and horses. She was soft and warm, utterly feminine, totally guileless. He liked that. He liked the feel of her in his arms. He liked everything about her.

By God, there was nothing he *didn't* like.

Not a deuced thing.

Her sobs were muffled against his chest. "Oh, Christian, ye don't know how lonely I've been withou' t'ye! I hate it here, I do! The birds're different, the animals're different, the people're cold 'n' unfriendly, and they talk funny, act funny. The air is cold, the grass is brown! Oh, Christian, thank God ye came t' take me back t' the ship! I'll surely die if I have t' stay here another day!"

He opened his eyes. "Deirdre, I did not come here to take you back to *Bold Marauder.*" He took a deep breath, his arms wrapping around her narrow shoulders. "I came here to ask you to—"

The front door of the house banged open. "Deirdre?"

A girl stood there, her curves tamed to modesty in a plain blue woolen gown and further concealed beneath a black cloak of linsey-woolsey. She had blond hair, not bleached and silvery like his own, but rich and tawny and yellow, worn severely braided and entwined around her head. Her face was plain, fresh, and unpainted; her eyes, smiling and knowing.

The eyes, bold and brimming with raw prurience, were what gave her away.

"Delight?" he gasped, shocked.

She picked up her skirts and hurried across the lawn, her finger laid across full lips that had been, at his last sight of her, red and painted. "Don't call me that in front of my mother—she'll have my hide!" Nervously, she glanced back toward the house. "It's *Dolores Ann!"*

Stunned, he helplessly peeled Deirdre off his chest just as the woman in question appeared on the threshold.

If Christian had any doubts as to where the Foleys' true loyalties lay, they were quickly put to rest by the woman's reaction to the presence of a king's officer on her front lawn. She had a pinched, worried look around her eyes that quickly turned to downright fear. Her face drained of color. Her eyes went wide, and a wet dishcloth fell from her hands and splashed into a puddle of mud at her feet.

Just as quickly, she regained her composure and stepped forward, only her darting eyes and high, jittery voice betraying her nervousness. "Why, Captain, 'tis not often we receive naval visitors out here in Menotomy! First Captain Merrick, now you. . . . I—I assume you must be, uh, Deirdre's suitor?"

Christian bowed gallantly and, tucking his hat under his elbow, stepped forward to take the woman's hand. It was trembling, the skin cold as ice. "Your assumptions, madam, stand you in good stead. I wanted merely to content myself as to the state of Miss O'Devir's happiness and well-being. And, of course, pay my respects to your lovely daughter and her obliging family, from whose hospitality my dear Deirdre has obviously benefited." He regarded the woman, his gray eyes steady and keen. "There is such tension in our midst, I can only thank God that my beloved has found sanctuary with a solid and upright family who is loyal to king and Crown. Pray, I hope I have not come at an inconvenient time?"

"Oh—oh, no, n-not at all!" Mrs. Foley said too quickly, her skittish manner as condemning as if she'd blatantly admitted that she and her family were anything *but* loyal. "Why don't you come in for some refreshment? A cup of chocolate, perhaps?"

A shadow flashed across her face at his reply. "I would enjoy that, madam. And if I may allow my horse a drink of water before I join you?"

"Yes, yes, please do! You may tie him up there, beside the watering trough. Dolores Ann? Please stop gaping and come with me—*now!*"

Christian's gilded lashes swept down to mask the triumph in his gray eyes. It was all too obvious that the woman had no desire this side of Hades to have him there, but to act in anything less than a hospitable fashion, especially toward a decorated and respected officer of the king's Navy, would certainly cast suspicion on the Foley name.

Had she acted this way toward Brendan, too? Bugger it, if only he'd thought to speak to the other frigate captain before he'd so hastily left Boston. . . .

Picking up her skirts, Delight's mother turned and hustled back to the house. In typical New England fashion, the structure faced south, its roof steep and sloping to rid itself of winter snows, its big chimney set squarely in the center. Five windows shone with sunlight at the top floor; four windows, divided by a door, looked out from the bottom. A barn stood a short distance away from the house, ringed by a fence containing two horses sleeping in the sun.

"I see you've bought yourself a steed, Captain Lord." Delight's eyes roved over the tall stallion, whose coat, glinting in the sunlight, was the color of rich cherry wood. The animal's ears were small, his eyes dark and intelligent. She quirked a brow. "But then, there are many activities besides *riding* that one can do upon a horse, no?"

Christian opened his mouth to reply with a sarcastic comment, but just then the door banged open. "Dolores Ann! You get yourself in here this instant!"

Delight sighed and rolled her eyes. "*God,* I really *do* wish I'd stayed in France sometimes." Still muttering, she sauntered off across the lawn, hips rolling. As she reached the door, Mrs. Foley yanked her inside. The woman's mouth was moving, her hands gesturing angrily, and Christian wished he could hear what warning the agitated woman was giving her daughter. Feigning indifference to them, he looked at Deirdre as she caught his sleeve.

"Oh, Christian, ye don't know how happy ye make me by comin' out here t'day! I've been so bleedin' lonely I can hardly bear it. I missed ye so much last night, I thought me poor heart would break!"

She leaned back and looked up at him, her dark lashes awash with happy tears. Her pale fingers rested against his lapels; her slim, lithe body pressed against his. Her heart was in her eyes, shamelessly reflecting love and joy, and again he felt his chest swell and threaten to burst with pride. She was *his*. She had given herself to him and, in her innocence, had made him a man once more, in all senses of the word.

And soon, she would be his in name as well as in heart. He thought of the ring in his pocket, and his heart gave a quick, eager flutter.

By God, I love her, he told himself.

Knowing that Mrs. Foley was probably observing them from her window, he gently pried Deirdre's hands from his lapels. "Come, dear girl. Let us go in and behave ourselves for a bit, eh?"

"Oh, Christian. Please don't ask me t' be behavin' meself for too long. I want t' be alone with ye and show ye how much I've been a-missin' ye!"

He swallowed hard, his loins tightening in instant response. As she took his hand and guided him to the house, he wondered how he had ever thought he might be impotent. "Well, then," he said, gazing down at her, his eyes darkening in desire, "perhaps you can borrow a horse from the Foleys and we can go, er, *riding* afterward?"

"Oh, Christian, can we?"

He thought again of the ring. It would be a perfect time to give it to her. "Aye," he said, tipping her chin up and gazing into her wide purple eyes. "Now let us go and be sociable."

But as they entered the house Deirdre fled up the stairs with an excited excuse about having to change her clothes, and with an equally excited Delight floating in her wake.

Christian stood just inside the door for a moment, his hat in his hands as he looked around. The house was small, plain, lived-in. He walked into the main living area, which obviously doubled as a kitchen, feigning casual interest while his keen stare searched for anything that would further boost suspicions that the Foleys were anything but Loyalists. But there was nothing incriminating. The house smelled of herbs, cooking, and years of fires burned on the huge hearth that dominated the room in which he stood. These were strange smells to his mariner's nose, just as the room itself, a palace compared with the size of his cabin aboard *Bold Marauder*, was strange to his seafarer's eyes. Wide boarded floors were scuffed smooth by the soles of many shoes. The huge, soot-blackened fireplace that dominated the room was framed by various cooking utensils of different sizes, shapes, and forms, and emanated the tantalizing aroma of baking bread. He peered into one ominous-looking black pot and saw a pudding boiling in a cloth. Herbs hung from overhead rafters; a set of chairs surrounded a rough-hewn table spread with elegant, pristinely clean linens that made a contrast of coarseness and refinement.

He looked at the chairs. In which one had his Deirdre taken her supper? Sat and talked to her hosts? Cried inside with homesickness?

By God and all that was holy, such was not a state she would have to endure for long. As soon as he gleaned the evidence Sir Geoffrey needed to brand the Foleys as rebels of the Crown, as soon as he himself learned what he needed to know to find and chase down the Irish Pirate—who was, as Sir Geoffrey had put it, "putting weapons in the hands of babes"—he would marry her and get her out of here.

That day couldn't arrive soon enough.

Mrs. Foley came bustling around the corner, absently patting her hair, her lips drawn tight, an anxious frown creasing her brow. Her hand flew to her chest at the sight of him.

"Oh! I hadn't realized you'd already come in—"

"My apologies, madam, for startling you."

She hastily indicated a chair. "No matter, Captain. As you know, things are so tense I suppose we are all in a state of agitation, what with those awful rebels rousing the country-side as they are!" She turned hastily away, unable to meet his eyes, and quickly changed the subject. "Dolores Ann tells me you took extraordinarily good care of her during the passage, and that your crew was most obliging to her *every* need."

Christian swallowed the wrong way, coughed, and out of the corner of his eye caught Delight's amused face as she entered the room in time to hear her mother's comment. "They were, uh, quite attentive," he said slowly, grabbing the cup of hot, steaming chocolate that was set before him. Bless him, if the woman only knew what her daughter's needs *were*—and how obliging *Bold Marauder*'s men had been to *see* to them!

"I'm glad to hear that," Mrs. Foley said. "Of course, one can never be too safe nowadays, what with such riffraff as that awful Irish Pirate terrorizing the seas! Why, I'm told that he struck again just last week . . . engaged himself in battle with an English frigate!"

Christian nearly scalded his throat at the woman's reckless taunt. He set the hot chocolate down. "I daresay he saw no battle with that English frigate, madam. The ship in question was under my command, and any damage she sustained was dealt by a Frenchman, not an overgrown brat playing at being a smuggler."

His remark, carefully delivered with just the right amount of anger and righteous British indignation, had the desired effect. He saw his hostess's eyes gleam before she swung quickly away and set a plate containing a slice of freshly baked pork pie before him. "Is that so, Captain? I don't think the Irish—I mean, the scoundrel—is 'playing.' In fact, I think he's become quite successful at his *game.*"

"I daresay," Christian said mildly, carefully sipping his chocolate and meeting her gaze over the top of the cup's rim. "Nevertheless, my admiral views his antics as a paltry inconvenience, and so do I. Really, the king's Navy and officers have better things to be doing than chasing after such vermin. A ghastly inconvenience to me, you know, having been sent across three thousand miles of stormy North Atlantic ocean for the sole purpose of apprehending this nuisance. Why, I could be home right now in England, enjoying the wind off my *own* seas, not chasing after some devilish rogue determined to get himself hanged."

His hostess took the bait. "You mean, you've been sent all the way from England *just* to catch the Irish Pirate?"

"Ghastly thought, is it not?" Christian gave a benign, planned smile. "Of course, one cannot blame me for my flagging interest in the assignment. As I said, there are matters of more importance than this . . . this *rogue*."

"Such as?" she prompted, trying to conceal her inquisitiveness.

Christian picked up his knife and fork and cut a piece of the pie. He allowed a gleam to come into his eyes. "Oh, such as the pursuit of other, more . . . shall I say . . . *romantic* interests."

She stared at him.

"Really, Mrs. Foley," he said, smiling patiently. "After that display on your front lawn, is there any doubt in your mind as to why I am here?" He clapped a hand eloquently to his chest. "I am in love with your guest and wish to marry her at the earliest convenience. My mind is too full of Miss Deirdre O'Devir to be entertained with notions of what little glory I would earn myself by catching the Irish Pirate."

Little glory indeed, Christian thought to himself. If he caught the notorious smuggler, he would earn himself a shamelessly flattering report to bring back to the Admiralty. But first and foremost, he had to gain the trust of the Foleys—and fool them into thinking he did not take his assignment seriously.

Apparently his plan was working; his hostess's face had visibly relaxed, and it occurred to Christian that marrying Deirdre, and thereby removing his excuse to visit the Foley household, would be quite welcome in Mrs. Foley's eyes indeed.

His suspicions bore fruit. "Well, then," the woman said brightly, "I shall not detain you in your courtship of the girl. Personally, I think you make a striking couple! Pity that she has no family for you to request her hand."

"Oh, but she does," Christian remarked, thinking of

Brendan—whose consent he intended to obtain as soon as he posed his question to Deirdre. But at that moment Deirdre herself came flying down the stairs, her cheeks pink with excitement.

"Ye like it, Christian?" She made a quick, childish pirouette, the skirts of her new riding habit flying to reveal shapely ankles. "'Tis Del—I mean, Dolores's. She gave me a bunch o' clothes t' wear till I can sew meself some o' me own."

Judging from the tailored fit of the bodice, and given the superior size of Delight's bosom, Deirdre had already been at work with needle and thread. Christian smiled wryly to himself. He pushed the plate of pie away, and drained the last of the hot chocolate. Then he stood up, six feet and two inches of handsome male power barely contained in the uniform of a king's officer.

"You don't mind, of course, if I take my beloved riding?" he asked of Mrs. Foley, his question more a command than a request.

"No, I don't mind at all, Captain Lord. In fact, do take one of our horses for Deirdre. Ah, would that we were all young again, and able to enjoy the fruits of our youth. . . ."

Christian nodded, took Deirdre's hand, and, gallantly kissing it, led her from the house, secure in the knowledge that Delight's mother thought him nothing more than a mildly arrogant, totally smitten swain of the lovely Deirdre O'Devir who had little interest in seeing to his duty of apprehending the Irish Pirate.

But as the Foley women stood on the porch, watching the tall and handsome officer escort his young love across the yard, Mrs. Foley was anything but calm. She waited until they were out of earshot, then turned frantically on her daughter.

"I don't like this one bit!" she cried, wringing her hands and dashing away the nervous sweat that dampened her brow. "That's all we need, to have a king's officer sniffing around here!"

"*Really,* Mama, he's a naval captain," Delight purred, forgetting to use her normal tone of voice and earning an instant glare of reprimand from her mother. "And naval

officers concern themselves with the affairs of ships and
sea, *not* with patriot gatherings such as those that you and
Papa have become involved in."

"Still, the man makes me nervous! He's too smooth. Too
controlled. And those eyes ... they see right through you!
He *knows,* Dolores Ann!" She gripped her daughter's arms,
her fingers biting into the soft flesh, her eyes wide with
fright. "He *knows!*"

"Pooh, Mama. He's knows nothing. He's merely in love
with Deirdre, that's all." Delight smoothed back a loose lock
of golden hair and tucked it under her mobcap. "Why, if
you'd seen the utterly *scandalous* way those two behaved
aboard ship, you'd know *just* what I'm talking about."

"Dolores Ann, everyone knows he was sent here to apprehend the Irish Pirate!"

"And by his own admission you heard how little the task
means to him." Delight gave a lazy, confident grin, and laid
her hand on her mother's arm. "Really, Mama, you worry
too much. Captain Lord may be clever, but he is nowhere
near as cunning as our Irish Pirate. Why, Roddy will run circles around him. In fact, he already has. Now come. Let us
go and see to supper, no?"

Taking her mother's arm, she led her into the house.

Chapter 25

They rode side by side, he gazing hungrily at her trim
form and loving her with his eyes, she admiring the
way the sunlight picked out every golden strand in the
bright hair that curled beneath his hat and lay caught between his broad shoulders. He smiled at her, and giddy happiness flooded her chest. Despite the hostile looks some of
the townspeople were giving Christian, she was proud to be

at his side, and never once felt ashamed to be in the company of this fine and distinguished king's officer.

Her heart swelled, and she felt her eyes filling with tears of love.

They rode onward, gazing at each other so much that it was left to the horses to choose their path. To Deirdre, America suddenly did not seem so bleak. She had been too homesick to appreciate her surroundings, but now, at the side of the man she loved, the sunlight looked brighter, the chickadees and cardinals and jays more colorful, the water of a nearby pond cobalt with brilliance, the scents of springtime—mud, melted frost, running water, fresh air—sharper.

And trees? She had never seen so many in her life, for the moors of Connemara were bleak and barren and empty of such thick woods.

"Christian?"

"Aye, my love?"

She was looking at a V of geese winging high overhead, their lonely honking drifting down in waves of sound. When she turned to look at him, her eyes were very wide, and suspiciously moist. "D'ye ever miss England?"

He smiled gently. "All the time."

"The same way I miss Ireland?"

"The same way. Though I daresay I don't carry a bag of trinkets with me to remind me of it!"

She frowned. "Are ye teasin' me?"

"Who, me?" His lips twitched suspiciously. "I simply find it a most charming trait, your sentimentality for home. But someday, you will learn that home is not where you happen to be living at the moment, or even where you hail from—but where your heart is. Home can be any place, so long as the one you love is there with you."

She raised her chin. "Then if that be true, Christian, I am home now."

He smiled at her, his eyes soft with love. "Was it very hard for you, being alone these past nights?"

"Aye," she said, the misery of those lonely hours nearly forgotten now that Christian was there with her. "But I managed."

"Oh?"

"I stole yer shirt," she admitted. "It weren't much, but with it in me arms, I felt as if I had a part o' ye there with me. And ye know what else I did, Christian?"

"Pray, do tell."

"I sat at me window an' figured out by the stars just where Ireland is—then I moved me bed so I can fall asleep every night with me face toward it."

He laughed in high amusement, shaking his head, but she merely scowled at him, undaunted. "Christian, d'ye think all th' Englishmen that're here—I mean, all the men in the ships, and all the men o' the general's troops—want t' go home, too?"

"I'm sure they do."

"I don't know why anyone would want t' live here, Christian. The land is ugly. And everythin's so cold, everyone so unfriendly."

"The people are unhappy with England's policies right now, Deirdre. When things are resolved, and agreements reached between the colonists and England, then you will find America a very beautiful place."

"'Tis nothin' like Ireland," she declared huffily.

"No, it is not. It has its own beauty."

"I see nothin' beautiful about it. The birds look different, the animals look different, the people talk different, and the grass is brown. Whoever heard o' brown grass? In Ireland right now, the grass'd be green and pretty!"

He slanted her a grin. "In Ireland right now, dear girl, it would be raining."

She clamped her lips shut.

"And," he pointed out with another gently taunting smile, "New England gets heavy snow in the wintertime—unlike Ireland—which is why the grass turns brown. But you wait. I daresay in a few weeks the grass shall be as green as it is at home!"

Her eyes widened, and again he saw the threat of tears. "Ye *promise*, Christian?"

There was such a look of childish hope in her purple eyes that he was nearly undone. "I promise, Deirdre."

She looked away, trying to hide her tears, and they continued for another half mile before she spoke again. "Christian?"

"Aye, my dear?"

"Have ye been thinkin' o' yer other promise? Yer vow t' help me find me brother?"

Guilt twisted in his chest, seeded so long ago when he'd gone to Connemara and taken the Irish lads in the name of the king. "Aye, Dee, I've been thinking of it. And so, apparently, has your cousin. I have not had opportunity to speak with him directly, and shall not for some time, as Sir Geoffrey has sent him out to patrol the coast. However, he did send me a note, pledging to do all that he can to help us." Christian did not add that locating her brother would be akin to finding a minnow in the vastness of the Atlantic, for that would only crush her. "When Brendan returns, we shall coordinate our efforts." He gave her a level look. "In the meantime, I will do everything in my power to restore him to you, so help me God!"

"If anyone can find him, *you* can," she declared, her eyes reverent and full of childish trust in what she obviously considered to be his godlike abilities. He swallowed hard, knowing he could never live up to her expectations of him, and swiftly changed the subject.

"Are the Foleys treating you well?" he asked.

"Aye."

"You are all right, then?"

"Aside from losin' me wool the first night, aye."

He gave her a puzzled, sidelong glance. "Losing your *wool?*"

"'Twas from Ireland," she said defensively. "It blew out the window when I was tryin' t' figure out in which direction Ireland was."

"I see." He hid a private grin.

"But I still have me Irish air left," she said, her face very serious. She patted her horse's neck. "And me pebble and me sand and shells. And, o' course, I still have me crucifix, which I *can't* lose because I *never* take i' 't'off."

"Never?" he teased.

"Never!"

He laughed, his eyes glinting with amusement as they left

the village behind them. The horses plodded along, their
ears flicking back and forth, their hooves thudding dully
against the road. In the distance purple hills rose against the
horizon, and here and there a farmhouse, spouting a curling
tuft of smoke from its chimney, made a splash of color
against the landscape. Christian turned off the road and led
the way down a small path through the trees, ducking beneath low-hanging branches. Deirdre followed behind him,
admiring the way his wide shoulders stretched the fabric of
his fine uniform.

So intent was she in studying him that she almost allowed
her horse to plow into his when he stopped.

He turned then, his eyes glinting, then darkening with unspoken desire as he gazed longingly, lovingly, at her trim
figure. "Do you find this spot as pretty as the loveliest one
in Ireland, Deirdre?"

She looked around. A bubbling stream, swelled with
spring thaw and rain, tumbled over a bed of brightly colored
pebbles and wound away into the woods. Sunlight shone
down through a stand of evergreens, making dancing patterns atop a russet carpet of pine needles and dead leaves
from the previous autumn. High above, a cobalt-blue sky
sparkled through the trees, and here and there large boulders
of granite, their color that of Christian's eyes, rose out of
the leaf-strewn forest floor.

She shut her eyes, listening to the happy babble of the
brook. "I think it might be," she admitted slowly.

"Do you find it a place that is suitable to . . . being *alone*
with each other?"

"Oh, aye, Christian. I wouldn't care if I was sittin' in a
mud puddle, long's I was with ye."

He gave a wolfish smile, and swung easily from his saddle. Her eyes hungry, she watched as he tied his horse's
reins to a nearby tree, loosening the girth so that the big
stallion could relax. She started to dismount, but he was
there, his hands reaching out to fasten around her tiny waist
and burn a hole right through her clothes.

His handsome face was only inches from hers, the gray
eyes dark with desire that made answering flutters of sensation dance between her thighs. A shaft of sunlight probed

down through the trees, falling over his gray irises and pick-ing out a hint of green there. "Please, love," he said, gazing into her eyes and pulling her down so that he could kiss her. "Allow me the pleasure."

She kissed him back, nearly toppling from the horse. Then she drew back, feeling those little flutters becoming the burning sensation that only he could evoke, and that only he could appease. Her heart pounded in anticipation. "Christian, ye don't have t' be always playin' the officer and gentleman, ye know."

"Dear girl, I am not playing," he said seriously, putting his hands around her ribs and plucking her from the saddle as though she weighed not more than the tuft of wool she had lost. She fastened her arms behind his neck and gazed up into his eyes, sighing with delight as he carried her to a sunlit spot a short distance away. "And though I intend to stretch the limits of the word 'gentleman,' I shall always be-have with your interests superior in my mind."

With that, he set her down, took a blanket from behind the cantle of his saddle, and spread it out over the ground. Somewhat shyly, Deirdre sat down and looked up at him. Dear God, she had never thought an Englishman could be so utterly, achingly, handsome. But as she gazed up at his tall form, stamped against the scattered blue patches of sky among the branches above their heads, she thought her heart would burst from loving him.

"Christian?"

"Yes, love?"

"I hate t' be bringin' up her name, but I think yer Emily was a fool. There be no man in this world as handsome an' wonderful as *you*. I'll never leave ye, I swear it."

The stern planes of his face softened with love. He took off his hat, hung it on a nearby tree branch, and, shedding his coat, knelt beside her. She was keenly aware of the mus-cled strength of his thighs, the heat of his powerful body, the fierce need that he had for her. He reached out and cup-ped her chin in his hands. "And I will not leave *you*, Deridre."

She swallowed hard, looking at every beloved feature of his face.

He gazed into her eyes for a long, intense moment. "Do you love me, Deirdre?"

She returned his stare unblinkingly. "I love ye more than I love life itself, Christian."

He took a deep breath. "Do you love me enough to . . . to become my wife?"

He couldn't have stunned her more if he had grown a third arm. Her eyes widened, her jaw went slack, and her lips moved several times before she could form the words. "Ye mean . . . ye want t' marry me, then? Ye mean I wasn't just hopin' against hope that ye'd ask?"

"You had hoped I would ask?" Eagerness threaded his voice, and his eyes were searching.

"I *prayed* ye'd ask, Christian. But I didn't think ye would, you bein' English, an' me bein' Irish 'n' all. . . ."

"Bugger that," he said. "English, Irish, it makes no bloody difference. I love you. You love me. I'd marry you tomorrow if I could, so much do I love you, so eager am I to take you out of this situation—"

"I know, Christian," she said gently, her hands coming up to touch the hard planes of his cheeks. "Brendan already explained it t' me, that yer Sir Geoffrey wouldn't like it none if ye kept a woman aboard yer ship who wasn't yer wife. He told me it might look bad for ye when it comes t' promotin' time. I don't like t' be away from ye, Christian, but I understand now why I have t' be." She shrugged. "Besides, the Foleys are treatin' me well."

His eyes were anguished. "God help me, I hate leaving you out here—"

"I can stand it, Christian, if I know ye're coming' back fer me. I can stand it if I know it won't be forever."

"By God, it won't be forever! As soon as your cousin returns to Boston, I shall ask him for your hand."

"Oh, Christian. . . ."

His hands moved to her shoulders. Slowly, he drew her toward him, and claimed her lips in a hungry, passionate kiss that burned away all memories of her loneliness. As it ended, he reached into his coat pocket and slowly drew something out. She looked down and saw that his palm was flat and turned upward, and a ring, as ancient and beautiful as Grace's crucifix, rested on its hard and callused surface.

Her hands went to her mouth, her eyes flashing up to his.

"This has been in the Lord family for hundreds of years, Dee," he explained, gently prying her hands away from her mouth. Her hand was shaking so violently he had to close his fingers around it to still it.

Then, he slipped the ring onto her finger.

She stared at it, holding her breath and unable to speak. There it was, proclaiming to the world that she belonged to this handsome, gallant, battle-scarred sea warrior. Tears filled her eyes, and he lifted her hand so that the sunlight caught the rubies of the lion's eyes, the diamonds of its teeth.

"You are mine," he declared.

Deirdre was crying now, unashamedly. "Ch-Christian, this be the h-happiest moment in me life." She wiped at her eyes and stared at her hand for a long moment to stamp the sight forever in her brain, then hugged her hand to her breast, mating the ring with the crucifix. It appeared to be a random gesture, but he guessed, knowing her penchant for sentimentality, that it was actually quite a purposeful one. The melding of Irish and English, one heart to its mate, one proud ancestry to another.

His heart twisted within his breast, aching with love for her.

"Christian. . . ." She looked up at him, her lashes drenched with moisture, her throat working helplessly. "I don't know what t' say. . . ."

He gripped her hands, his heart pounding. "Say that you will be my wife, Deirdre, and your words will make me a happier man than any who has ever trod this earth."

She looked into his searching gray eyes. "I'll be yer wife, Christian. From th' day the vows are said till the day I die." She placed her palms on either side of his face. His skin was freshly shaven and smooth, and she caught the scent of his shaving soap as she bent close to him, fastened her arms around his neck, and pressed her lips against his. He responded immediately, crushing her almost savagely in his embrace, one hard, hot hand coming up to cup her nape and draw her closer.

"By God, Deirdre, I've missed you," he murmured huskily as the kiss ended. "I daresay I can't wait until you are really and truly *mine.*"

"Do ye *have* t' ask Brendan, Christian? Can't we just get married and be done with it?"

"As the only known surviving male in your family, Dee, 'twould be devilishly improper *not* to ask him."

Her fingers were working on his neckcloth, loosening it, drawing it away from his throat. The heat from his skin seared her hands, and slowly, she spread her palms beneath the heavy weight of his coat and nudged it off his shoulders. It was a mild day, and he had left the long garment unbuttoned, but the waistcoat was not so; and, one by one, she worked her fumbling fingers against its gold buttons until that, too, was open, and his fine white shirt was all that stood between his powerful chest and her searching fingers.

She gave an involuntary shiver. "We're goin' t' freeze, Christian!"

But the sun was directly overhead, probing through interwoven branches and warming the blanket upon which they sat. "Dee, in a few moments we will be so devilishly *warm* that we'll be wishing it was a sight colder!"

She laughed, and slowly pared his white waistcoat from his mighty shoulders, taking care to be gentle where the musket ball had been lodged. Her heart caught in her throat at his handsomeness, and the burning sensation between her thighs grew moist and hot. He sat before her now in only his shirt, white breeches, shoes, and stockings, and she rose to her feet, taking his hands and coaxing him to rise with her.

He towered over her, his hair curling around his ears and making a brilliant display of pale gold against the whiteness of his shirt. Deirdre's knees were shaking, and it was all she could do not to lean into his embrace as she let her fingers wander down toward his waist, there to tug gently at his shirt until she had pulled it free of his waistband. Her hands slid beneath it, skimming the warm, scarred skin, the rock-hard muscles that sheathed his ribs and torso, the sharply defined muscles of his powerful chest that made such a contrast to the soft, curling hair scattered over its broad surface.

She lifted her hands and dragged the shirt up over his head, her eyes widening with wonder at the magnificent display of male power and beauty. Only a bandage, clean and white, marred that handsome perfection; and when it came off, only another scar would mark where courage and strength had seen him through another battle.

"The sight o' ye makes me burn for wantin' ye, Christian," she breathed, her eyes, then her hands, devouring his honed, sun-splashed body. She gazed at his massive, corded arms, the veins that stood in relief atop his forearms, the bronziness of his skin, the sparse, golden hair that roughened his battle-scarred chest and torso. . . . Sighing, she reached up and untied his queue, letting the rich, glorious strands of pale hair slide silkily between her fingers, against her moist palms. She cupped his hard jaw between her hands, her gaze mating with his; then he pulled her close to him and, bending his head, kissed her long and hard and thoroughly.

She melted against him, her hands drifting over the firm bulges of his shoulders, the flat planes of a belly banded in slabs of muscle. Her fingers found, and hovered at, the buttoned flap of his breeches; without further hesitation, she slowly slid each button through its hole. The breeches sagged around his hips; his mouth grew more insistent upon hers, his hands now roving up and down her spine and loosening her own buttons. She felt cool air drive shockingly against the back of her neck, and then she slid her hands fully beneath his gaping waistband.

His manhood, springing from a warm nest of silky golden curls, stabbed hot and hard against her hands. She groaned deep in her throat, dimly aware of his fingers freeing her hair from its confining braid and raking through the curling raven tresses. She broke the kiss and slowly bent, her lips trailing down his throat, the indentation between his collarbones, the deep valley between the muscles of his mighty chest, the flat slab of his belly. Her lips whispered over his hot, throbbing flesh, finding it softer than velvet between her lips, and she kissed him gently, lovingly, as her hands dragged his breeches, then his stockings, down his long and hard-muscled thighs. His hands caught her shoulders, pulled her back up, her clothes scraping every naked inch of him and heightening his desire for her.

"Christian . . . dear God, how I want ye," she murmured, just before his lips claimed hers.

He merely laughed against her mouth and kissed her harder. She felt him stepping out of his shoes, pulling off his stockings with his toes. She shivered in anticipation of taking that hard, heated length of him into herself, of welcoming every hot inch of his powerful body against hers.

His big hands worked to strip away her riding jacket, her waistcoat, her shirt; they lingered at the waistband of her skirts, unbuttoning them until they fell to the blanket around her feet. Soon, she stood naked and shivering in the cool spring air, hungry and hot for him and never wanting him more.

Slowly, he sat down atop the blanket, pulling her with him. Her hand came out, her palm splaying through the crisp hair of his sun-dappled chest, pushing him gently down so that he lay on his back beneath her admiring gaze. Her blood was tingling through her veins, her senses reeling, her inner thighs growing damp and prickly with heat. Her palm roved back and forth over his chest, down his torso, tracing each slashed scar, each indentation that marked where his life had come close to being snuffed out.

"My Lord and Master," she breathed, her gaze flickering up to devour every detail of his beloved face.

He smiled, lazily, wolfishly, confidently. His arms came up, and she shivered in delight as his callused palms scraped over her sensitive flesh, caressing her soft white shoulders, scattering her raven hair over them until they framed the creamy swells of her breasts. His eyes followed, and her nipples tightened to hard buds, tingling with response as he rubbed them gently between thumb and forefinger. Her mouth grew slack, her breathing heavy; her lashes fanned against her cheeks, a striking contrast of black against white, and her cheeks suffused with rosy color.

"I want ye, Christian . . . God help me, I do. . . ."

His voice was deep, smooth, low. "Believe me, dear girl, the feeling is mutual."

He placed his hands on her hips, lifting her up above his belly as easily as if she were a feather pillow. Then he gently lowered her down, until the velvety tip of his hard shaft just prodded the throbbing entrance to her womanhood. Deirdre gasped, her eyes going wide, her hands coming out to rest on the corded muscles of his arms to balance herself.

The gray eyes, dark as storm clouds over a roiling sea, met hers, and slowly, agonizingly, he lowered her.

She felt every hot, throbbing inch of him, sliding slowly into her and filling her, swelling mightily against the walls of her femininity, her soul. Her legs trembled against the raspiness of the blanket; muscles bulged in his forearms, and the veins stood out, faintly purple and thick with blood, as he lowered her but did not release her weight, then hefted her slowly back up. The slick friction was unbearable, exquisite, painfully joyous. She shivered, and felt the first spasms of heady, wild pleasure raking through her blood.

"Oh, Christian . . ."

"D'you like that, dear girl?"

"I like *everythin'* ye do to me. . . ."

His eyes darkened yet further, the pale gold lashes sweeping down and catching a beam of sunlight on their thick fringes. But Deirdre was lost to the delicious, shooting sensations of building pleasure as he lowered her once again, then raised her up, a little faster this time, then repeated the motion with increasing speed. Her fingers caught in the damp hair of his chest; her palms splayed against the hard muscles, balancing herself as he moved her up and down, harder, faster, faster, faster—

The building waves of pleasure crashed over her, and she cried out with the sheer force of them as her vision exploded in a showering burst of sunlight and stars. Her head fell back, her hair tumbling down her spine; then, when she thought she would die from the intensity of the feelings, she felt his body give a mighty lurch, and he drove savagely up into her, hoarsely crying out her name as his own release claimed him. The feel of his hot seed spurting within her thrust her over the edge once more, and her cries mated with his, finally dwindling to tiny, animal-like sounds of pleasure as she collapsed atop him, burying her face in the damp curls of his pale hair, the curve of his warm neck.

They held each other as the last blissful waves faded; then he wrapped his mighty arms around her shoulders, and with heartbeat against heartbeat, hair of sunlight entwined with hair of midnight, body heat and the juices of love melding them as one, held her protectively, lovingly, fiercely, against him.

In the distance, they heard the bubbling brook as it splashed over stones and sand, trying to burst the confines of its banks. Overhead, they heard the scrape of bare branches, the sigh of the cool wind dragging through the pines; sunlight streamed down upon their moist skin, warming them, and beneath the damp blanket the ground was earthy, warm, springy.

They slept, two people caught up in love, and when they awoke, an hour later, they came together again . . . and again . . . until the orange ball of the sun dipped below the trees and dusk began to blanket the woods.

They washed in the chilling crystal water of the brook, dried themselves with the blanket, and slowly dressed each other, their hearts heavy at the thought of parting. It was nearly dark by the time they rode into the Foleys' yard, and after a short apology to their hostess about keeping Deirdre out so long, Christian led his young love back out under the sharpening stars and looked long and hard into her eyes.

"I love you, Deirdre. As God is my witness, I love you."

"And I love ye, too, Christian."

They clung together, their hearts breaking; but finally, the moment came for Christian to leave. Slowly, reluctantly, he set her away from him, his hand lingering over hers, his eyes dark and sad as he gazed into her beloved face.

Then he mounted his horse and, touching his hat to her, rode off, leaving her standing there on the darkened lawn until his shadowy figure had disappeared into the night.

Chapter 26

Captain Christian Lord did not get very far down the Concord Road before intuition, opportunity, and the chance to carry out his own carefully laid plans made him turn back. Deirdre's warm body was still molded to his memory, and he ached for want of holding her, loving her, finding a deep, soft bed to sink down into with her. Soon, now, he would. But he had not been sent here for pleasure; he had been sent here to find and apprehend that known enemy of the Crown, the Irish Pirate, and as a good and dutiful officer of his king, he intended to do precisely that.

Acting upon a tip from his own spies, General Gage had informed him that there was to be a meeting tonight at which several known rebel leaders—Samuel Adams, John Hancock, and Dr. Joseph Warren—were supposed to gather. No doubt the Irish Pirate would make an appearance, too. The whereabouts of the meeting had not been known, but Gage had had his own nagging suspicions as to where it would be.

Christian halted his horse beneath the black silhouette of the branches of a sprawling oak and, rummaging in his saddlebags, found his wig, a bit crushed but perfect for his disguise. He took off his hat, smoothed his hair back, and put it on. Then he removed his naval coat and replaced it with a shabby green waistcoat, slightly rumpled from being stuffed into his saddlebag for so many hours. Only his hat gave him away, and this he wasn't quite sure what to do with. At last, he merely held it on the cantle between his

311

legs, thinking to hide it when he returned to the tavern and stabled his horse.

Back down Concord Road he went, a slightly rumpled traveler on a tired horse, nothing about him indicating he was a proud and decorated sea warrior in the service of the king. As he came around a slight bend in the road, he saw the golden lights of the Foley house; a single lantern glowed orange behind the curtains of an upstairs window, and his heart gave a painful lurch as he thought of Deirdre, up there getting ready for bed, and probably missing Ireland with all her young heart.

Did she miss him, too? he wondered. When she blew out the light, would she go to the window, pull back the curtain, and gaze out into the night, thinking of him as he had thought of her from the dark privacy of *Bold Marauder*'s cabin?

God love her. He might not be *with* her tonight, but at least he would be *near* her; not in her bed, but close none-theless.

He reined his horse in just outside the tavern across the road from the Foley house, his senses alert for danger, his carefully thought-out plan running through his head. Surely the same villagers who had glared disdainfully at a British naval officer hours ago wouldn't recognize this road-weary traveler as the same man. He hoped they wouldn't recognize his horse. But chestnut was a common color, and besides, he was more in danger of being recognized for his fancy, gold-laced naval hat. He dismounted, frowning, unsure what to do about the matter; finally, he hid the hat in a thicket of shrubbery and, leading his horse behind him, cleared his throat and pounded a fist against the tavern's door.

Several moments went by, long moments in which the only sounds were the wind moaning through the trees and the loud hammering of his heart. Then he heard footsteps, and the sound of a latch being cautiously lifted; he saw a sliver of soft golden light as the door was cracked, then opened wide. A woman, her dark hair covered by a mobcap, stood there, her eyes suspicious. She held a candle in a tin holder, and this she lifted, shining it fully into Christian's eyes until he blinked in pain.

"Good evening, madam," he said wearily, inclining his bewigged head. Behind him, the horse gave a weary snort, as though in full cooperation with his ruse. "Have you a room for a tired and sore traveler, and perhaps a meal to warm his cold bones?"

The woman lifted the candle higher, her shrewd eyes distrustfully taking in his slightly unkempt appearance. At last, satisfied, she lowered the tin holder and glanced quickly up the road whence he had just come. "Aye, we've room for ye. Nice, clean chamber upstairs, and some leftover stew still bubbling over the fire."

"Ah, I am much obliged, madam, much obliged. If you will allow me to stable my horse somewhere?"

"Aye, we've a barn out back. Put your nag away and then join us for a bite to eat. We're plain and simple folk, but you'll not find us lacking in hospitality."

"Thank you, madam. I am dreadfully weary, and would welcome nothing so much as a stout meal and a warm bed."

"That ye shall have, sir," she said and, turning away, left him to stable his horse.

An hour later, Captain Christian Lord, hero of Quiberon and pride of the Royal Navy, sat on the bare floorboards of his room, surrounded by darkness, the door locked behind him, his body well fed and wide awake. The bed was turned back, waiting for him. The dark orange embers of a fire glowed in the hearth. The window was open, and the captain had a small spyglass balanced against the sill and trained at the house across the road.

As he waited, his thoughts wandered back over the events of the day.

He thought of Mrs. Foley's look of terror when he had appeared, unexpectedly, at her door this afternoon, and her prevailing skittishness throughout his visit. He thought of Delight Foley admitting her desire for the Irish Pirate when she had cornered him aboard the frigate, and her plans to seduce and win him to her bed. He thought of the open hostility with which the villagers had regarded him, and the suspicious way the tavern owner's wife had studied him before finally letting him in. He thought of Foley's reputation as being loyal to king and Crown—and he thought of the re-

cent broadsides that Sir Geoffrey had shown him, broadsides most likely printed by Jared Foley and meant to in-
flame the rebels toward inevitable bloodshed.

Bloodshed that must, at all costs, be prevented—before
the Irish Pirate made the reputed rendezvous and succeeded
in smuggling arms to the rebels.

The Lord and Master's eyes hardened, and a grim
smile—the smile of the hunter—tightened his thin lips.

The Irish Pirate must be caught.

Shifting his weight to a more comfortable position, he
raised the glass once more, trained it at the dark house
across the street, and sat back to wait.

It was sometime around midnight that Deirdre O'Devir,
lying in a bed that faced toward Ireland—and Boston
Harbor—awoke.

The sounds drifted into her consciousness, thrusting rousing fingers into the haziness of her dreams, shoving the
handsome, fair-haired sea warrior aside. Low tones, of men
talking . . . A strangely familiar voice, heavy with an Irish
brogue . . . Not Brendan's. But familiar . . . As familiar as
that devil-may-care laughter that followed it.

Her eyes came slowly open, and she stared up at the dark
rafters above her head, wondering if it had been a dream,
wondering if it had been real.

Hugging her arms around the softness of Christian's shirt,
she turned her face back toward the easterly window and let
her eyes drift shut.

Again that reckless laughter.

Deirdre's eyes shot open.

It had been no dream.

Slowly, she peeled back the heavy blankets and quilt,
and, shivering, placed her feet, wrapped in thick woolen
socks, upon the coarsely braided rug that covered the chill
floor. She hugged her arms to herself, her ears alert for
sound, for that familiar voice.

She rubbed the sleep from her eyes, and went to the window. Outside, several horses stood tethered, dark shapes in
the gloom. Deirdre's eyes widened, and this time, she knew
she wasn't dreaming the sound of voices downstairs—or the

one that was hauntingly familiar, agonizingly unplaceable, and as Irish as hers. . . .

"He's nothin' but a buffoon, Foley! Christ Almighty, ye think I'm afraid o' some priggish, vain, out-for-glory, trophy-huntin' Englishman? Bah! Yer own wife just said he's more interested in this wee Irish guest o' yers than he is in the business o' his bloody king!" Deirdre heard the sound of a tankard banging boastfully down upon a table. "And don't ye be forgettin, I *know* the bloke, better'n any o' ye. I'll warrant. Besides, I've tangled with him once, an' showed 'im me heels. There's no ship afloat that can catch my sloop. Our pretty-boy naval captain may have 'imself a swift and powerful frigate, but 'e don't know what t' do with 'er. That bumblin' crew o' his can barely figure out a shroud from a sheet, let alone how t' use her guns!"

Deirdre, shivering with excitement and the overwhelming feeling that she was about to stumble upon something that was going to change her life, crept across the little room and, reaching for her robe, wrapped it around her. Slowly, she opened her door and slipped quietly down the stairs, hearing the voices getting louder and louder.

"Your swagger will be the death of you, man," she heard Mr. Foley say sharply. "Captain Lord is no buffoon, but an officer of unqualified skill and tenacity, highly respected by his admiral and his king. No doubt he has drilled that *bumbling* crew into one as smart as any in the king's Navy—"

"You mean there are any in the king's Navy that are smart?" another, mocking voice joked.

"Very funny, Hancock," Foley snapped. "And you, my fine Irish friend—you'd do well to cover your tracks and have a care about becoming too cocky!"

Deirdre flattened herself against the wall, just outside the parlor in which the men were speaking. Her heart pounded in her breast. That was Christian they were talking about, her beloved Christian. She clenched angry fists at her sides. How did they dare call him a buffoon! And who was this Irishman who boasted so recklessly, whose voice was so dearly familiar, but whose face she could not picture?

"Really, Papa," came the low voice of a woman, "you are as skittish as Mama. Our clever Irish Pirate will run circles around Captain Lord. Why, there is no comparison between their skills, their intelligence, the quality of their crews." She gave a rich, bubbly laugh of confidence. "Besides, as I told you, Captain Lord is, shall I say, *otherwise occupied* of late—too much, in fact, to be placing much attention on his task of apprehending my Irish Pirate. . . ."

Deirdre's eyes widened with shock. *Delight!* She swallowed hard, a thick, tingling wash of dawning realization sweeping her spine and radiating out into her blood, until even the tips of her fingers felt cold.

The Foleys were rebels.

And if Delight had just called the speaker *"my"* Irish Pirate, then surely the infamous smuggler—a man from Deirdre's beloved Ireland, whose rich, melodic voice evoked beautifully vivid images of *home*—was right there in the very next room!

She clutched at the crucifix, her brow damp with moisture. No wonder Delight's restlessness during supper . . . the pains she'd taken over her appearance earlier . . . the renewed interest in her *manuals* and her continued glances at the small shelf clock on the mantel. . . . Dear God, if Delight Foley was in love with a rebel, then wouldn't it stand to reason that *she* was a rebel, too?

"Oh, sweet Jesus," Deirdre whispered, suddenly terrified. It was all she could do not to flee the house and run all the way back to Boston, to the protective safety of Christian's arms.

"I met Captain Lord several years ago," came another, steady voice, "and he did not strike me as a buffoon, but a capable, clever, and unbending disciplinarian, entirely devoted to his king, his duty, and his command. I would not pass him off so lightly, my friend. Your English nemesis is not a man to be trifled with."

"Me God," the Irishman said on a note of reckless laughter, "if ye'd only seen that ship o' his takin' a beatin' b'neath the guns of a little French corvette, ye'd feel as I do! And *Bold Marauder,* a frigate, designed t' fight and kill and destroy! 'Twas almost pitiful, I tell ye, t' see a fine ship like that so poorly fought and sailed! So quit yer worryin', eh? The lovely Dolores Ann here crossed th' Atlantic aboard her. She knows what her Lord an' Master be like! Tell him, me love! Would ye say the man be single-mindedly determined? Obsessed with bringin' me down?"

"He is clever and tactical, but any single-minded determination and obsession he possesses is not directed toward bringing about the demise of the Irish Pirate, but winning the love of our guest. As long as he is so . . . *occupied*, I do not think him to be a particular threat."

"Regardless," Foley said harshly, "the man is well deco-rated, highly respected, and on the way to becoming an ad-miral someday. Your view of the Royal Navy, my fine Irish friend, may be soured, and with good reason—but do re-member Captain Lord's achievements when you call him a *buffoon*."

The Irish Pirate's proud voice came from just several feet away. "Ah, ye worry for naught!" He gave a rich chuckle of laughter. "And besides, 'tis not cocky I be, but confident." Deirdre heard his footsteps crossing the room, and, judging by their sound, he was not a slight man. *Oh, if only she dared peek around the corner!* "No one has been able t' catch the Irish Pirate, no' t'even me gallant cousin, who, thanks t' me own care in keeping me identity a secret, has no idea who I am!" Deirdre heard the thump of a fist hitting a hard chest. "And *he* is far more keen and clever than our bumblin' Captain Christian Lord!"

Another voice, thoughtful and obviously honed by a fine education, came through the ajar door. "You seem to have an active dislike of Captain Lord, my friend. Mind that such personal animosity does not dull your own keen edge and land you within range of his guns."

"Aye, you do seem to harbor a ripe hatred of the fellow!" came the jovial voice of the man called Hancock. "Perhaps you'd care to enlighten us as to the reason?"

"As Dr. Warren said, me reasons be purely personal, and none o' yer concern." Again, that melodious Irish voice. Deirdre shut her eyes, trying to place it, wondering where she'd heard it before, and desperately aching to pry open the door and just *look* upon her countryman's face. "But all I'll tell ye is that I'll not enjoy a better revenge than makin' the king's most revered captain look like the fool he is. He'll not catch me, by Christ's blood!"

"No, my handsome smuggler, he will not," Delight said confidently.

"Enough said, then." came another voice, hard with authority and full of barely reined zest. "You, my Irish friend? All I can say is to have a care for yourself. Captain Lord may be *otherwise occupied,* but still, he has a fine and deadly reputation that has not, to be sure, been founded upon *buffoonery.*" He paused, and Deirdre heard his footsteps, pacing back and forth, back and forth, with restless energy. "As for our own part in this plan, our minutemen companies have been drilling tirelessly, preparing for the worst. Captain Locke here has done an exceptionally fine job with his Menotomy men in such a short time. But we need more guns. As we speak, arms and ammunition are being hidden in carts and covered with straw, and transported by patriots into the countryside. Gage has wind of it, you may be sure. But of course, our own well-placed informants in the Sons of Liberty have ensured that the only information concerning the whereabouts of these stores to reach the governor's ears is erroneous."

"Of course, Adams," said Jared Foley. "And now let us hear of your fine plan."

Guns! Deirdre thought in alarm. And then her face went pale as she felt a high, itchy sensation beginning to burn the back of her nose. *Dear God, don't let me sneeze now!*

Panicking, she pinched her nostrils shut.

Adams's voice came from around the door. "I have written to my merchant friend in Philadelphia. He is a rather . . . *shady* sort, not above trading with pirates and other riffraff when the fancy suits him. In any case, he has agreed to ship a cargo of French muskets by week's end. Of course, if he were to try and land these guns in any of our nearby harbors, it would attract far too much attention. My plan, therefore, is to have our Irish Pirate here take his sloop out to meet him off Marblehead under cover of darkness. The transfer must be done quickly and efficiently. Not only is Captain Bishop's *Lively* patrolling these waters, but so is *Halcyon* under the command of Captain Brendan Merrick."

Deirdre bent her head, breathing deeply as she tried to control her approaching sneeze.

Adams continued. "Make the transfer quickly and cleanly, my fine Irish friend, and waste no time in pleasantries. Land the guns in Salem, where we will arrange for them to be met by trusted members of the Sons of Liberty. There, they will be transferred to wagons, covered with hay and vegetables, and transported directly to Concord."

"Nay, 'tis too dangerous!" Delight cried. "The British have stepped up their patrols!"

"I don't like it, either," said Jared Foley. "You get caught in that sloop under the guns of one of those frigates and it will be all over for you."

The Irish Pirate's merry laughter rang out. "Bah, I'll not get caught. There are scores of small fishing and trading vessels all up and down the coast. Mine is not so different as to arouse any suspicion!"

"And we *could* use those muskets," Hancock proclaimed. "I say let's do it."

"Are you up to it, my fine Irish friend?"

"For the love o' God, o' course I am!"

"Very well, then. My friend's ship is due to arrive on Saturday night. She will flash two lanterns at her bow, three times in succession. Your signal of acknowledgment is to be the same. Godspeed."

Deirdre shut her eyes, her hands clasped over her face as the sneeze grew closer.

"Should he learn of it, Gage will move to stop us," came the steady voice of the one who'd been addressed as Dr. Warren. "You may be sure of it."

Deirdre felt her chest convulsing. Her eyes watered. She gasped for breath, trying to still the sneeze—

"And when he does, we will be ready for him, you may be sure!" Adams cried, pounding his fist against the table. "The time has come to make a stand against tyranny, oppression, and the cruelties of unfair government imposed upon us by a dispassionate monarch grown fat on—"

At that moment, Deirdre sneezed.

It was not a small, feminine whisper of sound. It was a full-blown, silence-shattering roar that seemed to explode against the walls, the ceiling, the door that suddenly shot open to reveal a room of shocked and staring faces.

In the space of a heartbeat she saw them. Delight, sitting beside her father and mother and staring at Deirdre as if she were a ghost; several men, dressed in the decent clothes of merchants and the well-to-do, some with powdered wigs, others with their hair worn natural and clubbed at the nape; and, dominating the center of the room, a tall, forbidding man with snapping violet eyes and a wildly curling mane of black hair that lay loosely about his broad and muscled shoulders. He had a roguish smile, the coloring of a Celt, and a face of hard planes and sharp angles.

A face whose memory thirteen years could not dim.

Deirdre stood gaping, the blood draining from her cheeks, a thick roaring noise sweeping through her head. She swayed and clutched at the door for support. The occupants of the room came to their senses, some cursing roundly, some blanching with fear, some looking to the one who was obviously their leader—this Sam Adams—who stood, at a loss for words, beside the black-haired Irishman.

"Oh, dear . . ." Delight murmured, her full mouth going slack.

And then Deirdre, frightened and shivering in her nightshirt and robe, was seized and dragged forcefully into the room.

She stood staring at each of them in turn, the truth clawing at her breast, the memories exploding, finally, in her heart. She stared into the eyes of the legendary sea smuggler. Her hands came up, purposely drawing free from beneath the closure of her robe the glittering crucifix that had belonged to another Irish pirate. She let it rest blatantly, proudly, at her bosom, seeing the rebel smuggler's reckless, roguish eyes widen in horrified shock as recognition swept the color from his ruddy cheeks.

There were no secrets left.

Christian, unwittingly, had fulfilled his vow to her after all.

She swallowed on a choke, shaking so hard she could barely stand. Once more she met the eyes of the Irish Pirate.

Eyes that were as purple as her own.

"Roddy?" she whispered, the faces of everyone else in the room dropping away into nothingness, until there were only those darkly fringed violet eyes looking down at her. "Is it really *you*, Roddy?"

He stared at her, then at the crucifix.

"Aye ... 'tis me," he murmured, still in shock.

Foley leapt to his feet, scarlet with rage and fear. "Tarnal hell, she knows your identity, man!"

But the Irish Pirate straightened to his full height and laid a hand on Foley's arm. "Fear not that she'll betray me t' her fair-haired Briton," he said. He stared down into Deirdre's face, tentatively reaching out to touch one long black curl, and to wipe away the tears that spilled in hot torrents down her pale cheeks.

"What do you mean, 'fear not'? You're as good as dead!"

"Nay," Roddy said quietly. "The lass is me sister."

Christian's legs and feet had long since fallen asleep, but his mind was keenly alert, wide awake and sharp. He had not moved from his cross-legged position at the window, and the spyglass, trained with a marksman's aim at that single glowing square of light that was the Foleys' parlor, had not wavered so much as an inch over the past hour.

Though he could not yet know it, Roddy O'Devir, the handsome and swaggering Irish Pirate, had made a grievous error, for the English captain he'd written off as a buffoon had shown a cunningness far superior to that of the notorious rebel smuggler.

The Lord and Master of HMS *Bold Marauder* had seen it all. The first horse, its rider clothed in a dark jacket, materializing out of the night and turning unobtrusively into the Foleys' yard; another, and still another, until it was clear that Gage's suspicions about the whereabouts of the rebel meeting had borne fruit.

Christian harbored no doubt that these men were the rebel leaders. He had viewed descriptions and drawings provided by Sir Geoffrey and Governor Gage himself; one or two of them he had seen on the streets of Boston—the slim, young, elegantly handsome Dr. Joseph Warren and the outspoken patriot Sam Adams.

Adams's face, at the moment, was dead-center in the circular field of Captain Christian Lord's spyglass.

Other faces came into view as the rebels moved across the room. John Hancock, pompously dressed, wealthy, much given to laughter. The silversmith Paul Revere, middle-aged and leaning toward overweight. Jared Foley, his identity obvious by the ink stains that smudged his hands. Delight, his daughter, whose eyes had been following the tall, black-haired rogue whose face Christian did not need to scrutiny with his glass to recognize.

The Irish Pirate.

The memory of that same man, commanding a sloop that had brazenly attacked an English cutter in company with a lowly French pirate, burned him. Christian's hands clenched around the spyglass, his knuckles showing white in the darkness. How he wished he could go over there and arrest the bloody lot of the conspiring rabble. But no. With the exception of the Irish Pirate, the rebel leaders were in Gage's hands. His task was to apprehend the seafaring smuggler—something he could not do until he caught the blackhearted rascal at his game.

As for Jared Foley being a rebel, Captain Christian Lord had all the proof he needed.

He lowered the glass, rubbed at his aching eyes, and replaced it. Suddenly, the breath caught in his throat. There was a new figure in the room. A slim and fair-skinned woman with a spiral-curling mane of raven curls, a woman who, as he watched, flung herself into the arms of the man the Lord and Master had been sent to apprehend.

It was Deirdre.

The spyglass fell from his hand, nearly shattering on the floor. Shock tore through his body in great, awful waves of paralytic numbness, and he could only stare, blinking, at that pale square of golden light, seeing the small figures within through the daze of shock, disbelief, and denial.

No.

She was embracing him. Kissing his cheek.

His hands curling into fists, Christian stumbled to his feet, reeled against the wall, and nearly went down. His hand flashed out, gripped the headboard of the bed so hard that it cracked; his other hand pressed against a brow gone cold with sweat.

"Blind me. . . ." he whispered, staring fixedly out the window.

But the effort of holding his head up was too much. It drooped upon the broad column of his neck, the pale hair that she had once professed to hate, falling into his eyes. He brought his hand up to push it away and began to tremble so hard his legs would not support his weight.

No. . . .

But the awful truth raked through his heart with vicious, searing pain, leaving it little more than a bleeding pile of raw meat dying within his chest. He sat down heavily upon the bed, his disbelief giving way to logic, logic giving way to grief, grief giving way to anger, anger giving way to raw, white-hot fury.

She had betrayed him. She—his dear little Irish girl—had betrayed him.

I love ye, Christian. His chest convulsed on a choking sob of grief, of despair. *God help me, I love ye. . . .*

Raw agony, worse than the pain of a thousand knives, twisted his gut. "I trusted you," he snarled, his fist slamming into the wall and sending blood bursting in a spray from his knuckles. He never felt the pain, for it was insignificant in the face of the crushing blow he'd just been dealt. "Goddammit, I trusted you, loved you, *believed in you. . . .*" Blindly, he stumbled back to the window, seeing the Foleys' door open and spill a rectangle of pale yellow light upon the barren lawn. "How *could* you? Bloody, deuced hell, *how could you?*"

She stood there, her hands clutching the man who was his enemy, her lovely, traitorous face pale in the darkness as she turned it up toward that of her lover. He wanted to shut his eyes but he couldn't. He wanted to turn away but, sickened, found he could do nothing except stare at the two lovers as Deirdre's slender arms came up to wrap themselves around the neck of her Irish Pirate.

Betrayed.

He heard snippets of her joyous laughter, snatches of her happy sobs. The sounds drove another nail into the coffin

that contained his dying heart, then another, until he knew
that it would never, ever again be opened.

For Christian, there was nothing left. No feeling, no pain,
nothing. Just—emptiness.

He stood there watching them, until at last the handsome
Irishman mounted his horse and with a flourish rode away.
Deirdre remained, all alone in the road, the wind blowing
her dark tresses around her shoulders, her face turned toward the east.

Toward Ireland.

Toward where the Irish Pirate had gone.

Christian's gray eyes hardened to emotionless chips of
flint. Now he knew the real reason Deirdre O'Devir had
been traveling aboard his ship. To find her brother, eh? By
God, what sort of fool had she played him for? She had
only wanted free passage to America so she could reunite
with her Irish lover—and, no doubt, learn every secret of
the Royal Navy, and of Christian's own mission, that she
could pass on to him.

Fists clenched at his side, Christian turned away, his great
body shaking with a need to vent a violent, all-consuming
fury that boiled through every cell in his body. By a supreme act of will he controlled it. His mouth was a hard,
grim slash in the austere harshness of his face; his eyes
were colder than the North Atlantic, and where his heart had
been, there was nothing but a frigid, empty hole whose brittle walls of ice were even now collapsing in upon themselves.

The need for vengeance burned through him. "Two can
play at your little game, dear girl," he gritted through
clenched teeth. "So help me God, you will rue this day, and
so will your bloody lover." Apprehending the Irish Pirate
was no longer just another mission, but the only thing that
would keep him focused, sane, and standing.

He watched Deirdre lift a hand and wipe away tears of
sadness for her Irishman's departure, never realizing that
those tears were not for a roguish, black-haired Celt, but for
a fair-haired Englishman who was no longer playing by
anyone's rules but his own.

Chapter 27

The decks of HMS *Bold Marauder* were lonely and dark, with only a few lanterns hung in the shrouds to make a stand against the fog that lay damply over the still waters of the harbor. A few idle seamen swilled their grog and bemoaned the absence of Delight Foley. A marine stood leaning against his musket, his eyes scanning the mists, his thoughts far away. Ian MacDuff was the officer of the watch and, to relieve the boredom, had brought out his bagpipes, much to the dismay of those who happened to be on deck with him. For a short time the pipes had honked and croaked and moaned, until the accompanying curses and protests from his shipmates had sent Ian storming off in high Scottish rage.

Now, he stood sulkily beside Skunk on the empty quarterdeck, seeking shelter beneath the dripping tarp that had been rigged against the earlier, drenching rain. Lantern light caught the glimmer of moisture as it trickled down masts and tarred lines, pooled upon booms and yards, and made the decks slippery and treacherous. Skunk pulled his cap down over his grimy forehead and wiped away the moisture with the back of his hand. "Quiet night out there," he muttered. "Hibbert says the Lord and Master's still up."

Ian, shivering in the cold, damp rain that began to leak from the black sky above, cast a quick glance aft. Sure enough, a glow from the skylight confirmed Hibbert's observation. "Aye, I'd say he is."

"Somethin's up, Ian. He ain't said a word to anyone since

325

he got back from visitin' the Irish lass. Ye don't think somethin' happened between 'em, do ye?"

"I doona ken, Skunk. But 'tis right you are about something being in the air. The Old Fart came aboard this afternoon and he and the captain shut themselves up for over an hour. Evans was at his station and eavesdroppin' outside the door, and said that tomorrow night we'll see action."

"Action?"

"Well, I know I shouldnae be tellin' ye this, it probably being highly confidential and all, but we *are* shipmates. . . ."

Skunk swung around, his eyes eager beneath the brim of his hat. "Aw, Ian, don't start with that rubbish!"

The big Scotsman shrugged. "Well, the governor has his own system of spies, sprinkled throughout Boston and the surrounding countryside. Ye ken, in taverns, pretending tae be friends of the rebels . . ."

"Go on," Skunk urged, glancing over his shoulder even as Hibbert, his uniform dull and drooping in the mist, and Teach joined them.

"Aye, tell us, Ian!"

The Lord and Master would be furious if he found out that Ian was divulging secrets, but peer pressure overruled Ian's misgivings. Besides, the crew had long since abandoned their animosity toward the man who treated them with a respect and humanity not often seen in the Royal Navy. They would stand by him, no matter what.

"Well, it seems that these spies of Gage's have learned that the rebels are planning tae smuggle a whole shipment of guns ashore. 'Tis tae happen tomorrow night, off the coast of Salem." He glanced over at the riding lights of a nearby ship, the frigate *Halcyon,* now a ghostly smudge of darkness in the fog. "Ye ken how Captain Merrick returned from his patrol tonight? Well, apparently he sighted a large merchant vessel in the waters off Cape Ann. He tried tae hail the ship, but she took advantage of the dusk and fled. Kind of suspicious behavior, don't ye think? But Sir Geoffrey thinks her presence only confirms the rumors of an exchange tomorrow night. He wants the Lord and Master to be there to nail the rabble and catch them in the act."

"I wonder if it will be the Irish Pirate," Teach growled, swinging his tomahawk.

"I doona ken." Ian rubbed his beard. "But a dangerous mission 'twill be, whoever the rebels send. I canna imagine they'd entrust the job tae anyone but their best—the Irish Pirate."

Skunk's smile was wry. "And I can't imagine the admiral entrusting our job to anyone but *his* best."

As one, they glanced toward the dim glow of the captain's skylight.

"The Lord and Master."

The ship was nearly empty, for Christian was one of the few captains who trusted his company enough to allow them shore leave. Given the harsh life of the Royal Navy, many seamen deserted ship given the slightest chance, but Christian's humane efforts and relaxed methods of discipline had earned him the loyalty of his subordinates, men who, not a mere month past, had wanted nothing more than to make his life hell.

It was a triumph, yes, and so was his success in linking Jared Foley and the Irish Pirate to the rebel leaders. But Sir Geoffrey's praise for both accomplishments meant nothing to a heart that had stopped beating when Christian had seen the woman he loved in the arms of another man.

He got up and walked across the cabin to the stern windows, absently rubbing at his sore shoulder. Beyond the glass, he could see nothing but darkness and fog, punctured here and there by the fuzzy glow of lanterns hung in the shrouds of neighboring ships, and farther off in the distance, the lights of Boston. There were no stars. There was no horizon. Encased as the area was in a lonely cloak of mist and fog, it was hard to believe that thousands of British troops inhabited the town, trying to keep peace in a situation that was ready to explode into war. It was hard to believe that far beyond the fog, the shoreline, and Boston itself, rebels were secreting stores of arms into the countryside. It was hard to believe that, out to sea, a merchantman waited, carrying a vast shipment of arms—and it was hard to believe that the rebels would entrust anyone but the Irish Pirate to receive the musket shipment when the exchange was made tomorrow night.

In his heart, Christian knew that he would succeed in apprehending the notorious smuggler. He felt it as surely as he felt the damp tendrils of mist seeping through his clothes, chilling his skin, and making his hair curl damply, thickly, behind his ears and at his nape. But the assurance brought him no triumph, just a hollow, empty feeling of loneliness.

How would *she* react when he brought down this man who obviously meant a great deal to her? Would she come to him, begging for his release? Would she practice another form of deceit upon his scarred and wounded heart?

Christian lowered his head, staring out at the soupy blackness beyond the stern windows. His fingers brushed the bench seat where she had sat, touched the soft blanket that had once been wrapped around her shoulders. His throat constricted and he swallowed a thick, burning lump of pain, feeling empty and dead and alone. But from behind him came the soft whines of the puppies as they snuggled together for warmth, and the gentle sounds of Tildy's tongue as she washed one or two of the tiny, furry backs.

No. Not quite alone. Christian turned and went to them, his smile sad as he looked down at the little bodies that Deirdre had helped bring into the world. Bending down, he scooped up the runt of the litter, so small that it fit in the palm of his hand, and, tucking the animal beneath the lapel of his waistcoat to warm it, carried it back to his desk.

The puppy nuzzled against him, mewing like a kitten. Its small mouth fastened around his finger, suckling it. Closing his eyes, Christian laid his cheek, stubbled now with rough, golden bristles, tenderly against the tiny head. The fur was soft beneath his lips, sweetly scented and warm.

Like hers.

Again the choking lump of emotion rose in his throat. He swallowed hard, and reached for his inkwell and pen. First Emily, and now Deirdre. Both had betrayed him and sought the arms of another. Why? He cuddled the puppy and squeezed his fist around the pen, his eyes full of anguish. *Why?*

He cuddled the puppy to his chest. Thank God for animals. At least they were faithful and true.

It was too bloody bad that the same couldn't be said for
women.

Several miles away, in the little village of Menotomy, it
was cold and damp and dark. An icy rain fell from a black
sky, and wind drove the raw dampness into one's very
bones. But Deirdre, wrapped in a warm quilt and sitting on
the floor beside the open window of her bedroom, rejoiced
in it. If she closed her eyes, she could just imagine she was
back in Ireland. About the only thing that was missing was
the pungent, homey scent of peat fires wafting in the damp
air. . . .

Her bag of Irish mementos was at her side, nearly empty
now. The miniature of her mother, the model of Roddy's
long-ago sailboat, and the old sliver of wood that had been
part of her papa's boat were carefully arranged on the little
nightstand beside her bed. But apart from them, there was
not much left that was from home. She had given the felt
bag of sand and shells from the Connemaran beach to
Roddy, and even now her heart warmed at the memory of
how his eyes had misted over for the briefest of moments
out there in the starlight at her simple but generous gesture.
She had only the pebble from the pasture, and the flagon of
Irish air left.

Her fingers came up to touch the crucifix that never left
her neck.

And the legacy of Grace O'Malley.

She gazed off into the darkness, thinking of Christian.
She had not seen him since he had given her the ring, but
just having it on her finger assured her of his love, and was
a promise in itself that she would never again be alone.

But oh, what should she do about the awful predicament
she was now involved in?

She cradled her hand to her heart, her fingers roving over
the curved and sharp edges of his ring. Anxiety had prevented her from being able to eat; worry over the men she
loved robbed her of the happiness she should've felt at
thoughts of becoming Christian's wife. Should she send

word to Christian that her own brother was the Irish Pirate in the hopes that he would refuse to go after him? Christian was a king's officer; would he choose his duty over the vow he had made to restore her brother to her?

No.

He had made a promise to her that he would find her brother and make right the wrong he had done to her family. There was no question in Deirdre's mind that he would spare Roddy.

As for Roddy, his actions on behalf of the American rebels were his own way of getting revenge against the England that had press-ganged him and robbed him of his rights as a free person.

Deirdre was still dazed over the discovery that he was the Irish Pirate—and very, very frightened. Roddy had not changed much in the years since she'd last seen him; he was still rash and reckless, still full of bravado, still hot-tempered and volatile, but just as easily given to laughter. Such traits could, as the rebel leaders had warned, bring about the downfall of a man whose successes against the British had apparently gone to his head.

Deirdre's spirits began to plummet beneath worry for her brother. Captain Christian Lord was not one of the village lads with whom Roddy used to delight in getting into fist-fights. He was no puffed-up and swaggering braggart who couldn't see past the tip of his nose. He was no bumbling idiot, no incompetent idler. Christian Lord was one of the finest sea officers in the king's Navy, and he commanded a mighty frigate that was fully capable of smashing not only a formidable French corvette, but the little sloop Roddy would captain tomorrow night when the arms transfer was made.

Only Delight—who, behind her parents' backs, had given Roddy enough sultry winks, hot touches, and heated stares to entice him into asking her to accompany him riding to-morrow morning—seemed to feel no trepidation over the impending exchange. "Roddy has made many smuggling excursions, Deirdre," she'd said when she'd come to apologize for not revealing the Foleys' rebel tendencies. "This is just one more. The Lord and Master knows nothing of it, just as he knows nothing of our involvement with the patriot cause. You just watch. Roddy will get the guns, Adams and Revere and Hancock will meet him on shore, and the cargo will be safely transported to Concord. Lo, there is no need to look so scared!"

"I love me broth'r, Delight," she had murmured, staring down at the ring that weighed so heavily upon her finger. "But I love me future husband, too. And here I am, unable t' protect either one of 'em, and stuck in the middle o' hostilities b'tween two lands that aren't me own. Dear God, what a mess."

"You're not angry, are you, that I never told you we're rebels?"

"No. But please, don't try to draw me int' yer quibbles wi' England. I can sympathize with yer plight here in the colonies, for England treats yer people no better than she does mine—but th' truth o' the matter is that I love an Englishman, will marry an Englishman, and t' help ye in any way would be t' betray th' man I love."

Delight's eyes had rounded with fear.

"But please," Deirdre had continued, laying her hand on her friend's arm, "don't worry that I might betray yer family t' Christian. I'd prefer t' just keep out o' the whole mess, if ye don't mind."

"You'll have to choose a side," Delight had replied quietly. "Your *brother* is a rebel, Deirdre!"

"Aye, Roddy is a rebel now. And me future husband is an Englishman." Deirdre had raised her head, and her eyes had shone with pride as she met the gaze of her friend. "But I am *Irish.*" She'd pulled Grace's crucifix free of her shirt and wrapped her hands around it until the metal had glowed with warmth and life. "And as such, I'll stay true t' me own heart."

Her own heart. She did not have to take up arms against the English, even if her brother preferred to do so. Nor did she have to betray the colonists' secrets, even if her betrothed was a highly revered Royal Navy captain. All she had to do was stay true to her heart—and her heart lay nearly ten miles away, in the cabin of a mighty frigate, in the care of the most wonderful man in the world.

She pulled the quilt further around her, laid her forearms over the damp windowsill, rested her cheek against her wrists, and closed her eyes.

Moments later, she was asleep, her little bag of dwindling Irish mementos at her side, Christian's shirt against her skin, and her face turned toward Boston.

Chapter 28

Late the following afternoon, the dreary weather had not eased a bit, and it did nothing to dispel the worries of those who stood in the Foley yard, bidding good-bye to the Irish Pirate.

Rain had darkened his felt tricorn to a shade very near the inky blackness of his curls, caught in a thong of leather and hanging over his turned-up collar. Water dripped from the brim, trickling down his back and soaking his wool coat. The roan hide of his mare was wet and warm and steaming, and as Roddy swung up into the saddle, he slapped her neck and gazed down at the two girls who had braved the raw weather to see him off.

"Godspeed, my handsome smuggler," Dolores Ann murmured, letting her fingers rove suggestively over the length of Roddy's long, muscled thigh. She tilted her face up to his, her tongue suggestively touching the corners of her lips, then tracing their perimeter in a way that caused his eyes to darken and his blood to burn through his veins. A delight, was Dolores, Roddy thought, remembering their "walk" of this morning. That walk had given them both plenty of exercise—but not in the manner in which the elder Foleys might have been led to believe. . . .

He saw the worried eyes of his sister, who stood a little behind Dolores Ann. She was no different from the gentle,

frightened little sibling he'd known and loved in Connemara
when he was a mere lad and she barely out of swaddling
clothes. And she still wore that ancient crucifix, the first
thing she touched when fear overcame her.

With amusement, he saw that her fingers were wrapped
around it now with such ferocity it was a wonder the metal
didn't snap.

Reining his horse around, Roddy went to her, leaned
down in the saddle, and embraced her. "Please understand,
Deirdre. I know ye don't hold with the rebel cause, but 'tis
important t' me. That foolish British captain o' yers don't
even know I'm a-sailin'. So wipe that frown off yer bonny
face and send me off with a smile, eh?"

"That *'foolish British captain'* is to be my husband,
Roddy," she said quietly, the rain streaming out of her hair
and running, like tears, down her pale cheeks. "Please don't
talk o' him like that."

Roddy's jaw tightened. He had no love for Captain Christian Lord, and the rocks would be gone from the fields of
Connemara before he allowed the Briton who had pressed
him into the English Navy to wed his little sister. He'd see
the bastard dead before he'd allow *that* to happen! But for
now, he would keep his silence, trusting that separation
from the Englishman, as well as the gentle influence of the
Foleys, would bring Deirdre around to the rebel sympathies.
In fact, the Menotomy minutemen would be mustering tomorrow under the command of Captain Benjamin Locke,
and during his tryst with the lovely—and deliciously
skilled—Dolores Ann, Roddy had suggested that she take
Deirdre with her to watch the men drill.

He pulled his hat down over his eyes. If tomorrow were
anything like today, it would be a damned nasty day to drill.
But the wind was up and would be stronger near shore, and
he knew that it would be a fine night for sailing.

"'Tis sorry I be, Deirdre," he said, touching his sister's
cheek with his thumb and wiping away water that could've
been rain, could've been tears, could've been both. Beneath
him, the mare fidgeted, eager to be off. "But ye'll forgive
me if yer Englishman is not on me list o' favorite people.

Perhaps someday I can f'rgive him, as you have—but not now."

Straightening up, he gallantly tipped his hat to the two girls, blew Delight a kiss and a wink, and galloped off toward Salem, his cloak billowing behind him.

HMS *Bold Marauder,* her sails swollen with rain as she cruised slowly through the foamy, wind-ruffled seas a league off Cape Ann, had just completed another long tack in total, choking darkness when the lookout's voice came down through the thick mists that smothered the tops and yards so high above.

"On deck! Lights blinkin' two points off the starboard bow!"

On the quarterdeck, Christian turned to stare off into the night. It was the signal he'd been waiting for.

"Beat to quarters," he said quietly, "but no drums and no bosun's whistles. I want everything done in complete silence."

The Lord and Master's voice was barely above conversational tones, but so quiet was the ship, so eager and tense was every man in the crew, that everyone heard his command—and indeed, had been expecting it.

Anxiety instantly gave way to action. With hushed urgency and brisk efficiency, men darted through the darkness to their stations, some running to the huge guns that had been, on the Lord and Master's command, already loaded and run out. Others gathered near the pinrails, ready to grab sheets and braces in preparation to change tack, while others scrambled aloft with the nimble ease of monkeys. They needed no urging from their superiors to keep silent, no direction as to what to do, for the Lord and Master had had them rehearsing this moment from the time that *Bold Marauder* had slipped quietly out of Boston Harbor several hours before, unseen under the cover of night and fog.

He was a clever one, their commanding officer. He had ordered all lanterns to be put out before they had even left their anchorage; had made sure every man knew his place and station. Now they worked in a Stygian darkness that was blacker than Hades, but they knew their ship so well that they needed no light to traverse decks that were now treacherously slick with rain and mist and spray.

"We'll get that smuggler, you just watch," Skunk said to Hibbert, who had just come up from below. "Cap'n's rehearsed this moment all bleedin' day."

"Aye," Teach murmured from somewhere in the darkness. "He's out for blood. Pity the poor rogue who dares tangle with *our* Lord and Master!"

Christian, standing beside the wheel on the pitch-black quarterdeck, heard their comments as he stared off into the darkness, and those who saw his smile thought it as cold as the wind that ruffled his wet hair and made the folds of this heavy boat cloak billow around him. The mists made it nearly impossible to see anything off the starboard beam, but high above the deck in the maintop he knew it was clear, and the lookout had no such encumbrance to hamper him.

Christian clapped his hat to his head as a cold gust of wind and slashing rain drove against his cheeks, and considered going aloft with his glass to see for himself. But no. They would soon be needing him here on deck . . . maybe even sooner than he'd expected.

Forward, he saw movement as a ship's boy darted out of the shelter of the bulwarks and into the rain, but the lad was stopped by Skunk's meaty paw before he could ring the ship's bell to signal that another half hour had passed. No noises must penetrate the eerie silence of wind and wave to give them away. One wrong move and the Irish Pirate would escape them.

"Eight bells, sir," whispered Ian, coming up beside him.

Christian nodded. Midnight. He sensed the anxiety in Ian's voice, and saw it mirrored in the barely visible faces of those who surrounded them. "Very well, Ian." He turned to his first officer, his face grave and determined, his fair hair plastered damply to his cheeks. On land, it would've been a gentle rain, but the gusty sea wind drove the dampness against his unprotected skin and made his shoulder throb hellishly. Drawing his boat cloak around his shoulders, he walked to the quarterdeck rail and peered down into the gloomy darkness of the ship's waist, where the pale ovals of seamen's faces were all turned toward him, anxiously awaiting his command. Twin rows of dark, hulking shapes made up the batteries of the frigate's big guns. He heard the gentle hiss of spray at the bows, the soft drum of rain on the decks, and the whistle of the westerly wind high up in the tops. Water creamed softly along the sides and aft, the wake was lost in fog. *Bold Marauder* was ready. The guns were ready. His men were ready, and he had the element of surprise.

Tonight, he vowed, clenching his fist around his sword hilt, the Irish Pirate would pay the price of treason against the Crown.

Suddenly Ian gripped his arm and pointed out into the darkness. "Lights out to larboard now, sir! Looks like an answering signal from another ship!"

The Irish Pirate.

The fog had thinned, and now Christian could see out over the black seas and into the night, where the wink of a distant lantern pierced the darkness. Then the mists closed in again. He glanced at the compass, estimated the vessel's position, and looked at his officers, all awaiting his command. They were a formidable lot, and he harbored as much trust in this formerly motley crew as he had in any other he'd had the pleasure to command; Ian, his beard wet with rain, his eyes fierce and determined; Rhodes, quiet and competent and sinister; Wenham, chewing on the stem of a pipe he dared not light; and Hibbert, dressed in a uniform that was desperately in need of a wash.

"Mr. Hibbert!" he snapped, and the youth anxiously made his way to his captain's side.

"Aye, sir?"

Christian's eyes raked the middie's unkempt clothes with mock severity. Then he grinned, for his attempts to make the youth look the part of an officer had become a shipwide joke. "For God's sake, go change into a presentable uniform! This is a *king's ship!*"

Hibbert smirked, and scampered below. His captain shook his head, and opened his spyglass. Some things would never change. But this crew was a far cry from the one he'd left Portsmouth with. They had quit England in disgrace; soon, now, they would make both their Navy and their country proud.

He gave the order to change tack and take in the big, billowing courses. Moments later, HMS *Bold Marauder* was heeling over in the wind, slipping like a great, predatory hawk through the black mists of the night.

"Easy with those crates there, me lads," the Irish Pirate said, anxiously watching as the men, toiling in the rain, struggled to load the heavy crates aboard the sloop as quickly as possible. The transfer was happening swiftly, silently, competently, as it had been done countless times before, as it would be done countless times again. Boats, struggling in the swells, moved back and forth between the hove-to merchantman and the little sloop, their crews cursing and damning the wind and the rain. Above, the flapping topsail sent down a continued shower, and rigging banged noisily in impatience. A single lantern, set in the shrouds a foot above Roddy's head, provided the only light, and now it shone harshly upon the dark, bearded faces of men grown hard by living just beyond the reach of the law.

"One more trip and that'll do it, Cap'n," said a seaman, grinning up through the darkness as his boat nudged against the tossing sides of the sloop. He reached up and caught a wet line as one of his mates tossed it down, then hauled himself nimbly up the wet hull.

"Good," Roddy said, glancing nervously out into the misty night. A feeling of doom weighed heavily in his bones, and he would be happy when the exchange was done and he was safely back in Menotomy tonight. "Just hurry th' bleedin' hell up, would ye? 'Twill be dawn by the time ye laggards've finished!"

His good humor spurred them into even more haste, and a half hour later, the boats were back aboard, the merchantman was slipping away into the mists, and the heavy crates were being transferred to the hold.

Roddy wiped the rain from his face with the back of his hand, envisioned Delight's silky thighs spread beneath him, and, accepting a hot mug of buttered rum, went aft to join his first mate by the big tiller. Already his spirits were on the rise, and he breathed a sigh of relief as the staysail was backed, the sloop turned, and wind began to swell the big mainsail. The mists were clearing, filing away out to sea as though being towed by the forces of nature, and he could see stars beginning to shine dimly through the lingering vapors and sliding in and out of the fuzzy haze.

"'Twill be a fine mornin', eh, Stubs?" he said to the one-eyed, scar-faced thief who'd escaped debtors' prison only to find his fortune at sea.

"Aye, Cap'n. Stars are comin' out."

"In more ways than one, me lad, in more ways than one!" Roddy said, thinking of the woman he had once known as Dolores Ann and now knew as Delight. He grinned, his teeth flashing white in the gloom.

"Should I douse the lantern, Cap'n?" asked a seaman just coming up from below.

"Nay," Roddy said with an impatient wave of his hand. He gazed out into the darkness. More stars were crystallizing through the fading mists now, growing sharper and brighter as the night cleared. "There be no one out here but us."

"Adams is going to be singing our praises for sure," Stubs said, greedily accepting a mug from a passing seaman. "Christ, this is getting easier and easier. The Royal Navy just ain't what it used to be!"

"Well, with such incompetent dolts as Captain Lord to head it, what d'ye expect? He's probably out combin' th' seas off Cape Cod, th' fool!"

Several seamen standing nearby hooted with laughter. Stubs slapped his thigh, and Roddy raised his mug in a mocking toast.

"To th' Royal Navy and its ships o' fools!" he cried.

"Aye! A pox on the whole bloody lot of 'em!"

Harsh guffaws rolled out over the decks. Pipes were passed. More rum was poured; some was spilled.

And aft, the stars began to go out as a tall, dark shape rose menacingly out of the darkness behind them.

But no one saw the giant blocks of canvas blotting out the heavens.

No one heard the increasing roar of water as the bows of a mighty frigate swallowed the little sloop's wake.

And no one happened to look around to notice.

"I'll drink t' that!" Roddy cried, his eyes dancing. "A pox on th' Royal Navy, a pox on its bleedin' ships, and a pox on Captain Christian Bloody Lord, whose inability t' capture the dreaded Irish Pirate will land him straight in the annals of history as the most bumblin' buffoon the Royal Navy ever bred!"

At that very moment, the night blew apart in a deafening explosion of thunder and flame as the Royal Navy's finest—which had been silently trailing its quarry for the better part of a cable's distance—opened fire. In one deadly salvo from her bow chasers, the mighty HMS *Bold Marauder* smashed the mast from the little sloop and left her staggering helplessly in the water.

In disbelief, Captain Roddy O'Devir picked himself up from the deck where he'd fallen, and watched as the powerful frigate slid out of the darkness, her guns glinting in the starlight. He saw men behind their big muzzles, waiting for their captain's signal to fire. He saw marines gathered along the rail, their muskets trained down upon the shattered decks of his tiny command. And he heard the clipped voice of the English commander and knew that he had just made the most grievous error of misjudgment in his career as a captain—an error that would probably cost him his life.

"This is His Majesty's frigate *Bold Marauder!* In the name of the king, heave to and prepare to receive boarders! You are all under arrest!"

A grievous error indeed.

The voice belonged to that same *buffoon* whom Roddy had just scorned, a man who, he realized with a sinking, panicking heart, was no buffoon at all—but the shrewdest captain in the Royal Navy.

Christian Lord.

Chapter 29

❧❧❧

"*Deirdre!*" Delight's voice, shrill with panic, cleaved the darkness. "Deirdre, *wake up!* Oh, God, the Lord and Master caught Roddy! *He caught Roddy!*"

Instantly awake, Deirdre sat up just as Delight threw herself into her outstretched arms. The other girl buried her streaming face in the cup of her shoulder, her chest heaving with sobs. Outside, dawn was glimmering on the horizon, and the windows were gray with morning light. "Paul Revere just brought the news, Deirdre! Your Englishman caught him after he made the trade, and saw the whole thing. Roddy'll hang for this, Deirdre! He'll *hang!*"

Deirdre pushed the sleep-tousled hair from her brow.

Delight was sobbing hysterically. "Oh, Deirdre, you have to do something, anything, *everything* in your power to get the Lord and Master to release Roddy! There's no one but you he'll listen to, no one but you who can persuade him to let Roddy go!" Her fingers bit wildly into Deirdre's shoulders. "The man loves you, Deirdre! He'll do anything you ask!"

Deirdre embraced the other girl, her heart calm. "Aye, Delight, he will. Now stop yer cryin'. The Lord an' Master made me a promise tha' t'e'd find me brother and return him t' me t' make up for press-gangin' him all those years ago." She smiled, serene in the face of her friend's hysteria. "So see? 'Twill be no problem a'tall. I'll just go t' Boston, tell Christian who Roddy is, and he'll let him go."

Deirdre crawled out from beneath the covers and padded across the room to stand at the window. The floor was ice-cold beneath her bare feet, the dawn strikingly vibrant, but she was oblivious of both. *Ah, Christian,* she thought, hugging her arms to herself as she gazed out at the eastern horizon. There was no reason to be upset, no reason to fear that Christian wouldn't honor his word to return Roddy to her. But oh, if only she could make Delight believe the same.

She reached up to embrace the crucifix with both hands, her narrow body lost in the size and length of Christian's shirt, her black hair tumbling down her back in a cascade of a thousand ringlets.

"Oh, Deirdre, how can ye be so *sure?*" Delight wailed. "The Lord and Master is a king's officer! He values nothing as much as duty, loyalty, and service. What if he won't listen to you?" She burst into wild sobs. "Oh, God, what if he won't *listen?*"

Deirdre's head came up, and she touched the ring. "He is to marry me, Delight. He will listen." She turned confident eyes upon her friend. "I promise."

The puppies whimpered and squeaked in their box, tiny white blobs of fur that crawled over each other and pushed against their mother's pink belly as they suckled greedily at her milk-swollen teats.

The Lord and Master sat backward in a chair watching them, his chin resting upon his wrists, his wrists resting on the top rung. His coat was slung carelessly over the back of a neighboring chair, and his fancy, gold-laced hat rested atop one of its posts. Stripped down to white waistcoat, shirt, and breeches, he gazed sightlessly at the puppies, trying to glean some small sliver of joy from their antics.

It was useless.

He had been working on a detailed report to Sir Geoffrey all morning, and sheer exhaustion had forced him to take a break. He had not slept in two days, and his body was crying for rest. But he was afraid to close his eyes and give in to the sleep his body so desperately craved, for in his heart he knew that the nightmares would return.

Deep within the darkened holds of the frigate, somewhere forward and beneath him, was the man who was his Irish girl's lover. That he had succeeded in outsmarting and apprehending the rascal brought Christian no sense of triumph. Revenge had been empty, hollow, meaningless. There had been no action, for the Irish Pirate's sloop had mounted only a few swivel guns that would have been ridiculously ineffective against the strapping might of a king's frigate. The tall, wild-eyed sea rogue had surrendered without a fight, knowing that any efforts on his part at defending his ship against HMS *Bold Marauder* would only result in needless bloodshed of those who served him.

Now the rebel crew was in a Boston jail, the Pirate himself locked in what had once been the playground of Delight Foley. Christian was taking no chances. He dared not send the notorious smuggler ashore for fear that the angry mobs would storm the jail and free their hero. But those same people who might harbor thoughts of storming a jail would think twice about approaching a thirty-eight-gun frigate.

He stared down at the puppies, thinking of how Deirdre had delivered each one of the tiny bundles while he had fled topside to escape the frightful sight of Tildy crying in labor. He thought of how Deirdre had dug the musket ball from his shoulder, how she had loved him with her body, how her eyes had shone so brightly when he'd given her his ring.

To think that her actions had been superficial and false; to think that she loved not him but another, a handsome, reckless rascal with hair as black as his was fair.

The words she'd once spoken came back to him, mocking him. *"And I hate fair hair!"*

Pain twisted in his heart. He leaned down and carefully picked up two of the puppies. They cried like kittens, squirming in his big hands, their soft fur warm against the hardened calluses on his palms. Tenderness flooded his heart, and rising, he cradled the animals to his chest, then his cheek. The roughness of his unshaven jaw caught in their soft, fuzzy fur, and closing his eyes, he held the two babies against his skin. Instantly, they quieted. A tiny pink tongue came out to lick his face and he swallowed hard, feeling the sting of emotion like shards of glass behind his eyes.

Turning, he went back to his desk and sat down, carefully

positioning the puppies in his lap so they would not fall, and picked up his pen. Exhaustion made his movements forced and mechanical. He dipped his pen in the inkwell and willed the weariness from his brain, the agony from his heart, and took up writing where he'd left off. In his lap, the puppies fell asleep, contented and warm. Christian's head drooped, the fair hair falling over his brow. His eyes flickered shut, opened again, and jerking his head up, he wearily dipped the pen in the inkwell once more. He was just starting the next page when he heard the stamp of a musket against the deck outside his door. A moment later, the door opened, and Ian MacDuff, with Evans standing grim-faced behind him, stepped inside.

"Prisoner's asking tae see ye, sir."

The lieutenant held his hat respectfully in his hands, and the scent of his damp clothes permeated the confines of the room. Christian looked up and blinked, exhaustion making his eyelids heavy and his eyes achy. In his dazed, numbed state, it took a moment for him to realize that someone had spoken to him.

Cradling the sleeping puppies, he got to his feet and moved across the cabin to place them beside Tildy. Ian's eyes widened and he took a step forward, thinking to assist his captain, for the Lord and Master looked to be in a sorry state indeed.

"Be ye all right, sir?"

"Aye, Ian. Never felt better."

"If there be anything ye want tae talk about, doona hesitate tae ask. . . ."

Christian paused. He stared dumbly at the bulkhead, his throat working. Then he raked a hand through his hair and looked at the lieutenant. "Thank you, Ian. I shall remember your kindness, but I fear that talk will not aid me in the slightest."

"The Irish lassie, sir?"

Christian said nothing.

"I know ye be missing her, sir, but ye'll be back together soon, now that ye've accomplished yer mission—"

"*You do not understand!*" Christian's eyes were suddenly blazing. Then his voice softened, became dead and lifeless

once more. "Forgive me, Ian. I have no right to be sharp
with you, none at all." He put his hands on the back of a
chair and looked down at the puppies, his throat working as
he tried to say the words. "After I went to Menotomy to call
upon her—and ask for her hand in marriage—I—I saw her
in the arms of another man."

Ian's mouth fell open and his hat fell from his hands.
"A-another man, sir?" His great, beamy face went slack
with shock. "Why, she loves you. She wouldnae do such a
thing—"

"It was the Irish Pirate, Ian. And I shall take the memory
of her standing in his arms into the grave with me." He
looked at Ian, his eyes raw with anguish.

Ian saw the helplessness there, the need for consolation.
But he had no words of comfort, nothing from his own vast
experience with the bonnie sex to relieve the pain of his
commanding officer. "'Tis sorry I be, sir . . . I had no
idea. . . ."

Christian turned away to hide the sting of emotion that
plucked at the back of his throat and behind his eyes.
"Thank you, Ian. Your concern will not be forgotten."

"I'll let ye be, then, sir," Ian said, quietly, sensing Christian's need to be alone. "But please do think about getting
some sleep before ye have tae face the Old Fart. And I'm
sorry for disturbing you . . . I just thought you'd want to
know the prisoner's demanding to see you."

"Damn the prisoner. He can bloody well rot for all I
care."

"Aye, sir. I'll tell 'im that."

"Please do, Ian." Christian's bones and muscles were aching with fatigue; his skin was damp and cold and waxy. His
heart was a raw wound in his chest, its pain rivaled only by
the incessant throb of his shoulder. Dimly, he was aware of
Ian moving away and down the passageway, roaring for
Skunk and Teach as he went.

Soon the news would be known throughout the ship.
Soon every man aboard would know that he'd been neatly
deceived by a lovely Irish girl with innocent purple eyes.
But he found he was too tired to care. Too tired to fight the
anguish, the pain, the pity that would surely come his way.

And the nightmares.

Too damned tired. . . .

He stumbled to his bed and swayed on his feet with exhaustion.

Sleep.

He sat down and slowly bent to take off his shoes.

Sleep.

He was out before his head hit the pillow, and sure enough, the nightmares found him.

Only this time, the treacherous dream-woman who betrayed him was not the woman he had once wedded, but the one that he had hoped to.

Deirdre.

The summons to repair aboard the flagship *Dauntless* came shortly before noon, and Christian was gently shaken awake by a hand on his shoulder. He clawed his way out of the fog of oblivion, opened his eyes, and saw Rhodes standing there, the silver wings of his black hair shining in the hard sunlight streaking in through the stern gallery.

"Sorry to wake you, sir. Sir Geoffrey just sent his flag lieutenant across with orders to come aboard *Dauntless*. He wishes to speak to you about the Irish Pirate before dinner."

"Dinner?" Christian said, sitting up and rubbing his eyes.

"Aye. He's throwing a big celebration aboard the flagship in your honor. Gage will be there, and so will a host of other dignitaries."

Christian swung out of bed, alarmed to find himself in clothes that were now on a level of unkemptness with Hibbert's worst.

Rhodes added, "Gage wanted to give the party at his residence in Boston, but Sir Geoffrey thought it unwise, given the, er, present state of the people there."

"State?"

"Aye. The people are in an uproar, sir. You caught their hero. Adams and Hancock are giving rousing speeches and stirring up the rabble; Warren is demanding the prisoner's release. A fight broke out between one of our majors and a crowd of rebels, and there was a near riot in the streets. Our troops are doing all they can to contain the situation, but the people are screaming for your head on a platter to feed to the masses, and that's putting it mildly."

Christian sighed. "Very well, then. I shall be up shortly."

Rhodes's eyes grew uncharacteristically sympathetic. "I'm sorry to hear about the girl, sir."

"Thank you, Russell. You'll understand if I do not wish to discuss her?"

"Of course, sir."

His face solemn, Rhodes bustled out. An hour later, Christian had bathed and dressed. He trudged up the short corridor and went on deck, clad in his finest dress uniform and carrying his gold-tasseled presentation sword.

The sight that greeted him nearly did him in.

Seamen clung to the rigging, holding their hats to display their respect for him. Officers lined the rail, standing stiffly at attention, their eyes shining with pride and admiration. Even Hibbert had taken pains over his appearance. Whistles shrilled, drums rolled, and *Bold Marauder*'s people saw their captain over the side with a smart and moving salute that swelled his troubled heart. He blinked to cover his emotion, for he knew that they were trying their best to cheer him in the only way they could.

Even the gig's crew was smartly turned out, the oars rising and falling in perfect unison as the seamen rowed him through the harbor toward the towering hulk of the flagship.

Christian kept his eyes straight ahead lest someone see the anguish there—and thus missed the tiny rowboat that passed him just off to starboard, carrying a young woman with spiral-curling black hair toward the proud and mighty *Bold Marauder.*

"Christian!" she yelled, standing up in the boat and wildly waving her hat before Jared Foley or Delight could pull her back down. *"Christian!"*

She saw his back go rigid as he recognized her voice, but the handsome sea officer never turned.

"Christian!"

The little rowboat tipped dangerously in the water as Deirdre fought to keep her balance. She saw the proud shoulders stiffen and sudden, awful despair washed through her when he didn't turn to acknowledge her. What was wrong? Why was he ignoring her? Dazed, she sat back down and stared at Delight. "He went right by me," she whispered, her eyes filling with tears and her shaking hands coming up to touch the crucifix. "Sweet Mary, he didn't even turn around, and I know he heard me!"

"I fear we are too late," Jared grunted as he saw the side party preparing to welcome the British captain aboard the admiral's flagship with all the fanfare due a hero. The shrill of whistles cleaved the air, mocking their hopes of securing Roddy's release. "Your fine English sea officer has done what he came here to do, Deirdre—apprehend the Irish Pirate. It appears that he has no further use for you, or for anything but the glory such an accomplishment will bring him."

"But no, he wouldn't *do* that 't me, Mr. Foley! He has no reason t' ignore me like that! He loves me!" she cried, raising her hand and staring at the ring on her finger. "I *know* Christian, and he loves me!"

"But he loves his country more," the man said, resting on the oars and watching as the blue-and-white-clad officer scaled the great tumble home of the mighty seventy-four-gun *Dauntless*.

"No! He wouldn't cast me aside like this, Mr. Foley! He just wouldn't!"

"I beg to differ, Deirdre." The printer's sad eyes gazed hopelessly into hers. "He has just done so."

Chapter 30

The elaborate dinner that Sir Geoffrey hosted aboard the great flagship *Dauntless* to celebrate Christian's success had been more fitting for a king than a mere captain in the Royal Navy whose latest accomplishment was just one

more in a series of triumphs that marked a long and decorated career. Despite Sir Geoffrey's praise and General
Gage's pleasure, Christian was glad to see the evening finally come to a close.

Tired, weary, and wanting nothing more than the privacy
of his own cabin, he left the flagship to the piercing shriek
of the side party's salute and the stamp and clatter of Sir
Geoffrey's immaculate marines. Now, with the sea wind
driving the unpleasant scent of pipe smoke from his uniform, he stared longingly toward the glimmering lights of
the frigate he called home.

In the darkness, he saw figures moving on her decks,
along her gangways, gathering at her rail. His coxswain
called up to the frigate to alert the watch to his arrival, and
the decks became a flurry of activity. The gig moved into
the orange reflection that sheeted the water around the
ship's dark hull, passing beneath the long, probing bowsprit
and the figurehead crouched just beneath it.

The crew hooked onto the frigate's main chains, and he
leapt the short distance. But as he made his way up the
black, forbidding side, he suddenly wished he were back
aboard the admiral's flagship, where there were no memories to haunt him—and no nightmares waiting to torture him
the moment he closed his eyes.

For tonight, he knew, they would be worse than they had
ever been.

Christian pushed open the door to his cabin, and was not
in the least bit surprised to find *her* waiting for him.

She was sitting on his bed, her thick curls scattered over
her narrow shoulders. Tildy's puppies were cradled in her
lap and all but lost in the voluminous folds of her skirts.
Lantern light framed her face and hair in a soft, heavenly
glow, and his heart caught in his throat at her angelic appearance.

"Christian," she whispered brokenly.

"Get out."

He saw immediately that she had been crying.

"Did you hear me?" he snarled. "I said, *get out!*"

They stared at each other, his eyes blazing, hers wounded

and sad. She made no move to leave, and he didn't trust himself to touch her. A tantalizing bit of her ankles peeped above her mud-spattered shoes, and he turned away, furious that she could still arouse his interest after the treacherous way she'd treated him.

The silence stretched on, until tears began to stream down her cheeks.

"Why?" he asked, his voice tortured. He slammed his fist against the bulkhead and felt pain explode in his wounded shoulder. "For God's sake, Deirdre, *why?*"

Her lip trembled with suppressed sobs. She stood, carefully put the puppies back with her mother, and turned to face him. "I might ask th' same o' *you,* Christian." Her eyes were tragic. "Does glory mean so much t' ye that ye'd abandon those who love ye?"

"What?"

"Ye gave me yer ring, asked me t' become yer wife—then ye pretended I didn't exist. I didn't do anythin' wrong, but ye ignored me when I called t' ye in the harbor, treated me like I wasn't even there."

He glared at her, his eyes blazing. "Why the bloody *hell* should I have acknowledged you?" he roared, ripping off his hat and hurling it to the table. "After what you did to me!"

"I did nothin' t' ye! 'T'was *you* who treated me like I didn't exist!"

"Oh? And who is the one who is already cuckolding her future *husband,* eh?" he snarled, frightening her with the intensity of his anger. "Who was the one who professed to love me when all the time her heart belonged to someone else? Who was the one who worked so deucedly hard to win my trust, then betrayed it with no care for the consequences?" Her face went white with shock, confusion. "Don't sit there and pretend you don't know what I'm talking about! You came here to try to save your damned lover, didn't you!"

He lunged across the cabin and seized her shoulders, his fingers biting harshly, savagely into the tender flesh. *"Didn't you!"*

"Me . . . me *lover?"*

"A plague on you for your bloody deceit! The game is up, damn you! I *knew* you'd come to me today with some dastardly plea to release him, and that's the only thing you haven't disappointed me in, so help me God!"

"Christian," she whispered, her eyes brimming with tears, her voice trembling with hurt, "I have no lover 'cept you."

"How dare you stand there and *lie* to me!" He shoved her aside and stormed away from her, the lace of his handsome dress uniform glittering as he moved. "I *saw* you in the bugger's arms, by God! I bloody well *saw* you, Deirdre, so forget trying to tell me there's naught between you and him! I know now why you came to America! I know now why you finally consented to stay with Dolores or Delight or whatever the bloody hell her name is! You did it so you could be close to *him!* I should've figured it out before—you're Irish, he's Irish—by God, you even *look* alike—"

"Christian."

She walked slowly across the cabin toward him. Her face was very white, her eyes very purple, her lower lip very red and swollen where she had caught it between her teeth. The crucifix glittered from the folds of her shirt, a shirt, he saw now, that was achingly familiar because it was one of *his*.

Damn her. Damn her to hell and beyond!

She came right up to him and stopped. He caught the soft scents of her soap, her damp woolen waistcoat, her rain-washed hair. Tentatively, she reached out and placed one hand upon the handsome gold insignia of his sleeve, the other against his thundering heart. His jaw hardened and he clenched his fists at his sides, every ounce of will straining to hold his temper in check.

"The Irish Pirate is not me lover," she said flatly. Her eyes flashed up to his, beautiful, brilliant, and crystalline with tears. "How could ye even *think* I'd betray ye like that, Christian?" Her throat worked; tears clung damply to the fringes of her lashes, then began to roll down her cheeks. "'Tis you who has me love. It hurt me t' think ye'd have so little trust in me that ye'd think I'd do anythin' t' hurt ye. . . ."

"*I—saw—you*" he gritted out, shutting his eyes and turning his head so he wouldn't have to look at her. "Damn you,

I didn't go back to Boston the other night after I left you! I turned around and took a room in the tavern across the road so that I could spy on the activities of the Foleys." He felt her tense, saw the stricken horror dawning in her eyes. "Sir Geoffrey had intelligence that they were rebels; Gage's spies learned there was to be a patriot meeting that night; and given that it was *my* task to apprehend the Irish Pirate, and that he was suspected to be in league with the rebels, I felt it prudent to learn all I could." He tilted back his head, unable to look into her eyes, unable to stand the soft pressure of her palm lying possessively against his heart. "But never did I expect to see *you*, of all people, standing out in the road embracing the bastard. I *saw* you, Deirdre. I saw you hug him, kiss him, give him one of your precious Irish mementos." His eyes darkened with anguish. *"Damn you, I saw you!"*

For a long moment she said nothing. Then she gave a heavy sigh and, trembling, bent her head until her brow rested against his crisp lapels. "Aye, that ye did, perhaps," she said slowly. "Ye saw me in the arms o' th' Irish Pirate, I'll not be denyin' it. And I'll not deny that I love him, too, but not as a lass loves her man, as I do you."

"What other bloody way *is* there to love a man?"

"A moment ago," she whispered, "ye said that the Irish Pirate and I look alike. Did ye ever stop 'n' consider that I might love him not as a lover . . . but . . . but as a *broth'r?"*

He stared at her for so long, his heart seemed to stop beating. The breath caught in his chest, hanging there suspended until speckles of darkness danced across his vision. Her words hung heavily in the room, and her eyes were steady, unwavering, questing.

"Did ye ever stop an' ask yer prisoner what his real name is?" she asked gently.

"Dear God . . ." he said, paling.

"And did ye ever stop an' recall the face o' the lad yer press gang took from Connemara all those years ago, Christian?"

He shut his eyes.

"Did ye?"

"No," he murmured, passing a shaking hand through his hair. "Oh, dear God, Deirdre—"

More tears were falling softly, wretchedly, down her cheeks. "I would never, ever do anythin' t' hurt ye, Christian," she whispered, reaching up to dash away the tears. "But t' think that ye trusted me so little as t' think I would, breaks me heart."

He collapsed into a chair, his eyes anguished. "Why didn't you *tell* me, Deirdre? By God, why didn't you tell me the Irish Pirate *was your brother?*"

"I didn't *know* he was me broth'r until I saw him at the Foley house," she confessed. "And I haven't seen *you* since ye left that evenin'. How was I supposed t' tell ye?" She came closer to him, her hands tightly clenched together, her lips white with pain. "And would it have made a lick o' difference if I had?"

"What do you mean?"

"Would ye still have gone after him, Christian?"

He stared at her, then looked away.

"*Would* ye?"

He set his jaw. "I am a king's officer, Deirdre. I had no choice but to go after him."

The breath left her chest in a deep, ragged sound of defeat and despair. Slowly, she said, "And does that mean that, as a king's officer, ye can do nothin' t' free him?"

Emotion warred in his face, and again he raked a shaky hand through his fair hair. Then he lunged to his feet and began to pace. "I must abide by my duty to king and country, Deirdre." At the windows he turned, his eyes dark with torment. "I cannot release your brother. He is an enemy of the Crown and therefore must be punished for his activities against it."

She raised her chin. The hope was fading from her face, and terror began to fill her eyes. He turned away so he wouldn't have to see that, his hands curled into fists.

"They will hang him, Christian."

He whirled. "By God, Deirdre, what am I to do about it? I can do nothing to help him, not now!"

"Ye could just let him go."

"And face a bloody court-martial?"

"No one has t' know about it."

"I am a king's officer, Deirdre! You don't understand, damn you!"

"Oh, I understand, all right," she said bitterly, her wounded eyes flooding with fresh tears. "Ye speak o' duty an' gallantry an' bein' an officer an' a gentleman. Aye, ye be an officer, all right, and a fine one at that—*but ye be no gentleman.* Yer word, yer honor, be as hollow as a rotten oak."

She moved toward the door, her face tight, her chin high. His hand flashed out and caught her arm. "What the bloody hell are you talking about?"

"Ye're no gentleman," she whispered tremulously. "A gentleman always keeps his word. Ye *promised,* Christian, tha' 't'ye'd help me find me brother. Ye promised t' return him t' me, but now ye're goin' back on yer promise. Ye're goin' t' stand mutely by an' let him hang, just so ye can gather all the glory yer bleedin' Navy can bestow upon ye. Another medal f'r that fine and decorated chest, another step up th' ladder t' promotion. Aye, ye'll be an admiral someday, I've no doubt. But if it be men like you who make admirals, then I pity England.

"Ye're no gentleman in *my* book, Christian. Ye're breakin' a promise ye made t' *me.* But I guess I don't count, do I? I guess because I ain't some highfalutin admiral—and because I be *Irish*—I just don't count." She pried his ring from her finger and held it in the palm of her hand, lamenting all that it had meant, all that it *could* have meant. "I've no wish t' marry ye now, Christian. I'll not have a man as me husband who lacks honor, a man who breaks his word t' the woman he wants f'r his wife."

"Deirdre, please, let me explain—"

"There be nothin' t' explain, Christian. Ye made me a promise t' help me find me broth'r. Ye found him, all right. But if he is hanged an' put t' death for believin' in a cause that in his heart be righteous an' just, then ye've robbed him from me not once, but twice."

He stood, paralyzed, only his eyes moving as they flickered to the ring.

She turned and walked slowly to the door, choking on

tears while her heart screamed for him to say the words that would bring her back to him, the words that would keep her from walking out of his life, the words that were the only thing standing between Roddy and a hangman's noose.

The words that, once uttered, would mean a lifetime of happiness for both of them.

She paused, her hand on the doorlatch while her eyes beseeched his. "Let me broth'r go, Christian. Please . . . say ye will. I beg o' ye. . . ."

He set his jaw and turned away.

Taking a deep, shaky breath, Deirdre plucked the ring from her palm, laid it on the table, and quietly left the cabin.

Chapter 31

"**C**aptain, sir?" Midshipman Robert Hibbert stood in the doorway, his eyes probing the cabin's gloomy darkness until he spotted the form of his commanding officer sprawled in his chair. The Lord and Master had been down here for a week, ever since the Irish girl had left; now he stared dejectedly at the half-empty bottle of brandy, his arm cupped around Tildy, sitting in his lap and staring at young Hibbert with sad eyes.

In their box, the puppies whined pitifully.

"Captain?" Hibbert repeated, stepping into the cabin.

Slowly, Christian raised his head. His eyes were lifeless, bleak, his untouched breakfast congealing on a plate near his elbow. "Pray, what is it, Hibbert?"

The young midshipman frowned at the sight of the brandy bottle. "Uh, Mr. MacDuff's respects, sir, and says to tell you a barge is setting off from the admiral's ship. Sir Geoffrey is aboard, sir."

"Thank you, Hibbert."

The Lord and Master remained unmoving, his eyes staring dejectedly out the stern windows at the gray, rain-pocked sea.

"Uh, begging your pardon, sir, but don't you think you might want to, uh, maybe make yourself look, uh, um, presentable?"

The gray eyes remained fixed on the sea. "Have a care whom you are talking to, Hibbert."

Hibbert's young stare met his captain's. "I am, sir." He drew himself up proudly and smoothed his own smartly pressed uniform. "But this is a *king's ship,*" he said slowly, pointedly, "and we wouldn't want our captain taken aback."

Christian turned his head and stared at the boy. Then he looked down at his own uniform. He wore only his shirt and breeches, and both were badly rumpled and in need of a wash. A large spot of spilled brandy—or was it rum? he couldn't remember—stained the front of his shirt, and his hair was uncombed and unqueued. He swallowed hard and looked at his hands, gripping the edge of the table. "Thank you, Hibbert."

Drawing himself up, Hibbert flushed and swelled with pride. "I'd be happy to help you buckle on your sword and clean up the cabin," he offered, with a fleeting glance at the bottle of brandy. "Ian says we have maybe ten minutes before Sir Geoffrey reaches us. It's kind of windy out there, and his crew's having a hard row."

"Yes, of course," Christian said woodenly. He got to his feet, swaying a bit unsteadily. He could feel the midshipman's worried eyes upon him. He was not making a very good role model for the young officer, or any of his men, he knew.

He didn't give a bloody damn.

Topside, he heard the sounds of feet running over the deck as the side party was mustered and the crew prepared to receive the admiral. Shaking his head to clear it, Christian set Tildy back down with her puppies, and, pouring a pitcher of water into his basin, plunged his hands beneath the surface and scrubbed at his unshaven face.

Hibbert saw his predicament immediately. "Would you like me to shave you, sir?"

The tired smile was answer enough. Christian sat down and closed his eyes, allowing the lad to lather his face. From above, he hard Ian's gruff voice coming down through the skylight as he ordered the side party into position.

"I know you're feeling poorly about the girl," Hibbert said suddenly, bravely, as his captain's eyes opened to regard him with anger. "And we're all proud of you for outsmarting the Irish Pirate and bringing him to heel." The razor passed slowly over Christian's chin. "But don't you think you might just consider letting the man go? I mean, I've talked to him, and we've been playing cards with him every night—"

"*What?*"

"He's really a nice fellow, Captain O'Devir. Not a criminal at all, sir, but a man who believes as strongly in his ideas as, and pardon me for saying so, sir, you do in yours."

"He is a treasonous rebel and traitor to his king," Christian snapped, "and do not forget it!"

"Aye, sir." The razor scraped over Christian's cheek, but the youth's hand was surprisingly steady. "I know you might be thinking you can't let Captain O'Devir go, because *we* might be angry with you, but we held a meeting, sir, and we don't want to see him hang. He's really a fine fellow."

Christian seized the midshipman's wrist. "Why the deuced hell does everyone on this bloody planet seem to think I can just release the bastard? Such decisions are not mine to make! And, by God, this is a king's ship. I have a code of honor and duty to attend, and so do the bloody lot of you." He shut his eyes, cringing as he heard the bosun's whistles shrilling on the deck above. "Besides," he added in a gentler tone, "I can't just *release* him. You know that, Hibbert."

"I know, sir. But you've got to do something. . . . We know you're loyal to the king; we know you're loyal to this ship and the flag that flies above her decks. But in the end, who wins if the Irish Pirate is hanged? No one. The rebels are still going to transport arms to Concord; everyone knows that Gage will soon have to move against them."

"Hibbert, you show a devilish amount of knowledge for one so unadvanced in years."

"And pardon me, sir, but you show a devilish amount of stubbornness for someone as advanced in yours."

"Pray, go to hell."

The midshipman laughed, wiped the razor clean, and toweled the streaks of lather from the Lord and Master's austere face. "Well, sir, I just wanted you to know that *we* won't think any less of you if Captain O'Devir ... *escapes.* And—" He paused, looked away, and then, unflinchingly, met his captain's steely eyes. "I know this has been a long time in coming, sir, but I have to say it. You're the best Lord and Master we've ever served under ... and we only want to see you happy."

Christian looked down. He took a deep breath, then raised his gaze to the youth's. "Thank you for that, Hibbert. That ... that means a lot to me."

"It's the truth, sir. Now, if you'll just stand up, I'll help you into your dress coat. I do believe I hear the Old Fart's voice outside now—his barge must be bumping our hull, I'd say."

Christian rose and allowed the young midshipman to help him into the heavy blue coat. He pulled his lacy sleeves free of the cuffs and buttoned the coat to conceal his stained shirt. Then he tied his hair back, picked up his hat, and raised his arms so that Hibbert could buckle on his sword belt.

"You will make a fine captain someday," he said as the midshipman stood back to survey his handiwork.

"Thank you, sir. I have had a good example to follow."

For the first time in days, the Lord and Master's severe face broke into a grin; then he abruptly turned and exited the cabin. Hibbert stood there for a moment, his eyes moving almost reverently over the captain's family coat of arms that hung on the bulkhead, the painting of the king, the crossed swords, the set of fine pistols.

Then he walked to the table, picked up the bottle of brandy, unlatched the stern windows, and flung it outside.

"I say, Christian, the governor has not stopped praising you," Sir Geoffrey said, his shrewd eyes raking *Bold Ma-*

rauder's decks for signs of laxity, and finding none. "He toasts you at every meal and has written letters to the king commending your apprehension of the Irish Pirate."

"I am flattered, sir."

"Don't be—you earned it. Damme, you are a fine candidate for flag rank, Captain Lord, a fine candidate indeed." Aware of the eyes of the frigate's crew on him, the crusty old admiral straightened his back and followed *Bold Marauder*'s captain below. "As you know, my flag captain has proven to be most incompetent, and I must choose another. Captain Merrick comes immediately to mind, as he is a fine young officer, but I've already been accused of showing favoritism where he is concerned. But then, he has earned his laurels, too."

Christian pushed open the door to his cabin and uttered a silent prayer of thanks. Young Hibbert had done a fine, albeit hasty, job of tidying it up.

The admiral's words suddenly hit him. "What are you saying, sir?"

Sir Geoffrey beamed and clapped Christian between his shoulders. "I'm offering you the position of flag captain, my good man."

Christian stared at him, a tide of emotion sweeping through him. He'd carried the flags of admirals before, but still, it was another step toward raising his own broad pendant. Another step toward becoming an admiral. Another way the Royal Navy had of thanking those who were loyal to the Service.

Loyal.

There, that word again. He fisted his hands, the force behind the unseen gesture causing ripe, hot pain to burst in his shoulder. He hadn't felt very loyal these past few days. . . .

Ye speak o' duty and gallantry an' bein' an officer an' a gentleman—

He swallowed with difficulty.

—but ye be no gentleman. Yer word, yer honor, be as hollow as a rotten oak.

"Well, my good fellow?" Sir Geoffrey said, his craggy face set in a hard grin. "What d'you say, eh, Christian?"

Another medal f'r that fine and decorated chest, another step up th' ladder t' promotion.

Christian turned bleak eyes upon Sir Geoffrey. To be asked to carry the flag of his admiral was the greatest honor that could be bestowed upon a captain. There were those in the fleet who'd give their eyeteeth to be in the position he now found himself.

. . . yer honor be as hollow as a rotten oak.

He met the admiral's eyes. "I am deeply honored, Sir Geoffrey," he said quietly, knowing, even as the words left his mouth, that the decision he had made—and was about to carry out—did not entitle him to carry the flag of any admiral, let alone wear the coat of a king's officer.

But it would allow him to live with himself.

To spend the rest of his days knowing that he had done what was morally right. To be able to face himself in the mirror every day. To know that he had made his decision, based not on the decree of the Navy to which he had devoted his life, but on the code of honor that he—as an officer, as a gentleman—lived by.

Honor. It went far beyond the service a man gave for his king and country; it encompassed his thoughts and deeds in dealing with his fellow man. Long ago, he had committed an unpardonable sin against an innocent family when, in the name of the king's Navy, he had taken young Roddy O'Devir from his homeland.

It was time to atone for that sin.

"Well, Christian?" the admiral said, grinning.

The Lord and Master's gray eyes were steady, resigned, proud. "Thank you, sir . . . but I'm afraid I must decline."

It was dingy and dark, musty and damp in the tiny room in which the Irish Pirate found himself. He lay on his back, staring up into the darkness, a scratchy wool blanket draped over his body and a small felt pouch of Irish seashells clenched in his hand.

Down here in the depths of the frigate, sounds were distant and muffled. Thrice a day, a young midshipman brought him a meager meal of bread and cheese and salt pork. He was afforded a small jug of water, a few blankets, and all the privacy he could possibly want. But for the past few hours, the ship had been as quiet as a tomb.

Roddy's fingers curled around the felt pouch, feeling a shell that his little sister had plucked from a beach that he would never see again in this lifetime. Emotion clogged his throat, and he suddenly wished he could turn back the clock and make up for those lost years with her. Caught up in the patriots' cause here in America, he had used it as a sort of strange revenge against the English for what they had done to him. Now he lay moldering in the orlop of a king's frigate, and the only reward for his actions was the hangman's noose.

Roddy had had many days to think about his life, his plight, the foundations and workings of his own heart. His hatred for Captain Christian Lord had faded to grudging respect, for the man had outwitted and outsmarted him. The English captain lived by a strict code of honor and duty honed by many years in the Royal Navy. Just as he had merely been following orders when he had pressed Roddy so many years ago, so he was only doing his duty in apprehending the notorious Irish Pirate.

A man could not be hated for doing his duty.

But Roddy, too, had done his duty. He had smuggled food to the hungry, out-of-work people of Boston after the British had closed the port down as punishment for the Tea Party incident. He had worked side by side with Adams, Hancock, Warren, and Revere to bring about fair treatment for his adopted land, a land whose plight closely mirrored that of Ireland's. He had done his duty, and followed the decree of his heart.

He would die with a clear conscience, and perhaps someday he would be remembered as a hero.

Outside, he heard footsteps detaching themselves from the weighty silence, and his stomach gave a hearty rumble. It would be young Hibbert, bringing him his supper. Pork and bread and cheese, or maybe dried peas boiled into edibility. It mattered naught. He would eat it. And later, perhaps, some of the English lads—who really weren't such bad fellows after all—might sneak down with a tot of rum and a deck of playing cards.

The door opened and a hook of light cleaved the darkness. "Hello, Hibbert," Roddy said, still staring up at the deck beams above his head.

There was no sound but the closing of the door, the quiet hiss of a lantern.

Roddy shut his eyes. "Wha' 'tis it t'night, laddie? Boiled beef and hard tack? Dried peas and hard tack? Cheese and hard tack?"

"Leg of mutton," a voice said quietly.

The Irish Pirate's eyes shot open. His head turned on the damp pillow and he sat up, staring at the man who stood there, a tray in one hand, a lantern in the other.

"Christ Almighty!"

The English captain gave a tired smile. "No. Merely Captain Lord, come to bring you your last meal."

Roddy's jaw hardened and he clenched his fists, feeling the chains biting into his skin. "Are ye mockin' me, Brit?"

The gray eyes regarded him steadily, taking in Roddy's filthy shirt and breeches, his damp and unkempt hair, his angry purple eyes that were so much like those of the girl the Lord and Master loved. "Nay, my good fellow, not at all. I merely thought you might appreciate something a bit more bracing than our normal fare."

He set the tray down on the floor, because there was no table in the tiny room. Roddy's mouth watered. On a fine plate of what had to be the captain's china was a juicy, sizzling, hefty club of baked lamb, dripping with a mint glaze and sprinkled with an assortment of fragrant herbs. A wreath of boiled potatoes surrounded it, and there was a steaming chunk of fresh bread that looked suspiciously like the type he used to enjoy back home in Ireland, so many years ago.

"Be this some sort o' joke?" Roddy snarled, his Irish temper leaping to the fore as he saw the bottle of fine wine set on the tray.

The English officer reached into his pocket and drew out a key. He moved slowly across the small space between them, the lantern's glow probing the brilliant azure depths of his gold-laced coat and glinting upon his fair hair. He grasped Roddy's chains, fitted the key into the lock, and snapped it free. "No joke, my dear fellow," he said quietly. "As I said, this is your last supper aboard *Marauder.* Sentence has been passed upon you . . . tomorrow it shall be carried out."

"Hangin'?" Roddy asked nonchalantly, lifting a proud chin that was now heavy with beard.

"No. An execution squad, of Sir Geoffrey's own marines."

Roddy swallowed, a cold prickle of terror shooting up his spine. He eyed the plate of hot food that rested on the floor. The English captain eased himself to the decking, leaning his broad back against the bulwark and letting his hands dangle over his bent knees. "Pray, eat it before it grows cold," he said, motioning for Roddy to join him. "My cook went to a devilish lot of trouble to prepare this for you."

Warily, Roddy slunk down from the bunk and joined the English captain, facing him across the plate of food. His stomach growling, he picked up the fork and knife, and sawed into the juicy chunk of lamb. "Looks like the fare me mama used t' make back home," he muttered, brushing his errant, dirty hair off his brow with the inside of his elbow.

"I am glad."

Roddy bit into a chunk of mutton and shut his eyes in bliss. "I haven't been in th' Navy for many a year, Brit, but I do know this isn't customary, a king's captain goin' t' all this trouble t' make a prisoner feel comfortable."

The Englishman spread his hands in a gesture of innocence. "'Tis a humane thing to do, I should think. And my methods have never been regarded as . . . customary."

Roddy sawed off another piece of the mutton. He raised his gaze to the Englishman's, and found the sea-gray eyes regarding him steadily. Between swallows, Roddy said, "I ain't goin' t' waste time in pleasantries, seein's how I don't have very much of it left t' waste. But I know th' two o' us go back a long ways, an' I've had a good many hours down here t' think about things. I hated ye, truly I did, f'r all o' th' past thirteen years. I lived f'r the day I could cross swords with ye, an' run me blade through yer heart." He bit off a piece of the bread and washed it down with a long swallow of the wine. It was an expensive wine, and had no doubt come from the English captain's private stores. "But now I find I've lost all me taste f'r revenge."

The gray eyes regarded him thoughtfully. Wisely. Steadily.

"I know, too, tha' 't'ye have yer eye on me sister," Roddy said, waving his fork. "She be a fine lass, a wee bit on the sentimental side but a warmhearted girl who'll make ye proud." He cut a piece of potato and put it into his mouth. "If ye give me yer word ye'll treat her as a lady, an' honor her f'r the rest o' yer days, I'll be consentin' t' let ye have her hand in marriage."

The Englishman smiled a sad, private smile. "Thank you, Captain O'Devir. That is most gallant of you."

"I mean it. I told ye I hated ye, but I don't any longer. Besides, any lad who can outwit and outsmart th' Irish Pirate deserves t' win the hand o' his sister."

For some reason, the innocent remark seemed to distress the captain. He looked away, and for the first time, Roddy noted the deep lines of strain and sorrow etched into the austere, handsome features.

Long moments went by. Abruptly, the Englishman said, "I have allowed all of my crew a well-deserved shore leave."

Roddy's brow puckered. *"All* of 'em?"

Captain Lord began to idly pluck at the lace of the captain's insignia on his sleeve. "Aye, all of them."

"That ain't customary, t' let yer entire comp'ny go."

The gray eyes lifted to regard Roddy. "Again, my actions have never been considered *customary,* Captain O'Devir."

Roddy stared at him. If he didn't know better, he would swear the Englishman was trying to tell him something, but damn him if he knew what it was. . . .

"Yes, Captain O'Devir, I let them all go, with the orders that they are to be back by midnight. General Gage has been making some secret plans, which I am not at liberty to disclose, but ones that will require my crew to return to their vessel before the night has waned." He continued to be markedly interested in his sleeve. "Pray, that leaves just the two of us here."

Roddy bit into the mutton.

Captain Lord gave a heavy sigh and kept his head down. "Just you and me . . . Roddy. Two captains with naught but the other for company. . . ." He glanced at the shackles which had bound the Irishman, now lying slack across the bunk. "Pray, you could rise up, knock me in the head, and be away from here with no one the wiser for it."

Roddy stopped chewing. He looked up and saw the Englishman regarding him steadily.

Slowly, Roddy put the lamb down on his plate and wiped greasy fingers on his breeches. "Aye . . . that I could."

"Of course, you would have to make neat work of it. My admiral would not take kindly to the fact that the Irish Pirate has escaped. Nor, for that matter, would General Gage." He gave another heavy sigh and continued to pluck at his sleeve, his fair hair glinting in the lantern light, his pale lashes sweeping down to conceal the expression in his gray eyes. "To overpower me and render me totally senseless would be the only faintly acceptable excuse, I should suppose . . . but, of course, I am talking silly, am I not?" He looked at Roddy and grinned, and the simple gesture transformed his face—the face of a man who had known much pain and suffering in his own right—into that of a youthful lad on the eve of discovering something wild, forbidden, and tempting.

"Quite silly," Roddy agreed gravely.

"But still, 'twould be an easy matter," the Englishman mused. "We are of like height and build, and therefore a fair match of strength. Why, you would only have to get in a lucky blow in order to make your escape. . . . Pray, I shall have the devil of a time explaining the incident to my admiral, but then, I have had worse times explaining worse things to both him *and* other superiors."

Their gazes met, deep purple against flinty gray. Roddy picked up the bottle of wine, drank long and hard from it, and passed it to the Englishman. The other captain did the same, and passed it back to Roddy.

Again their gazes met.

The unspoken bargain was sealed.

The sins of the past had been forgiven.

The hope of many tomorrows shone brightly.

The Englishman got to his feet, tall and proud and strikingly handsome. He reached up and removed his fancy cocked hat, baring his hair to the shimmering glow of the lantern. Then he looked deeply into Roddy's eyes and smiled.

"And, of course, not a deuced soul shall ever know the truth," he murmured.

He turned, presenting his squared shoulders, his broad back, and moved slowly toward the door.

The Irish Pirate wasted no time. Raising the empty wine bottle, he brought it crashing down on the back of the fair head and caught the Englishman as he fell, gently lowering his heavy, sprawling body to the deck.

He stood for a moment, looking down at the unconscious officer and silently thanking him for giving him back his life. "God love ye, Cap'n Lord," he said, then, without further pause, was on his feet and racing topside.

Chapter 32

War broke out two days later.

On the previous Friday, a warship from England had arrived in Boston, carrying orders from Lord Dartmouth, Secretary of State for the Colonies, to General Gage, directing him to waste no further time in breaking up the rebel network. Gage, fearing for his position as military governor, was quick to act. Intending to arrest the rebel leaders Adams and Hancock, and to seize the buildup of stores the rebels had reportedly secreted in Concord, he chose the fateful night of April 18 to make his move.

Though he took every possible pain to keep his plan secret, telling no one but his wife and Hugh, Lord Percy, of the impending march on Concord, Gage had unwittingly alerted the watchful eyes of the rebels during the preceding days by activities that were suspiciously suggestive of an impending military activity on the grandest of scales. Spies, mounted messengers, and intuition on the part of the rebels guaranteed advance knowledge of Gage's plans, and days before the British troops began their fateful march, the patriots had already transferred their arms stores in Concord to other secret sites. They hid sacks of bullets in nearby swamps, melted their pewter plates down into musket balls, and devised a set of signals so that, when the British soldiers made their move, the information could be quickly passed on to Concord and other outlying towns.

By the time Gage's select troops of grenadiers and light infantrymen, numbering some eight hundred, stole quietly out of Boston on the night of April 18, under the command of Lieutenant Colonel Francis Smith, and were ferried in the warships' boats across the Charles River to begin the sixteen-mile march to Concord, rebel messengers were already galloping from Boston to spread the midnight alarm.

The American War of Independence had begun.

Deirdre was awake and sitting at her window, staring out into the crisp, moonlit night, when Paul Revere galloped through, shouting hoarsely at the top of his lungs.

"The regulars are out! The regulars are out!"

The hoofbeats rose in crescendo, growing louder and louder, peaking, and then fading away into the distance. In their aftermath, she saw lanterns being lit in the windows of the neighboring houses, the inn across the road. People began to wander outside, staring off toward where Revere had gone and straining their ears to hear the last vestiges of his voice as it died away.

It was finally happening.

Deirdre shut her eyes, dipped her head, and, with the crucifix clasped between her hands and its chain wrapped around her fingers like the beads of the rosary, prayed.

For the safety of Roddy, whom she had not seen or heard from since that rainy afternoon when he'd left on his final mission as the Irish Pirate, and who, according to Jared Foley, was hiding at the Boston home of Dr. Joseph Warren following the brief scuffle with the captain of HMS *Bold Marauder* in which he'd made his escape.

For the safety of her adopted family, who had spent the night preparing for war, rolling powder cartridges for the two muskets the Foleys owned, cleaning and oiling them, and maintaining a state of watchfulness.

And most of all, for Christian, whom she missed with every shred of her lonely, aching heart. If only he had released Roddy, and honored his promise to her. But how could she have expected him to forsake the values, traditions, and honor by which he had lived the past twenty years of his life, turning his back on his own principles of what was just and right? He was a king's officer.

Bitter tears stung her eyes, and she pressed her lips to the spot on her finger where his ring had rested for so brief a time. How stricken he'd looked when she'd taken it off and laid it on his desk, then turned her back and left him. The memory brought the tears streaming down her cheeks. At least he would be safe behind the mighty guns of the frigate should the worst happen.

She raised her head and looked out into the night. Figures moved in the darkness, their voices hushed and excited. More and more people, alerted by the night messenger, were trickling from their houses and standing dazedly along the road, some staring fearfully toward the east, whence the British would soon be coming.

Deirdre shut her eyes once more. Her lips moved against the hard edges of the crucifix, and salty tears wet her suddenly cold hands.

"Please, God, watch o'er all those I love, an' those I do not love, those I know, an' those I do not know. Please, dear Father, keep ev'ryone safe, especially Roddy, wherever he may be, and me beloved Christian. I love him, Father, I love him so very much—even if he *did* put his Navy before me. And please, oh, Father, don't let th' minuteman have t' take up arms against th' British, for there be good and decent men on both sides."

She paused, shivering in the night air that wafted in through the open window. The acrid scent of woodsmoke hung in the air, making this lonely countryside seem homey

and lived in and united. She heard a faint breeze rustling the
dead leaves on the trees, and knew that the swelling buds
that clustered on their branches would soon be as brilliant
and fresh as those that, by now, would herald the arrival of
spring back home in Connemara. She saw the grass shining
silver in the moonlight, and felt a pang inside at the memory
of Christian's promise, for that grass—so brown and dead
and ugly when she had first arrived in America—was now
every bit as lush and green as any lovely field back in Ireland.

Downstairs, she heard Jared quickly snapping orders, instructing his wife and daughter what to do when the British
came. Soon, she knew, someone would be coming up to get
her, but she had a few moments left. Precious moments before she had to leave the sanctuary of her little bedroom.

Her gaze lifted to the horizon beyond the trees. She
thought of the British troops, making their way even now
through the moonlight toward them, and a prickle of doom
made the hairs rise on her neck and shivers dance the length
of her spine.

Her head dipped once again, and squeezing her eyes
tightly shut, she prayed, "And oh, Father, please, oh please,
please, please—don't let anyone get killed. . . ."

"Deirdre?" It was Jared, calling from the foot of the
stairs. "Gather your things together and come down here
with us. The regulars are out!"

As though she didn't know.

"Aye, Mr. Foley . . . I be awake."

Standing up, she moved across the room, her limbs stiff,
her muscles cramped from sitting at the window for so long.
It took her a while to dress. She put on a simple skirt of
brown wool, a green jacket, a pair of boots, and a thick,
quilted petticoat. She had gone to bed in Christian's shirt—
and she left it on beneath her snug waistcoat, keeping the
only part of him she had close to her heart. Then she picked
up her canvas bag, nearly empty now except for the flagon
of Irish air, and smoothed her fingers over the rough canvas.
That little bag had traveled the vastness of the Atlantic. It
had never left her person since she had bidden good-bye to
her beloved Ireland. It would not leave her now.

She was just moving down the darkened staircase when the first dogs began to bark wildly in the distance, piercing the quiet of the night. Fear rose within her and a deep rumbling began to sound from the east. The Foleys raced to the front window and peered out into the moonlit night. And in the little cupboard, the plates began to vibrate. Louder and louder and louder—

"Dear God above," Mrs. Foley breathed, paling with fright.

For just outside the window, the measured tramp of their feet vibrating the very floor upon which the Foleys stood, was a vast, unending river of red-coated soldiers marching past, their bayonets gleaming in the bright shards of moonlight. Here and there an officer rode, his steed's hoofbeats thudding like the knell of doom. The dark line stretched as far as the family could see, and the rattle of wagons, the stamp of the war-horses, the measured thunder of booted feet were enough to send Mrs. Foley reeling back from the window, closing her eyes in terror.

"Dear God," she repeated, and leaned heavily against her husband. "Dear God, have mercy on us. . . ."

They dared not light even a candle. Some of the troops broke rank and darted across the lawn, stopping to drink from the well before racing to catch up with their comrades. It seemed to take forever for them to pass, and it was a long time before the frightened Foleys dared to leave the safety of their house and venture outside to join the neighbors.

All up and down the Lexington Road, the townspeople were streaming from their houses, standing in the moonlight and pointing toward the west, toward Lexington, where the soldiers had gone. Lights began to glow from windows, and somewhere a baby wailed. Then Solomon Bowman, the lieutenant of the Menotomy minutemen, went racing from door to door, summoning the minutemen and instructing them to assemble on the green at the crack of dawn to march to Concord and Lexington.

Jared Foley wasted no time. Gathering the powder cartridges they'd been making ever since the first rumors of Gage's planned raid on Concord had reached them, he laid them on the table and turned to his wife. "Throw all of the pewter and silver into the well," he told her, gripping her trembling shoulders to steady her. "Gather up everything of value, then take the girls and go to the Prentiss house with the other women."

"Oh, Jared," she said, on the verge of hysteria, "please do not ask me to leave my home!"

"I do not ask it, Joanne, I demand it!" He lowered his voice. "There will be bloodshed this day," he murmured. "I feel it in my bones. You will take the girls and go to the Prentiss house with the other women and children, out of sight and away from the road when the British pass through on their return to Boston. Do no defy me in this, Joanne."

He turned away, missing the mutinous set of his wife's jaw, and the exchange of glances between Deirdre and Delight, both of whom knew she had no intention of carrying out her husband's wishes. He picked up the rolled packets of black powder and began to stuff his cartridge box. "If blood is shed today," he said, setting the case aside, "then I pray that those who die will not do so in vain. This moment has been a long time in coming, Joanne." Straightening up, he gazed at her face before folding her quickly to his chest. Then he set her back, and looked deeply into her eyes. "Whatever happens, keep the girls safe. I will leave you with one of the muskets in case, God forbid, you are called to defend yourself."

He handed her a Brown Bess, stolen from a drunken British soldier several weeks ago, and showed the three women how to prime and fire the weapon. It was a needless gesture, for he had already done so many times in the past few days, and the motion was made more to reassure himself than to teach the women anything they didn't already know.

And then dawn began to glimmer on the horizon, and the urgent beat of a drum rolled across the fields, calling the brave minutemen of Menotomy together. Grim-faced fathers and eager-eyed sons bade good-bye to wives and children and sisters, and, toting muskets and ammunition, raced to the town green to answer the call to duty, never knowing that for some of them, it would be the last dawn they would ever see, and that their farewells to loved ones would be their last.

Shortly thereafter, the farmers were marching toward Lexington under the command of Captain Benjamin Locke, leaving behind only those who were too old to fight, and the women and children. Carrying their valuables, they left their homes and gathered at the house of George Prentiss, there to await their fate.

For the people of Menotomy, it would be a day of bloodshed and death.

The nightmare had come to him last night, more intense, more vivid, more frightening than any that had ever preceded it. A nightmare of blood and fighting and death, only this time the victim was not the woman he had once married—but the young Irish girl whom he loved.

And he, bound to the frigate by the command of duty, was unable to save her.

On the deck of HMS *Bold Marauder,* Captain Christian Lord paced agitatedly. His face was pale with tension, his eyes bleak, his mouth a grim slash of worry.

The morning brought no sense of serenity to the Lord and Master's troubled heart. Dread tightened his gut; foreboding tingled in his spine. Several hours ago, eight hundred troops led by Lieutenant Colonel Francis Smith had left Boston under cover of darkness with the intent of seizing the rebels' military stores in Concord. And now, reinforcements of some twelve hundred more, under the capable command of Hugh, Lord Percy, had just left to join them.

Deirdre was out there. Alone. Unprotected. In the middle of it, should that spark explode into flames.

He shut his eyes against the vivid memory of the nightmare, its message clawing at his heart until the nausea of worry overtook him. Taking a deep, shaky breath, he wrapped his hands around the tarry shrouds that climbed skyward to support *Bold Marauder*'s proud masts, and shut his eyes. The nightmare was meaningless, merely a product of his own worry—surely, things wouldn't go that far, would they?

Those eight hundred select troops, tense and eager for action, had left Boston in the dead of night and by now should have reached Concord. They would already have passed through the little West Cambridge village of Menotomy. Had the awesome and terrifying might of nearly a thousand armed soldiers awakened his beloved Deirdre as they'd marched through in the moonlight on their way to Concord? Had she looked out the little window and trembled in fear? Where was she now? What was happening?

And oh, God, what the deuced hell was he doing here aboard his ship when he ought to be with her?

Cursing desperately beneath his breath, he leaned his brow against a tarry shroud. *Go to her. Tell her you did release her brother, after all. Damn your bloody pride, man, just go!*

Footsteps sounded on the ladder that led up to the quarterdeck, and he turned, seeing Rico Hendricks crossing the deck toward him. Christian frowned, and the bosun yanked off his hat and belatedly saluted the quarterdeck.

"Sorry, sir."

The Lord and Master merely gave a tight smile and resumed his pacing. Finally, he returned to his spot near the shrouds, feeling Hendricks's eyes upon him. The big Jamaican cleared his throat, the noise unusually loud in the stillness of the morning. "Er, how're you faring this morning, Captain?"

Distractedly, Christian reached up to touch the hard lump on the back of his skull, wincing a bit as his fingers found the tender area. "Devilishly fine, Rico," he murmured, his gaze flickering once more toward the horizon over Boston. "'Tis my heart that worries me, and the dread that darkens it."

Hendricks joined him, his face grave as he let his hands dangle over the rail. "I'm sorry about the prisoner escaping," he said, keeping his face carefully averted, for he had been the one to discover his friend and captain sprawled senselessly in the brig, the shackles mysteriously loose, and the prisoner gone. But he had been with Christian long enough to recognize the inner war he'd been fighting in the days immediately preceding Roddy O'Devir's escape. He knew his captain well enough to know that he was not so careless as to turn his back on a dangerous prisoner. He knew it was far too coincidental that the entire crew had been on shore leave when the Pirate had escaped. And he knew that pride would never allow his commanding officer to admit that maybe, just maybe, he'd had a hand in the escape of Roddy O'Devir. . . .

No, there was more to it than that, and every man aboard the frigate knew it—though none dared mention the matter to the Lord and Master. Sir Geoffrey had been enraged to learn of the Pirate's escape, and only the persuasiveness of his favorite captain, Brendan Merrick, had saved Christian from a court-martial. It had been the younger officer who'd reminded the admiral that Captain Lord had, after all, accomplished a miracle in making something out of *Bold Marauder*'s hopeless crew.

Such was cause for recognition in itself.

Abruptly, Christian said, "*The* nightmare returned last night, Rico."

Rico said nothing, merely standing beside him and looking down into the gray water that swirled so far below.

"For five years, Rico, I was plagued by torment because I was unable to rescue Emily from that burning house. For five years, I have gone to bed every night knowing I would see her standing in those flames once again, trapped, screaming as they consumed her . . . *burned* her." He fisted his hands around the shrouds and shut his eyes, his voice harsh with agony. "For five years, I have lived with the anguish and guilt of not being able to get her out of that house."

Rico looked down, pretending to study the calluses on his broad hands.

"Now the nightmare is back, Rico, but this time it is not Emily who is trapped and dying . . . it is Deirdre." Christian took a deep, ragged breath, the shadow of his hat falling over his hands as he bent his head. Rico heard him swallow once, twice. "And again I stand here, helpless."

Rico said nothing, watching the morning light glittering like diamonds on the gray sea below.

"I shall not remain helpless this time, Rico." The shadow fell away as Christian's head came up. "I must go to her. And"— he looked away, his features contorted with anguish—"and I must tell her the truth."

Rico looked into the steady gray eyes, at the determined set of the harsh jaw.

"Aye, Captain," he said slowly. "Perhaps you should."

Christian straightened up, the pink-and-gold light of dawn shining upon the crisp whiteness of his waistcoat and breeches, the fine snowiness of his stockings. "If I don't go, Rico—if I don't go tell her the truth and win her back—I will spend the rest of my miserable days in anguish, better dead than alive. I cannot live without her, you see? By God, Rico, I love her." He turned, and gripped the bosun's broad shoulders, his eyes desperate, his voice nearly breaking. "*I love her!*"

"Aye, Captain."

"I was wrong to have such little faith in her as to think she had taken a lover! I was wrong to allow her to believe I cared so little for her happiness that I would not honor my word and release her bro—"

He caught himself too late. But Hendricks was smiling knowingly, for he knew well what *truth* his captain was agonizing over. "Have no fear, sir," Hendricks said, his teeth white against the darkness of his face. "Yer secret is safe with us."

Christian stared at him for a long moment—then he looked away. The wind came up and blew his hair around his cheeks, his brow. He gazed off toward the west for a long, anxious moment, and then he turned.

His gray eyes shone with resolution. "I'm going, Rico," he said quietly.

The big Jamaican smiled and shrugged. "I knew ye would, Captain."

"Aye, as Sir Geoffrey does, too. He'll not be happy, I daresay. But I cannot stand here and wait. I cannot stand here and do nothing to protect her. I cannot wait here, wondering, praying, wishing, dreading . . . I must go, by God!"

Ian's voice boomed suddenly from behind them, making Christian whirl around. "Well, sir, if ye're going, ye'd best be off. Lord Percy and his reinforcements are long gone. But if ye hurry, you should be able tae catch up tae them."

Ian was not alone. Behind him, the entire crew had gathered. Christian swallowed hard, knowing they would support him in any decision he made, whether it be good or bad, wise or unwise. He knew they would defend him when Sir Geoffrey learned that he'd deliberately disobeyed orders and abandoned his ship. He knew that he had won their trust, their loyalty, and, perhaps, even their love.

The Lord and Master straightened up, the strain easing from his austere face. He went to Ian and laid his hand over the big Scot's shoulder. "I may return as your commanding officer," he said quietly, "or I may return in irons for disobeying my admiral. Either way, Ian, I leave *Bold Marauder* in your hands."

He strode resolutely down the quarterdeck stairs, his back rigid and proud. Hibbert, who'd obviously been eavesdropping, was standing there, the Lord and Master's sword belt in his hands, the gleaming blade catching the stabbing rays of dawn. Already the crew was assembling, needing no commands to organize them into tight lines of discipline and respect. The sight brought the sting of emotion to Christian's eyes, for he knew it might very well be the last time he was ever honored so.

His gaze moved over these men who had come to mean so much to him. Teach, huge, and bristling and formidable, his belt strung with weapons of every size, shape, and kind. Hibbert, trying hard to emulate what he thought a good officer should be, his uniform fresh and clean. Ian, his red curls glinting like fire in the morning sunlight, and Skunk, his pungent scent enough to give him a private standing space of several feet. Wenham, sad-eyed and hulking. Rhodes, tight-lipped and unsmiling. Evans, standing at the forefront of his grim-faced marines, and Rico, his dark eyes shining with pride as he came forward to present Christian with his sword.

The boat had already been lowered, and far below, the oarsmen waited.

Slowly, Christian passed the carefully formed lines of seamen and officers, smartly returning every salute. At the rail he paused and looked up at the giant, billowing Union Jack—the flag that he had spent his life defending, the flag whose honor he had sworn to uphold, the flag that would always swell his heart with pride.

Then Rico was handing him the sword and Ian was touching his hat to him as he accepted command of the king's frigate *Bold Marauder*.

"Godspeed, sir. I hope ye find her, and may the both of ye return to us safe and sound."

Christian smartly returned Ian's salute. Then he turned, climbing down the side of the ship and into the boat that waited below.

Huddled in their homes and in the crowded rooms of the Prentiss house, the women and children of Menotomy paled at the first distant boom of gunfire to the west.

The alarming reports had already come trickling in as horsemen raced through the village, shouting the news. Fighting had broken out in the dawn hours at Lexington, and both colonists and British regulars had been killed. There had been a skirmish at the north bridge in Concord. The British had failed to find the stores of munitions and ordnance, and now the weary troops were on their way back to Boston.

Early in the afternoon, a twelve-hundred-man relief force under the command of Lord Hugh Percy had marched past on its way to aid Colonel Smith, their horses' hooves raising a thunder of sound, their bayonets glinting in the sun, their mighty field pieces rumbling along on giant carts made especially to carry them. And no one would ever forget the sight of a little girl, attending her mother's cow as it grazed by the side of the road, looking up to see the oncoming redcoats. As the animal plodded through the ranks, the child, heedless of the danger, followed it fearlessly. The Britons left her alone, and one or two even paused to ruffle the child's hair. Then the main column of Percy's men had passed, their measured footsteps sounding like the tread of one monstrous leviathan. They were flanked by officers on handsome horses, and trailed by carts and wagons laden with supplies. It seemed to take forever for the road to empty, and still stragglers came galloping by in their wake for hours.

At four o'clock in the afternoon, the bloodshed hit Menotomy.

In Concord, Colonel Smith's exhausted troops, bitter over their failure to capture the rebel stores, and growing increasingly alarmed at the sight of minutemen pouring in by the thousands from all over the countryside, had turned and headed back toward Boston. Incited by the bloodshed at Lexington, the rebels began to fire on them from behind stone walls, fences, and trees. British regulars fell, dying. They tried desperately to pick off the minutemen, but found it impossible to hit men who fought like Indians, hiding behind trees and stone walls, only to pop up and pick off their comrades. Panic rose, took over, and what had begun as an orderly march back toward Boston soon became a downright flight of terror. By the time the soldiers met up with Lord Percy's relief force outside Lexington, all semblance of order had been lost. After a brief rest of a half hour, the British regulars resumed their hasty retreat toward Boston—but this time, there was no sympathy spared for the Americans.

As Smith's weary soldiers fled down the Lexington Road, desperate to reach the safety of the guns of the men-of-war stationed in Boston, Major Pitcairn, knowing that the men needed an outlet for their fear and frustration, cunningly sent Percy's fresh troops ahead and outside of the main column with permission to burn and pillage everything in their path. By the time they hit Menotomy, they had carved a path of violence and destruction before them.

And Menotomy was not to be spared.

Deirdre, huddled at the window with Delight and her mother and several neighbors who had joined them, felt her companions' hot breath stirring her hair, warming her neck; she smelled the sweat of their fear and heard their sobs of terror, a terror that was reflected in her own heart as the sharp crack of gunfire and the boom of cannon heralded the approaching arrival of the British forces.

With a sound like rising thunder, they came around a bend in the road, nearly two thousand men running as fast as their legs could carry them. Officers galloped past, their coattails flying, their hoarse voices shouting for order. Wagons toting the dead and wounded rumbled by, their wheels lodging in mud and spinning free once more. Gunfire cracked around them, and Deirdre saw a British soldier fall, only to be trampled by the river of red-coated regulars. A horse reared up and plunged over backward, crushing the officer who had been mounted so proudly atop its back. Minutemen, mere shadows in the haze of gun smoke, darted from behind trees, their muskets spurting flame and smoke.

Mrs. Foley's screams pierced the air as she saw her husband and Captain Locke dive headlong over the stone wall that bordered the house, popping up to train their muskets on the fleeing troops. Thunder cleaved the air, and more British fell, some wounded, some dying, some dead. Flames and clouds of roiling black smoke burst from the windows of a nearby house as the soldiers ransacked the building and then set it afire. People ran screaming out into the road. Minutemen raced into the nearby house of Jason Russell, and Deirdre saw the old man die on his front steps as a wild-eyed redcoat cut him down, savagely bayoneting his body.

"Lock the windows!" Joanne Foley cried, and sobbing, they slammed the shutters shut against the sounds of the carnage outside. Tears streaking her cheeks, Deirdre closed her eyes and clung to Delight. The windows rattled in their casings with the reverberations of thunder. One shattered with a piercing explosion as a musket ball burst through, flinging the shutters wide and slamming into the mantel just above their heads. Fists pounded on the door and curses rent the air. Joanne Foley hefted the musket and swung it toward the door, the thunderous blast exploding in their heads. Outside, a man screamed in agony and another hurled himself through the open window, only to be brought down by the musket of an old man who took careful aim at the redcoat from his place on the stairway. Blood exploded against the wall. Flashes of red drove past the window. Horses screamed in fright, bellowed in agony. Smoke tainted the air, and the dying cries of those who had been shot, those who had been bayoneted, those who were dying, pierced the walls of the little house.

The sounds of gunfire roared from the house of Jason Russell, where the minutemen had made their stand, and with each hollow boom, each crack of a musket, the women sobbed and cried and huddled together. The horror seemed to go on forever. Then the thunder began to fade as the fleeing British raced on toward Boston, leaving the wounded and dead in their wake.

Like a land savaged by storm and just opening its terrified eyes, Menotomy began to stir. The fields were strewn with bodies, some clad in the king's colors, some in the ragged wool and homespun of local farmers. Outside, in the muddy road where puddles of water were now stained crimson with blood, the dead and dying lay. A few last shots pierced the air as minutemen fired upon straggling British troops who, carrying their wounded and dead, were too exhausted to fight back as they trudged past.

Bitter crying and long, keening wails came up from the townspeople as, here and there, someone recognized the corpse of a loved one. Women crushed screaming babies to their breasts, comforted sobbing children, began to stagger out of the houses in which they had barricaded themselves. The wounded and dying lay in the road, in the fields, draped over fences and walls. A red-coated figure stirred in the yard outside and reached for his musket, only to fall back, his legs jerking, as a single shot cracked out.

And then, from the distance into which they had gone, Deirdre heard the rolling hoofbeats of a single, approaching horse.

She knew. She knew, even before she lunged to the door and flung it open, who it was. She knew, even before she saw him, that he had come looking for Roddy. And she knew, even before her mouth opened in a desperate scream of warning, that it was already too late to save him.

The glistening, foam-flecked hide of the big chestnut stallion swept around the bend and burst into view. And though a dark boat cloak covered the fine uniform beneath it, it was all too obvious that the militaristic figure who sat so tall and straight in the saddle was no less British than those who had slashed a murderous swath through the helpless village a mere half hour before.

"Christian!"

The horse kept coming, the dark folds of the rider's boat cloak billowing in the wind.

"Christian, *no-o-o-o-o!*"

She was racing across the lawn, her skirts flying, her hair streaming behind her, before anyone could stop her. The breath whistled through her lungs. Wind caught her tears and ripped them from her eyes. She stumbled once, fell, picked herself up, and kept on running, even as she saw a minuteman stand up from behind the shelter of a stone wall and carefully, deliberately, bring his musket up to bear on the lone rider.

Purple eyes met gray.

"*No-o-o-o-o-o-oooo!*"

The explosion seemed a thousand times louder than the mightiest of *Bold Marauder*'s broadsides. She saw the flames spurt from the lock and muzzle of the gun in a brilliant cloud of smoke and orange fire. She saw the minuteman raise his fist and shout with triumph. She saw the rider jerk in the saddle, a streak of blood rippling along his white thigh, his hand going for his sword a moment before another shot tore a swath of bloody flesh from his temple and sent his cocked hat spinning away into the mud.

He tumbled from the horse, his bright hair glinting in the sunlight.

Screaming, she raced to him and bent down, her knees sinking into the bloody mud where he had fallen. The big stallion bolted, thundering back down the road, the irons of his empty saddle slapping his sides. She heard Jared Foley yelling hoarsely, and the boom of cannon and gunfire, far off in the distance now. She smelled the acrid stench of blood and death and war, tasted it upon the wind.

Sobbing bitterly, Deirdre sat down in the mud, took Christian's hand, and cradled it to her heart, to the crucifix, rocking back and forth, the sunshine glinting upon the lace of his coat where the boat cloak had fallen open.

"Christian," she sobbed, tears streaming down her dirty cheeks and dropping upon the insignia on his sleeve that marked him as a king's captain, "don't die on me. Oh, dear *GOD,* don't take him from me, *please,* God, don't take him ..."

Shadows stamped out the sunlight. Concerned hands grasped her shoulders, tried to pull her away. She heard Delight's voice, saw someone poke a musket at the officer's chin, and, satisfied that he was no threat, move away.

"Don't die, Christian . . . oh, please, don't die." She crushed his hand to the crucifix, never seeing the little drops of blood that the sharp points raised, never feeling it trickle down her hand, staining the whiteness of her shirt. "Dear God, please, don't take him. Dear God, please, oh, Father, restore him. Don't take him from me—he was just doing his duty, God. Oh, God, oh, God, *please*—"

Far off in the distance, the last sounds of gunfire faded.

Jared Foley bent down and grasped the captain's wrist, his thumb pushing up Christian's sleeve to find a pulse. His eyes grazed the bloody slit that cleaved the white breeches; his fingers touched the wound that carved a shallow path of blood at the temple. "Your man's alive," he said, releasing Christian's wrist. "Merely a flesh wound. Lucky he is, too, for *he* will live to see many tomorrows."

"Don't know what the tarnal hell a sea officer's doin' out here," muttered another, peering down at the gold lace of Christian's coat.

"Aye, 'tis rather strange, eh?"

But Deirdre, staring down into the Lord and Master's still face, knew why he had come. In that brief, awful moment when their gazes had met just before the minuteman's musket had felled him, she had seen the truth.

He had come for her brother.

Her throat constricting, she reached out and touched the blood that trickled through the fair hair at his temple. Bitter, choking shame coursed through her. She had tried to make him choose between his promise to her and the principles by which he lived his life. How could she have thought he would abandon his values? How could she have thought he would turn his back on the Navy, on his duty to king and country? In his eyes Roddy was a traitor, an enemy of the Crown.

It was unfair of her to expect him to abandon his values, just for the sake of love. It was unfair to think that the two of them would ever have a chance to be happy together.

But the fact that she loved him would never change.

Slowly, Deirdre O'Devir reached up, drove her hands beneath the heavy fall of hair at her nape, and lifted the chain that had kept Grace O'Malley's crucifix against her heart for so many years.

The crucifix that she had sworn never to take off for as long as she drew breath.

She shut her eyes, her lips moving in silent prayer. Then she pulled the crucifix off, enfolded it in her palm, and pressed it to her lips for a long, tremulous moment. It was warm with the heat of her body, and before it could cool, she lifted the Lord and Master's head, drew the chain over his hair, and carefully eased his head back down, her lips lowering to touch his pale skin, his parted lips, in a final kiss of farewell.

"I love ye, Christian," she said brokenly. "Dear God, I love ye. . . ."

She looked at the crucifix, lying against his heart and glittering as proudly as his buttons, his lace. Then she stood, her hand coming up to touch the strangely empty, naked area at her throat. But what she had done was right. What she had given him was lasting proof of her love. Her eyes streaming, she turned to Jared Foley, knowing that he and his family would take care of her captain until he recovered.

There was nothing left in America for her, and the colonists' war was not her own. If she and Roddy stayed here any longer, Roddy would surely be caught and hanged—if not by Christian, then by someone else.

She had come here to find her brother, and that she had done. She had come here to fulfill a vow to her dying mama—and now it was time to honor that promise.

Find m' son, Deirdre, and bring him home to Ireland.

It was time to go home.

"Mr. Foley?"

He was staring at the crucifix nestled between the English captain's lapels, and watching his daughter try to stanch his bleeding. Dazedly, he looked up at Deirdre.

"Please take me t' me broth'r," she said quietly, her proud, Gaelic face shining with courage and misery beneath her tears.

"What?"

At her feet, Christian was beginning to stir. She looked

down at him through blurry eyes, her heart breaking. "Christian'll only hunt him down again, ye see? He's smart an' determined, Mr. Foley. He's th' finest officer in th' king's Navy. He'll find Roddy and take him from me, only this time, 'twill be forever."

"What are you saying, girl?"

She looked up, turning her face toward Boston, and Ireland beyond. A gust of wind came up, carrying the smoke of battle and tugging at the raven curls at her temples.

Brokenly, she murmured, "That it's time for me t' go home."

She stood on the shore at Boston Harbor, her eyes seeking the British men-of-war anchored there. Her gaze moved over each of them until it finally settled upon the one that was different from the rest . . . leaner, lither, with more sharply raked masts. The one with the pointer crouched beneath its proud bowsprit, the one that had brought her here to America, the one that she would never, ever forget.

HMS *Bold Marauder.*

The wind blew from the east, ruffling the frigate's furled sails, kissing the gleaming spars and yards and masts. It continued on its zephyrous journey toward shore, dancing over the waves and making them crest with merriment, playing across the glistening blue waters of the harbor until it finally caressed her tear-stained cheeks.

She threw back her head and opened her arms, embracing the wind for a final time.

And then she uncapped the glass flagon, letting the Irish air escape to be forever mated with its American cousin. She allowed the flagon to fill with wind, then tightly capped it once more.

Her brother stood nearby, uncharacteristically quiet, and solemnly waiting to take her out to the little brig he had procured to bring them home. His face was a mix of conflicting emotion, his heart in turmoil, for only he knew of the unspoken promise he had made to the man who had once been his enemy.

A promise he now considered breaking.

Roddy stepped forward, biting his lip.

And then he stopped, his eyes tragic.

He couldn't do it. For he had made a promise, and Roddy O'Devir always kept his word.

Chapter 33

Connemara, Ireland

The press gang was in.

One could tell by the way a thick pall had settled over the land, cloaking the rocky green hills with darkness and shadow, like damp mist snuffing out the noonday sun. One could tell by the way the little village had grown quiet and seemed to huddle within itself, the people slamming shut the doors of their whitewashed cottages and fearfully watching the roads from behind slitted curtains. One could tell by the way the taverns had emptied and the menfolk had fled into the hills that rolled away from the slopes of the purple mountains, where they would hide until the threat was past.

And one could tell by the big, three-masted men-of-war that filled the harbor.

This time, England was at war with America . . . and not everyone wanted to fight.

It was an infrequent threat, the Royal Navy seeking its unwilling recruits from this western part of Ireland, but here in the peaceful village in Connemara, it was not unheard-of. No able-bodied young man was safe from the press; and so it was that Deirdre O'Devir solemnly watched her brother shake his head with exasperation and leave, grumbling as he headed into the hills where the others had already fled.

Then Deirdre locked the doors and waited.

So many years ago, this same scene had enacted itself, just as it was happening now. She pulled a chair up to the fire—a good, Irish peat fire that glowed warmly in the hearth—and sat staring into the flames.

A single, swelling tear leaked from her eye and splashed down upon her hands.

Another.

A flagon sat in a revered spot on the table before her and she reached out, touching the cold glass, staring into its seeming emptiness and remembering that last day in Boston, several months ago.

She would never uncap the flagon and let the American air out.

Just as she would never empty the vial of American water scooped from that same harbor, toss away the felt pouch containing Boston sand and seashells, discard the tuft of hair combed from the Foleys' plow horse, or eat the bread—made of corn grown in Massachusetts pastures and milk gleaned from the Foleys' cow, and baked over a good, American wood fire—that was carefully wrapped in a square of linen and tucked away in her bedroom.

The tears came harder.

Home was where the heart was, Christian had once said; home was whom the heart belonged to. Home could be any place on earth, as long as it was shared with the one you loved. And it wasn't until Deirdre had returned to her beloved Ireland that she realized the place of her birth was no longer her home. It wasn't until her heart began to pine for a handsome Englishman whom she could never have that she realized that her heart belonged not to Ireland, but to Christian.

The fire had grown too warm, and she stood up, the heat fading instantly from her face to leave her cheeks cold and empty. She hugged her cloak to herself and stared morosely into the smoking fire. There was a decided nip in the air, and in America, as Roddy had told her, the leaves on the trees would just be starting to take on the glorious colors of sunset.

She walked to the window and looked off toward the sea, where she could see the towering masts of the men-of-war silhouetted against the black-and-orange-streaked sky to the west. Over thirteen years ago she had seen masts very much like these, from this same window, and had gone to see for herself just what was so terrible about the English and their Navy that everyone so feared and hated.

Now she knew there was nothing terrible about the English, nothing terrible about their Navy.

She had learned a lot in the thirteen years since she had first learned to hate the British and their Navy.

Outside, the wind began to rise, moaning around the little cottage as it had done for centuries. The clouds grew thicker, heavier, darker. She thought of Roddy, hiding up in the hills with the others. She thought of her neighbors, terrified of losing their loved ones to the dreaded press gang. And she thought of the new horse in the stable, a gift from Roddy that she had named Booley in remembrance of Christian's pony from his childhood.

A desire to relive painful memories finally got the better of her. Huddled in the cloak, her thick raven curls blowing madly in the rising wind, she hustled across the yard, saddled the horse, and, once away from the cottage, kneed him into a gallop and raced him headlong over the hills toward the sea.

Night was coming on; huge black clouds dragging damp feelers of mist were filing in from the ocean, their shadows trailing over the land. Recklessly, Deirdre urged the horse faster, not pulling him up until they had crested the last rocky hill.

There she sat, a pale, ethereal beauty, her hair whipping around a face dominated by the haunted, tragic eyes of a grieving soul. Far below, the sea swapped kisses with the base of the hill, thundering and booming and sending up great silver mists of spray. She licked her lips and tasted salt, and drew her cloak more tightly around her.

Then she clawed the wild snarls of black hair from her eyes and gazed out over the ocean.

A half mile out in the bay, a British warship lay, majestic in all its dread, frightening in all its beauty. And another, its pale sails furled upon spiraling masts, its anchor cables stretching down into the sea. And still another, sloop-rigged and nimble, and all but dwarfed where it lay in the shadow of the fourth and final ship, a mighty, towering wall of wood pierced by the snouts of what had to be a hundred guns.

Its mastheads seemed to scrape the bellies of the low-hanging clouds themselves, and from one of those masts flew the broad pendant of a commodore.

Not just a single warship this time, but a squadron.

Behind her, a stone, loosened by the horse's hooves, skittered down the hill, the sound cleaving the tense stillness. Deirdre gave a start and spun around, her skin crawling with the uncanny feeling that she was being watched.

But there was no one there, and the wind, peppered with rain, was suddenly cold and damp.

Beneath her, the horse began to fidget. Then his ears pricked forward, his head lifted, and Deirdre's breath caught in her throat, for a boat had been lowered from the flagship, and was plunging through the breakers toward shore.

She forgot the oncoming storm. She forgot the approaching darkness. She forgot the feeling that she was being watched.

The boat—not just any boat, but a smartly painted one that was surely the pride of some high-ranking officer—was nearing shore now, its crew having a rough time of it in the heavy seas. Oars rose and fell in perfect rhythm, and every so often the boat's bow would nose up as it plowed a wave, drenching the men and the tall officer in the stern with spray.

She shut her eyes, emotion choking her throat. A drop of water splashed upon her hand, another upon her wrist, and Deirdre never knew if it was rain or her own tears, for as she edged the horse toward the edge of the cliff she saw that the officer—over thirteen years older than he had been that other time, but no less handsome, no less proud—had a telescope to his eye and was training it on *her.*

Deirdre leapt off the horse and dashed down the cliff, her skirts flying, the tears streaming down her cheeks. The officer jumped from the boat. She plunged into the surf and flung herself into his arms before the seamen could even pull the boat up onto the beach.

His brows were blond and haughty, his fancy, gold-laced hat covered richly gilded hair that was caught at the nape with a black ribbon. He had long golden eyelashes, eyes the color of fog, and a profile that reminded her of a hawk.

He clasped her to him, nearly crushing the breath from her. And then he drew back, his heart in his eyes. She had expected cold fury, but there was only . . . love.

"Really, dear girl, you have given me the devil of a time trying to catch up to you!"

Behind him, the seamen, grinning, exchanged happy smirks as they drew the boat up onto the beach. She saw familiarity in the richness of a red beard, the rumpled unkemptness of a midshipman's uniform, the stench of a huge, barrel-chested body, the fearsome countenance of a piratical fiend—and the yellow hair of an aspiring courtesan.

In the midshipman's arms were three half-grown puppies.

Her eyes filled with tears. "Oh, Christian, there be nothin' for ye here! Let me brother alone, I beg o' ye! He'll not be goin' back to Amerikay. He'll not be causin' any more trouble—"

He laid a finger over her lips.

"I did not come here for your brother, Deirdre."

She stared at him.

"I did not come here to press more Irishmen."

She couldn't move.

"I came here, dear girl, for *you.*"

He gazed solemnly down at her, his hands very warm upon her shoulders. She felt her heart melting, breaking, swelling; saw her emotions reflected in his gray eyes. "Ah, Dee . . . I thought you had deserted me—until I found *this* around my neck." He reached up and lifted the crucifix, hanging against the buttons of his waistcoat. "I may have wagered all in coming here, but I took this to mean that you really *do* love me."

"Christian, I never *stopped* lovin' ye. 'Tis just that—"

He silenced her with a finger against her trembling lips. "Dear girl, I did not go to Menotomy that day to recapture your brother, as you believed. Delight told me, you see? Nay, I went there to get *you,* and make a confession . . . one that I should have made long ago, but one that I refrained from making because of my foolish pride."

She swallowed hard, searching his face.

"Regarding that, er, *scuffle* your brother and I engaged in when he made his escape?"

"Aye. . . ." she said slowly.

"Well, 'twas no accident. I *allowed* him to overpower me." He looked a bit sheepish, and had a sudden interest in his sleeve. "In fact, I daresay I asked him to."

Her eyes widened with shock. "But I thought—"

Again he laid his finger over her lips. "I know, love, what you thought. And if Roddy made no mention about what *really* happened between us, 'tis because he was more attentive to his promise to *me* than I was with mine to *you.*"

Tears spilled down her cheeks, and he wiped them away with his thumb. Then he reached into his pocket and slowly drew something out, looking at it for a long, reflective moment. "I . . . I hope you still want this."

It was the ancestral ring of the Lord family.

"*I love you,*" he said quietly. And then he took her hand and slid the ring onto her finger.

Behind them, the seamen erupted in wild cheering, Delight clapped her hands in glee, and the puppies yapped with excitement.

"Oh, Christian. . . ."

He smiled down at her, achingly handsome in his blue-and-white uniform.

She reached out to touch the fabric that stretched across his powerful chest. Then she looked at the ship that filled the harbor, her eyes widening at the sight of that stately leviathan.

He noted her confusion. "Sir Geoffrey was so irate that I'd abandoned my command, he kicked me out of Boston and sent me back to England, vowing he hoped to never set eyes on me again."

She stared at him.

"And, dear girl . . . I am a commodore now."

"A *commodore?*"

"Aye. 'Twas Elliott's doing." He smiled. "You see, love, when I returned to England, I learned that my manipulative brother had gone to great lengths to amuse himself in giving me command of *Bold Marauder.* No one could make something of the frigate, and the Navy had all but given up on her. Unbeknownst to me, Elliott made a bet with the first Lord of the Admiralty that I could succeed where the others had failed. A bet that would earn me the rank of commodore."

"Ye mean t' tell me they made ye a commodore f'r straightenin' out *Bold Marauder?*"

"Aye ... but lest you think Elliott is one to show favoritism, do know that our family relationship has never stopped him from disciplining me in the past. In fact, he made quite a public display of doing so the day I tried to leave Portsmouth."

"But I don't see *Marauder.*"

"Nay, she is at Spithead, being refitted for a voyage to the West Indies. She will join us shortly, under Captain MacDuff's command."

"Captain MacDuff? The *West Indies?*"

He smiled, and touched her cheek. "I will not fight the rebels, Deirdre. Had Sir Geoffrey not kicked me out of Boston, I would have handed in my resignation, for the Americans have my sympathies. Nay, my squadron will be deployed to the Caribbean, there to monitor French activities. They are sure to throw in their lot with the Americans sooner or later, and one can never trust the French, you know!" He sobered and stared down at her, taking her hands in his own and raising them to his lips. "As soon as *Bold Marauder* is ready, we shall be away. But I will not leave this land until I have replenished my full complement of persons aboard my ship."

"And ... and how many d'ye lack ... Commodore Lord?"

"One."

She stared up at him, her heart filling with love and pride and joy. He was all that she could ever want. He was all that she would ever need. The tears rolled down her cheeks as he reached up and drew off the crucifix. Slowly, he settled the heavy chain over her head, positioning the crucifix back where it belonged, between her own breasts, against her own heart.

She swallowed tightly. The rain clouds were moving away, and bright, golden shards of light stabbed through their parting masses, kissing the harbor with the promise of a golden tomorrow.

The promise of a lifetime of golden tomorrows.

"What do you say, dear girl?"

She smiled up at him, twisting the ring around her finger, unable to speak for a long, long moment. The big flagship waited. The three accompanying vessels waited. The seamen waited, the puppies waited, her future waited—

He waited.

"Just let me pack a few things, Christian," she said, "an' leave a note f'r me brother."

Leading the horse, he walked with her back to the cottage, and two hours later she was being rowed ceremoniously out to the big man-o-war that flew the proud broad pendant of a commodore.

Around her neck was Grace's crucifix.

In her lap was a little chest containing the miniature of her mama, the wood from her papa's boat, and a square cut from Roddy's shirt.

But there was no canvas bag, for this time there was no need of any Irish mementos.

Deirdre O'Devir was finally going home.

Avon Romances—
the best in exceptional authors and unforgettable novels!

THE LION'S DAUGHTER   Loretta Chase
76647-7/$4.50 US/$5.50 Can

CAPTAIN OF MY HEART   Danelle Harmon
76676-0/$4.50 US/$5.50 Can

BELOVED INTRUDER   Joan Van Nuys
76476-8/$4.50 US/$5.50 Can

SURRENDER TO THE FURY   Cara Miles
76452-0/$4.50 US/$5.50 Can

SCARLET KISSES   Patricia Camden
76825-9/$4.50 US/$5.50 Can

WILDSTAR   Nicole Jordan
76622-1/$4.50 US/$5.50 Can

HEART OF THE WILD   Donna Stephens
77014-8/$4.50 US/$5.50 Can

TRAITOR'S KISS   Joy Tucker
76446-6/$4.50 US/$5.50 Can

SILVER AND SAPPHIRES   Shelly Thacker
77034-2/$4.50 US/$5.50 Can

SCOUNDREL'S DESIRE   Joann DeLazzari
76421-0/$4.50 US/$5.50 Can